THE SLEEPING BOY

THE SLEEPING BOY

a novel

BARBARA J. STEWART

SEAL BOOKS

THE SLEEPING BOY
Seal Books/published by arrangement with Doubleday Canada
Doubleday Canada edition published 2003
Seal Books edition published April 2005

ISBN 0-7704-2973-4

Cover images: (cityscape) Kim Steele/Getty Images
(woman with gun on bed) © Paul Vozdic/Photonica
Cover and text design: Kelly Hill

Seal Books are published by Random House of Canada Limited.
"Seal Books" and the portrayal of a seal are the property of
Random House of Canada Limited.

Visit Random House of Canada Limited's website: www.randomhouse.ca

PRINTED AND BOUND IN THE USA

OPM 10 9 8 7 6 5 4 3 2 1

To my mother, Lelia Marion Bugden Stewart,
who always wanted to sing like Maria Callas
and dance like Tina Turner.

Sing. Dance.

ACKNOWLEDGEMENTS

To those whose varied and patient support has made an incalculable difference—let me count the ways: dinners, movies, café mochas, guest rooms, wine . . . well, you get the idea. Denise, Gerri, Harry and Bette, Jan, Jane, Laurelle, Linda, Meg, Michael, Michèle, and Scarlett. If there's a theme here, it's in the quality of my friends. I choose to think I deserve them. But maybe I'm just lucky.

To my mentors, who may not yet know they were: Don Nurse and Ches Yetman and Kathleen Shannon.

To Maya Mavjee, Suzanne Brandreth, and Nick Massey-Garrison at Doubleday, elegant in their conviction that books do matter and ideas are important.

To my agent, Helen Heller, fierce, principled, and ferociously funny, who treated me like a real writer before I was.

And Devan Towers, with her own strong faith in new beginnings, who said to me if you don't like where you're standing, move your feet. Then bought me boots.

"Liberty is liberty—not equality or fairness or justice or culture, or human happiness or a quiet conscience."
—Isaiah Berlin, *Two Concepts of Liberty*

PROLOGUE

She was the sort of cat that people think of when they say they don't really like them. Named Emma by her owners and Shit Machine by the neighbours, she dominated the whole of her suburban Arcadia throughout the long night. One unrecognizable creature left in pieces under the spirea in the corner and, beneath the butterfly bush—the *Buddleia davidii*—a yellow songbird who'd never sing that particular song again. But the rain was almost here. And soon the can-opener in the kitchen would be whirring out its seeming unending supply of salmon bits and grain filler.

Emma slipped into the still-quiet house, enjoying as she did the familiar, even strokes from the plastic flaps in the all-weather door installed solely for her convenience. There was only an absence in the kitchen. No slippered feet showing yet. No flannel-covered legs to push against in an act of proprietary aggression that they chose to interpret as affection, while they mumbled on, unintelligibly. No whirring.

From a static standing position Emma leapt on to the sleekly smooth granite countertop beside the sink. Normally a forbidden area, she was prepared to vacate it if necessary, a split second ahead of any hand raised in her direction. Her peripheral vision described an arc of more than 210 degrees. But she sensed no threat in this place any more.

A thin sheen of spectres and auras filled in all the corners of the room, their colours slowly fading as the level of watery daylight rose behind them. Her eyes were already narrowed to slits against it. She could make out some new outlines from yesterday. Shapes, still distinct, hard and bright. The softened, more pastel ones of last week were beginning already to blend with layers left by years and hordes of others. Shadows, in *this* place at least, were made of something other than light. The infinitesimal movement of ethers, liquid currents curling up against the ivory-painted ceiling mouldings. Mere remnants of heightened moments and loud words. The things only a cat really cared to see. For her, and for all her kind through the millennia, it was the means of simple survival.

Emma slid within her own skin loosely, comfortably. The fur was merely a sheath laid over harder bone and muscle. At the touch of her tongue it was reduced to pure texture, attached but apart, the sensation a combination of delicious and disgusting. Irresistible.

One or two single raindrops struck the glass and ran like syrup down the window nearest her, which overlooked a carefully sculpted garden. Under a high, polished pearl grey sky, the colours of the now visible landscape folded into one another. This birth time of day.

In late spring it was formed of myriad shades of green—sea green, emerald green, linden green, jade, moss, chrome green, olive, khaki, kelp. The cat perceived a world of difference among them, her palette a substantial and generous one, expanded a hundredfold in the water-washed air. Add cilantro and catnip. Emma's senses blended the sights and tastes into an intense combination that lifted each element high above any singular aspect.

She willed herself to relax now, though her thoughts still fluttered up like high-pitched birds. She settled in place and studied the view. Icy turquoise, bronzed green, celadon, acid, pistachio, ivy, kiwi, mustard, celery and apple green, tangy green, porcelain green, pale green milk.

Still no legs or hands or big-eyed faces up and about yet. Admittedly, they were loud and they were disruptive. But they were late. The coffee pot, with a series of wet pops, had filled now, its brown fragrance confirming her own sense of the time. Emma went looking for someone to feed her, up the silent stairs.

A hundred yards away, at the school-bus stop out front on Scott Boulevard, it was the usual Monday morning near-catastrophe of straining children and taut-faced, strained mothers. One seven-year-old whining that she'd forgotten her lunch and blaming everyone. Another finding the entire contents of his knapsack covered in spilled contact cement. Dean Hartwell, age nine, had just discovered his Friday homework assignment, due today. He was ready to start crying, right here, right now, if his mother even *looked* like she was thinking of getting mad at him.

A comfortable street. An appearance of openness in the well-done women and carefully arranged offspring, even now, in the pouring rain. Gore-Tex and Burberry and Aquascutum in fortunate plenty.

The children were decorated in colourful slickers. Most of them just wanted to go home and watch TV, have another bowl of Cocoa Puffs and milk. Each mother smiled tightly and rolled her eyes at the others, knowing that briefcases and laptops and—hopefully—enough time for a mocha latté from the drive-through waited in the length of Cherokees, Sidewinders and Magic Vans idling up and down the block.

One small boy, already inside the bus, was waving for his mother's attention. As usual she was occupied with everything else. Finally, another interrupted the conversation to point out the boy's flagging efforts, the shouted, unheard words. This other woman was better at lip-reading too. "He's saying Kyle's not here." And out of habit the entire group, as one, looked resentfully towards the big house just across the street.

"The Mallick kid again," the boy's mother muttered under her breath. Then she spoke to her son through the window, enunciating each word distinctly. "Just go on. You'll see him at school." She backed further away from the bus and continued in a hushed tone to the others, "The usual. You've got to wonder, though—her being a doctor and everything." She made a slight face.

Her own son, unfortunately named Orion, settled back into his seat, unaccountably angry. OK, let's get this show on the road, he thought. What the hell were they waiting for, anyway?

At the same time, only one street away, a stranger's car had already turned towards them all, heading at a speed more than twenty-two miles an hour over the posted limit. It was easy enough to overlook the traffic cone, even the sign warning drivers to watch for children and pets. On a normal day it wouldn't have mattered that the tires were nearly bald. But this morning, rain was falling. And by now Melissa Redmond was already jumping out of her mother's temperamental red Audi, slipping out from under the seatbelt by herself. She didn't need help. She'd been diagnosed as quite advanced for seven. And Melissa was in a hurry to show off her new Xena Warrior Princess doll. None of those waiting on the other side even noticed the car approaching until it cut out suddenly from behind the school bus.

The driver's face widened in surprise and the cellphone fell from his hand. The slick pavement might have been a sheet of ice for all the purchase it gave. The car began its inexorable, slow drift to the right and, very slowly, stopped. There was one loud shout from someone in the crowd.

In the end the distance between them was approximately fifteen feet. It would grow shorter, of course, in all the retellings over the next few hours, down to the point where the bumper actually nosed against the little girl's raincoat. But for now, at least, Melissa was entirely safe, heedless of the drama.

Her mother, however, Alicia Redmond, was a full shade lighter than white. A stray bit of her dark hair whipped out from under the hood of her jacket and plastered itself against her damp forehead. She grabbed Melissa, wanting to frighten her. "Don't you ever, *ever,* cross a street like that alone again." Alicia knew she couldn't actually smack her daughter. Not with all those eyes staring in their direction. But she really, really wanted to.

And as nervous giggles replaced gasps, she heard one mother exclaim to another, "Isn't it weird how things can happen?"

"Just like *that,*" and someone else snapped her fingers.

Orion stubbornly remained in his seat, even as all the others crowded against the bus windows to gawk at the near tragedy. It was his accustomed place, two-thirds of the way down, and just one row ahead of the bigger, mean kids. He usually spent his early morning ride scrunched down and squinting in anticipation of whatever was going to hit him from behind that day—a paper clip flung from an elastic band, part of an old orange, something sticky scraped from under the seat.

At least when Kyle was there, the negative attention got spread around a bit. They'd talked about trying to grow a minimum of a foot over the coming summer, ready to start doing something about this crap by the start of fifth grade. But Kyle was away too much. And even though they were the only fourth-graders on the route, Orion knew he would never have picked a loser like that on purpose anyway. Almost nine and still getting weepy in the mornings.

When she did bring him, Kyle's mom was standout pretty. But the other mothers watched her in a way that told him something was going unsaid. And she always seemed in a bigger hurry than everyone else. Orion wasn't sure that he liked her, either. But Kyle—he wouldn't even look away from her face until she'd actually pushed him backwards up the steps. He would still be trying to get off by the time the bus driver was ready to pull the door closed, and she'd have to spend the next fifteen seconds herding him towards his seat with big wide motions through the window.

It had become a regular, if embarrassing, morning tradition.

Orion thought of that little pasty face and those round, sad eyes—like the one puppy you wanted to rescue from the shelter—and decided it was time to toughen him up, or fifth grade would take him out. Ultimately, as everyone had to learn, the schoolyard was not a level playing field.

The driver shut the door with a big wet clap. Orion was left totally on his own again.

OK, then. Just get it over with. Let the big kids take their best shot. At least he wouldn't have to sit there and pretend to care about star charts or rising constellations, or whatever else Kyle said he could see at night through his telescope. Orion decided he wasn't going to waste any more time looking for things that were never as good in real life as they were in pictures. Kyle was just another version of a loser.

The bus pulled out. Those left standing at the curb parted from each other, smoothly melting into their separate vehicles. One more step completed in the complicated choreography of the day. And the street became empty and quiet within seconds.

Inside the house, a hundred yards distant, Emma the cat felt their leaving as a slow fading away of vibrations.

She liked this place best when she had it to herself. And but for those eddies and drifts and old sounds left standing in the corners, she was, essentially, alone.

She wandered along the upstairs hallway, towards the largest of the three bedrooms. The door was very slightly ajar and could be moved open with a firm push. The only sound inside was the bedside radio, which now shut itself off. The curtains had been left open and the window's light framed a large, elongated pool of red on the hardwood floor.

She took one step to cross it, startled to find her paw tugged, caught by something there. The small hairs between her pads clung together with a jellylike stickiness. All cats—and this part is pure instinct—hate to walk on sticky things. She touched it delicately with the point of her tongue. Salty. Vaguely like the juice of the lamenting songbird, though finer, richer, with a somewhat metallic bottom note and the bouquet of meat. And it certainly *was* thicker than water.

Emma backed away from the congealing stain, stepping around it to head directly for the high platform of the bed in the centre of the room. If they weren't moving already—and there was nothing to indicate that they were—then it was one of those days when there was still ample time to disappear into the thickness of the goose-down duvet. She loved to settle there, floating just below their level of consciousness. Breakfast could wait.

She flew upwards to land lightly at the foot of the bed, and waited. No reaction. No movement. Only the distant sound of the phone ringing downstairs, a machine picking up and recording a call from Blockbuster Video. *The Prince of Egypt* was overdue and they'd be charging the full rental price for every day the tape was late.

Emma purred loudly and walked among the two pairs of legs outlined under the bedclothes. She lay between them, ready to rest after her long night out. Then her attention was drawn to something glinting on the pillow.

Between here and there was a pair of hands to cross, the fingers tightly interwoven, two bare arms reaching towards each across a white space. She carefully stepped on to a woman's still-beautiful face, a few strands of blonde hair settled lightly across the blue eyes. It was like mounting a stone. Hard and cold, yielding nothing to the pressure of her steps. Emma extended her claws reflexively, sinking them a fraction of an inch into the glossy white skin of the forehead. She stood there for a moment, enticed by the mix of smells.

Beside her, the man's marble white back shone in the morning light. He was resting partially on his side, most of the contents of his head spilling across the fresh country prints of the bed linens. Feathers from an exploded pillow adhered to the edges of the small black hole on one side of his head. This, or rather its exaggeration on the other side, was the source of the still-soft sprawl of red on the floor below, the threadlike tail petering out halfway up the built-in bookcases on the far wall, across the chronologically ordered back issues of *Metropolitan Home.*

There was a froth of soft vomit around the woman's smooth, slightly parted lips. Emma cleaned it off for her. Fur and flesh met at the top of the food chain.

The cat scooped the shiny metal cylinder out of the folds of the Ralph Lauren 300-thread-count Egyptian cotton fabric and batted it around a few times, finally sending it flying off the bed. She followed quickly after, her paw prints left behind, faintly outlined in rust on the sheets. Once on the floor, and soon bored, she forgot the new toy and instead began to lick herself clean of the remains of the blood. The radio came on again, forcing her from the room and down the long hallway in search of simple warmth, peace and quiet.

The door to the second bedroom tapped loosely in its frame. Back and forth, staccato, in the strong breeze that Emma felt coming from the crack underneath it. But the door itself remained stubbornly closed to her. She slid back down the wide staircase. There was always another way.

Although it was now full daylight, the overcast sky had lowered dramatically and darkened in the last hour. Emma kept tight to the side of the house, sheltering herself under the eaves. Here the ground was still dry, though mere inches from her it was soaked, running with rainwater. Anticipating the climb ahead, she recalled a clear route from sometime in the ancient past. Where once had stood a rain barrel, there was now a slope-roofed shed. Then a trellis. Then a low-angled gable to a window that stood already half opened.

The heavy rain came straight down at this point.

So it was only the growing wind that moved the curtain aside. Emma insinuated herself into the room. Past the sill. Past the mirror-like eye of the telescope on its pedestal, pointing upwards.

There, she jumped effortlessly on to the small, single bed in which the child lay. She pushed her face up against his, roughly. No response. She finally settled into the available curve of his shoulder, against the fading pulse in his throat. There was still a faint warmth there, at least.

She reminisced about the thrill of the dying songbird, then went to sleep. It had been a long, full night and Emma's heightened senses, like those of all her kind, were finely attuned to disaster and dislocation. Something seemed out of place here though it was all where it was supposed to be. Whatever. Even the most disturbing shadows would fade in time.

Downstairs, the phone rang again.

1

If it was early enough in the day, you could still see the city it had once been: mist coming off the river and drifting up the valley, Lockport settled secure above it—a stirring, potent bulk of brick and steel. The sun hitting the windows at exactly the right angle to turn all of them to gold.

But by late afternoon you would see instead the city it had become: the golden buildings, now exposed as underused, eviscerated or abandoned, the emptiness having somehow resolved itself into a kind of disappointed acceptance. And all so slowly revealed—over decades, really—that no one had noticed until it was far too late. Except when campaigning politicians came to town and used it as the backdrop for stories unveiling pockets left behind by The New Economy, or whatever had come next to take its place. One of the have-nots, in an entire country of must-haves. The Stoney River, no longer the source of a fresh and clear breeze. As they say, when steel goes, only rust remains.

Looking over it all as she drove across the river, Annie still saw the whole. Maybe it was nothing more than middle-aged inertia that kept her there. Or that, in every neighbourhood she passed through, she'd always know someone or recognize a local phrase or the trace of a familiar accent pointing back to immigrant parents. It was still easy to guess who had gone to which parochial school. Some neighbourhoods changed less than others because people generally stayed where they started.

Not Anne Shannon, though. She'd made it all the way to South Navy. Not far—still on the same side of the river as her old neighbourhood—but further than most who came from her background ever really expected to get.

In the next moment it was all behind her. The water disappeared below and Annie coasted smoothly off the bridge into the luxurious greensward of Belford.

Annie knew Belford best from her earliest years, when she had travelled through as a kind of tourist; remembered it when she used to follow her two older brothers through this same neighbourhood, sliding precariously along icy ruts cut into the freezing brown slush. Those were the dark winter afternoons when they rode their bikes over to look for Fred James. In those years, Fred James had been the only real celebrity in town—a legendary defenceman for the New York Rangers. She hadn't really understood very much at all about Fred James or his place in the pantheon of hockey, but it was something the boys wanted to do, and she always followed.

The three of them would gather on the sidewalk in front of Fred James's big house, in the damp early evenings of winter, hoping to pick out the familiar figure moving behind the windows. In the off-season, the summer, they knew that Fred James went away to Florida to play golf. But by October he'd be back here, visiting his family, and they might be able to see him. Though all they ever really saw was the cool blue light of a TV, casting reflections on the living room ceiling.

Back in their own neighbourhood, they practised like it mattered, every night the same eight or ten kids, in the few hours between school and supper. The net was set up in the middle of the icy street, forcing traffic to slow around them. With every set of headlights coming towards them, a wail of mixed impatience and resignation. *"Car!"* Always someone's father behind the wheel, so they couldn't get too mouthy. The net dragged back and forth in the same place, carving out a path in brown slush that usually lasted until spring.

Now, even *she* was famous, after less than two years as director of communications for the Lockport police department. On TV almost every night. Trotted out on the local news to explain one tragedy or another. Trying to answer the often unanswerable.

As she neared the address she'd been given, Annie reached over to click on the radio. Nothing yet but weather reports, commodities prices, an ad for one of the lube shops on the bypass. For something like this she was half expecting to drive in under the glare of lights and microphones already extending towards her out of the gloom. But then again, she reminded herself, "something like this" hadn't happened for a long time. Maybe everyone was just out of practice.

Almost reluctantly, she switched to the police band. Things were being ordered in as others were dismissed. The coroner's office was—*definitely* was—required. She translated the codes without thinking. After almost twenty years it was a language as familiar to her as the Latin liturgy had once been. Rare, though, to find herself at an active crime scene these days. Usually, by the time she showed up, the debris was already cleared away, its pertinent details set out in sharp relief, ready to be ordered into another tidy narrative, reduced to the substance of clean-typed summary reports. They weren't paying her for her investigative skills anymore.

This time, it was different; they wanted her there as soon as possible. It meant she was going to have to approach the situation from another perspective. Rely more on older habits—calculating how best to enter the scene, the most immediate concerns of preserving evidence. Prepare herself for whatever atrocities she could expect to see, then get ready to spend the next few nights trying to push those same pictures out of her head. Maybe *she* was the one out of practice.

The disembodied voice on the radio was now saying that the streets were clear. Just keep it that way, Annie thought, and she pulled into the driveway.

It was Fred James's old house, of course. She knew that before she saw it. The same large trees. The same vine-covered, half-timbered walls and mullioned windows, gabled roofs, the curved walk up to the big wooden door. A mansion well suited to a childhood hero. Now, more notoriously, the home of a murdered family: husband, wife, eight-year-old boy.

Maybe it was fame itself that had now come to inhabit this house, and forever after it could be referred to simply by its provenance, its lineage—a brand name, like those belonging to long-forgotten Hollywood movie stars. The Gary Cooper. The Carole Lombard. Maybe in time this would become The Mallick.

Police officers were pulling a roll of yellow plastic tape across almost the entire front of the house, stringing it between the big trees to block anyone who might try to approach the scene from the sidewalk.

The school bus had returned only a few minutes earlier. The tribe of mothers was again assembled, but more quietly this time, holding themselves in a tight group on the other side of the street. As the bus was unloaded, each child in turn stared at the big house, now surrounded by police, gas utility trucks and other unidentified vehicles, the front yard—even in the early darkness—brightly outlined in yellow tape.

All the children were excited and demanding. Their mothers tried to hustle them away, refusing to answer their high-pitched questions, separating from each other with meaningful, self-important glances and terse comments above their children's heads.

Then Annie's view of them was cut off by the arrival of the WAZL news van, which blocked her from behind. The cameraman had already jumped from the vehicle to grab establishing footage—the house, the garage door, the yellow tape stretched tight between the trees—all of it in the kind of hysterical bobbing and weaving that had become the hallmark of the station's overheated coverage. Callie Christie, WAZL's features reporter, was still busy checking her makeup in the rear-view mirror. Annie moved away quickly, trying to cut across the lawn towards the front door.

Too late. "Lieutenant Shannon," a voice called out. "Hey, Annie. Wait up." Callie Christie had spotted her and was waving cheerfully as she hurried towards her.

Annie took a deep breath. She just wanted to go home, maybe have another bowl of bran flakes and milk. Instead she forced herself to stand and wait, her high heels slowly sinking into the rain-soaked grass.

That was the deal. She'd made herself one promise before agreeing to step into this job: to always deal with the media as straightforwardly as possible; to take the longer view in establishing trust, no matter what the short-term pressures. Most of the time, as it turned out, the real pressure came from irreconcilable demands inside the department itself. On other days it seemed like everyone in Lockport had already staked some kind of personal claim to her. But you bought that kind of attention with the ride, she reminded herself. It was foolish to try to duck it. The best policy in the end? No speculation, no spin. And, mostly, she'd kept to that.

"How many dead?" The vintage Callie Christie opening. Optimistic as always. Ready to do whatever she could to provoke a spontaneous emotional reaction. The camera light was on, and the front yard of the house lit up like a stadium.

Annie took a deep breath, giving herself a moment to set aside her automatic irritation. She knew they'd be happy with a little something for the suppertime news, nothing more than a short sound bite until the next report. "At this time," she began calmly, "we are able to confirm only that there are three people in the house, all members of the same family. We have no indication, as yet, of their condition." Then she stopped.

Callie feigned surprise. The camera ran on, her none too subtle signal that she was waiting for something more. Tape was cheap. And most subjects finding themselves trapped in that light *would* ramble on, she knew, usually digging themselves into a deeper hole.

Not Lieutenant Shannon, though. It seemed that she could outlast any silence. With a grin, Callie finally dropped the microphone to her side. The cameraman cut and everyone blinked in the sudden darkness.

Annie smiled, adopting a lighter tone. "Give me about an hour, Callie, and I'll do your eleven o'clock."

Callie shrugged and waved the cameraman away. Then she turned back to Annie, more eagerly. "You *do* know, right? That it's Leah Mallick. The doctor?" Just the way she said it made it sound important.

Annie had discovered early on that it was usually worth her time to trade a little of this lifestyles-of-the-rich-and-famous with Callie. She lived for the stuff, apparently, and her inventory of trivia about them was positively awe-inspiring at times.

"Yeah, so I understand," Annie responded. In truth, the name didn't mean anything to her. After a while the social pages tended to blur from one gala into the next. But she knew Callie was well connected and, right now, seemed conspicuously excited as well. "So, what do we have on them?" Annie said it casually. Funny, she thought, in this town it was usually the reporters who didn't know when to shut up.

"Well, he's some hotshot financial investment type. Rolled out some high-tech thingy as soon as he got to town. Hooked up from the get-go with all the right people. In fact, they were *both* major social when they first arrived. Out of the blue, right? About a year ago. They were, like, a real power couple, you know? *Crème de la crème* type of thing? Absolutely gorgeous, too—in fact, that's really what you first noticed. But then, a few months ago, they seemed to drop out. Of everything. Charities, clubs. Just sort of disappeared." Callie stopped long enough to register bewilderment.

Annie could easily guess what Callie was thinking: why would *anyone* want to step off the merry-go-round like that? And the likeliest answer came to Annie in the same instant: money problems. She had nothing specific—the details would inevitably flow over the next several hours—but she easily recognized the *type*.

One of the unexpected obligations of the job was that she put in at least a token appearance at almost every charity gala, exhibition or sporting event held in town. She regularly rubbed shoulders now with the kind of people she'd only ever heard of or read about before. People like these. *The Mallicks.* "Well, anyway," she said, "we don't have the formal IDs yet. So let's keep quiet about that for now. My guys haven't even finished the preliminary inside." She shrugged, smiling slightly again. "Listen. You know you got here the same time I did—"

She was about to go for her standard just-between-us pitch—the "can you at least *try* to keep the speculation to a minimum until I get back to you" one—but was interrupted by the sound of another siren floating to them from less than a block away. A tune composed of new notes.

Callie turned to Annie, surprised. "That's the paramedics, isn't it?"

Annie said nothing. Callie was right. But why would *they* be on the way? She'd already been told there was nothing left for them to do here.

Annie sucked her brand-new Ferragamos out of an inch of wet turf and headed towards the house, the reporter practically climbing her heels as she walked. Ignoring her own growing unease, Annie stepped through the doorway without a backwards glance, leaving Callie on the front step, barred from following by a wall of three uniformed officers.

Annie stood in the entry hall for a moment, looking around. But it was nothing less or more than what she'd expected: the controlled intensity of a first walk-through, playing out in a kind of slow motion. A couple of cops standing watch. A few plainclothes detectives moving deliberately through the downstairs rooms.

Everyone glanced up quickly when they heard her come in. A few greeted her with a friendly wave. But then everyone returned to their work, with one exception—a young cop, a regular patrol officer who continued to stare at her, impressed to see her there, in person.

She'd noticed that kind of thing happening more and more. People were always making too much of her appearance at a scene—if not another cop, then the "lookie-loos" crowding the edges of every incident. Calling out her name. Even asking for her autograph. She showed up, it meant lights, cameras and action; something better, anyway, than a B & E or a prostitute's overdose. Real street theatre. But her sharp impatience with the phenomenon was new, even to her.

Out here, she felt like something apart from the real work, her presence an afterthought, almost an intrusion. No matter how much lip-service they gave to abstract ideals about informed public relations, she was nothing more to them than another flack, despite all her years out on the street, in the department. When she knew she'd earned every right to walk into 'something like this' as one of them.

Just calm down, she told herself. One young, star-struck recruit wasn't to blame for her bad mood. Stress was. Being in this kind of place was. Maybe just the thought of going upstairs was, her own reluctance to take the first step to becoming a new, unexpected failure.

A second later it was the arriving medical crew that stopped her, pushing her out of the way as they barrelled through the front door at a near run to disappear up the staircase before she could even begin to climb. Without having to ask, Annie knew that Bill Williamson was already supervising whatever was happening up there. And he'd tell her whatever she really needed to know as soon as he had it. It made it easy to justify staying out of the way a little while longer. More politic. Detectives, even long-time friends and former partners, didn't appreciate an envoy being sent in by management to look over their shoulders.

So Annie found the doorway leading out to the double-car garage.

It was frigid. The temperature had dropped more than ten degrees since three o'clock and everyone's breath clouded the air. A group of three investigators was already at work on the two expensive vehicles—one a European sedan, the other a high-performance sports car. Combined value, she estimated, at least $150,000.

It would have been obvious to anyone exactly what had happened here. Annie was sure she could still detect the faint smell of exhaust.

Two detectives were examining the tailpipe of the car closest to the door into the house—a silver Porsche Boxster, still attached by a flexible hose to the outlet of a built-in vacuum-cleaner system. They recorded their low-key conversation as they documented and catalogued the evidence, working quickly to determine its probable connection to the drama unfolding upstairs.

One detective looked up and met her with an easy smile. "Hey, Lieutenant. This must mean we're going to be on TV tonight."

Annie nodded shortly. No one could really be surprised at that, she thought.

He gestured towards the car. "This is the one—actually ran out of gas. Just enough though," he said. "These things don't get many miles to the gallon." He looked, laughing, towards the other two officers.

The second detective was John Bartlett. He glanced up at Annie now, unsmiling. "So, how goes it upstairs? We heard the medics pulling in outside."

Annie shook her head. "I don't know yet. I was just on my way up there when they arrived."

Not strictly true but it was only what her Aunt Ell would have called a simple sin of omission. She should have added that she didn't really need an excuse—that she would've given anything not to have to go up there. Anything, not to see a murdered child. She'd already set her expression to neutral. "So, anything jump out?" You always looked for the anomaly, she remembered.

Nearly hidden on the other side of the vehicle, the third detective piped up in a Mr. Rogers-like singsong voice. "Can you say open-and-shut, Bunkie?" He was lifting fingerprints from the car, its silver finish already marred with untidy smudges of what looked like black soot. They'd be working out here for hours yet.

"So, anything unusual?" Annie said. John Bartlett glanced up at her again. It took her another second to realize that she'd said the same thing only a moment before.

The other detective waved his hand, covering the general scene. "Nothing you can't read about later. Hewitt'll have our stuff in a couple of hours." Dan Hewitt was homicide's chief investigator. She knew he'd be arriving any moment now.

The thought of that made her nervous too. Annie never counted on getting much help from him. Rarely more than a basic incident report. His attitude towards her was clear to anyone who bothered to listen. And if they didn't exactly share Dan's opinion, they certainly weren't willing to go too far out of their way to buck it. It had led to an almost continuous series of unnecessary confrontations between her and Dan over the last eighteen months. What use could she possibly have for the details, Hewitt complained loudly. It wasn't up to her to decide what they meant. But this time, Annie thought, *this* time, she was going to need a hell of a lot more than just the *Reader's Digest* version.

Bartlett had already gone back to cataloguing various pieces of evidence. Annie looked around, automatically filing away a few key details for herself—the most visual things, the ones which provided the easy hooks reporters tended to hang their stories on. It always helped to have a solid mental picture. She'd given them dozens of catchy lead paragraphs in the past year or so, framing the story the way she wanted it to be presented.

Only a half-hour ago she'd received the phone call—hardly more than an address and a name. But the urgency in it was obvious and the implications immediately clear: this event mattered a great deal to some important people for whom even the *potential* of expanded media attention was entirely unacceptable, people grown accustomed to the soft strokes of more malleable locals like Callie Christie. But they knew as well as Annie did that these were the first murders in Belford in a generation. This time it was a prominent doctor, a well-connected businessman and a child. Increased scrutiny was inevitable.

"Listen." John Bartlett led her away from the others. He looked at her now, dead serious. "Him, the wife—they're gone, that's for sure. But it's the kid up there. That's who they're working on." His own expression softened. "I thought you should know."

It shouldn't have made any difference—tragedy was tragedy. But Annie knew what he was really thinking: that it was different for her.

"It's okay, John," she said. "No one has to walk on eggshells around me." Another lie.

But, then who among them could claim to be prepared for this, despite the show of easy, bantering sameness? If nothing else, that's what her presence here really told them—that they were *all* being watched, very closely, and that management was very nervous.

Annie took in the garage once more with a single dismissive glance, then turned to go back into the house, letting the door sigh closed behind her.

She went through the formal dining room to have a quick look at the kitchen.

It was magnificent, of course.

Through a large window it overlooked the lush back garden. A green and verdant land, she thought, something completely rational. Yet the Mallicks would have looked out on exactly this same view only yesterday, she reminded herself, and found precious little peace in it.

Annie turned her back to the window and began her own careful survey of the room.

In front of her was something straight out of an expensive lifestyle magazine. A large centre island covered with imported granite, expensive cookware hung on display, a restaurant-size Sub-Zero refrigerator and a Gaggenau cooktop. Every bell and whistle. What was it that Callie had called them? "A power couple." Gorgeous, rich and connected. With confident good taste, and the means to impose it upon the world. No wonder the media was gathering. However lurid the details of their deaths, their lives appeared perfect from the outside. Fantasy incarnate.

Annie heard loud voices start up in the front hallway. Some reporter had planted himself firmly on the threshold and was arguing with the same young cop she'd noticed on arrival. The cop was flustered but equally determined. "Sir. No bodies can be moved until we're completely finished," he said, his own voice rising in competition with the reporter's. Annie stepped in between them.

She wasn't surprised to see that it was Sandy Galloway trying to push the line, this time with an inexperienced cop. A bit of a fast-hander that way, always testing the limits—of taste *and* security. She drew him aside, if only to get him to suspend his posturing.

"Come on, Sandy, give us some room here," she said quietly. "Let me do my job and I'll try and give you what you want in a few minutes."

Galloway hesitated for a moment, unwilling to be pushed back without something to show for it. "It's getting pretty late. Can't we move just *one* out?" Not a trace of irony in his voice. He needed the pictures.

She punched the words out more forcefully than she really meant to. "OK. Who do you want first, then? Tell me. What can I do for *you,* Sandy? Which one would *you* like?" It was only the startled expression on his face that stopped her from going further.

He was already backing up now, hands raised in mock surrender. "OK. OK. Jeez, just relax, Annie. I'll step back. But you know I'm still gonna be waiting right outside this door."

She could see that the crowd behind him had grown substantially, despite the efforts of several posted officers.

Dammit, they couldn't even handle street traffic properly. What made anyone think they could really control this story?

"On the sidewalk, Galloway. Now." One of the older, uniformed officers took him by the arm and had him out the door in the next moment.

The young cop was left standing there, not knowing what to do. *So* new. Annie smiled sympathetically and motioned to him. "Hey, could you do a favour for me? I'd like you to make sure there's no kids left over at that bus stop across the street when we have to start moving them. OK?"

He shot a look in the direction she was pointing, then nodded, his face serious. He could be depended upon for *that* much at least, she guessed—probably the type who'd want to be able to tell friends that he'd worked with Anne Shannon at the actual murder scene. As he left, he offered her a small, self-conscious salute.

Annie climbed the stairs, hearing her own words echo in her head. "Which one . . ." she repeated to herself, embarrassed that she'd actually said it aloud, and to a reporter. It was always the flippant remarks that came back to bite you in the ass, she knew. Aside from the fact that other than the memorable mound of John Belushi under a stretched white sheet being carried out of the Chateau Marmont they all looked pretty much alike—in pictures, anyway.

She suddenly found herself standing at the top of the stairs. Something was still going on in the room to her right. She caught a brief glimpse of the paramedics bent over a small figure laid out on the floor.

Bill Williamson glanced up the moment she arrived, staring at her with a mixture of surprise and discomfort. The crew was already clearing out of the large master bedroom. They'd just hauled the two body bags into the hallway.

Something clicked in her. "I think I'd like to hold these until . . . that's finished and out of here," she said. She lifted her thumb over her shoulder in a quick gesture towards the other bedroom.

Bill immediately reached over and tapped the coroner's assistant on the arm. "These stay here until I tell you otherwise," he said.

The assistant straightened up. Didn't matter one way or the other to him; in another ten minutes he was collecting overtime. "No problem. Time for me to go out for a quick smoke?"

"Yeah, but go out the back."

Bill led Annie into the large bedroom.

Having the bodies gone made it easier to move around. They'd taken the photographs they needed for follow-up on positions, distances and angles. She saw that the blood-splash pattern was in one clear direction—across the floor and up the wall. It started at the bed and flew, the bulk of it landing about three feet out from where the man's body had been found on the bed.

"Sorry. I wasn't even thinking what that might look like," Bill said quietly. He understood as well as she did that it wasn't a good idea to have the live one transported out after the corpses. The optics were all wrong, as though they had their priorities confused.

"What's taking them so long, anyway? With . . ." Annie didn't finish, just loosely indicated the direction of the other bedroom. They could both hear the commotion down the hall.

Bill looked at her more closely. "You gonna be OK with this one?"

Jesus. If only people would stop asking. Annie nodded stiffly. "I don't get to choose, Bill. Any more than anyone else." As a distraction she picked up a large framed photograph of the Mallicks and studied it for a moment.

It wasn't just hype, she saw now. They were, or had been, extraordinary to look at. In a moment of perfect ripeness, tipped with sunlight and glowing. Clear eyes, perfect teeth. He, prematurely silvering, still boyish. She, sweeping planes of cheekbones and a pronounced widow's peak of platinum-blonde hair above a high forehead, her generous mouth, an enigmatic smile. Hard to reconcile that with the contents of the two anonymous body bags stored in the hallway. Annie carefully set the picture back in place. "Anyway, I think we're right to worry this time. The media's going to be all over it. I have to grab as much as I can before Dan gets here. You know what he's like when I'm involved."

Bill rested back against the door frame for a moment, his arms folded across his chest. He stared at his feet before speaking. Then he looked directly at her. "OK. To tell you the truth, he was gone. Blue as a coot by the time we got here. Cold to the touch. No heartbeat that anyone detected. We'd already called for the wagon. Then my new guy, Ellison, he thinks he sees some pupil reaction. Before

I know it, he's down there on the floor with the kid, shouting and praying like a son of a bitch the whole time. Started CPR right away while someone gets on the radio for an ambulance. Then the paramedics—they want a real response before they bother to make a run for it. Only got a heartbeat about five minutes ago."

"Their only child?"

"The Mallicks? Yeah . . . about eight years old, from what I can tell." Bill made a dismissive, circular motion beside his own head. "Ah, everything's pretty well shut down, I'd say. There's nothing there to bring back. But I guess you gotta try." He rubbed his eyes, tired. "So the big guys called you, eh?"

Bill rarely referred to department managers as anything other than "the big guys." Faceless, interchangeable. He liked to keep his distance from them.

She shrugged. "They're a little overexcited, maybe. But they haven't had anything like this for quite a while." It was an impressive understatement, she knew.

"Well, tell 'em they can see it downtown, any time they want," he drawled with slight sarcasm.

"Yeah, maybe. But those ones don't have pretty houses with pretty wives in them," Annie said, smiling faintly now. She indicated the large photograph again, one amongst several others like it displayed on an antique side table. The couple. The family of three. The boy alone. The woman, looking straight into the camera. Incredibly striking eyes.

The loud movement in the hallway startled both of them. The ambulance crew was getting ready to leave.

Annie looked at Bill with dismay. "They're really going to do this to him?"

He shook his head, his own face grim. "I know."

They were both thinking the same thing: let him go.

Someone walked into the bedroom as Annie turned away. Another detective, she guessed, but one she didn't recognize. By her rough calculation that made at least twelve personnel in total on scene. It was already a circus, inside and out.

This man had to be Bill's most recent partner, Eric Ellison, recently transferred in from rural upstate. A long-time cop, she'd heard, but new to homicide. He'd probably awakened one morning and figured it was about time to find a career made up of more than stolen trucks and shot-out stop signs. She noticed that he had one part of it down cold already—attitude. Without missing a beat, he was picking up, right where he'd left off, just before he'd pulled the boy back from the dead, with some story about another murdered family. Maybe this room was more luxurious, he allowed, but whatever the demographic, people were dead, exactly the same way.

Bill finished a last notation in his notebook, then looked up at Annie and shrugged. "Well, unless we find a bloody glove that doesn't fit, it's pretty straightforward from here on in. His gun in his hand . . . and . . . *that.*" *That* was the brain matter scattered in a cumulus-shaped cloud. No signs of a struggle in the room. "I figure he must have sat himself down there in that garage, in his fancy car, just waiting until he calculated they were pretty well gone, then wandered back up and finished himself off. Pretty cold bastard, I'd say."

They heard the phone ring in the distance. The one beside the bed remained silent. As the red light on the answering machine blinked, Bill leaned forward to turn up the volume.

A woman's voice—Leah Mallick's presumably—crisp, professional-sounding. But low and slightly roughened. "Hello. You've reached the Mallicks. Please leave a message and someone will get back to you as soon as possible. Thanks for calling." The context was unique, but there was absolutely nothing unusual in it. The beep sounded, followed by an amplified squeaky, complaining adolescent voice. Blockbuster Video. *The Prince of Egypt* was still accruing overdue charges. And it was their only copy.

"Isn't that a little unusual—no ring?" Annie commented. "For a doctor, I mean?"

"Psychiatrist. Probably regular office hours. None of that middle-of-the-night stuff, I guess. Apparently, they all just waited for Monday to come calling," Bill said offhandedly. "There's nine messages. What do you want to bet they're all from today?"

There's a good reason why everyone hates Mondays, Annie thought.

Ellison spoke up from near the window. "You know, one thing—I can't figure out how the casing made it this far. It should have fallen either on the bed or right beside it. Even if it bounced, it wouldn't likely go twelve or thirteen feet in this direction, would it?" His voice was a careful monotone, the comment deliberately phrased as a question. Obviously, he didn't want to look pushy, his first week on a new job.

Annie glanced over at him. The ID tag for the shell was set on the floor on the far side of the room. He was right—it was too far.

"We haven't had a chance to analyze everything yet. I don't . . ." Bill paused.

Annie narrowed her eyes slightly, trying to recall the detail of something she'd seen downstairs, in the picture-perfect kitchen.

The radio came on again, unexpected and startlingly loud, the voice of a hyper drive-time announcer blasting from some all-news super-station in the Midwest. Annie glanced at her watch. Six o'clock—probably the time the Mallicks walked through the door on an ordinary day. Then a few minutes to come upstairs, change into something more comfortable for the evening, catch up on the news. Old habits died harder than people.

Annie reached over and turned it off. The mocking normalcy of it seemed more inappropriate than all the other evidence of death around them.

They heard voices in the hallway. Ellison went out to check. Annie looked around the large bedroom once more. Everything was ready to remove in careful order. Full scene analysis in about a week. Lab results a couple of days later. Autopsies, if they pushed for them, probably by late tomorrow.

Bill started out, then stopped short in the doorway. Just over his shoulder Annie caught a glimpse of two paramedics lifting a stretcher over the railing to force it around the corner. They left a long scuff mark on the creamy yellow wall.

Ellison followed behind them, a big cat draped loosely in his arms. "This guy just ran from under the kid's bed. Making some kind of weird noise."

From the gagging, cacking sound, Annie knew it was nothing more than a hairball. The cat looked sleepy and evil to her. But then, she was a dog person.

"Seems pretty groggy, too," Ellison said to Bill.

"Yeah, well, maybe it got some gas when it settled in for a nap. Have someone drop it off at the ASPCA." Ellison started downstairs. Bill called after him, "And get a receipt."

In the next moment the bank of television lights came on again outside, and Annie saw the light from several flashes—still cameras this time—bounce off the wall. Seconds later the siren started up.

Bill turned away in disgust. "Vultures still circling out there?"

"Yeah. They're waiting for me. I have to go back out and talk to them in a few minutes, anyway." She glanced at her watch. "OK, I want to take a quick look." She headed down the hallway towards the boy's bedroom.

"Annie—c'mon . . ." Annie looked back to see Bill shaking his head. "You don't have to go in there."

"Yeah, Bill, I do." She entered the room.

Reluctantly, he followed her.

Once inside, she could see that there was really nothing. Nothing untoward, at least—no blood or gore. Only elegantly framed science posters and models of the space shuttle. And an elaborate, expensive telescope standing at the window, aimed at the sky.

She let out a long, slow breath.

"It's really something, though, isn't it?" Bill said quietly. It was reflex—he'd dropped his voice to a low whisper as he waved a hand around at the whole expanse of the house.

And he wasn't the only one impressed. Let's face it, she thought to herself, if *we* weren't cops and *they* weren't dead, none of us would even be invited inside a place like this.

Annie nodded. "Fred James's old house. When I was a kid."

Bill smiled slightly. "The hockey player? With the Rangers in, what, the late fifties?"

"Something like that." She'd already moved away from him, to the other side of the room near the window. She was now standing there, staring out.

"Annie, what's going on? Why are you here—really?" He'd put a slight, if unintended, emphasis on the "you." The real question was, Why are you putting yourself through this?

Unexpectedly, a fleeting thought formed whole. *To bear witness.* Where had that come from? She buried it again.

Without turning, she knew exactly what Bill's face looked like in this moment, mouth drawn down in embarrassed, misplaced sympathy. Like John Bartlett's. Like a few of the others she'd seen walking through this house who knew something of her history. They all wanted to jump to the same conclusion—that this amounted to a kind of test for her.

They weren't wrong. Even now, a subtle tremor was working its way through her body. Sheer tension. She only hoped Bill couldn't see it.

"Look," she began, "If I didn't think I could handle it, I wouldn't be here. It doesn't take something like this to remind me. Everything does. It always will," she said. "A highway accident. Or some kid goes missing in a shopping mall. Or I pass a sandlot baseball game on my way home." She stood facing him directly, her voice firm now. "Charlie's been gone for ten years, Bill." She indicated the room. "*This* is not my problem. You are. You and all your friends—watching me, just waiting for me to fall apart."

A simple overstatement this time. And they both knew it.

Bill protested. "That's not true. Or fair . . ."

After a moment Annie made a slight gesture of apology. "You don't need me to tell you what's going to happen here. Look out front. They've got it *all,* this time, everything they could possibly want." More than enough to feed the whole voracious frenzy of overheated commentary on TV, in the tabloids. "You saw what the Mallicks looked like—that alone would put them on the front page of every newspaper in this state. *And* they were rich, they were successful, and they were important enough for someone to want to send in half the department. Maybe you don't need to be here. But I do." She almost smiled. "All this, combined with violent trauma? Absolutely irresistible, I would imagine."

She looked out the window again, over the back garden, now sunk in shadows, disappearing into a deep river ravine. She felt Bill brush his hand lightly against hers. "Well, we sure as hell don't need to *stay* in here," he said.

Annie allowed him to guide her away from the window. At the doorway she turned one more time to look at the room, wanting to take in all its details. The small, single bed. The slight, rounded indentation in the pillow, the bedding dishevelled as though kicked off in the night. Star Wars sheets.

She squared her shoulders. Now she was ready to confront the hovering hordes.

Annie started slowly down the staircase, still mulling over one lost detail. She looked up to see Bill leaning on the railing above her. "Hey, were the doors closed?" she asked. "To both bedrooms?"

"Yeah, I think—" he said, then hesitated and checked his notes. "No, wait. The master bedroom was open."

That was it. She recalled a small animal entrance cut into the back door, in the kitchen. One of those little plastic things with the weather flaps. That's how it would have happened, the bullet shell. A typical cat, letting himself in and out, maybe a dozen times in the night. It was the cat who'd probably knocked the casing off the bed, in some atavistic ritual of domination. Nothing more than a new, shiny toy . . .

Annie stopped herself. A cat who'd magically found some way to dematerialize through a closed door, then reconstitute itself in the room of a sleeping boy . . .

She shook her head, then dismissed it. The ways of cats are mysterious. And it wasn't in her job description to come up with all the answers.

"Well, I *will* bet you ten bucks on one thing, Billy Boy," she said.

Bill was watching her now with a cautious smile. "Yeah? On what?"

"The cat'll lead the broadcast."

There was another sudden flurry of activity on the stairs. The two body bags were being carried down and placed on stretchers waiting in the entrance hall. Through the living room windows Annie watched as the TV lights came on again in anticipation. The folding stretchers were snapped up to full height and paraded down the curving path into the ambulance, the attendants carefully ignoring the cameras and the people from the neighbourhood gathered on the sidewalk. The ambulance took off immediately. No flashing red lights this time. No siren.

Five minutes later Annie stood in the same glare and a light rain, ready to wrap it all up for an audience she knew wanted only to retire in peace for the evening. Three other TV stations had joined the small assembly of media which now included all the local and area newspapers.

Annie stood calmly in front of the house, waiting until she saw they were ready for her. She felt no particular anxiety, had never been susceptible to stage fright. She hardly bothered to look at herself in the mirror any more. Her only concession to vanity was that she habitually removed her glasses before being photographed, though it left her slightly nearsighted. When strictly necessary—maybe for a studio interview—she applied makeup to a face she regarded as not quite her own. It was a face, though, that—surprisingly to her at least—happened to work for television.

The secret, she had learned, was not to care. This translated well on camera. Almost anything could be projected upon it: calmness, credibility, assurance and confidence.

Annie offered her opening statement matter-of-factly: "Police arrived at approximately 3:30 p.m. today, to a home in the two thousand block of Scott Boulevard, in the Belford district of Lockport. Attending officers found the bodies of two deceased, a man and a woman, both apparent victims of foul play. A third person was removed to Riverview Hospital. The condition is unknown. None of the victims has yet been identified."

"One of them is a child? A little boy?" It was Callie Christie.

Annie glanced sharply into Callie's eyes behind the camera. *Leave it alone for tonight.* The reporter cleared her throat and waited.

"We're not prepared to confirm any of the identities at this point," Annie repeated coolly.

Callie pressed another button. "Why did it take more than an hour to transfer the third victim to hospital?" Annie knew they would pick up the requisite shot of the reporter's concern on a reverse later.

Don't you see the damn utility trucks? "The scene was being assessed for a possible gas leak. We also had reason to believe that there were registered weapons on the premises. We were unsure how many people were actually in the house at the time, and where they might be located."

"When did you realize there was a problem?"

"Our department was contacted around 2:45 p.m. today. Concern was expressed when various appointments were missed and several phone calls made to the home weren't returned." Shit! *There's* your answer, she thought—we called out the cavalry because someone missed brunch.

"Did you enter with a search warrant?"

"No. No warrant was issued. We had probable cause and entered the premises when there was no response to our initial approach."

"Did you suspect someone might be in trouble inside?"

Annie looked at her this time with barely disguised contempt. *No, we just happened to be passing by.* "Yes. That's why we were investigating."

"What about the victim still in hospital? Do you have any information?" It was another reporter asking.

Annie was getting wet and rapidly losing patience. "As I said, we haven't received a report on the medical condition at this time. There'll be another statement as soon as we have anything else." She walked away before she'd confirmed that all the cameras had cut. Dammit, they'd probably choose to leave *that* in—her back disappearing into the dank night—making her look slightly evasive, if nothing else. Well, it was out of her hands now. And at least the rain was fading. She kept walking.

Over a short time the job had become almost too easy for her. She'd quickly learned that most stories can be controlled simply by conducting the available elements into an easily understood narrative. She was successful at that too, always managing to frame tragedy and happenstance as a natural, completely rational cycle of apparent cause and effect. It was only a hint of confusion that could cause her any serious problems afterwards. It was apparent ineptitude that they jumped on, not purposeful deception. And, as it turned out, almost every story was negotiable.

At least she made sure never to use words like "paradigm," "Zeitgeist" or "synergy."

Alone in her car, she waited for the other vehicles to clear the driveway behind her, for things to settle down and become quiet again. She imagined the house continuing on by itself—automatically making coffee, turning lights and radios off and on, running the VCR, regulating heat and answering phones. Then, growing cold at last, slowing, the machines would finally become still, as everything inside ceased and composed itself into silence. After all was said and done, how would these particular people be missed in the world, she wondered, and by whom? What specific *absence* would their deaths create?

After half a minute, she roused herself and leaned on the horn, hard, to clear the traffic jam the media had built around her. One crew was still out there, shooting God only knew what.

Finally, one car left. A news van pulled away. It was almost over. She noticed, with some surprise, that her knuckles were white where she gripped the steering wheel, and she realized that she couldn't breathe properly. On top of it all, she felt the start of another hot flash. Not even the decency to come in the middle of the night this time . . .

Dan Hewitt, the chief investigator, rapped sharply on the driver's side window. She rolled it down a few inches. "Follow me to the office. I'll give you the briefing details tonight. Tomorrow's my day off," he said.

Annie hadn't noticed him arrive at the scene.

Her hand shook a bit as she inserted the key into the ignition. Metallica blasted out of her speakers. That wasn't her regular station. She switched over to soft rock, coming in on the anthemic, see-sawing shouts of the Righteous Brothers. "Baby. Ba-by." Then Elvis Presley's "Kentucky Rain." Poor Elvis, she thought. She turned it off completely and pulled out on to the boulevard.

Belford's quiet streets had always represented the silence of luxury to her—better, certainly, than the screaming of too many kids crammed into a series of small bungalows, ruled by shouting mothers fighting to be heard. Now, that same silence spoke more of retreat. There was no one out on the street here any more. All apparently tucked away, safe inside their houses.

Fifteen minutes later she drove into the parking lot at Division Seven. It was a large pile of a building completely dominating the street front on three sides of a city block. It served as Department headquarters too, though large sections of it now were used for storage or simply left empty. The building sat squarely in the middle of downtown, next to the most crime-ridden section of the city. No one in the Department was unaware of the irony in that. But none of them lived here any more; they commuted in from the suburbs.

Early evening, relatively calm on the first-floor Operations, with a smaller night shift coming in. Her own office was away upstairs in the administrative section, but Annie crossed through the hallway into the main room. She saw a crowd of five or six moving slowly in her direction, talking loudly. It looked like the typical tour, some retired cops just dropping in for a visit.

Fewer people actually worked in the building these days. Satellite offices, community policing—it spread the available force a bit thin over a broad, expanded area. Most long-timers retired away from here, no longer bothering to come back, even to reminisce. They had their RVs parked now in Florida or Arizona. They golfed or went to the dog track. They sent sunny, smug photos back to family and snow-bound former neighbours in the middle of winter. There were only a few still left around.

As the group passed her, she heard them talking to each other in loud stage whispers. "That Bud's girl? The one from the TV?"

Her father had been retired from this same division for a little more than fifteen years, and there were very few she remembered from that time still on active duty here. But those who had remained in the city liked to drop in sometimes, get the "inside skinny," as they called it. They told the same stories, to anyone who would listen, every time. She usually managed to avoid them.

Dan Hewitt was at his own desk on the other side of the floor. His assistant, Randy Bellows, was working with him, printing out materials from the laptop they shared. Hewitt set a few of the finished pages to the side. He looked up briefly as she arrived.

No preamble. "Here's my notes. Williamson's." He laid them out as he spoke. "Names. Our call-sheets. Anything else?" He didn't wait for her answer, but turned again to Bellows. "Get these to the lab. And you can follow up with the coroner first thing tomorrow." Hewitt sat on the edge of the desk and pointed to the computer screen. "Check on business registrations in either of their names. And get a hold of any bank account numbers held in the state. Credit cards, that kind of thing." Hewitt was already assuming money problems. "Anything on next of kin yet?"

The other officer shook his head. "We've started contacting California. Nothing we can find so far."

Hewitt finally spoke directly to Annie. His tone, as usual, was carefully measured, entirely reasonable-sounding whenever anyone else was around. "They moved here about fourteen months ago. No one can tell us much about them."

"Neighbours?"

"As usual, they're worth a big bucket of warm spit," he growled. "None of 'em heard or saw a thing. The ones that *wanted* to talk to us had nothing to say. One of them spent the whole time complaining about the dog next door barking all night. All those houses over there are spread out on half-acre lots. They're not going to know anything."

"But the Mallicks were fairly active socially," Annie said. "At least, initially—"

"Yeah, I know. I heard the same thing. Real society money types." Hewitt glanced at his watch. Far too late to disturb that particular type of person and ask about their late friends. It wasn't worth the rash of complaints to the mayor's office. "Someone'll have to check them out first thing in the morning too. Anything else *you* need?" An edge of sarcasm in the way he said it now. He glanced up.

"Maybe we could discuss how you want to handle this—like, release the information."

He waved his hand at her dismissively. "That's up to you."

Bellows was almost finished. He held out a few more pages to Annie. "Quite a little mess there," he said.

"Does anyone have any real idea why he did it yet?" she said.

Dan Hewitt sounded completely uninterested. "Mallick? It'll come out. It's always the same thing with ones like this anyway. We'll have it tomorrow or the next day."

Bellows looked up from the keyboard. "What about *her*—did you get a gander at those pictures? Man!" He'd seen the photographs displayed throughout the house too. He shook his head. "And the kid. If he just wanted to off himself, why them?"

Annie had her own idea: that Tim Mallick simply hadn't wanted to leave them behind. Instead, they were just all going to go to sleep. Travelling away together. Sliding into unconsciousness, while he awaited the end alone. A warped kind of tenderness . . .

"I hear you tore a strip off Sandy Galloway. Getting a little pushy, was he?" Hewitt asked. He seemed almost amused for a moment.

She blushed slightly. Someone must have overheard that hissy fit. "Yeah. I just had to push back a little."

"First high-class murder these guys have had in quite a while. Maybe he just forgot where he was for a minute."

How could anyone "forget," she wondered. There wasn't one person there tonight who hadn't taken a moment to imagine what it would really be like to live in a big, fancy house like that. A beautiful garden, an interior designer's fantasy, a boy's own wet dream of a high-performance sports car in the garage. The only thing that could disturb the perfect picture was tucked way upstairs. Everywhere else, it was quiet and order.

Bellows finally indicated that he was done, with a long list to start on, first thing in the morning. He said good night and left.

Once they were alone, Annie felt an immediate shift in Dan Hewitt's attitude. He didn't look up when he spoke. "So why were you there, anyway? You know you always get our briefing as soon as it comes out."

"Just trying to keep my hand in, Dan," she said, hoping to sound more at ease than she really felt. The response was glib, she knew. But she was weary of the constant low-grade tension between them. Management had sent her in. He knew that. The situation was significant enough to warrant her direct involvement, the first murder in Belford in years. In fact, it was potentially explosive. These particular dead people had been well connected. She wasn't given a choice. "You know, filling in the colour commentary."

Hewitt raised an eyebrow briefly, then closed his notebook. "Well, you'll have the rest of it before the end of the week. Anything else?"

Annie hesitated for another moment. Dan didn't welcome interference from anyone, especially her. "Just that I think we're going to have to be ready for an unusual amount of attention on this one."

He glanced up at her again, his eyes narrowing now. "Oh? And why is that?"

She knew this wasn't the time to become defensive, but he always chose to make her fight for every inch of ground.

"You saw the media out there tonight, Dan. And it'll be twice that by the end of the week. With something like this . . . Look, Tim Mallick was some big-shot consultant, with important local connections. His wife was a prominent psychiatrist. Who knows what either of them was really into, what was going on between them? The simple fact is that people are going to ask—"

Hewitt slammed the drawer of his desk with some force. He drew out his words as though speaking to a child. "Well, I'll tell you. And you can tell them. I am not prepared to spend any more staff time on this than I have to. We've got enough going on down here. Once the coroner's report is filed, it's done. We got the bad guy. He's dead. So we know who. We know where and when, and we know how. I figure that's as much as we get paid for these days. If they want more, they can take it to a grand jury. But if you're going to have trouble with this . . . ?"

She couldn't let him think what he was thinking. "I'll be fine," she said. "But you know why they sent me in tonight. And what I need to discuss right now is how we should be working this one."

Hewitt pretended surprise. "'We,' Lieutenant? What reason could we have to work together?"

"Because we don't know why, Dan," she said flatly. "And 'why' is all the public's going to be asking. No one's seen anything like this for a long time. Everything you, I," she pointed vaguely in the direction of administration, "or *they* do, is going to be on the front page."

"Can't say I give a particular shit." He refused to look at her now. "Isn't that just bread and butter for you PR types?

Lucky for us we've got someone like you protecting the good of the department."

She knew they were both being more knee-jerk than usual, but at least everyone was warned for this round. And his implication, patronizing as he intended it to be, was straightforward. She was one of "them" now.

"You're right. I'll handle it," she said tightly.

He pushed the chair into the desk. "Well then, I guess I can head out."

She spoke more firmly. "I'll be releasing the names at the press conference. Whatever else your guys come up with. Unless you can give me some reason why I shouldn't . . ."

"You do what you have to do, Lieutenant," he said. "You know it's just a relay this time, anyway. We're passing it upstairs. And they can all take it and twist it into anything they like up there. I'm going fishing." He left her standing.

As she watched him walk away, she recalled a dozen summers when she'd been invited to tag along with her dad and Dan Hewitt, in that old twelve-foot aluminum boat of his. On the early morning water, through the years when the Stoney River still flowed with fish. A five-horsepower engine putt-putting them up against the slow current. Drifting back, as the sun finally rose. Those were the only times the grown-ups would let her drink coffee.

Someone called out to Hewitt as he passed—one of the visitors. She watched him stop to talk with them, all still gathered down at the other end of the floor. They were right in the thick of reminiscence now, she knew, everyone repeating the same stories she'd once memorized. The ones they'd all heard themselves, too, a hundred times. Legends and fables of being a cop in Lockport, everything she'd once believed, accepted, without a second thought. Most of them down there had come up through the ranks together, the last of them now a year, maybe two at most, from retirement. She heard some loud talking, followed by a big shout of laughter. She left by the other stairs.

Annie could easily imagine what her job looked like to most of them: unlimited social swilling at white-wine receptions, little speeches, rubbing elbows raw with uninformed elected officials, visits to school kids, always out promoting charity events and bicycle rodeos. Maybe they were right—maybe it was nothing more than a kind of limbo with a clothing allowance.

At least most of the working cops were polite to her face, agreeing to co-operate whenever she asked. Some even seemed flattered to be involved. Otherwise, she supposed, they didn't really notice one way or the other what she did, as long as it didn't get in their way. But Dan Hewitt was something else. And tonight she felt spent and empty and exhausted. The last thing she'd wanted was another fight with him.

Annie took her usual route through the downtown core. It made for an easy commute. A few sleazy dance clubs and bars the only real action showing down here at nine on a weeknight. Knots of patrons at the doors, flashing colour and cash. She knew, though, that a single raid on any one of them could net at least twenty illegal weapons charges and probably five or six arrests for trafficking. Forget simple possession—they'd have to charter a bus.

But unless something big happened, cops didn't bother going in that much.

Hitting the four-lane, she noticed only that the rain had ended. Everything else outside the car quickly retreated to a straight line of strip malls and car lots. The same pattern reproduced with relentless economic efficiency in a million other places just like this one.

Lockport was divided cleanly in half by the Stoney River. Where it passed through town, the Stoney appeared, from almost every angle, like a still and stagnant pond, ready to disappear in the next heat wave. Distant street lights reflected off it now as she passed over. From this height the water looked as hard and slick and unmoving as a sheet of black plastic—a river so abused it no longer knew which way to flow.

Annie's house was on the opposite side of the river from the Belford district, in the neighbourhood still known as South Navy, a name given it after the First World War. It was the second of Lockport's two oldest districts, and its once gracious homes had quickly filled with the large families of European immigrants who arrived in the years when a canal to the lake was promised and great shipyards were planned.

These days, South Navy was composed mostly of obstinate left-over seniors living on low fixed incomes. Over the years, its larger houses had been divided into suites to help carry heating costs and taxes. It was a neighbourhood that found itself in a constant state of unwanted change, barely accommodating the influx of older welfare recipients and mental outpatients, even as it tried to push its own drunks and drug addicts further to the west.

In some ways though, the neighbourhood reflected a small part of the movement to urban gentrification. Her own remodelled house, a pseudo-Victorian, was a mid-sized two-storey, built around 1922. Nondescript, rundown in the beginning. A "character" home, the real estate agent had said—as though the very act of its possession would give her one. Annie's interest in it as a project waxed and waned with the seasons and the weather.

She climbed the steps to her expensively restored porch. With a sigh that sounded alarmingly like a groan, she bent down to pick up two days' worth of water-soaked newspapers.

Her overweight English springer spaniel flung himself at the front door as she opened it. He gave her the same rapturous, unconditional welcome at her every return. It sometimes seemed worth coming home for.

Ben was making it very clear that he needed to go out. It would probably do both of them some good, she knew. She gathered up his leash and headed back out.

They walked slowly along the wet sidewalks, beneath shadows of dripping chestnut trees, under the dim, old-fashioned street lamps the city hadn't yet got around to replacing in the area. The streets were mostly empty. Ben trotted up ahead of her, carrying the end of his leash in his mouth. It was his only trick.

Annie tended not to go out this late alone. It was her job to reassure residents that they were safe, yet even as a cop she sometimes felt uncomfortable walking at night on these old, familiar streets. She knew she was being as obstinate as the rest of them, staying on against her better judgment when she could probably afford better elsewhere. She was in danger of becoming one of those despised, stereotypical white-painters, with her carefully restored gingerbread house, banking on promises of urban renewal while the neighbourhood collapsed around her.

An elderly woman was walking fifty or sixty feet in front of her, pulling a small cart loaded down with bags of groceries. It was far too late for her to be out alone too. The woman looked stiff and nervous from behind, obviously listening for any threatening movements. Annie watched her deliberately ignore the passing of one or two cars.

Annie and the woman arrived at the corner at the same time. They both stopped on the curb, waiting for the light to change, though there were no cars coming. Old habits. The woman didn't acknowledge her presence, and looked determinedly ahead.

Wanting to reassure her in some way, Annie spoke. "Hard to believe it's spring already." An innocuous remark, but it sounded too loud in the dark, even to her.

The woman glanced quickly over at her, softening only slightly when she noticed the dog. Still without responding, she crossed before the light had changed. On the other side, she turned down the street, moving as rapidly as she could manage away from the stranger.

Annie considered offering to walk her home, then decided a second approach would probably make it worse. She turned to the right instead, with a good long block left to go.

Reaching home, Ben raced inside before she could grab him, leaving wet footprints the entire length of the hallway to the kitchen. Annie hung up her coat, checked the mail and walked into the dark living room, immediately turning on the television. She didn't bother with the sound; it usually wasn't necessary right away. She found the remote in the seat cushion and slowly climbed the numbers on the dial, studying the silent screen intently.

Who was covering what? And what pictures were they using?

Eventually, she wandered out into the kitchen, finally ready to admit that she was ravenous. For the last hour Ben had been padding quietly back and forth between the living room and the fridge. Together, they'd ended up watching parts of two or three movies, checked out an infomercial that promised to reshape double chins without surgery and enjoyed what had to be the fiftieth rerun of an episode of *Mad About You.*

Annie stood in front of the fridge with the door hanging open. It was filled with carefully labelled containers. Low-fat, high-protein, no carbs. None of it looked appetizing. She gave Ben half of her only piece of Swiss cheese while she archived the rest. Some cold salsa. How old was that Szechuan chicken, and was it worth the risk? She settled for the last of the deli turkey. No bread, no mayo. Like it made any difference.

The answering machine was blinking. As she reached to press play, the phone rang in her hand. Her heart jumped hard in her chest. Still a little tense, she thought.

"Kinda late getting home, aren't you, Lieutenant?"

She could hear the grin on the other end. Greg Bauer. He was a young cop in the division, second lead on the tactical squad. Athletic. Good-looking. And all of thirty, maybe thirty-one years old.

Surprised, she checked her watch. Almost one. Apparently, she'd been stationed in front of the TV for more than three hours. "Yeah. Long day."

"I just got off too," he said. "I thought maybe I could bring by a pizza or something. I don't have to work tomorrow . . ." He waited.

For a moment she considered the possibility. It wasn't the first time; she'd spent most of her working life around groups of healthy men. No strings, she knew, for either of them. It was a straightforward proposition, one even she recognized.

Annie relaxed a little, enjoying the normal, easy give-and-take of it again. It had been a long time. Obviously, fame had its privileges. "So this must be one of those—what do they call them—'booty calls'?"

She heard a low chuckle, followed by a feeble protest. "I . . . uh . . . no. I was just thinking about you. And, ah, hell, you don't really want to be alone, do you?"

Yes. As a matter of fact I do, she thought. "Can I take a rain cheque?" She waited for the argument. It wouldn't take much—

"OK," he said. "Sounds good."

Then silence. Neither of them knew what was supposed to come next. "We got a lot going on at the office," she said, after a moment. Maybe they could have a conversation and consider *that* foreplay.

"Yeah? Anything exciting?" He was trying to be polite.

But she could tell by the sound of his voice that he'd

already moved on. Unless it involved some combination of extreme sports, with mountain-bike riding and whitewater rafting thrown in, a guy like Greg would never find much of what she did very exciting. "No, just a few things in play," she responded.

"Sounds good. Well, listen . . . I'll catch up with you later, then, eh?"

Annie held the phone until she heard the click. These young guys give up far too easily, she thought. Or maybe it was just that they had so many other options.

She extinguished the kitchen lights and stood in the quiet darkness for a long time. The only illumination came in, cool and blue, through the old-fashioned pantry windows set high in the thick walls—an original feature of the house, and a good part of the reason she'd bought it in the first place. That, and the oversized backyard.

After a few minutes she lay back on the living room couch, with Ben sprawled across her lap. He was making little licking noises in his sleep, probably already dreaming of breakfast. She closed her eyes. This was fine. Whenever she was in the house, the television was on. Twenty-four seven. Usually a radio playing somewhere too. She found it comforting.

"And now our latest on the tragedy in Lockport tonight . . ."

The news report was the same. Onscreen, Eric Ellison and the cat stared into the TV camera, two pairs of eyes glazed in the bright lights. Every time, it was the first image. At least she'd won her bet with Bill.

"A family pet has survived a horrific murder-suicide in the Belford area of Lockport tonight. Police made the grim discovery late this afternoon when they arrived at an address in the two-thousand block of Scott Boulevard."

There again were the two body bags being wheeled out the now familiar front door of the Tudor-style house. This was followed by the image of a stretcher, the small figure nested at its centre obscured by drip bags and blankets, swaddled beyond recognition. The intense faces of attendants studiously ignored the camera's lights carving them out of the darkness.

But they'd fucking *changed* it, she thought, irritated for the hundreth time that evening. Didn't they understand—first the survivor, *then* the corpses? They'd deliberately reversed it, probably because someone thought it made a better "throw" to the anchorman.

It wasn't even news any more—just endless repetition of the same headline, over and over again, underlining a garish subtext. Identical to an hour ago. And an hour before that.

"Two bodies, those of a man and woman in their early forties, were found in the upstairs bedroom of a luxury residence. Though as yet unconfirmed, early reports suggest that the prominent financial consultant died of a self-inflicted gunshot wound after murdering his wife, a leading local psychiatrist. The third victim, the couple's nine-year-old son, was removed to Riverview Hospital, where he is now listed in critical condition. Police can still offer no motive for the killings. The names have not yet been released, pending notification of next of kin."

Obviously, a zealous reporter had cornered someone working the scene, someone who'd let slip that they'd pretty well concluded Mallick was the murderer. Probably that assistant from the coroner's office, she thought, the one who'd just stepped out "for a smoke." But the worst part was that there was no one to call and bitch at; it was still only two o'clock.

All it did was destroy every effort she'd made to keep a lid on things until they knew what had really happened. This was Belford, after all, and no speculation was welcome. It also blew apart her own judiciously worded statement, the "disconnect" further emphasized when they chose to show her slinking off into the darkness. Even she could see that. Everything about it—her posture, her body language—was terrible. It looked like a lie.

The piece ran again, at least twice. Annie finally fell asleep on the couch, drifting away to the sound of her own calm, reassuring voice. "The scene was being assessed for a possible gas leak . . . weapons on the premises . . . how many people were actually in the home . . . we haven't received a report on the medical condition . . . we're not prepared to confirm any of the identities . . ."

Bullshit, she thought sleepily.

2

From a mile away, the capital dome of the statehouse seemed to rise above the fog with all the expectations of the First Republic. At this distance it looked almost more impressive than the federal monument it self-consciously imitated. Legend had it that, while passing through on an early whistle-stop tour, President Calvin Coolidge had eyed it, then light-heartedly suggested perhaps servants shouldn't have better quarters than their masters.

Susan Shaw sat on her apartment balcony, watching it glow against the purple sky. The image floated up, as insubstantial as a plaster-and-plywood stage set, lit for only an hour at each dawn and dusk. That was the administration's latest PR move—to save on electric bills when everyone started pushing the environmental hot buttons again for the upcoming election.

Half asleep, she pulled an old sweater up around her shoulders and shivered in the morning damp. She'd spent the night here, curled up in an old lawn chair left by previous tenants, her hands at first wrapped around a large mug of hot chocolate, the same CD—a baroque concerto—repeating for the last three hours. The music was drowned out by a single phrase loud inside her head: Leah Mallick is dead.

It seemed like years ago now. Someone had casually called to her across the nearly deserted cafeteria, pointing at the headline story on the late edition news displayed on one of several TV monitors in the room: *Lockport Couple Found Slain in Home.* "Doesn't that sound like that doctor you got chairing your commission . . . Mallick, right?"

Susan watched the rest of it without comment, then excused herself to spend the next three hours processing a thick stack of files alone in her office. Blind both to the words on the pages and the simple passage of time. When, eventually, she'd found herself standing beside the one window on the floor that still opened, she took up smoking again.

Now, she was well into her third pack. Sitting here, holding the phone, feeling her circulation slowing to zero, her pulse almost flatlined. How, she wondered, could her heart still be pounding like this? Just breathe, she told herself again.

She stared at the skyline. Someone, please, tell me that the entire world isn't about to disappear . . .

The phone had been resting in her hand for the last hour. She gave it another moment, then dialed, listening as it clicked through. Barely six o'clock, far too early for anyone with good manners to be making a call. But on the fourth ring someone answered.

"Hello?"

"It's me."

Immediately, the businesslike tone on the other end gave way to something warmer. "Hi, sweetie. *You're* up early."

Susan waited until she was sure she could speak calmly. "Georgia, I think I'm really in trouble this time."

~~~~

By 6 a.m., Annie had faxed the official release to every news organization in the region. Only one paragraph, and she'd sent that out without getting the usual management approvals. No conclusion—that awaited final corroboration from the medical examiner—but everyone had read between the lines anyway. There wasn't much else. Nothing more than names, address, occupations, ages. Gunshot. Two deaths. Gas. A child in intensive care. There was no point in holding it back now. If it proved necessary, she could arrange a formal press briefing for first thing tomorrow morning.

By eight, she was entering headquarters through a side door, climbing the stairs to the third floor in order to avoid the several reporters already staking out the front lobby.

Tina, the administrative assistant, was standing in the middle of the hallway, waiting as Annie approached her office. She flourished a thick block of messages. "Your voice mail is completely full," she said. "And I've already got fourteen of these. All from people who say they want to adopt—thirteen for the cat, and one for the boy."

Annie held up a hand. "Whoa. Just . . . just . . ." She took a deep breath. "Gimme a sec. Anyone else in yet?"
~~~~

What she *really* wanted right now was a coffee. Didn't dare ask Tina to get it for her.

Tina's animated expression darkened impressively. "Well, the commissioner certainly wants to talk to you." Emphasis on the "you" again.

DeVries was here already? Annie sighed and headed down the hall to her office. "OK. I just need a minute."

"Oh, and by the way—you might like to know there's already someone in your office," Tina called after her, the shrill excitement rising again in her voice. She was practically singing now.

The moment she walked through the door, Annie saw why.

There was a woman sitting there, a woman who stood to meet her, graciously extending a hand heavy with a two-carat diamond. "Lieutenant Shannon? I'm April Vaughan."

Of *course* you are, Annie said to herself. Who *else* would be here, waiting for me?

No introduction was necessary. Like everyone who owned a television, Annie recognized her immediately. April Vaughan—the long-time star of *BackPage,* a national newsmagazine that ran in every market, in every city. Every prime-time Thursday.

And here you are. In my office. Well, la-di-da, la-di-da.

Rake thin. A lavender blue suit—Armani, as far as Annie could tell. A dark teal-coloured pashmina shawl thrown perfectly over one shoulder, held in that careless way Annie knew she could never have pulled off. Not without duct tape, anyway. The shoes alone had to be worth a month's take-home pay. Only then did Annie realize she was actually staring at the woman, like some star-struck teenager. April Vaughan seemed accustomed to it.

"Thank you for seeing me so early in the morning," she said.

Annie could almost hear the martial blare of the familiar theme music rising behind that famous voice. And it's not as though anyone gave me a choice, she thought. Then she saw that April Vaughan had left a bright lipstick stain on the cup now sitting empty in front of her. Apparently, Tina *didn't* mind getting coffee sometimes . . .

Annie slowly took off her coat and set her briefcase on the desk, playing for time. Just calm down, she told herself. You do this every day. "You must have had a long drive," she said pleasantly. It was better than six hours from New York.

"Actually, they chartered a plane for us," April Vaughan said, laughing modestly.

Annie winced. At least she hadn't guessed Greyhound.

"You know, just one of those small ones," April Vaughan added. "I have to be honest, though—it still absolutely scares the hell out me. A good friend of mine was killed in one a couple of years ago."

Annie knew she was referring to a three-term U.S. senator on his way to a major White House policy announcement. A crash in the night in an Iowa cornfield. Then coverage of the funeral on TV when Annie, along with most of the country, had watched the evening news as April Vaughan, among a large crowd of famous mourners, made her way down the steps of St. Patrick's Cathedral to the line of limos waiting below. Supported on one side by the number two box-office star in the world. On her other, by the vice-president of the United States.

"Could I offer you another cup of coffee?" Annie said as casually as if she entertained a major TV celebrity in her office every day.

April Vaughan's face almost betrayed her for a split second. Barely short of curling her lip, Annie noticed. So, maybe it wasn't exactly lattés at Le Cirque.

"Sure, that'd be wonderful," April responded brightly.

Annie stuck her head out the door. "Tina, would you get us a coffee, please—two of them?" Annie settled in behind her desk, trying to compose herself. She'd warned them that the TV tabloids would be interested. And local coverage overnight guaranteed that anyone could figure out who it was—a brilliant investment consultant, who'd murdered a prominent and beautiful psychiatrist. It was Lockport. They were big wheels in a small pond, to mix the metaphors a bit. But it was still happening so much faster than even she'd anticipated. "So, then. What can I do for you, Ms. Vaughan?"

Vaughan lifted one perfectly shaped eyebrow—*don't play it too cute, Lieutenant.* "We're very interested in doing a piece on the Mallick murders."

Well, knock me over with a feather. But it was only one, Annie thought. *One* murder, one suicide. And one damaged child left behind. Annie nodded again, vamping for time. Remember, this is a professional colleague, she told herself. Just one peer to another.

"I admit it's a difficult situation," she began smoothly enough. "It's quite a shock to the community, of course. As you can probably guess, we don't get a lot of that kind of thing around here. But, let's be frank, Ms.Vaughan—you and I both know it's not a particularly unique occurrence in this country any more, an incident of domestic violence. Why would you be so interested in this specific case?"

She heard the echo of her own words: " . . . but *they* don't have pretty houses with pretty wives in them . . ."

April Vaughan almost smirked. "Lieutenant, I've seen those pictures, too," she said. Obviously, she felt that was explanation enough. "And they certainly travelled in all the right circles—to use a slightly discredited cliché." She raised the eyebrow again, more suggestively.

"Well, I don't know how much of that is relevant, really. I'm sure the social life of Belford can't mean very much to anyone beyond our city borders. And from what we *do* know, they were fairly ordinary people, not celebrities, after all. I wouldn't think it offers any real potential for you."

April Vaughan pursed her lips a bit. Annie could picture her making the same gesture just before springing a surprise question on a woefully unprepared starlet. "Well, *we* happen to think the issue of domestic violence is important," April said.

Jesus Christ. "No, I—"

"And we *are* a newsmagazine." Another brief, gimlet-eyed smile.

Ahh, then, Annie thought, that would explain the story they'd put at the top of the program last week: a special on celebrity plastic surgery. Strictly Page Six stuff. "Yes, I—"

"And, believe me—it's still news when a beautiful *woman* does it."

For a minute Annie thought the audio portion had been turned off. She could see April Vaughan's lips still moving, but she was now saying something Annie couldn't hear; her own heart was pounding too loudly in her ears. Obviously, April Vaughan had made some mistake. It wasn't *Leah* who'd done this.

The silence stretched out all around her. Annie spoke at last. "Sorry. You were asking me . . . ?" Her own voice had become dangerously thin and reedy. She kept her hands out of sight, knowing they were beginning to shake slightly.

April Vaughan appeared to be deeply engaged in the leather-covered notebook she'd taken out. Could she really be so unaware of the effect she had caused? And now she was holding a gold pen, poised to write whatever came out next. She glanced up at Annie again with her glimmering smile. "I just said that we're going to be in town for a few days. What's the best restaurant?"

Annie looked at her numbly. "I don't think there *is* one," she said at last. Then someone spoke loudly from the doorway. Annie jumped slightly.

It was Tina, glancing eagerly from the cop to the TV celebrity, announcing everything a little too distinctly as she held out more messages with an extravagantly formal gesture. "You will have to clear out your voice mail, Lieutenant. I haven't time to take any more of these. We've got people calling in from all over the country this morning." She placed the new stack on the corner of Annie's desk, pulling out one in particular to wave in the direction of April Vaughan. "I mean, look at this one, Ms.Vaughan. This is the kind of thing we have to put up with."

"Tina . . ." Annie protested weakly.

April Vaughan's hand stopped halfway to it. "May I . . . ?"

Annie sighed, shrugged. Shit. What difference did it make? "Sure. Go ahead."

The message was an inquiry from out of town, someone wondering whether the Mallick house was up for sale yet. It looked nice in the pictures—maybe it was available cheap "because of the recent tragedy?"

"Jesus," April Vaughan said sympathetically as she passed it back. "Takes all kinds."

Tina nodded furiously. "I know." Then to Annie, "Don't forget your e-mail either, Lieutenant. You know if you don't answer them they phone me anyway."

Annie allowed herself an edge of sarcasm. "Any faxes?"

In answer, Tina dropped a mass of them, on top of everything else. "And Commissioner DeVries called you again."

He *would* phone rather than walk the thirty feet to her office, she thought.

April Vaughan surveyed the growing piles of paper. "Well, I'd say it looks like you're going to be very popular for the next little while."

Annie riffled through the stack pointlessly. Some of it was related, perhaps; most of it probably wasn't. But she knew she couldn't afford to say one more word right now about Leah Mallick. Or anything else. Clearly, April Vaughan had had this information several hours ago. Even a flight would have taken *some* time.

Annie checked her watch openly, well aware that she was being watched. The famous eyes had become even more penetrating.

She had an out. "I'm sorry . . . April, but I really will have to excuse myself right now. I have to meet with the commissioner this morning, and I've got a taping scheduled for my TV spot—" She stopped, suddenly self-conscious again. She was looking at a genuine multi-million-dollar television star. "I sometimes do a little . . . thing. For our little . . . local Crime Stoppers program."

April Vaughan nodded agreeably. "I certainly know what *that's* like. I started in local news too. About a million years ago. Maybe I could join you? Get some real idea of how you all work up here. Is it a piece about Leah Mallick?"

How could it *possibly* be about her? Annie thought. Who'd had any time to even think about that? "No, of course it isn't," she said shortly. "No, I mean, it's . . . it's for something else . . . another crime, that happened a few months back." *Yeah, we try and space them out a bit.*

"An *unsolved* case . . . ?"

Why had April chosen that word?

"Yeah—but not a big one." *There, now. That was fairly stupid.* And far from true. If anyone cared enough to check, they'd find out that it was arson, an attack that had in the end destroyed a family's entire livelihood, along with a couple of designated heritage buildings. *Someone, please, get me out of here before I start babbling uncontrollably.*

"I suppose *that's* good," April Vaughan responded pleasantly. Then another silence.

Annie began to gather her papers, offering a professional smile of her own. Maybe there was a way they could still work this out. "This Mallick thing, you know—it really *is* pretty straightforward. Granted, we don't have every detail yet, but I fully expect it'll be wrapped up fairly quickly. A day or two."

Now it was the "Mallick thing," probably well on its way to becoming "Mallick-gate" if April had her way.

April Vaughan's eyes locked on hers for just a moment. *Don't fuck with me.* "So, you're saying you do know who, what, where, when. And why." Her tone had become icy. It wasn't exactly phrased as a question, but Annie knew one was being asked.

April wasn't stupid. She knew she'd caught them out. All this was some weird cat-and-mouse game they'd agreed to play before they settled on any rules.

"Well, we've still got a lot to go through, but, essentially, yes—we do know what happened."

"And, as you say, it was 'a shock.'" April Vaughan flipped to another page in her notebook. "Well, I know you're busy, so I'll get to the point. I've seen your work and you'd be very good on our kind of show. Genuine. Down-to-earth. It comes right through on the screen. So, I'm here, hoping you'll agree to be the one to help us explain it all. We've booked a studio at our affiliate in town, and I'm setting up a couple of interviews. I'd like to have one of my producers give you a call and we can do something together."

Do something together? Annie recognized that, if anything, April Vaughan was "doing" her, right now. "I don't think I—"

"What I need, of course, is the real inside story, what your people are learning about the issue as they go along.

The conclusions of the inquest, when there is one. Domestic violence resonates for a lot of our viewers. The impact this kind of thing has on families—you know, on kids."

This wasn't about an issue. And the impact on kids is that they die. But Annie nodded, feeling cornered now.

"Good. I'd like to start with the list of people you've questioned so far. We've got some coverage in California, but it sounds like you've done the local side. Wasn't Dr. Mallick associated, in some way with—" April Vaughan consulted a note she'd made, "—Riverview Hospital, for example?"

It hasn't even been eighteen hours, Annie thought. "I have to go through the rest of the reports yet. They're still coming in this morning."

"Yeah, I know what you mean. My research staff has been scrambling a bit too. Certainly inconsiderate of the Mallicks to leave us all flat-footed like this, wasn't it?"

Annie recognized the technique; it was the "just-between-us" two-step. She searched for anything else she could use to buy herself a little time. "I do understand that they'd pulled back in recent months—from all the, you know, the 'social swirl,'" she said. Pronounced aloud, the phrase sounded trite, almost condescending. And it wasn't exactly hard news, by anyone's standard. In fact Callie had said something just like it—was that only yesterday? "I'm just suggesting maybe they didn't find the local scene very interesting. Not what they were used to in California."

"Yep. The Golden State's Golden Couple." April Vaughan threw the phrase out like an epithet as she snapped her notebook closed. Her face had gone rock-hard now. "You people don't really have anything on them, do you?" Finally, the real question. "You don't have any idea why she did it."

It was like someone starting brain surgery without an anaesthetic. Annie could practically feel the scalpel descending. "We will," she said. At least her voice sounded firm.

April Vaughan had narrowed her eyes. "Uh-huh. By the way, did *you* know her? Leah?"

Annie simulated what she hoped was a sophisticated smile. "I think you'll understand when I say that Dr. Mallick and I didn't travel in the same social circles."

April Vaughan returned exactly the same smile. "Well, I suppose you had little reason to. Up till now." At last she stood to go. "But I'm sure there are a few people around here who did. Lockport's not that big a town, is it?"

No, it's not, Annie thought. In fact, at this very moment it's far too small.

April Vaughan laid her business card on top of the mess in the middle of Annie's desk. "Anyway, I've written my personal cell number for you on the back there. You can reach me any time. And I'll see you on Thursday . . ."

Annie couldn't recall actually agreeing to an interview. "Listen, I might have to hold off until—"

"I'll even send a car for you." April Vaughan was making another note in her calfskin Daytimer.

And exactly when *had* she arranged to be the one hung out to dry?

In the next moment, April Vaughan had turned back

into TV Person. "Don't worry, Lieutenant. You'll be great. We'll just have some fun with it. I'll give you a cheap promo jacket. You give me a toy badge. We take some pictures together. We both get to do the jobs we're paid for and the public is dutifully informed. Everybody wins. So, Thursday, then."

Annie watched April Vaughan approach the small clutch of people now lingering self-importantly around the reception desk. A Polaroid camera had been produced from nowhere and everyone was jockeying to have their picture taken with the visiting celebrity. For each, a flash of light, a flash of the famous smile. Tina actually squealed with excitement as she led the short burst of applause that followed April Vaughan down the staircase.

Annie waited at her third-floor window until she saw April Vaughan slide into the stretch limo idling in the police parking lot below. If it was true that Leah Mallick was the murderer, how had *she* found out? Ahead of Dan Hewitt, ahead of Bill—ahead of them all? And if it was true, it meant they had a real problem this time. There was an informant working against them in the medical examiner's office; it was the only possibility. More than just gossip this time.

But there was no point in asking. She knew that any reporter, even that one, would hide behind some pat statement about confidential sources. Everyone had their own Deep Throat now. Or deep pockets.

Aprilvaughan. All one word. One phenomenon. On a collision course with another. One murder, one suicide and one sleeping child.

The limo was gone by the time Annie had pulled on her trench coat. She dialed up her voice mail. An electronic-singed voice informed her that she now had twenty-eight new messages waiting. She hung up without listening to one of them. She needed the time to tell the commissioner what was happening.

As she neared DeVries's office, Annie heard other voices coming from within. The loudest of them was a distinctive and familiar bray. Annie put on her own TV face, squared her shoulders and walked in.

Two people were standing with Paul DeVries. One was the chief, Roy Warren. Annie gave him a cautious glance. Maybe no one else knew.

The other—the short, large woman in the fuchsia pantsuit addressing both of them now—was Deputy Mayor Rita Graham. And Rita was, as usual, in full throttle, holding forth on the well-worn subject of her boss. She continued unabated.

"And *Harvey,* that silly prick, is terrified that his 'enemies' will attempt to exploit this in some way. Though how, God only knows." Her laugh was big as well. And her contempt for the current mayor widely publicized. She turned towards Annie now. "*You* certainly know it, Annie. None of us has to get involved if we all do our jobs right. We keep ourselves strictly at arm's length. *I* will, anyway. But some people—you know they're gonna want to stick their fingers in, all the way up to their armpits. That's how it goes. So the way I figure, it's really just a matter of creating an atmosphere of confidence. And I'm the royal pain in the ass who gets to 'drop in' just to make sure we're on the same page. Nothing more than that. Roy here has been telling me y'already got it all under control, so . . . ?" She seemed to expect a response.

Annie stared back. Where to start? "I suppose I can—"

Rita nodded with satisfaction and gathered up her purse to leave. "Oh, no fears there. I know you'll handle it great. You always do. It's these new fellas here—I don't think they really understand this kind of thing at all. It's just a natural instinct we old Lockport gals seem to have, eh?" She actually poked DeVries in the ribs with her elbow as she passed. He looked startled. "And so we'll just leave you your head for now, shall we?" The deputy mayor wrapped a raincoat around herself and exited, trailing an overpowering scent of gardenias behind her. "After all, in the end it really comes down to nothing more than simple human tragedy, doesn't it?" Rita's voice faded down the hall.

In the silence Roy Warren allowed himself a grim smile. "Imagine being trapped with that at every council meeting."

Annie turned to face both of them. "She's the least of our problems. I've just been given some interesting new information. And if there's any possibility that it's true—"

DeVries held up his hand, speaking for the first time. "I presume you're referring to Leah Mallick?" He took note of her reaction. "Yes, Lieutenant, it is true as far as we know. Don't ask how—but we just found out ourselves a few minutes ago. And now we have to look at all our options before others find out too. I don't want to act in a precipitant manner. There are local factors—"

There always were, Annie thought. But there were only a few that ever really counted in this town. Annie let out a groan of disgust. "You can't be serious. What do *they* want now?"

He was referring to the Island Boys, of course—the wealthy members of an exclusive refuge that had stood for generations on a private island in the middle of the wide Stoney River. And why be surprised that they would have a hand, even in this? What had they'd gotten themselves up to, this time?

It was Roy Warren who spoke now. "Well, it turns out that a few of them," he began cautiously, "they placed a lot of money with Tim Mallick's company, about six months ago. And apparently lost it all. We believe we can put it down to a bad land deal or something. At worst, they were probably just dumb-ass stupid." Warren shrugged uncomfortably. "Anyway, we told Rita that we didn't see any real need to go down that road if we can be assured there's nothing too much in it."

From the sound of his voice Annie knew full well that this wasn't Warren's own idea. Paul DeVries was the politically bent one here. But it meant that, from this point forward, the department was going to have to run some serious interference for the Island Boys, the same ones who wouldn't appreciate *any* connection to the Mallicks being drawn to them right now. And Rita Graham was their hand-picked messenger, eager to protect larger political ambitions of her own: everyone knew she was looking to replace the current mayor in the next election.

Roy Warren rubbed his eyes. "So, we just suggested they stay out of our way and let us manage it." He looked at

DeVries again, who was, as usual, impassive, fingering invisible levers.

Annie finally lost it. "Then please tell *me* how we do that. How are we supposed to 'manage' this when I'm already getting blind sided in my own office by some tabloid reporter? A nationally known TV star to boot, who obviously has her own pipeline right into the medical examiner's office. And God only knows what else." One who could apparently charter her own fucking plane, any time she wanted to. "Because if there *is* a connection to the island—"

DeVries actually tried a smile. "There isn't. None of them ever intended to bring any action against Tim Mallick anyway. The regulations class them as 'sophisticated investors,' so there's no securities violations that we can tell. And, supposedly, they're not even looking to recoup now. They just don't want it spread around that they got taken by some slick Young Turk. All I've agreed is that we'll try to keep it away from them. If the road leads to the island, we'll take it at the right time. But until then, Roy here will arrange to have the incident file disposed as quickly as possible to the coroner's office. And unless someone else chooses to take it further, we'll be clear of it inside two weeks. I don't see that there's any real reason for this department to be further involved."

But she knew *that* wasn't where the media attention was heading. And they were all standing here, trying to ignore the elephant standing right in the middle of the room.

"We can't just negotiate some gentlemen's agreement, Commissioner. It wasn't him—it was *her*. You have to realize that will change everything. It was a mother doing what mothers don't. It was Leah Mallick. That's what makes it a national story. And I heard *that* from a reporter. They already know—"

DeVries held up his hand to stop her. "*Who* knows? Specifically, Lieutenant. Who? Us. And April Vaughan. And I'm fairly sure *BackPage* is prepared to do whatever it takes to protect their exclusive. After all, they probably paid a lot for it." DeVries laughed sharply, turning to Warren again. "Who do you think? MacLennan?"

Who in the ME's office might have collected a little unexpected bonus for talking? Who was the perpetrator who would probably be flushed out and finished in a matter of hours, with the appropriate amount of shit hitting the fan? DeVries didn't countenance disloyalty, even of the most banal variety. He was the type prepared to use a sledgehammer to kill a fly. If only as warning to the rest of the flies.

Warren stood by, resolutely expressionless. Clearly, he wasn't finding this nearly as simple as the commissioner did.

DeVries gave Annie a harder, more calculating look now. "So it *was* her. The beautiful Dr. Mallick was a murderer. Maybe a hysterical woman, reaching 'a certain age'—worried she's losing her looks or her husband. Or maybe just a sudden hormonal imbalance. I don't know. We *don't* know. But does it matter? Let them speculate. It'll be titillating for the tabloids, but it represents exactly nil long-term impact for us.

"Because what it really means is that this isn't hard news anymore, Lieutenant. And it certainly isn't police work.

When the time comes, you'll do everything necessary to keep it light. Give the media exactly what they're asking for. I'm sure you can dig up the tears and flowers to throw to them. Make some new friends. Get it shifted over to the Lifestyle section. After that, it's just a matter of minimizing media treatment. It'll last the requisite fifteen minutes."

He noticed her hesitation. A new expression of irritation crossed his face, then disappeared just as quickly. He glanced away. "Something else, Lieutenant?"

"Why *not* tell them right now? Obviously they don't know yet that it was Leah," she said. "Why didn't you say something to Rita just now when you had the chance?" Why *not* tell City Hall, Rita Graham, the Island Boys that they wouldn't have to lose any more sleep over this? That, in the end, it wouldn't involve them or their money. Or any connection to the Mallicks. Why just leave them twisting in the wind?

"Timing, Lieutenant. It's all in the timing," he replied with a thin, private smile. "I don't think we should say anything until the formal ME's report actually comes out. And that's scheduled for . . . ?" He turned to Roy Warren.

"Friday morning," Warren finished.

"Friday. So until then, I imagine we'll look quite invaluable, in some quarters." Time enough, she knew, to gather some favours while appearing to keep the lid on it.

"Spin some local colour. It's nothing but strictly over-the-backyard-fence gossip. Give *that* to them. As much of it as you want." Deliberately, DeVries picked up another memo and began reading it. Annie knew she'd been dismissed. In more ways than one.

But when she turned to go, she caught Roy Warren's eye again. He looked like a man with something more to say too.

Because he knew, as well as she did, that within only a few hours, floral tributes large and small had begun to appear on the front steps of the Mallicks' house in Belford. And that every time the images were broadcast, those same piles only grew larger. Adding to them, dozens of notes and letters and balloons. Handwritten signs. Even some stuffed animals. People seemed determined to possess a part of it, to express something of themselves in what was already becoming an increasingly common ritual of public mourning—a kind of 'communion' with those at the centre of tragedy.

They, the ones standing in front of those make-shift shrines, were the ones who would ask, and have answered, their questions. And no matter how she handled it, Annie knew this wasn't going to go away, simply because someone willed it to.

∿∿∿

Annie settled into what she'd lately come to think of as her favourite spot, balancing precariously on a small wire stool at a ridiculously tiny table. It had become her secret vice—an ice-cream emporium only a few blocks from home. Though maybe not *much* of a secret any more, she conceded, whenever she saw herself on television these days. Those two extra chins had to have come from somewhere.

All around her she heard parents telling their kids to "leave room for supper." The logic of that had always escaped her. Why the hell were they in here at quarter to five? All the mixed messages we give them, she thought. All the contradictory things we represent. Do what I say, not what I do. Enjoy yourself, but not too much. Hurry up and wait . . . We tell ourselves that children are our greatest gift, then we leave them sitting in neglect, or, worse, poverty or hunger or war.

Or a woman, some mother, like Leah Mallick, sets out to kill her own child.

Through the window she watched Bill's car pull into the crowded lot. After a minute or two he got out, leaving his jacket behind, sizable patches of sweat marking his shirt. The temperature had hit a new record for the day—over eighty degrees, and not even summer yet. Bill was carrying a large brown envelope with him.

Whatever else might lay between them, they still found themselves looking out for each other. He made sure she got everything she needed on all the cases before them; and she kept the media out of his hair.

This time, though, she wasn't going to be able to do that.

He stood in the doorway now, looking exactly like what he was—a broad-shouldered, no-nonsense cop with something on his mind. He spotted Annie immediately and, without saying a word, pulled up a chair for himself. It was ridiculously small for him. But he was clearly uncomfortable about something else. She noticed immediately that his eyes were a little bloodshot.

"I was a little surprised when you suggested us meeting here," he said after a moment. He glanced around at the lights and the noise, uncharacteristically distracted. She could tell he didn't know where to start, whatever it was he wanted to say.

She shrugged as she licked her spoon. "You don't look like you're getting much sleep, Bill. Why don't you let me treat you to a Chocolate Bunny Delight?"

He smiled weakly. "I don't think I'm going to be able to squeeze into my summer clothes as it is." It didn't really matter, of course. Summer or winter, Bill always wore the same thing.

He looked tired. He set the package he was carrying on the table between them, then looked up at her. "I just want to apologize—" He drew out one thin file from among the rest of the materials in the envelope.

Annie glanced at it impassively. "So that's it?" she said after a moment. The ME's report. "Then it's true." Against all evidence she'd still wanted to hold on to some faint hope that it wasn't Leah.

"Yeah. I mean, I don't know where DeVries got it from—*this* isn't even finished." He flicked the file cover. "They only faxed it to me an hour or so ago. A friend of mine inside the coroner's office had to 'borrow' it from the ME as it was. They're still planning the official release for Friday, like they said. But I guess someone figured I deserved a bit of a heads-up."

Bill propped his elbows on the tiny table and opened the file. It contained only three or four loose, handwritten pages. "Bobby Canon's going to say we screwed up at the scene. That we jumped the gun. Even contaminated some evidence. That's how we missed it." He traced the words with his index finger, then looked up. "You know he's been looking for something like this for years. Here's his chance, I guess."

Annie took the draft pages and started reading. Canon's motives aside, the forensic evidence seemed clear: Dr. Leah Mallick had done it. She was solely responsible. Whatever her reasons, she had murdered her husband and then started the car, running enough deadly carbon monoxide into the house to kill both herself and her son.

Well, she succeeded partly, anyway, Annie thought bitterly. At least she can't do any more harm. Annie pushed it away again. They expected her to lay this off on some version of hormones?

"And there's absolutely no suggestion that there's anyone else involved in this?" Annie asked.

"Well," he admitted, "we don't have everything yet. But I'll swear the only people concerned were the ones already inside that house. It was locked down like Fort Knox."

She looked at him questioningly.

Bill opened his own file. "State-of-the-art security throughout. The system probably cost six, seven thousand dollars. Motion detectors. The whole enchilada. It was hooked into their computer, in fact. They ran the whole house off it. Lights, thermostat, everything."

Annie remembered another detail. She was back in that late afternoon in Belford, the last suggestion of light in the sky. The rain nearly at an end and the sound of it rolling soft through the window. The curtains saturated and limp with water, slowly dripping on to the floor. The telescope angled upwards, the line of sight just clearing the treetops.

When she looked again, Bill had spread his large hands on the table in front of him, examining them as though they could hold a different answer. He said as much. Sure, the police could always claim that their early crime-scene examinations were only preliminary, but they hadn't looked very hard for any other possibilities. "It's the bush leaguer's trap. We just assumed."

She knew it happened more often than they liked to admit. Faced with a heavy caseload, gut instinct counted for a lot. You couldn't go out every time trying to reinvent the wheel. If she'd been there, she might have seen the same thing.

Bill was turning over another page, jabbing a finger at it. "An abrasion ring on the scalp, a small concussive fracture from the barrel, just above and in front of the ear, his prints on the weapon, minor residue on his hand . . ." Unconsciously, he was miming the actual motions as he read aloud to her. It was an old habit. You could always tell what Bill was thinking by watching his hands.

Memorably, once, he'd given an extended middle-finger salute to a defence attorney while being cross-examined in court. A row of cops attending the same session were left snorting like school kids. Bill probably didn't even notice he was doing it. His face had remained a placid mask, his voice as smooth as an FM radio jock's.

But now what he was thinking was that, even in hindsight, the details still supported his conjecture. Snap judgment or not, what they'd seen had led them straight to Tim Mallick. As, perhaps, Leah had intended." Well, I guess there's a couple people who're gonna be real relieved to learn that it had nothing to do with him after all." Bill sighed. "You know what those guys are like over there." He'd been given the same picture Annie had. And Annie *did* know what they were like. The Island Boys. The people like Lewis Stephens, who ran them. She'd grown up knowing them, knowing who was in charge. It was unspoken. And unspoken *about.*

She couldn't stop the sharp edge of frustration in her voice. "So what do we say, then? An act of God?" PMS. Low self-esteem. Give it to the media, DeVries had said. As much of it as I want to. As much of it as I can stomach. "Shit. If only someone hadn't stupidly put it out there before we knew for sure. Now I've got to backpedal like some circus act."

She finally noticed that the noise around them had become a steady roar. It was time to go. Things weren't getting any better sitting here. She started to stand up. "OK, if that's it—"

"No, I have to talk to you about something else," Bill said. Unconsciously, he'd reached out and taken her hand in his own, the way he always used to when they were alone. "I want to explain it to you before someone else does. You know how you get to talking when you're out there. And it seems to be a big deal, so maybe you show off a little . . . You remember what that's like, right? Thinking there's nothing left to surprise you anymore. And so you throw a long pass. Maybe a little careless. Before you know it, you've shot your mouth off, and someone else overhears it . . ." His voice petered out.

It took her a good long moment to absorb what he was really saying. He was trying to tell her that *he* was the one who'd given Tim Mallick to the media that night. Bill himself who'd told them that it was "the husband" who'd done the shooting and tried to kill his own son. She could hear him saying it, in a mixture of grief and honest anger: *Then the son-of-a-bitch, he starts up his fucking sports-car . . .*

And as uncharacteristic as it was—Bill had always been as careful as anyone in the department—it emphasized a stark truth: no one could have reasonably expected that Leah Mallick had deliberately set out to deceive the world.

Annie sat back, thinking hard. She didn't hesitate. Even now, it was still her instinct to try to protect him. She wouldn't have lifted a finger if it was just some smoker from the coroner's office . . .

"What finally confirmed it *was* her, anyway?" Annie asked quietly. Whatever happened next, it was going to go hardest on Bill. It was inevitable, given the way DeVries was planning to play this one. For a time, they might successfully swamp Leah Mallick in trivia, but when they had to start looking for a scapegoat to explain why they'd arbitrarily cut off any further investigation of the Mallicks' local involvements—and it *would* happen, she knew—it was Bill they'd point to. To what Bobby Canon had termed "overconfident incompetence." They'd find one way or another way to make it Bill's problem—not the department's. She was learning how people like Paul DeVries worked.

Bill continued, his voice flat. "Two things, really. A large chunk of his dura mater was slightly crushed under her body. We assumed that the piece had just blown there. But the conclusion is that she had kneeled, or maybe stood, to use the gun on him and then . . ."

Bill didn't say what they both knew came next: that Leah Mallick had lain down again, amidst that shiny, blackening viscera, the detritus of their marriage and their ended lives, and waited. Who's the "cold bastard" now, Annie wanted to say.

"It's funny. In the end, they were holding hands. Like—" He reached for her hand again to illustrate, holding his palm against hers and lacing their fingers together into a version of the child's game: "this is the church." After a moment, Annie pulled away.

Bill gave a bitter laugh. "There's something else that should have given us an idea, I suppose. The fingerprints. Out in the garage. Bartlett couldn't find any that mattered—on the car, the hose into the house, the exhaust pipe. Maybe if we hadn't been so sure about him—it should have tipped us all off. Mallick had no reason to cover his tracks at that point."

Annie didn't contradict him. Because it was true. Tim Mallick would have had no motive to hide—not if he'd been the one making all this happen.

But why had Leah Mallick wanted the world to believe it was him? She must have worn disposable gloves, then flushed them down the toilet. Surgical gloves, like the ones a doctor would wear. A dime a dozen in any drugstore. Maybe she was only following her instincts.

"The real thing, though—" Bill paused. "There was a glass of water beside the kid's bed. We asked for a routine analysis on the contents—you know, maybe there was an attempt to drug him too. But it turned out that it had residue of Tim Mallick's blood on the outside. A microscopic trace. She must have carried the glass in to him. After . . . it happened. Probably the noise woke him."

Annie thought back to the touch, the texture, of the chilled after-rain air blowing into the room. "Who else was drugged?" she said. Bill had said "too." She felt herself going numb, but something inside was still trying to kick in to function.

"Aw, shit, they're saying now she had enough junk in her own system to be out for eight to twelve hours. At minimum. You know, some regular over-the-counter stuff, some prescription—we don't have everything back yet. The gas would have been enough, eventually. But the combination is what really did her in that fast. They figure now it probably took less than two hours." Unconsciously, Bill flexed the fingers of one hand, holding it out in front of him and examining it. "She didn't have it—the colour." The usual cherry red lividity in the extremities that marks carbon monoxide poisoning.

"Who else knows about this?"

"The ME's office. My friend in the coroner's—there's gotta be bits and pieces floating around all over the goddamn place now. We don't even know what's going to hit next." He sighed, then tried to sound hopeful. "At least it'll all be over by Friday. And I move on to the next mystery. Like Batman." He leaned back in the chair.

Annie didn't want to be the one to tell him that this wouldn't end on Friday. She didn't want to say that what was going to hit was like something none of them had ever seen before. April Vaughan was breaking her exclusive on

Thursday evening's edition of *BackPage*. This was just the calm before the storm.

They sat together, watching the kids and their parents for a few more minutes. Enough sugar and clowns and noise in the place to overstimulate anyone under the age of ten. It was all threatening to kick off the migraine she knew was on the way. And where she clutched the file, her fingers were damp. Another hot flash too.

A four-year-old was sobbing now at the next table. Sitting in front of him was one of the world's biggest banana splits, but he was demanding his sister's caramel fudge cake instead. In overly patient tones the parents were trying to reason with him, to explain that what he had was exactly what he'd ordered. The sister, obviously, was refusing to trade, share or negotiate, little arms folded. She looked to be about three. Henry Kissinger himself couldn't have moved her.

Bill half laughed then, weary and depressed. "You know, it was just so goddamn easy to buy that it was him. Guy takes a gun . . . It happens all the time, doesn't it? But it's not something you ever picture a normal, intelligent woman like that doing. I didn't see it coming. None of us did." He looked at Annie with reddened eyes, clearly exhausted. "I'm only sorry you had to hear about it—like *that.* From some son of a bitch like DeVries."

An invisible hand tightened around her throat. It didn't take him to remind her that no "normal, intelligent" mother could reasonably be suspected in the death of her own child.

They'd danced their scripted parts for almost ten years now. Coming close, moving away and never saying what they were always thinking. And for ten years Bill had looked for some way to turn back the clock, to a time before everything had gone wrong. He couldn't. He still wanted to care for her, and she would never again let him. Their own shattered history was a testament to the fact that you can't always get what you want, she knew. Sometimes only what you deserve. If she ever allowed herself to remember any part of the good that had once been between them, she would have to face, in that same instant, the truth that it had destroyed the rest. Bill didn't understand that you couldn't have one without the other.

People had been driven apart for less—but that's all she had to measure the world by. And in the deepest recesses of her heart she felt hollow whenever she faced him. They'd turned away, not towards each other when it had mattered.

Her stomach was in knots now. All around them kids were screaming with excitement. A clown was giving away balloons.

"Why, Bill? You think you're the *only* son of a bitch who's allowed to give me bad news?" It came out before she knew it.

He slumped back in his chair as though she'd slapped him. "Annie . . . I was there, too, that night. You're not the only one who made a mistake." Soft, and careful.

But she'd already risen quickly from her seat and grabbed the package he'd brought her. "And—just for the record—it wasn't Paul DeVries who told me. It was April Vaughan," she said, turning away before the expression on his face registered his shock.

No, normal, intelligent women *don't* do that to their own children, she thought to herself as she started her car. No mother intentionally ever would.

Someone had left a half opened window. With a telescope aimed at the sky.

3

"You know, I came from a town just like this," Georgia said.

She said the same thing every time they met. Always in some old diner on the outskirts of the city, a place where no one they knew would have been caught dead. Something that sat at the junction of two forgotten roads, while everyone else stuck to the Interstate. It was the atmosphere she enjoyed, apparently, not the food. The mile-long counter, the smell of a greasy grill, a picture window opening on to a street filled with dusty pickups.

Susan knew most of Georgia's likes and dislikes well enough by now, this straightforward woman of modest habits and strong loyalties who loved to talk about her family and pets.

She'd been nervous approaching Georgia the very first time, intimidated as much by her reputation as by the woman herself. Then surprised when it was Georgia who gave her the most practical advice, who took the necessary time to explain the arcane and unspoken of state politics. Georgia too who'd pushed her hard to understand that intelligence was at least as useful an asset as her faded beauty-queen looks—as she said, to put paid to the idea that the only viable positions in politics were fetal or missionary.

It had taken Susan a long time before she could believe that of herself—that her expertise was worth anything to important people. Until she no longer felt like an imposter at every meeting. And it was always Georgia backing her, encouraging her at each step, urging her on to the next.

Lately though, Susan had noticed that Georgia looked more like someone's aging grandmother. Older, tired. Maybe finally ready to admit that she wasn't up to another hard campaign. That was easy enough to understand; everything else had already changed.

It was pure, undiluted ambition gathering around Thomas Acton this time. Everyone knew the same thing—that a popular second-term governor was a strong starting point for presidential primaries. But first they'd have to win the second term.

And it was with the expensive addition of David Pearson as the director of Acton's gubernatorial campaign that they were given as close to a guarantee of that as possible. Pearson, the "pro from Dover," had arrived only six weeks ago to formally take over, bringing a fully staffed, portable war room—everything from private pollsters to direct-mail specialists. And a long string of recent electoral successes behind him. Four governors in four races. A couple of U.S. senators on the west coast. A total of eight congressmen elected, in six key states. Ready for the big one, with a lot of good quality chits to cash in. Assuaging wounded sensibilities wasn't part of the battle plan, and

Pearson didn't seem to care much about anything else. It wasn't personal.

Even Susan recognized that much. She'd become Tom Acton's point of vulnerability. The old rumours still followed her. Almost from the moment of her appointment there were snickering asides whenever she happened to appear in public with the governor, at each speech and presentation, every fundraiser she attended. Pearson and his crew would have heard the same stories by now. It wasn't money she could raise any more—just questions.

She saw the subtle signs everywhere. In the past two weeks alone, all her calls had been returned by a series of low-level staffers. And Pearson himself had left her cooling her heels in a dirty, crowded hallway before permitting her the professional courtesy of a private meeting.

Georgia was the only one who could allay her fears, who could always be expected to come up with something reassuring. *Lay low, sweetie, they'll forget about this the second there's a real crisis . . .*

Instead, Susan found herself waiting nervously, studying Georgia's face in profile—the mouth set firm, eyes half closed in weariness. Or disappointment. It was hard to tell what she was really thinking this time—maybe just that things had run their natural course. And aging star-fuckers like Susan Shaw were a dime a dozen.

If Georgia refused to help her this time, she was out. Maybe not out of the fancy corner office, not out on the actual street—but *out* in the only way it really mattered. Far enough to make her irrelevant again.

Leah Mallick's death was the real issue.

Susan tried to laugh now, bent over her second coffee and fourth cigarette. The ashtray was already piled high in front of her. They were in the kind of place where no one bothered to empty it until it actually interrupted the view. "Maybe it's not as bad as we think. I could wait a couple months, then put another commission together, when they aren't so preoccupied with publicity. Just sit it out. They'll forget about her." She reached down the counter for an clean ashtray. "I've already got my own little piece of the pork barrel anyway, right? Good job. Useful contacts. My ludicrously overpriced car's almost paid off. And even *you'd* have to admit, I've got a great wardrobe." She smiled weakly. Her addiction to shopping had been a long-standing joke between them. But brittle cynicism couldn't completely disguise her present reality. The minute that commission fell apart, Susan Shaw had risen exactly as far as she was ever going to. And if you weren't climbing the ladder, you were sliding down the snake.

This time, Georgia was looking at her with something akin to pity. Finally, she spoke. "Oh, honey . . . do you really think they'll let you keep *that* now? A political appointment?"

Susan fingered her cigarette, irritated to see that her nail polish was chipped in a couple of places. "Why should that matter? They tell me to set up one of the most high-profile commissions ever convened in this state. They want diversity. And I do it—all of it—in record time, thank you very much. I get blacks, whites. Hispanics, Asians. Men, women. Rich and poor. Old and young. Urban and rural. It's like a goddamn Noah's ark in there. And you know as well as I do what's supposed to happen next. They write their report. We put it in a drawer. If there wasn't an election coming up, no one would even notice it."

Susan stopped herself. Georgia didn't consider any expression of anger, even of the mildest variety, entirely appropriate right now. There *was* an election coming up and, like it or not, everyone was noticing everything.

Georgia spoke more deliberately, in a careful monotone. "But you saw that story . . . ? How they're saying that—"

Susan cut her off sharply. "Georgia, I read it. He committed suicide, after he . . ." Susan's voice faded for a moment. She cleared her throat. "But you damn well know that I'm the one who told you all, from the very beginning—including Tom—that I had serious concerns about her husband's business dealings. I *said* that it could come right back on us if we weren't careful. I said to anyone who'd listen that I needed more time to check him out. But Pearson and his group gets here—and they're so damned determined to push this whole thing through as fast as possible. And now when it turns out . . ." She couldn't finish the sentence. Reservations or not, in the end she'd gone along without another word of protest, on the record, anyway. And only victors get to write the history.

Georgia carefully stirred her tea. "Well, as it turns out, it was her." She looked past Susan for a moment, glancing furtively around the diner.

Susan could feel the tension inside her suddenly twist. "What do you mean . . . ?"

Georgia hesitated before quietly repeating, "Leah Mallick. It was *her,* not her husband."

Susan leaned closer. "I don't understand, Georgia. What are you saying?"

"Someone owed us a favour. We got a phone call from one of the networks early this morning. She's the one who shot *him,* then killed herself. Apparently, she even tried to make it look like he did it. And . . ."

Susan could feel the blood slow in her veins again. Everything was coming full circle. "And everyone will want to know if it has anything to do with us," she said slowly. Her voice had taken on a dry, distant quality.

Georgia laughed bitterly. "Well, they certainly won't have far to dig this time, sweetie. All they'll need to know is that we were about to name Dr. Leah Mallick as the next Secretary of Health and Human Services."

Susan stared at her, unseeing. Only one move, but it put Leah Mallick at the very centre of every proposed program for high-tech research and health care development in the state.

Susan knew she sounded panicked. "*I* was told it was to chair a goddamn community committee, Georgia. When did they decide to give her the entire fucking department?"

The clatter of plates and cutlery around them stopped abruptly. Everyone in the diner was watching now over their morning newspapers.

Let them look, she thought. It wasn't much of a secret any more anyway that the election campaign was being capitalized on a single idea: the Health Sciences Corridor, the New Technology hub, at the heart of a so-called economic Renaissance Zone. A strategy designed to resuscitate the northern industrial sector of the state and, incidentally, secure the political fortunes of Thomas Acton. That was the entire platform—the real reason the circus had come to town. It was how they were going to turn a governor into a president.

Susan recalled something Georgia had once told her: an election campaign is no place for policy debate. The specifics don't matter, she'd said, except to a few pointy-headed paid commentators and ivory-tower academic analysts. Voters would always buy a campaign platform for what they thought they saw in those standing upon it.

So someone had decided they needed a "star" to help sell this one. And a high-profile commission had been created simply to serve as Leah Mallick's walk up the red carpet.

Georgia sighed deeply. "Well, after all, *you're* the one who vetted her, sweetie. That's all it'll take. It's the only thing the opposition is going to have to hear—that we were *this* close to appointing an unstable, irrational killer to head up the most important economic initiative undertaken in this state in a generation. In another twenty-four hours David Pearson won't let you back inside the building."

Susan could feel it—everything, all of it, slipping away. "Then why didn't you tell me what the commission was really about? How could you let her get that close?" It was the whine of a plaintive child.

Georgia said nothing for a moment. Another sigh. A slight stoic shrug. "Remember that Eagleton schmozzle in '72? McGovern's own running mate? Electroshock treatments for a proposed vice-president? Sometimes these things just slip through . . ."

Susan crushed the empty cigarette package. Maybe Georgia could afford to be more philosophical about this; she was nearing retirement. She had her family and pets.

Georgia turned away to signal the waitress at the end of the counter,

Taking her own sweet time, the waitress eventually drifted away from her conversation with two truckers and approached. Georgia spoke to her in a voice as firm as steel. "Listen, honey. I want you to make me a real cup of tea this time. I want you to scoot in the back there and find a kettle. And I want you to bring cold—*cold*—water to a boil. Then you put it in the good teapot, the one you keep up on some shelf for yourselves. And you bring it to me, with a decent cup and saucer, and a nice little pitcher of milk on the side. Just like you'd make for your mother. All right?"

The waitress, whether surprised or just confused, backed away and disappeared obediently through the swinging door into the kitchen.

Georgia had always been considered an anomaly in the business. No one would ever mistake her for a sophisticated political operative. No Atwater, Carville, Rove or Matalin here. She was, in fact, plain-spoken to the point of bluntness, uninterested in the usual easygoing sociability practised around the executive branch. Certainly, a less than obvious choice for an up-and-coming politician's staff. Especially in the beginning. Because, even then, Thomas Acton could have had his pick. From the moment he'd entered his first race, he seemed favoured. Glamorous and exciting, energetic—some even believed brilliant. And aimed unerringly, most agreed, towards higher office. The betting line began almost immediately.

But inside closer political circles Acton was often seen as uncertain and wavering, too easily characterized as unorganized or undisciplined. Conventional wisdom had it that he could always be swayed by the last person he spoke to. And, encouraged by little else, potential rivals always started out full of promise against him. Many had actually judged him vulnerable, at least in the early days. Their real mistake, Susan had learned eventually, was in underestimating Georgia.

Georgia never lost focus, never gave it away. Georgia Gagnon. Plain and ordinary, with the unassuming manner of a small-town bookkeeper. But it wasn't long before everyone knew *exactly* why Acton had chosen her. In time it had even become part of the crude political dialogue around the capital: some secretaries were employed to give their bosses a hard-on, Georgia was there to give hers a backbone.

The waitress was returning from the kitchen, balancing a full tray. She carefully set out a complete tea service on the counter, smiling. "And I even found you ladies some nice cookies." She said it cheerfully. It had a certain novelty in this place. Cups, saucers, small silver spoons. The Queen of England couldn't have complained.

While Georgia occupied herself, Susan desperately searched for an answer in her view of the street beyond the diner's plate glass window. There were two choices. She could walk out now and keep on walking; or she could fight to stay, grabbing the only real option left open to her. She didn't have to be alone in this, she told herself. She didn't have to be that plaintive child any more.

Susan took a deep breath, stiffened her shoulders and turned back. "Then, Georgia—it really *isn't* just about me any more, is it? If they think they can afford to let this one get out of the bag . . ." Even Pearson and crew wouldn't be able to fix that election.

Alive or dead, Leah Mallick *was* the race. They'd tied themselves to her, and to everything she was capable of doing for them. That was the plan. And without her, Thomas Acton's campaign wouldn't make it out of the starting gate.

Susan peeled the Cellophane off a new pack of cigarettes. "And I sure as hell didn't come all this way to quit now."

Nodding slowly, Georgia took a careful sip of her tea. A small smile of satisfaction crossed her face. "No, sweetie," she said. "I didn't think you had."

~~~

Annie finally agreed to hold a media conference, scheduling only ten minutes for it and crossing her fingers. Everyone she expected—and a few she didn't—was already squeezed into the press room by the time she walked in, the crowd considerably larger than the usual one she faced.

She read the news release aloud. It was nothing more than what she'd already sent out to them the previous day, in that hour before dawn. The names and ages of the deceased, their occupations, address. The few details the department actually had in hand. No reference whatsoever to the ME's report. It didn't leave them with much, Annie would have admitted if pressed. And there was nothing in it that was
~~~

wrong or deliberately misleading. It just wasn't everything she knew. And this time, there was no way she was going to be able to wrap it up in a nice, neat bow.

She felt like someone left holding a live hand grenade with the pin already pulled. She knew she could end the suppositions, the rumours, all the speculation right here and now. She could pull her arm back in a graceful arc and lob the truth right into the centre of the room—that Leah Mallick was the murderer.

Instead, flailing against her better judgment, she would await the release of the ME's report along with the rest of the world. And, until then, discount everything as an unsubstantiated rumour. No one in her department had ever *said* that it was Tim Mallick—not on-record anyway; the media, everyone else, had apparently just jumped to their own conclusions. If they chose not to challenge certain widely held assumptions—well, that was up to them.

Just one more sin of omission to add to her list.

Within seconds she could see that very few of the reporters in the room were satisfied. In fact, as she'd expected, the questions began immediately. She looked towards the back of the room where three senior managers were standing to watch this play out. DeVries was one of them. Pointedly, she raised an eyebrow at him before dozens of hands waving in the air obscured her view.

No, she couldn't suggest any motive. No, the child was not able to provide further information. No, they did not believe any other parties to be involved.

Yes, it appeared to be a murder-suicide. Yes, it was a surprise to their neighbours. Yes, the county medical examiner's report would be released as soon as possible. Yes. Yes. Yes.

And no again. No. The child would never, ever wake up. She didn't need a hospital report to tell her that. It had been hours; Bill had described a dead child.

It would have to do for now.

Several reporters tried to delay her as she left the podium. One wanted to "just explore the possibility," as he put it, that Kyle Mallick had suffered because of the length of time it had taken to have him removed to the hospital. The early television reports had served to feed that rumour. She refused comment. They'd have to let the hospital handle any medical assessments, she suggested.

Another told her, more quietly and off the record, that a full-time investigative reporter had just been assigned to look into Tim Mallick's "unusual" business dealings.

And why not, she thought?

That was the story being left out there, if only by implication. That Tim Mallick—a heretofore loving husband and father—had simply decided, one night, to blow away his family. The department hadn't said it; it wasn't the official line; she'd refused to confirm it. But the media had bought it because it was a user-friendly answer. And because maybe someone had let a detail slip carelessly in a casual conversation.

Annie saw herself launch another grenade through the room. DeVries really believed he could cut off all further investigation. If nothing else he was being obtuse. It wasn't like cutting off air to a fire. Isolating Leah posthumously wouldn't work for long—she'd left them too many questions.

And it was probably a very short leap to connect Tim Mallick to the money in town if there was even the hint of something untoward. It would come out, one way or another, no matter how hard she—or anyone else—tried to manage it. Then she reminded herself—maybe he was only waiting for a better time. Or a better deal.

She passed Paul DeVries, lurking in the press room doorway. "Well, that seemed to go pretty well," she said. Then, with a thin smile she leaned towards him to whisper in his ear: "A bit of professional advice, Commissioner. I wouldn't stand there too long if I were you. It looks like they might still have a few questions." From the corner of her eye she could see a handful of reporters already crowding towards him, microphones extended.

Annie evaded them herself by fleeing down the hall and slamming the office door behind her.

~~~

She recognized the older-model, unmarked police car sitting out in front of her house. It was Greg Bauer's. No surprise. *Don't think about it too hard. You can afford to enjoy this.*

Annie crept up and rapped on the window sharply. Greg sat bolt upright, looking dopey and dishevelled. Some stakeout. By the looks of it, she'd awakened him from a coma.

"Hi. Looking for a big bust in South Navy?"

He was already grinning widely. "Sure. What size are you?" Real subtle.
~~~

She paused, still undecided. But then, why *not*? Why not make tonight pizza night? she asked herself. "C'mon in. I'll fix us something to eat."

He seemed impossibly pleased with himself. "Great. I don't get much home cooking."

"Surprise—neither do I," she said.

She opened the front door, sending Ben running in frantic circles around them until she could corral him out into the backyard. Then she busied herself in the kitchen, leaving Greg to turn on the television in the living room.

It took only a few minutes. So much for "home cooking." She brought out a plate of sandwiches, a quick side salad. It was enough for now, still too hot for anything heavier. Greg was already half asleep again, in front of the TV. She sat down on the couch beside him.

He roused himself. "They just ran that new Crime Stoppers thing," he said, indicating the screen. "You're pretty good. I bet you whip those things out now, like, in ten minutes."

"About that," she said. "One-take Annie."

Together they half watched the last inning of some baseball game while Greg finished off most of the sandwiches. He didn't seem to care much about the game; too slow for him. And they both knew that wasn't why he was here anyway. After a few more minutes he yawned again and stood up to stretch. "Come on, babe. I've only got a few hours before I have to go back out and fix the world," he joked as he reached down to pull her up. It was nothing more or less than she'd expected. But she pointedly ignored his hand, remaining seated.

She realized she wanted someone to talk to tonight. It could've been anyone. Just his luck. "Speaking of work, I was thinking of trying something new." That was almost true, though the idea seemed to arise out of nowhere.

He stopped. She could read the confusion in his face: you want to have a *conversation?* Right *now?* "Yeah? Like what?" he said gamely. "Haven't you been in that job for—like—ever?"

Annie almost laughed aloud. As *if.* Not unless the concept of "forever" had grown so much shorter since she herself was young. No, it wasn't even two years yet. Two, in the entire span of a more than twenty-year career.

"Actually . . . I've been thinking about it for a while, getting more involved in some other things again. Maybe even get re-qualified." Really? Until this very moment she'd never considered a return to active duty. So why was she standing here, trying to convince someone else?

Greg was frowning now. "I guess so . . . but wouldn't it take a lot of work?" He was probably trying to summon up what "supportive" sounded like—and that wasn't it. "And, anyway, it isn't anything like you remember. They got us doing mostly all shit work now. Gangs and low-life dealers. You left Operations a long time ago."

According to his concept of history, probably right around the time the earth was cooling . . .

Annie was already sorry she'd started this. Here was a straight, good-looking, healthy, sports-watching, warm-blooded carnivore. And she was doing a bad imitation of Bette Davis in mid-life crisis.

She huffed loudly. "Well, I certainly don't mean out on

street patrol tomorrow. Maybe just some way to combine the Operations stuff with all the community work I'm doing."

"But you're management, babe. Why would you even *want* to go back out there?"

"Christ! I'm already out there every day."

"Yeah, but not chasing scum with a gun."

"I could. I did it for ten years. Bill and I were pretty good, you know."

"You wanna work homicide again?"

He was right—it sounded ridiculous.

Then, surprisingly, he leaned back and laughed. "Hey, I know . . . This is because of those murders over in Belford, isn't it? You gotta little taste of it again, didn't ya? Got your juices going—" He was already moving towards her. Interest, excitement. Juice. It always came down to some version or other of testosterone.

Annie regretted even mentioning it and moved away from him. "Maybe it's just that I feel a responsibility to use my skills for something more than bike rodeos and Rotary luncheons once in a while." True. "And Cher is still doing disco," she added sullenly. Where had *that* one come from? And why in the world she thought it would mean anything to him, she didn't know.

He blinked. "Cher?"

"Yeah, she's over sixty and she's still straddling boy toys in music videos. Wearing leather things."

"Cher's sixty?"

"Yes. Probably more like sixty-five. And I *can* meet specs, you know—I just need to work out a little first."

Greg stared, then, grinning, pulled her up. "I'll just bet you can. Well, let's us do a little workout upstairs. Put you through all your paces. See what you got there, Lieutenant."

She stood stiff and sulky inside the circle of his arms. Just let it go for tonight, she told herself. Who was the one doing the counting, anyway? He shook her playfully from side to side until she finally began to relax.

At least I'll always be younger than Cher, she said to herself, allowing him to lead her up the stairs. Younger than Cher, and only a little older than Methuselah.

It was still and dark. Without looking, she guessed it to be about four o'clock. Greg had already left, suddenly remembering he had an early morning basketball game.

Unable to sleep, Annie sat down at the kitchen table, ready to organize all the materials Bill had given her. Everything was spread out in front of her now.

She began in the same way she'd always approached a formal investigation: rebuilding the files slowly and deliberately, reading every word again as she went. Physical scene observations, day logs, shift reports—front-line materials—all went in the first pile. The second she designated for the technical studies as they became available: ballistics, toxicology, blood splatter analysis, medical examiner's notes. The third she used to build a kind of thumbnail sketch of the victim or victims: previous arrests, if any, education, employment records, a quick bio of pertinent places and dates.

The last group comprised interviews with any witnesses. Annie called that her People Pile, usually the one of most interest to the media. There wasn't much in it this time, of course. Available witnesses: just two or three neighbours who thought they might have heard something that sounded kind of like a gunshot, sometime in the period between eleven at night and seven in the morning. The Walther nine-millimetre Leah Mallick had used would have made little more than a popping noise anyway. Any car that dared to backfire in that neighbourhood would be louder. Even an expensive car.

The only other piece in the pile was a transcript of the messages left on the Mallick's answering machine. Mostly missed appointments: a school meeting, a hairdresser, a late lunch with an acquaintance. Blockbuster Video.

The large envelope included a full collection of photographs taken at the scene. Brutally clear, they still pointed to the same conclusion any experienced detective would have reached—that Tim Mallick had blown himself away and conspired to take both of them, his wife and his son, with him. Sometimes it happened.

Annie hesitated for a moment. There was another set of photographs she wanted to see. She leafed quickly through the package again. They'd been removed. Or at least, there were none here. None of the boy. None, even, of his room. Maybe it was only because Kyle wasn't dead yet; he wasn't yet one of the victims with whom they were supposed to concern themselves.

Looking beyond the strict fact of death, Annie knew that a different kind of attention was going to begin to focus almost exclusively on the child, the only witness left in their midst. The hospital had already been warned to increase its security. And there was a whole new range of media questions to prepare for. She stopped and stared at the empty sheet of paper. What do you put in a bio for an eight-year-old—his favourite colour? And, they'd taken forty minutes to remove him to hospital, so that was a problem . . .

A moment later Annie had shoved everything aside. Something more unsettling was sweeping over her now, disturbing and unexpected. It was a wave of utter disgust.

Christ, I'm even starting to think like all of them, she said to herself. How will they react? What's their lead going to be? What can I bury or leak or spin most effectively? What strategy can I work to keep it all under control? Because now here she was—actually calculating how to put the best possible light on the imminent death of a child.

If nothing else, she knew this wasn't who she'd set out to be, all those years ago. And it certainly wasn't why she still wanted to be a cop.

Abruptly, Annie pushed herself away from the table.

The grey morning light was expanding. She stood in the open doorway, welcoming the cold, damp air that rolled in against her. It was a foggy morning. The mist wrapped around the piles of lumber, tarps and machinery scattered about the yard, waiting to be incorporated somehow into her new addition. The contractor had dubbed it—somewhat pretentiously, she thought—a "winter room." One more folly among so many. But the project had already taken on a life of its own. In this light the backyard looked like a relic site, an archaeological dig. The evidence of any neighbours drifted at an oceanic distance, their houses only intermittently visible, quiet and looming, like other ships spotted through the fog.

She'd often stood here, waiting for dawn. Since the onset of menopause her sleep disruptions had become more profound. A long-time tendency to insomnia now set whole nights in a row of almost constant borderline wakefulness. Dreams went on and on, like epic movies or serials. She usually awoke ahead of the alarm clock, exhausted still by the day before, forced forward to deal with the next.

It had all started years ago, when Annie found herself adrift—more, actually overtaken by the endless days she could count but not remember. And despite the perils of dreams, she'd never feared any unlit night half so much as that unreasonable brightness gathering on the next horizon. Watching it even now, she remembered how it had felt—the almost Shakespearean weight of Nameless Dread. That had been Lady Macbeth's most human and poignant complaint too. And who could blame her, murderess or not? The spirits having already foretold that all light would fall upon a chaos that she herself had fomented in the night's most secret hours. Naturally, that lady craved peace, and the darkness again, even as she sleepwalked through rivers of imagined blood.

And what of Leah Mallick's own haunted wanderings? What horror had she conjured up on her last night, as her own child slept in a room down the hall?

I'll give you Leah Mallick, Annie thought. You can have her. Just leave *him* alone.

She looked down at what she was still holding in her hand. It was the medical examiner's confidential notes, the ones Bill had given her. *This* was the kind of stuff they really wanted, she knew. This she could use. For the first time, Annie felt the great weight lighten inside her.

~~~

Susan Shaw walked down the unlit hallway, grey under a murky sky lowering outside the row of tall windows. Her heart thumped uncomfortably under a new suit. Dark red. The skirt probably an inch too short. Silk blouse, clinging with the unexpected humidity. It hadn't stopped raining all night, hadn't dipped below eighty degrees. She tried to ignore the fact that her stomach was still rolling from the burnt coffee she'd had at the hotel restaurant less than an hour ago.

She had no doubt she was about to step into another upcountry quagmire. There were more than enough people in Lockport who believed they had every good reason to hate the current governor of the state. After all, they'd been on the receiving end of Thomas Acton's opening salvo in his term as the state's youngest attorney general. In a bid to grab the political agenda, his office had decided to target a series of minor irregularities within the police pension funds. And whether it was bad advice or just bad luck, Lockport had attempted to stonewall his state-wide investigation. He'd burrowed in and before it was over, Acton had successfully prosecuted criminal indictments against two high-ranking officers in the local union leadership and recommended ten others for immediate suspension. The case, played out on every front page, had set him on the course for the governor's mansion.
~~~

And they certainly liked to harbour their grudges up here, she knew, with all the blood-deep tenacity of an inbred mountain clan. Despite substantial changes in the years since, up and down the entire chain of command, there were still some in this very building who wouldn't lift a finger ever to help Tom Acton. Or anyone associated with him.

Susan approached the front counter in the administrative reception area behind which was a young girl seated at a computer, half-whistling, half-singing to herself and sporting one pierced eyebrow, a nose stud, henna-coloured hair.

"Good morning. I'm Susan Shaw."

If she'd really anticipated any reaction, she was disappointed. The girl just looked at her dumbly, as though trying to resolve some complicated puzzle.

Or maybe she'd just interrupted a video game. "I'm here to see Commissioner DeVries," Susan said. "Could you tell me where I can find him?"

The girl roused herself at last. "Uh, yeah. Sorry. Sure." She pointed down the hall. "Right at the end there. Through those big double doors. Should I tell him you're on the way?"

"Thanks. No." Susan was rapidly disappearing in the distance. She'd learned long ago that if you didn't appear to require an appointment, you usually didn't have to make one either.

Pretty snotty, Tina thought. Nice suit, though.

∿∿∿

At noon, Annie found herself wedged in tight among the several hundred members of the Lockport Businesswomen's Association for the annual charity luncheon for breast cancer research.

Early on, she'd accepted that a large part of her job was attending events like this. And the appearance of normalcy was helpful right now. But why did everything have to involve pantyhose?

Annie looked around. Tickets alone were a hundred bucks a pop. Everyone was beautifully dressed. And they could all afford to take a leisurely, long lunch in the middle of a regular workday. These women were, by every applied standard, successful and well off. Yet something was feeding a palpable sense of fear in the room.

You certainly didn't have to be a cop to feel it. It was drawn on almost every face around her. Fear for friends, for relatives, for themselves. What if chemo treatments didn't go well over the next few weeks? What if the surgery was further delayed? What were the statistical probabilities of survival past one year . . . two . . . five? "Fear" wasn't an abstract theme for them. At least here it was given name and reason.

For now, though, they seemed happy to await the distraction of their advertised speaker—a famous radio talk-show host who'd flown in specially to give a first-person account of her own battle with breast cancer.

Annie was seated at a front table, slightly to the side of the stage, from where she could view the whole of the room. Not surprisingly, she was surrounded by all the same people she saw at every local event. A kind of girls' own party circuit. Some were displaying so many ribbons and buttons in support of one cause or another that they could barely stand erect.

And the wine was flowing freely. Meg Compton, seated directly across the table from Annie, was determinedly getting loaded. She kept repeating the same thing: "Thank God for all these fucking benefits. At least I can get out and talk to someone. Cut loose once in a while."

Dessert was followed by the requisite short break for networking. Then the headliner, national personality Regina Welles, was introduced to extended applause. Her radio talk-show was one of the most successful in the country, carried on more than three hundred stations. Her latest, very slight, very thin book was already quickly climbing the best-seller lists. She was sharp and shiny, with an outsized smile and professorial-looking glasses.

Within moments, she had skilfully put herself right in among them, describing exactly the same difficult process of discovery and denial, doubt and diagnosis they'd all been through. She seemed to share everything, the physical and emotional degradation that sometimes—if you were very fortunate, she added—paid off. One of the lucky ones, she said. A survivor. Knock on wood.

"I knew that I'd be leaving my children, my husband, everyone I loved. I had a lot of trouble coming to terms with the simple idea that they were perfectly capable of going on without me. That someone else could hear Elgar's *Enigma Variations,* or listen to Glenn Gould's early recording of the *Brandenburg Concertos,* and be moved to the same tears. Those were *my* tears, dammit! Hell, it really bugged me that someone else would get to see a Garth Brooks concert I'd never managed to get to.

"And—I'm not kidding—my particular coping strategy was to actually plan my own funeral. I created guest lists so that I could exclude all the people I didn't like—I wasn't going to give them *that* satisfaction. I designed the seating plan as though it was for some dinner party. I chose an attractive colour scheme. I talked about it incessantly, with anyone who'd listen. Normal conversation was something completely beyond me. Everything else became trivial. I worked hard to drive my family away. They might have still been in the same room, but I made sure they couldn't relate to me as anything but a disease. And it turns out that it's really difficult to go out in great style when your head's in the toilet all the time."

All around her, women began tearing up. Annie watched as a few others used the opportunity to quietly pass out more business cards.

"Every night, I was so scared that I was afraid to close my eyes. But during the daytime I began to find a new way to be brave. Endless hours were spent in doctors' offices and hospital hallways. And I started to use a lot of that time listening to other people. Somehow, I found the productive energy for others that I couldn't find for myself.

"And I learned that it was in listening to others that I was able to make some kind of positive contribution. *Surpri-i-ise!* For all the credit I'm given today for what I do, ninety percent of my time on air is still just that—listening. I can't say for sure that's what saved my life—I was lucky that I had a very special doctor—but it certainly helped.

And it got me the most unbelievably freakin' huge contract for a nationally syndicated radio talk show I've ever seen." That was her expected big laugh. She appeared happy and grateful when she got it.

"But I *know* it's got to be really difficult for some of you right now. One of our hard-working organizers here today"—and Welles turned to survey the head table—"was telling me earlier that she'd just completed her own six weeks of chemo. That leaves you feeling like a piece of shit, doesn't it, ladies?" There was a chorus of scattered hoots and cheers. "Where's . . . ? *There* she is. Let's all give Dorie a big hand. Stand up, honey." Dorie stood shyly. Applause erupted. Welles waited, smiling.

When it was quiet again, she leaned into the microphone, her voice perfectly modulated, obviously preparing to wind it up.

"So, that's my advice. If you have someone, a friend or a family member going through this, *listen.* It's the best thing you can do for them. Don't bring flowers—lend them your ears." She gave them another large smile, one big enough to cover the whole of the room and every individual within it, and spread her arms wide to take all of them in. "See what a gift it is? You're all doing me the greatest favour today—you're *listening.* Give yourselves a hand. You did a great job."

There was thunderous applause, a standing ovation. There was open weeping. Then there was a rush to the ladies' room.

Annie waited until the crowd had thinned out a bit. After a few minutes she walked in to see two women standing at the mirror, still discussing Regina Welles. One of them was busily repairing the damage done to her mascara. "Gawd, that was wonderful . . ."

For some reason, Annie had found herself strangely unmoved by the speech. It was dramatic and effective, but a little too calculated, too "show-bizzy." Or maybe she was just becoming overly aware of the skills it took. It was a trick, something *done.* From the opening moment, Welles had held the room in the palm of her hand. Celebrity helped, of course. The woman made millions doing exactly the same thing every day.

The other two were still talking as they left the washroom. "But you know, I really thought she'd be a lot taller—"

"And a *lot* younger, eh?" the other added loudly. Their laughter faded as the door closed behind them.

Annie stood alone at the sink for a moment, regarding her own reflection in the mirror. Then a toilet flushed and Regina Welles herself emerged from one of the stalls.

Welles quickly looked around. "Is it safe?" she said in an exaggerated stage whisper. Satisfied they were alone, she walked over to rinse her hands at the sink and glanced up at Annie. "I thought I was going to have to stay in there forever. People sometimes forget you still have to go to the bathroom." She was leaning close to the mirror, reapplying her lipstick, but stopped to look at Annie's reflection. "You're Anne Shannon, aren't you?"

Annie was embarrassed that she found the recognition flattering. "Yes, I am—"

Welles nodded firmly. "I thought so. Someone pointed you out to me earlier. You're PR for the local police here, right?" She turned to face Annie, all business now. "There's something I wanted to ask you."

"Sure—"

Welles raised one hand for a moment and closed her eyes, as though having to steel herself for what came next. "Someone at my table told me that you had a murder out here . . . on Monday? Is that true—that it was a Leah Mallick who was killed? A *psychiatrist?*"

Just how many other Leah Mallicks had died recently? Annie blinked again. "Yes. It was."

Welles's reaction was immediate and impressive. She gripped the hard edge of the counter, allowing herself to sag slightly. "Oh, my God." Her distress, while theatrical, looked genuine. "I can't imagine why *no one* told me about this sooner."

"You knew her?" Annie wondered why that didn't come as a complete surprise.

"Yes. Very well, in fact." In the next moment Welles's glance had unconsciously slid back to her own face in the mirror, perhaps only to confirm that the shock had done no permanent damage. "Well, not so much lately. We lost touch a few years ago. But she was the doctor I was talking about—you know, the one who directed my own medical treatment? Eight years ago?"

Annie vaguely recalled that Welles had mentioned some doctor during her speech, someone who listened well. "Dr. Mallick was a psychiatrist, though, not an oncologist."

Welles flicked her hand impatiently. "That's just it. We were still in Santa Barbara at the time. They brought a small group of us together—over a period of, oh, maybe three weeks. It was a series of special counselling sessions. But done at a very high level. I mean, it was all tied into some advanced medical treatment and in-depth psychological testing." She stopped and nodded her head at some private memory now, then shook it off.

"I can tell you, here and now, Anne, I still remember the very first time I set eyes on her. She was probably fifteen years younger than me, but even then she was the most assured presence I've ever seen—simply walking into a room. And I've seen a lot of entrances, honey," she said with a practised laugh, turning back to the mirror.

Annie found herself staring at Regina Welles now. Mallick was forty-three. That made her—

"I'm fifty-eight." She'd caught Annie's assessment of her in the mirror. "Plastic surgery. A bit of work around the eyes. A personal trainer." She shrugged. "California." Welles turned towards her again, relaxing against the counter. "But by the end of it all, at the completion of just those few weeks, they'd somehow convinced me to undertake a completely experimental program. Me—always *so* into control, you know. And I actually beat it—knock on wood. But right up to those particular sessions with Leah, I'd been one of those patients ready to give up, if you can believe that. Some do. Give up, I mean. They say you never know which way you're going to go until you get there.

"And I have to tell you—it *was* quite extraordinary. With her. Almost psychic, if that doesn't sound too la-la-land. More than anyone else I saw, all during that time, she was the one who seemed to understand so completely—almost presciently—what I was really going through. Right at the bottom of that trough, you know, when I couldn't even risk bringing it up with my own family any more. She was always there, even when I was absolutely at my lowest.

"Somehow she managed to turn the old girl around. And—well, I understand they've established it as some kind of a new specialty. 'Psycho-oncology.' Sloan-Kettering heads most of the work on it now." Welles turned back to the mirror, lost in thought again. "My God. What in the world was she doing *here?*"

Annie noticed that, as she spoke, Welles reached up very carefully to arrange a stray strand of hair. Suddenly everything on top of her head appeared to slip sideways. It was a wig, obviously, a very expensive one. Annie looked quickly away. Regina Welles deserved her privacy certainly. And perhaps it was no one's business if she was undergoing cancer treatment again. But maybe she should have tacked an addendum on that luncheon speech—that knocking on wood didn't always work forever.

Then Welles must have realized what she'd just said aloud. "I mean, don't get me wrong, this place is darling, of course. But I would have thought she'd be set up by now in a major practice of her own, in New York or L.A. or Chicago. Such a brilliant woman. Absolutely stunning too. European-looking—rather Catherine Deneuve-ish." Welles examined her own face more critically in the mirror. She seemed satisfied. And why not? There wasn't a line on it, that Annie could see.

Welles spoke again to Annie's reflection. "Some of them *didn't* make it, you know. From that same group I was in?

At some point they just seemed to give up. It was like all the air went right out of them. I guess I have to give myself credit for hanging in. But maybe I *was* a little luckier," she laughed. "After all, I found *her.*"

~~~

Twenty minutes later, Annie found herself cornered by Callie Christie, exactly as Annie had planned. It had required nothing more than a casual suggestion that they carpool to the luncheon together.

She knew that Callie was unlikely to see it as anything out of the ordinary; people socialized outside work all the time. To Callie it would mean nothing more than a heaven-sent opportunity to squeeze a backgrounder out of her, in advance of the formal release of the medical examiner's report.

Well, she had absolutely no idea how very easy *that* was going to be over the next few minutes.

Callie's instincts for light material were good, but she demonstrated little interest in or patience for anything more complex. In fact, her idea of vigorous reporting was to unearth a press release—and every once in a while to ambush some unfortunate victim with the revelation of a personal peccadillo. She'd found a way to make it work for her, straddling both sides of the backyard fence—gossip in, gossip out. To her credit, she didn't pretend it was anything else. When she was frank, or drunk, Callie would freely admit to anyone within hearing distance that her real ambition was to replace Mary Hart on *Entertainment Tonight.*
~~~

However, she could certainly *imitate* a real news reporter, Annie knew. And she was smart enough not to look a gift horse in the mouth.

Everyone had heard that *BackPage* was in town. A stretch limo wasn't the most discreet form of transportation in a place like Lockport. And it was already going around that April Vaughan had paid big for interviews with anyone who'd had anything to do with the Mallicks—none of whom would agree to speak to the local media any more. Local reporters were being frozen out of their own market while they watched *BackPage* locking down an exclusive.

Annie casually suggested that Callie drop off her two other passengers before circling back downtown. It would save time, she said reasonably. And it would leave them alone, for a fifteen-minute drive.

Callie wasted the first five on small talk—the luncheon menu, Regina Welles, who was wearing what. Then she turned on the car radio. It was the Beatles and "We Can Work It Out." "I hate that old shit," she said impatiently, punching the buttons. She looked sideways at Annie. "Sorry, you probably still listen to it."

Still. Annie smiled wryly. "No. Fine, whatever you like. I listen to just about anything, anyway. Eric Clapton, Rod Stewart, the Stones. 'N Sync . . ."

"Yeah?" Callie spent a few more seconds looking for something she could handle, finally landing on Phil Collins. "This OK?"

Annie sat and waited. She knew Callie was searching for an opening.

Then Annie heard a small intake of breath. "So, what are they going to do about that boy? Kyle Mallick?"

Annie watched her careful plan slide off the rails in the next moment. She said nothing, willing her almost instantaneous headache to fade before she was forced to respond.

Callie was *supposed* to ask about the ME's report, pretend to be nonchalant, even ingenuous, and only vaguely interested, with something like "So, what about this report coming out on Friday—any surprises in it . . . ?"

And Annie would carefully hesitate, appearing a little unprepared perhaps, taking a good long minute to deny that there was anything out of the usual. That sure, maybe there were a couple of contentious points, but it would all be worked out by Friday. "We usually have such a *good* working relationship with Bobby Canon's office," she'd say.

That would be Callie's cue. Any normal reporter hearing that would burrow in like a rabid ferret. "Why the hesitation there, Annie—why say there's nothing out of the ordinary? You got some glitches, maybe?" Any normal reporter would take note of her slight nervousness and inquire about *that,* at least. And not let her out of the car until she'd confessed. To something.

Instead, Callie was opting for the boy . . . ? It was things like this that just proved she'd never make a real reporter, Annie thought. Damn her.

There were only nine minutes left on the drive. "I don't know. I expect social services is handling it," Annie said quietly.

Callie nodded. "Yeah, that's what I thought too." Another pause. "So, you're not still involved?"

What did "involved" mean anyway? "I never was," Annie said shortly. Putting out media releases, waving reports in front of the news cameras, didn't amount to an "involvement" in anyone's books.

"It *is* kind of weird, though, isn't it?" Callie mused aloud. "You always think people like that have everything going for them. But it must have been an absolute zoo in there at the end. And then he finally snaps . . ."

Callie was right, of course—even in the best of homes, murder-suicide wasn't exactly a viable lifestyle choice. "Why would he have snapped?" Annie said. It was the word "finally" that she couldn't resist. And Callie knew it.

Callie was smiling faintly. "The way I hear it, she was looking for some new action on the side. Shoving his face in it too. That's really why they had to leave California."

Annie nodded, saying nothing. She'd already begun to consider that possibility herself. Had there been someone else? In Lockport? Maybe the capital?

As though reading her mind, Callie Christie snickered now. "Yeah, eh? In fact, one woman I was talking to—who claimed to know her really well—and the way *she* put it was that Leah Mallick was 'just too good-looking and too smart for her own good.' She actually described her as 'uncannily gorgeous.' Isn't that amazing? Apparently, Leah always projected herself as a real innocent, but she just didn't know when to turn it off. And then old Tim, well—he must have, you know—he just *did* it."

It made perfect sense, of course. In fact, the only problem Annie could see with that theory was that it wasn't Tim Mallick who had snapped. It was Leah.

And Annie was carrying the irrefutable proof of that in a briefcase that now rested on the seat between them.

It was true—the pictures did show an uncommonly beautiful woman, looking with her disarmingly direct gaze at the camera. Someone who could just lift a finger . . . Yet, from all accounts Leah Mallick had withdrawn willingly from whatever social life was available in Lockport. She'd chosen her exile. And there was nothing, even now, pointing to cavalier, jet-setting trips out of town to any secret rendezvous—no line of jilted suitors and jealous wives left stretched out across the country.

Whatever she had done in the past, it was becoming increasingly clear that Leah Mallick could still provoke strong reactions in others, intended or otherwise.

Then Annie had to listen as Callie went walkabout again. "Did you know that Eric Menendez' mother typed out a script for him, just before he and his brother Lyle killed them? And it was *exactly* what the two boys ended up doing to them. The whole horrible murder, the insurance—it was all there. Everything." She glanced at Annie with grim satisfaction.

Annie rolled her eyes. She'd always suspected Callie's primary research source was *People* magazine. "So you think there might be a hidden screenplay . . . ?"

"No, I mean it just backs it up," Callie continued. "Statistically, of course, the most dangerous species on earth is the young human male. I'd be afraid even to have kids now." Apparently, she felt there was some connection, though to what, Annie had no idea. Kyle Mallick posed no danger to the world any more.

Annie smiled tightly. "Ah, Callie, you can't believe everything you read."

This was incredible. Here she was, ready to give Callie everything a reporter could ever ask for: the chance to hijack April Vaughan's exclusive and earn the enmity of a powerful network; the opportunity to sabotage a growing conspiracy of silence. And all Callie wanted to do was . . . *schmooze.*

Annie had envisioned an entire scenario for her. Callie would immediately assume the official role of paid mourner. Easy enough—she identified personally with every story she presented. And this one fit her like a glove, like all the other ones constructed of kittens stranded up telephone poles, a family's gifts stolen in a Christmas break and enter, yellow ribbons tied 'round the old oak tree. It was the only perspective from which she ever chose to interpret the world, invariably the most sentimental one. Never anything to which she couldn't easily attach vibrant, outsized personalities, wring out every heightened emotion. Leah Mallick as murderer was everything a Callie Christie could want.

"So, you think they're just going to leave him like that, then?" Callie wondered aloud.

Another dive back into the non sequitur pool. For a moment Annie felt defeated. Then she realized it didn't signify anything; everything out of Callie's mouth was served at exactly the same temperature. It just made it harder to judge what was actually sinking in.

"How long do you think *that* could go on?" she added, back to her mental picture of Kyle Mallick dying in the hospital, worrying at it again like a puppy with a bone. "That's the real story, isn't it?"

Annie took a deep breath. If she was going to do it, it had to be now. Maybe it would mean the end of her job: DeVries was about to lose his temporary advantage over the Island Boys after all. And it'd be easy enough to figure out how Callie got it. But what were all their small-town machinations against something like this anyway? Hers or DeVries's or Rita Graham's or the Island Boys'. How could any of them *really* believe that it would simply blow over in this fecund, close atmosphere? Even if what they were saying this time was true—that there was a "casual relationship" between the money in town and the death of Tim Mallick—it was coated in so many of the right elements that it almost didn't matter *what* they said this time. It fed directly into what news directors referred to as an "event fixation," and you had to at least acknowledge that before you could ever hope to dismantle it. They were all swimming out of their depth.

Paul DeVries could just go piss up a rope.

Because no—Kyle Mallick's not the real story, Annie said to herself. And I'm not going to let you turn him into one. His fate, for better or worse, was going to be left in the hands of doctors and state social services. Not turned into commentary. Not debated in the frenzied indignity of some media scrum. Not if she could help it.

Annie knew now that she was going to have to lay everything out, twirl something shiny and bright right in front of Callie's eyes. No subterfuge, no pregnant and brilliantly timed pauses. They'd still be sitting here next Christmas if she waited for Callie to *infer* a fucking thing.

Annie cleared her throat. "No, it's not. In fact, no one's uncovered what the real story *is* yet . . ." She wanted to appear tentative, even a little upset. "Callie, I've got a bit of a problem. I've found out something and . . . in the next two days . . . well, I think someone's going to try and use it to set us up. I mean the department. April Vaughan is threatening to come out with some story about how we screwed up." She intentionally added a bitter laugh. April Vaughan couldn't have cared less about the local police, but it helped to create a common enemy.

And at the mere mention of April Vaughan, Callie bolted upright in her seat. "Wha—?"

"She's putting together a major piece about what *they* told her is supposedly happening here. They've got it wrong, but I'm worried it could get in the way of the real investigation, big time. I heard she's going to broadcast it . . . tomorrow night."

"What is it?" Callie's eyes narrowed.

"I don't know if I really can . . . Look, I *will* tell you it's something significant. And—well, let's just say there's always a few local types who want to play politics with things like this. You know who I mean. They want to tie it up, drag it out as long as possible. Anything to make a big splash." This was nudging it close enough to be credible. She deliberately left it vague; there was always a "they" you could use to fill in the blank: the coroner, the mayor, the military-industrial complex . . . "We can't violate protocol without creating a real problem. Or, at least, *I* can't. Not publicly."

Annie waited, trying to hide her impatience. *For God's sake, ask me something.*

"So, you're saying you guys have something else . . ." Callie said slowly. Then the penny dropped with a loud clank. "This is about Leah Mallick, isn't it?" she said at last.

This time, her unnatural leap of logic was worth it.

Annie nodded and carefully inspected the passing scenery. "But if I give it to you, it has to stay 'deep background.' Do you understand what I'm saying?" She turned to look at Callie. "And I'm going to need some help here too. Quid pro quo . . ." Was that *too* blatant?

"OK. Sure. We can do that."

Apparently not. "So I give you everything, and you take us off the hook . . . ?"

Callie stared blindly at the road ahead of her. "And you want me to say 'sources in the department—'"

"Why don't we use 'high-level sources in the department,'" Annie interrupted. It suited her to let DeVries take the credit for this, even if unwillingly. Then he couldn't leave the cops on the line holding the bag. And Bill would be clear of it.

"City Hall doesn't know you're talking to me, do they?" Callie said more slyly. She was starting to sound almost like a real reporter.

And she'd jumped to a useful conclusion this time. The Lockport council was a fetid swamp anyway—no possible way to trace anything back. Callie could believe it was the Department of Parks and Recreation for all the difference it made. "You *know* they'll tear us apart if it comes out that I was the one who gave it to you . . ." Annie said encouragingly.

"Yeah. No love lost there, I bet." Callie gave her a smug little grin now. "This isn't really your usual style, though, is it? Off the record like this? Aren't you the one who always wanted to play it so straight . . . ?" No spin. No speculation. Past tense.

Annie felt a sudden stab of doubt. This was how Callie always did it. Stumbling, however accidentally, on a hard kernel of truth—that she would then use to beat you with. She might grow up to be an April Vaughan yet, Annie thought more grudgingly. But she was right: Lieutenant Shannon was about to break her own unbendable rules.

Annie smiled back uneasily. "Let's just say I finally took the stick out of my butt."

Callie snorted.

They were nearing police headquarters. Annie indicated a side street. "Take the next left here." It pointed them in the opposite direction, away from her office, down towards the river.

Callie signalled a turn. "Then what?" she said.

"Then . . . ? I let you buy me a cup of coffee."

~~~

Tina was coming straight for her as she exited the elevator on the third floor. "Someone was here a little while ago."

"A-a-nd . . . ?"

"I don't know. She just looked kind of familiar. Like—" Tina glanced aside before speaking again in a near whisper. "Maybe you should get on down to the commissioner's office. I think she might have something to do with the media."

Annie sighed loudly. A police station and they couldn't maintain even minimal security. The lobby had already
~~~

been declared off-limits to the media, one ancient security guard left on the front door. There were at least five full news crews hovering around on a daily basis now, and the building wasn't designed to accommodate the traffic so everyone was being forced to camp outside. But it didn't seem to matter.

"OK." She passed her briefcase to Tina. "Hold on to this for me for a few minutes. She's already in DeVries's office?"

"Yeah," Tina said. "In fact, they *all* are."

Annie entered to find half the department already jammed into DeVries's small reception area. She slipped inside the door, moving quickly off to one side. DeVries was making his introductions.

He pointedly ignored her arrival, waiting until he'd finished the round of everyone else in the room.

"And *this,*" he said finally, "is the late Lieutenant Anne Shannon, Director of Communications." His tone set her aside as clearly as if she'd been tagged irrelevant.

Susan reached over. "Susan Shaw, Department of Business and Professional Regulation," she said. A firm handshake. A brief, cool smile. Good, level eye contact. In terms of style, she was well, even expensively, put together. Across a room, Annie would have guessed mid to late thirties. Up close, she saw, it was more like mid forties.

Noticeably self-conscious too. Annie had the distinct impression that Susan Shaw would rather be anywhere than here. And no wonder. Superficial manners aside, everyone in the room was already regarding her with undisguised suspicion.

But her voice, when she addressed the room as a whole, came as a kind of surprise. "I know I'm probably the last person you all wanted to see when you walked in here today." Light. Detached. Almost amused. "The governor sends you his warmest regards. He specifically asked me to assure everyone that your pension funds are all now safely invested in high-ratio margin accounts on the Nikkei commodities market." Pointed enough. At least she'd acknowledged that they might have some reason to hate him. She even smiled slyly.

There were some uncomfortable laughs in response. But at least a few shoulders dropped a couple of inches.

Susan seemed to relax too. "Commissioner DeVries has been kind enough to give me this opportunity to speak with you. I'll try to be brief. We understand that a current case in your division is about to be put over. Tim and Leah Mallick. We know that you've already considered all reasonable possibilities: money problems, family conflicts, trouble in the marriage. We'd like to be able to put it to rest as well. But there's a lot of unexpected attention out there that isn't easily going away." She appeared to glance in Annie's direction for a split second. "And of course, the child is still alive. That alone will attract the press . . ."

Annie felt the air sucked forcibly out of her lungs.

Susan gazed down at the floor, appearing to weigh her words carefully before continuing. Annie doubted that any of this was extemporaneous. "Bluntly," Susan said, looking up at them again, "my office is interested because Dr. Mallick had agreed to head a community commission we'd created to look into some grassroots possibilities for managed health care in this state. It's only a small part of a proposed economic initiative for the administration's second term, but . . . well, I'm sure you can all understand that there would be several long-term fiscal policy issues under consideration. And not a few reputations at stake. Dr. Mallick had already been involved in certain . . ." Inexplicably, she hesitated. " . . . several policy discussions," she finished quietly.

As vague as it was, Annie could feel a threat building behind her words.

Susan seemed to be gathering herself for what came next. Her voice rose again. "So, I've come today to ask all of you—does anyone have any idea yet what's *really* behind this? Why here? Why now? Was there some concern about Tim Mallick's business involvements, for example? I understand they were fairly extensive."

"Concern" wouldn't explain it, but there it was, playing across the faces in the room. Annie saw more than a few people shift uncomfortably: the commissioner, the chief, several others she noticed now, any of whom could have had dealings with the Island Boys at some point in the recent past. The chickens were coming home to roost. Susan was telling them that the real professionals were ready to plunge into their own version of spin control.

And they wanted public attention to go elsewhere—not on the dead woman they had chairing a high-profile commission. Whatever the facts, the backroom types down at the capital were saying that they didn't want Leah Mallick laid out for tabloid fodder, just another *cause macabre.* Find something else. And they'd put Susan Shaw in charge of finding it—just in time for the next election.

Annie looked up to see DeVries glance towards her. They'd both come to the same conclusion in the same moment: that Susan Shaw already knew Leah Mallick was the real murderer. And if she did, then so did the governor. Her polite appearance here was a political charade. But the threat was real: give up Tim Mallick and the Island Boys or Acton's pit bull of an attorney general would be coming back here with a steam shovel, digging for bodies in the mayor's front yard. Doing whatever it took to divert media attention away from Dr. Mallick.

One detective, blithely unaware of all the implications, cleared his throat, summoning up phlegm from last week. "If you're talking about some kind of major fraud here . . . we don't have a large commercial section—"

Susan interrupted him cleanly. "I don't know *what's* at issue, Detective. Honestly. I can't even guess. I assume that you want this one off your books as soon as possible. It's a small department. You have limited resources. And I understand the medical examiner's report is expected Friday . . . so it's over. And maybe your job is done up here. But give *me* a reason to walk away."

Susan had moved over to the window and was looking down at the sidewalk in front of the building and the small crowd of media clustered there.

"It looks like you've already got a PR mess on your hands. Everything suggests you're about to be overrun by every major network before you can begin to turn around.

I don't think any of us can afford for this one to get blown further out of proportion. Not *this* time."

Annie watched almost everyone in the room flinch. Don't overplay your hand, Ms. Shaw, she thought.

Susan continued. "The more press involved, the worse it's going to look. And whatever conclusions the tabloids may come to, there's a real reason why this happened. Is it in the possibility of substantial fraud? Who's to say?" Susan gave a small shrug. "But I'd suggest that's our likeliest starting point."

"What about the kid?" It was Bill speaking.

Susan shook her head. "I believe it's about the husband."

From across the room, DeVries had settled his gaze on Annie again. She felt it.

Susan continued. "I know none of us wants the feds drawn in here. I'm confident we can still keep it quiet, share whatever information we do have between us. Maybe we can wrap it into your ongoing investigation for the next couple of days? It might mean fewer red flags going up." She stopped for a second.

Who'd said anything about an ongoing investigation? And exactly what "PR mess" was she referring to anyway? Annie could feel her own resentment growing in the same moment that she became aware of something else starting up inside her. As usual, she'd chosen to ignore the early warning signs, but she could no longer pretend that it wasn't happening. The dampness was already breaking out on her upper lip. She recognized it for a real, full-blown, raging hot flash. The boiler was stoked and she knew she was only seconds away from soaking through her light linen jacket. She could feel her face glowing bright brick red as she looked longingly towards the door; maybe it was still possible to quietly slip out. Except that her way was blocked by the cop beside her, looking at her with a big grin. And when she turned, she saw Susan Shaw casually observing her too.

Susan spoke again. "I realize that you people don't have the highest regard for Tom Acton. But as someone involved in politics, I can tell you it's better to have him with you than against you. All I'm asking is that if anyone has any new ideas, maybe you could let me know. I've set myself up at the Creighton Hotel, over on Fourth, and I'll be working out of there—at least until Friday." She wanted to do it while the media attention was still focused on Tim Mallick.

As she spoke, Susan moved slowly towards the window closest to Annie. Reaching it, she stopped and, without interrupting her own summary, pushed the window all the way up, wide open.

With it came a rush of fresh air. Annie's relief was nearly instantaneous. She felt the cooler breeze rush in, carrying its faint metallic tang off the river. She closed her eyes momentarily, grateful beyond all measure as the heat inside her began slowly to subside.

Out of the side of his mouth, and more than loud enough for everyone in the room to hear, the big cop beside her spoke up again. "Funny, when that kind of thing happens to my wife, I open a window too—and just crawl out it myself." There were choked guffaws.

Yeah, well, Annie thought, come and talk to me, you son of a bitch, when you gotta pee every twenty seconds.

They fell into silence again.

By the time Annie noticed, Susan Shaw was on the other side of the room again, standing beside the commissioner. "So, does anyone have anything that they'd like to discuss now?" She looked around expectantly, meeting only blank stares from most of them. The others were quietly checking out her legs.

This time Susan didn't bother to mask her growing irritation. "Then I'll lay my own cards on the table: I think all of us have a lot to lose here." She seemed to be looking only at Annie.

DeVries cleared his throat, waiting an awkward few seconds in the suddenly still room. Everyone was nervous now.

Then, abruptly, they were all dismissed. Annie trailed out behind the rest, listening to them all repeating the same thing—that it looked like the governor just wanted another excuse for another cynical dirt-digging exercise as he entered yet another political campaign. Probably ready to call for an internal audit on the division this time someone suggested. And who the hell was Susan Shaw, anyway?

Annie passed two detectives talking intently outside the men's room. One pumped his fist up and down forcefully a couple of times, in a vulgar gesture. They both laughed.

Annie crowded past them, pretending not to notice. In the end, that's all they could see in a woman like that.

At the end of the long corridor she saw DeVries accompany Susan from his office. They stood together at the top of the stairs, talking for a few minutes. He seemed considerably more animated than usual. Then she saw Susan rest a well-manicured hand very casually on his arm. Getting along like a house on fire, apparently.

Don't blame the guys, Annie reminded herself. It's what women like Susan Shaw *want* them to see.

~~~

Annie lay on her living room couch and followed every news report from the beginning of the evening. The narrative she'd designed with Callie built steadily, starting with the first bulletin cutting into *Wheel of Fortune*. Then other stations started scrambling to catch up. Annie's phone began to ring almost immediately.

In total, Callie made a half-dozen separate appearances, each time adding another piece to the picture. By the end of the night she'd hit every duck Annie had set up: a whole series of full-screen images of Leah Mallick, some the public hadn't seen before; new footage from in front of the house; a pinpoint-accurate artist's rendition of the location of the bodies; details of the full extent of trauma; toxic levels reported; confidential sources quoted. The microscopic blood speck on the water glass. That police suspicions were raised early on when they found no fingerprints in the garage. That gut instinct had told them the rest, Callie said with some admiration. They looked like geniuses, with all discrepancies magically dissolved.

Well, Annie thought, if the latex glove fits . . .

At the conclusion of the final, eleven-thirty broadcast, Callie all but made a thumbs-up gesture to the camera. She'd broken her first news exclusive—the local Lockport
~~~

police had identified Leah Mallick as the murderer. And April Vaughan was probably hanging herself right now with her pashmina.

Everything Annie had wanted was there. " . . . revealed today, when Lockport police concluded their investigation into Monday's Belford tragedy. Police spokeswoman Lieutenant Anne Shannon refused to confirm or deny the story. Police declined further comment, indicating their intention to await the conclusions of the formal medical report. The medical examiner's office has yet to release the results of its own investigation, after several days." Callie punctuated the last comment with a rueful little shake of her head. Poor Bobby Canon, Annie thought.

After this, Canon would be left scrambling to bring out even the semblance of a report in time, all the while trying to explain why it was "late." And he'd have to start by rewriting everything in the current one. No more fulsome regrets about "contaminated evidence," sly editorial accusations of a "dangerous rush to judgment." He could only agree and go along with the police. Canon was more than welcome to make a play for chief coroner, but it would have to be on some *other* case of "institutional incompetence." And as far as he would ever know, the leaks had sprung directly from his own office—maybe even from April Vaughan's "secret source." Or whoever it was who'd informed Susan Shaw. There were a lot of possibilities. Let them look. Annie turned off the TV.

DeVries's cold-blooded politicking was the more serious issue now. He'd been prepared to stand back and watch as his own officers were publicly humiliated by an ambitious

ME exploiting a stupid slip, instead of stepping in and quietly looking for a way to downplay the error. DeVries had wanted the media to blow the story up into something big and threatening, all too willing to abandon his own people out there for nothing more than a scant few days of perceived advantage over the Island Boys and their friends. It made it tougher to believe that they were all working on the same side.

Annie smiled grimly to herself. Well, at least he couldn't say that she hadn't served up a full helping of Leah Mallick—just not in quite the way he'd anticipated or hoped for. Nothing left for him now but to take credit for it and smile through gleaming, gritted teeth.

Even DeVries was right about *one* part: everyone would steep themselves in Leah Mallick for the next few weeks, combing through the soap opera libretto, constructing yet another cautionary tale of the favoured few destroyed by envious gods.

And as a bonus, Callie Christie was firmly and forever in her pocket. Who knew how useful that might be eventually? For the moment, though, everyone could carefully step back. She had managed to "manage" it.

And that's what you call spin, she thought. Amateurs! Whose PR problem was it now?

Annie stepped out of the shower and stood in front of her bathroom mirror. It was almost two in the morning. Nothing left on TV. Probably suppertime in Japan. Maybe there's someone *there* I could phone and talk to, she thought. Then shook her head. Someone to talk to . . . *If it wasn't for those fucking women's charity luncheons, I wouldn't have much of a normal life either.*

But what constituted "normal" any more? Annie studied her own image in the mirror, the edges of it smudged by steam formed on the glass.

Cancer. What exactly would it *feel* like? Actually to touch it? She began to explore her left breast with her right hand. Smooth, soft, a perfectly rounded shape, now newly full of vague menace. She took it wholly in her hand, trying to imagine what a man felt and wanted in that caress. She flexed her shoulder muscle and touched what could have been a lump. It disappeared, sliding away under her fingertips. Would it feel like a small ball bearing in the beginning? A dried pea? Like a golf ball or a grape? Hockey puck or orange? Was it more appropriate to compare it to food products or to sporting goods?

She pinched the loosened skin in her fingers, the stuff under her arms, felt for the multiplying folds and creases around her back as far as she could reach. She turned slightly under the high bathroom light, lifting the other breast, looking for a telltale ripple or dimple or indentation. Maybe a garbanzo bean. The marks of her bra straps still showed pale red. There seemed to be nothing.

But that was just it: it was nothing you could possibly have known about, then something you could no longer deny. What were the statistics? How long was she obliged to stand there looking, searching? A two-percent possibility? Then maybe five minutes a week was enough. If you were in a high-risk category—an hour every second day? If you checked too often, would it make you too casual, a little nonchalant, maybe miss the inconspicuous start of change?

Cheer up, she told herself. Summer's coming, and soon you can start checking for irregular moles.

Her arms still raised behind her head, she shifted her glance upwards to her face. She looked hard, noticing for the first time her mother's features emerging from her own, like an island slowly revealed by the ebbing tide. She had grown up being told that she looked just like her father, his side of the family. With his blue eyes, his sharp angles and hard ways and obstinate propensities. The man she and her brothers had always secretly referred to as Tough Meat.

But those were definitely her mother's crow's feet coming in now. Her grandmother's softened jawline. A spinster aunt's furrows developing nicely along the nose. Her own face was quickly disappearing into an album of family photographs. She had inevitably joined a resolute line of matriarchs marching through history behind her.

You know you're middle-aged when the pillowcase creases on your face in the morning are still there at bedtime. You know you're middle-aged when sales clerks don't even bother to offer you extended warranties on major appliances any more. You know you're middle-aged when you finally give up any idea that you could look like Michelle Pfeiffer if only you knew how to use eyeliner. Or when you figure time available by calculating backwards from death.

She lowered her gaze again to her breasts. And felt, rather than saw, a baby drawing milk into his whole length, with uncertain power. His mouth a source of unexpected, subtle pleasure. All flesh a need, so gratefully met. How long was it since she'd even allowed herself to remember something so plain, unequivocal, unambiguous?

Then Greg, cloudy with sleep, was standing behind her.

She'd completely forgotten he was still there. Just another pizza evening. He laid his head on her bare shoulder and turned his mouth to warm the curve of her neck. His hands reached around to take her breasts and gently round them in his touch. She noticed in the mirror that she had cleavage again. She leaned back into him. He was only half awake, but certainly willing. They went to bed.

It didn't help. Afterwards, she lay awake for hours more, unable to sleep. Waiting in the dark for the alarm to go off.

Maybe her body was riddled with every disease on the face of the earth. Or maybe she could live to be a hundred. There were so very few things you could ever know.

And maybe Leah Mallick *had* suffered from nothing more than an unpredictable, intractable hormonal imbalance.

But Annie was sure of one thing: if she didn't try to find out the real "why" of what had happened that night in the house in Belford, something far more important would be lost to her again.

4

April Vaughan laughed.

The host of the network morning show had convinced her to join a cooking segment with Wolfgang Puck, and Vaughan had just managed to dot her Prada with crème fraîche. She indulged a few weak double entendres as the host offered to clean it off for her. And, always expert with a segue, Vaughan played along until she could bring it around to the purpose of her appearance. She was here to pump Thursday evening's *BackPage.*

"Last night, of course, local police in Lockport finally had to admit that—" she said, only to be interrupted again.

The host plucked the newspaper off the coffee table in front of them. "Our own viewers might have already seen this, this morning," he said, holding the page up to the camera. "Lockport's not that far from here, is it, April? We all heard how a prominent psychiatrist committed suicide there a couple of days ago?" There were murmurs of recognition from the studio audience. "But this is the part that's really troubling—before taking her own life, this doctor, Dr. Leah Mallick, actually shot her husband to death. Then she tried to kill her little boy. And came very close to succeeding." The host shook his head ostentatiously, his face grim. The audience responded with a collective *Awww*. "That's tough," he said, leaning close and lowering his voice. "How is the boy doing now, April?"

"His name's Kyle—and he's in what doctors term a persistent vegetative state. A PVS. All the medical experts I've consulted tell me he's never going to wake up—we're even going to be taking a look at new allegations that local emergency workers didn't get to him in time—and how the hospital is now being forced to keep him alive artificially."

The host wrinkled his nose as though at a bad smell. "You mean with all those tubes and wires and everything?"

April nodded. "Just another element in this very troubling case—maybe another debate. But tonight, on *BackPage,* for the first time we're going to tell you *why* Leah Mallick did it. Why someone as intelligent and compassionate as everyone says this woman was obviously felt *forced* to take her own life and lead her family into deadly disaster."

The host looked off-camera for a moment. "Do we have the clip set up . . . ? We do? Good. April, maybe you can describe what we're looking at here."

Their faces were replaced with close-ups of the Mallicks together. Then Leah alone—

"A beautiful, beautiful woman," the host murmured.

Tim Mallick. Kyle. A final portrait of the three of them, looking picture-perfect, mournful music under. There was an audible reaction from the audience, and the camera cut to a few of them shaking their heads. The stills dissolved into a video clip of the house in Belford, crawling with cops, EMTs and news media.

"Just part of tonight's documentary on *Back Page*. But, April, they tell me you have something else to share with us . . . ?"

The picture cut to April Vaughan, now crisp and energized. "*BackPage* has obtained its own copy of a confidential medical report which I'll prove put this entire train of tragedy into motion." April flourished a sheet of white paper. "In the past twenty-fours hours I've learned that Tim Mallick was already suffering from what was diagnosed as a terminal neurological disease. I'm going to have some of the country's best experts with me to describe what these people might very possibly have been facing. Some very terrifying symptoms—maybe the same ones challenging some of our own loved ones. Graphically."

The host mugged to the camera. "What, again an exclusive? You people have your own SWAT team over there?"

Vaughan smiled thinly at him, then continued. "In the end, we'll show that it's really more a kind of love story. Because Leah Mallick was a doctor herself, she had to understand what that diagnosis could mean for her husband. And what we've also learned is that it's often doctors as a group who are the least mentally and emotionally equipped to deal with a terminal diagnosis. As a society, we don't recognize that. In some ways, death represents much more than a personal loss to them. It's a professional failure. And that's not something we train the medical profession in this country to accept. In fact, statistics suggest that in hospitals today, eight out of ten doctors refuse to be the ones to tell their patients the truth if the news is bad."

April looked out over the audience, nodding sagely, while the host expelled a shocked, "Really! So maybe that's how we end up with all these cases now, where doctors choose to keep patients alive like that—"

She took a sip from the coffee mug at her elbow. "Exactly. Leah Mallick knew better than anyone what he would be left to face inside the medical system—and she took a different path. We'll tell you all about that tonight, on the show." Vaughan settled back into her chair.

The host carefully gauged his audience now. "Hmm, maybe just as much a victim?"

Vaughan nodded slightly. "In the end, I believe it's a story about personal choice."

"Well, April Vaughan—controversial as always. I'm sure we'll all be tuning in tonight. That's *BackPage,* at ten o'clock, folks. Thanks for being here, April." He grasped her hands and kissed the air near her cheek. "And, hey, send that dry-cleaning bill to Wolfie, eh?" They laughed into the applause as it went to commercial.

Sitting alone in her hotel room, Susan switched off the television. And picked up the phone.

~~~

It was barely seven o'clock when Annie climbed the stairs. There was almost no one else in the building. She had the running track to herself this morning.

Her intention was to take it slow, discover a comfortable pace. Annie glanced up at the large clock on the end wall.
~~~

The minute hand floated towards the twelve as she began her first lap.

All those half-hearted attempts in the last few months, running in clumsy spurts between the house and St. Edward's Park, meant absolutely nothing now. Any claim to "service readiness" paled in the face of this: the circuits of an oblong track. Here it was reduced to an unequivocal number. She was pretty sure she couldn't do it.

Easy, steady, measuring her breaths to her stride. Trying to settle into it. She'd already done two laps before she saw another police officer coming up the stairs to the track. A young woman, probably mid-twenties, who, judging by the pattern of sweat on her T-shirt, had already done a warm-up in the weight room downstairs. She stretched now in a graceful way that looked more like ballet. Then simply started running.

Annie found she was able to keep the other woman at the same distance, neither losing nor gaining ground against her. A little short of ten laps, Annie saw her passing exactly the same point on the other side of the track. Still matching her, step for step.

Specs required twenty-two circuits. Annie checked the clock and was surprised to see only a little more than half her time was gone. It was worth a try. She increased her pace slightly.

Then there was nothing left to consider but the sound of her rhythmic breathing. She knew that her legs were slick with perspiration. She could feel the shirt clinging to her back. She tried to distract herself from everything that was starting to hurt. Tomorrow was Friday. A weekend with a good book . . .

Annie heard footsteps directly behind her. The young officer was passing on the outside. She went by without glancing over. She wasn't even breathing hard. Within seconds Annie saw her on the opposite side again and decided against trying to keep up. All that counted, she reminded herself, was the time on the clock.

At the three-quarter mark the woman was beside her again. "Hi, Lieutenant Shannon. I wasn't sure it was you at first. I'm Lisa Taylor. FCU." Financial Crimes Unit. The other cops referred to it as the Fuck You. Her tone was friendly, conversational. Annie had heard something like that was possible—that you would be able to talk if you were jogging at the right speed for your fitness level. She was fighting for her life here. Lisa, apparently, was jogging. Annie nodded a greeting.

"I was taking a look at that Mallick case. You know, that murder over in Belford? Just out of interest. I thought maybe there was something in there for us. But you know how it goes. Unless someone turns up the heat—" Lisa shrugged and smiled. So, she could do *three* hard things at once, Annie thought.

Annie felt her own face frozen in a pleasant grimace. Even through the fog that was building behind her eyes she understood the point being made: unless someone higher up supported a formal charge, they were given no room to investigate. And Paul DeVries had already made it clear that anyone who might have been caught out by Tim Mallick had very little interest in publicly pursuing a complaint. Then she forgot why it all mattered. I can breath or I can think, she said to herself.

Lisa Taylor reflected for another moment. "Oh, well," she said lightly. "Too bad. It might have been fun." She was subtly extending her stride, Annie noticed. "Well, I've got to get in a bit of a workout here. I'm only twenty off minimum."

What does that mean? Annie thought. Miles, repetitions, hours, percent? Years? She watched Lisa pull away, until she was a distant speck on the horizon, like the Road Runner.

As they neared the end, Lisa passed her once more, forced to call out a warning. "Track!" Annie was now wobbling from side to side.

Lisa picked up her towel, draping it around her neck, before she gave a small wave to Annie and disappeared down the stairs. Annie still had one more lap to go. And less than two minutes. She tried not to think of her breathing now. There was no point. Do—don't do—there is no try. Who was it who'd said that, anyway, she asked herself through the pain—Yoda?

Half a lap to go now. The clock showed fifty-one seconds left. Annie plunged towards the spot on the wall that marked the end.

She crossed the imaginary finish line, her arms raised overhead, hearing the music, floating at least a foot above the track. Her picture would be on the Wheaties boxes. She'd replace that "thrill of victory" guy on *Wide World of Sports*. Wilma Rudolph. Flo-Jo. Babe Didrikson. A blend of Hillary Rodham Clinton and Annie Morrow Lindbergh. On steroids.

She didn't have to look at the clock. She'd beaten it—destroyed it—annihilated it. Pounded it into submission.

They'd have to send the parts back to Switzerland for repair.

The only thing close to this must be a heart attack or stroke, she thought—either of which could come at any moment.

Specs in two more weeks. Maximum, maybe three. Add a few chin-ups every day . . .

The gym was empty. She went down to the main floor and paraded around it in tight circles, clutching her fist. Grinning. Gasping. This was what winning felt like.

She finally collapsed on a nearby bench.

Then looked over to see Roy Warren standing against the far wall, silently observing. She hadn't heard him come in. But she watched now as he walked slowly towards her and sat down on the other end of the bench, straddling it to face her, like a coach with a troubled player between quarters.

"Quite a workout," he said.

She nodded and wiped the towel across her face, holding it there for a moment. She didn't want him to see how hard she was breathing. She forced a laugh. "Stupid impulse, I guess. I wanted to see if I could still do it."

Warren nodded. "And apparently you can." But his smile was unconvincing. "I admire your determination, Lieutenant. After all, you're pushing fifty this year."

I fucking know how old I am, she thought. "Well, I figured it was now or never." They sat in uncomfortable silence for a moment. She looked away from him, ducking her head so he couldn't see her face. "Actually, I was thinking about maybe trying to find a way to get a little more involved in

Operations again." Casually. "You know, combine some of what I used to be . . ." She'd meant to say "to do . . ."

When she glanced up, Warren's expression was unreadable. "That's fairly unusual for someone in your position," he said. Then the silence stretched out again. He coughed and cleared his throat. "But now that you mention it, it reminds me—there's something I always meant to ask you, about your work back then. When I read all the personnel files, I still remember how yours stood out. From what I saw, you were one of the best out there. Solid. Smart. It's a good advertisement for being brought up in a family of cops, I guess."

She heard again the faded anthem: "*My sons and my son's sons. My father, and his father before him . . .*"

He leaned back casually. Roy Warren was one of the agents of change DeVries had brought with him at the time of his own appointment as commissioner. A new captain for the department, someone with no local ties.

Warren shifted on his seat. "One thing always stuck with me. Given everything *I* could see, anyway, you should have gone a lot further. Nothing stopping you from becoming the first female captain in the department. But for some reason, you suddenly took yourself out—and nothing in that file told me why. Instead, you disappeared into a straight admin job . . ."

Her heart began pounding hard again.

"When I talked to a couple people—there wasn't one bad word against you. So I'm left thinking it's the typical stuff. Politics, a bit of disciplinary action—I don't know, maybe the old glass ceiling thing. Distractions from a boyfriend or a husband, family . . ."

Annie looked away, knowing what was coming. It can never be over, she thought. Not as long as I am on this earth. She felt the trickles of sweat running down her stomach and back, soaking the waistband of her gym shorts.

Warren's expression subtly altered. "It took me a while to put two and two together. Then I found out what happened to you. To your son . . ."

He waited. There was no response. "I'm sorry. I know I should've said something to you sooner. But I was a stranger, and I thought maybe it was better to leave well enough alone." He glanced around uncomfortably before speaking again. "But we're not strangers any more, are we?"

She shook her head.

"So if I had to guess . . ." He looked at her appraisingly. "You still see yourself as a cop. A good one, with a need to find out why things like this happen in the world. But that's a problem for this department because it means maybe you're not doing your job objectively. As it is, I've already had to do a bit of a soft-shoe to stop the commissioner going after you."

It has taken only a couple of hours to figure out that she'd leaked the information to Callie. Annie made a face. "DeVries can't really expect—"

"Look, DeVries isn't your problem. He may be a royal pain in the ass, but he's not stupid. You've already played him for a fool once this week. I wouldn't try it again soon." He looked at her meaningfully. "And this Mallick case isn't yours to solve."

They sat, silent. There was nothing more to say.

Then he stood up and checked his watch. "And I've got a shitload of stuff on my desk that I have to get rid of before I can even start my day. It seems to grow there overnight, doesn't it?" He put his hands on his hips and sighed before glancing up to the lap clock above their heads. "So, what was your time?"

She cleared her throat. She wasn't sure any sound would come out. "Twenty-nine thirty-three."

She'd beaten the minimum departmental requirement by twenty-seven seconds. He allowed himself a small smile. "Pretty good. I should probably get out there myself and start doing it again too—a new hobby." He squeezed the couple of inches overhanging his belt. "It really creeps up on you at this age, though, doesn't it? Anyway . . ." He glanced at her again. "Look. You're good at what you do. That hasn't changed. At a police board meeting a couple nights ago they made a special point of saying how they liked the new Crime Stopper spots."

She grabbed her towel and leaned over to wipe down her now throbbing leg. "Thanks, Captain."

His street shoes clicked loudly across the wooden floor of the gym. Then he stopped and looked back at her for a moment. She hadn't moved from the end of the bench. "By the way, Susan Shaw called me. She thinks we're holding out on her—a little too much 'ambiguity' is how she put it. Whatever the hell that means. Do your job, Lieutenant." The double door clanged shut behind him.

It demonstrated a deft touch for political shading. Susan Shaw had gone over her head, but only by a little. To Roy Warren rather than DeVries. Or the governor. A warning shot.

Annie shivered. She'd allowed herself to cool down too fast this time. And the smell of her own sweat, sharp and sour, was making her nauseated.

∿∿∿

"So, we're agreed." DeVries straightened his glasses. "We'll co-operate with her—for the time being."

Annie knew he didn't mean *co-operate* as much as *distract.* "You know, Commissioner, trying to delay this isn't going to help us. Just let them ask the questions they want," Annie said. She was tired. They'd already been going back and forth for more than an hour. "They're going to do whatever it takes to move the media attention off Leah Mallick now. Why make ourselves the target this time?"

He looked at her warily. He knew what she was really thinking—that it was too late. That they'd been overtaken by circumstances. And that she really *did* mean *co-operate.* Like the Vichy government, if that's what it was going to take.

Within only a few hours Callie Christie's evening exclusive had been replaced by April Vaughan's early morning shocker. And now the case had circled back again to Tim Mallick. It was the needle stuck in the record, one thing running into the other as though it made one continuous story. And maybe it did.

She knew that most of the country would be watching *BackPage* tonight for more news about Tim Mallick's sickness. Yet even now, all DeVries seemed to want to focus on was that he'd been hearing from the Island Boys again.

As long as there'd been a Lockport, there'd been Island

Boys. Always with some shell game or another running over there. And now, somehow, they'd got themselves wound up in a national story. But this time, as far as Annie was concerned, Susan Shaw could have them all.

"Maybe it's time to really think about giving up Lew Stephens," Annie said. "He can afford a good lawyer. And you know he's behind whatever bizarre scheme they've got going on in that little enclave of theirs. If the governor even *wants* to suspect that we're stalling them this time, he'll be all over us like flies on sh . . . on a dirty shirt. They already think we're a bunch of hicks up here anyway. And what happened last time is *nothing* compared to what they'll make out of obstruction of justice or conspiracy. The governor's campaign will be using *us* as the bumper sticker this time, if we force their hand."

DeVries discounted the idea almost immediately. He shook his head. "Not right now. We know this Mallick stuff has to die down. But I do agree—let's view it as an opportunity to build some bridges. I believe we can satisfy her inquiries fairly efficiently—let her see we're holding nothing back. There's no charges, no indictments, no complaints filed, nothing outstanding. Then we send her on her way," he said. "Anyway, this department's clean now. And Tom Acton damn well knows that."

On the surface of it, he was right. No Lockport cop would dare accept a free coffee in a doughnut shop any more. Over the last three years DeVries had overseen substantial changes in every area of the department. And his public reputation was still squeaky clean. He'd avoided every potential for scandal so far.

At the time of his appointment DeVries had been loudly trumpeted as a "good get," with all the fanfare the mayor and the police board could bring to the announcement. And however grudgingly she admitted it, Annie knew that his past performance warranted it. She was still riding in a Lockport patrol car by the time he'd already made sergeant in Chicago. A captain less than ten years out. Now the Boy Wonder Commissioner—and not yet forty-five. It was unprecedented. And it made him almost untouchable. But his antennae never stopped moving. Nose to the grindstone, lips to someone's ass.

You know you're middle-aged, she thought, when the guy picking up the lifetime achievement awards is younger than you are. "But what if she really *is* expecting a full investigation?"

In light of April Vaughan's revelations, that seemed inevitable. And if Susan Shaw decided there *should* be one, Annie suspected, there would be one.

For the first time a cloud of impatience swept across DeVries's face. "You don't seem to understand the nuances here, Lieutenant. If *I* wanted an investigation, I'd send someone else. *You're* the one I want to handle this." He shot her a meaningful look. *Stay on message.*

Annie nodded. Oh, yeah—God forbid it should be a real cop, she thought. Give it to Nancy Drew.

"Just hand her the file and offer to stay in touch," he said. "The two of you can talk this through. Then let them do with it what they will. Just as long as they do it elsewhere and we continue to be apprised of any developments. I don't really have to tell you your job, do I?"

It wasn't an explicit threat, of course. That wasn't his style, she knew. But he certainly seemed to want to keep her off balance. Not one word about the ME's report being leaked to Callie Christie.

No, his control was impeccable. His tone might be solid ice, but he was proposing a reasonable exit strategy: as far as the Lockport police were concerned, the Mallick case held no further interest. The lead characters had switched places, but it was no different than three days ago—nothing more than an incident of domestic violence gone very wrong. And now April Vaughan had conveniently provided the motive. Everyone could say they knew "why." Whatever happened next didn't have to involve them—if they were smart and silent.

Or unless it turned out to be useful. She'd overheard DeVries promising the mayor "no more surprises." He'd said exactly the same thing to Rita Graham only a half-hour earlier. His bread, it seemed, was being buttered on at least four different sides. He'd painted himself a very fine line to walk.

But this time, she knew, if it went wrong, she would be the one publicly pilloried. "No, Commissioner. No one has to tell me my job."

As she rose from the small conference table, she saw DeVries take a moment to make another neat notation in his Daytimer: Shannon—Shaw. The third word might have been *handled.* Reading it upside down, she couldn't be sure.

Then DeVries spoke again, from behind her. "After all, Lieutenant, if the Island Boys go down, how long do you really think you and I will be here?"

~~~

Annie drove the few blocks to the Creighton Hotel. The elderly doorman waved her right up to the curb as usual, into the open spot generally reserved for a taxi stand. At this time of day, there was little call for cabs.

"Well, Annie Shannon. How's your father, then?" He always asked.

"He's good, Mr. Cook. I'm OK here for a few minutes?" She always asked.

He waved her off. "No problem, darlin'. I'll look after it for ya."

Annie stopped at the ornate front desk that dominated the large, old-fashioned, high-ceilinged lobby set with forty-year-old plastic plants and cracked leather chairs. It had a certain charm, she supposed—if you'd never been elsewhere. A high-school boy was running it, dressed like a Mormon on a mission. Or an assistant manager at McDonald's.

She began to reach for her identification.

"Lieutenant Shannon," he said. "How may I help you?" His big, toothy grin reminded her of someone she'd once known.

She found herself smiling broadly in return. "Susan Shaw's room, please," she said.

The clerk attacked the computer like a PlayStation. Obviously, she was his first celebrity.

"Ms. Shaw is in . . . yes, Room 535. Take the second elevator and turn to your left on exiting." He was still looking at her, expectantly.
~~~

She glanced down at his name tag: James S. Trainee Assistant Manager. "Have we met?" she said after another moment.

The boy seemed thrilled. "Not me. But you went to high school with my dad. Roger Sills . . . ? He talks about you every time you're on TV."

Roger had been the linebacker on the school football team. Annie remembered him—the first guy she'd ever let get to third base. Closer to shortstop. The same wide grin as the boy in front of her now. The same six foot three.

Annie smiled and nodded. How was that possible? But then, some of her friends were already having grandchildren. "Oh, really? Of course. Well . . . well, please say hello to him for me." She could feel herself blushing. Those crisp, long-ago autumn nights under the grandstand . . .

James spoke in a rush. "I'm hoping to get into police work too. I'm starting at the state college in September. This is just my summer job. I'd like to maybe go on to the FBI academy. But local police work really interests me too. Maybe I could ride with you sometime?" He probably imagined himself in one of those scenes on TV—where after a suitably high-speed chase, they'd drag down a half naked offender with a blurry dot imposed over his face, screaming bleeped obscenities.

"Well, actually, James, I don't 'ride' any more, so to speak. But maybe I can set up something for you with one of the officers in Division." They could drive him fast enough to push his eyeballs into the back of his head. She smiled as she passed him her business card.

He stared at it, silly with pleasure. It looked a little like her own reaction to getting a Sky King decoder ring when she was six.

"Just give my office a call. And say hi to your dad for me and . . ." She couldn't recall who it was that Roger had ended up with. " . . . and your mom." Probably that chesty cheerleader, she thought.

"Thanks. I sure will."

Room 535. Left from the elevator. Susan Shaw opened the door at the first knock, as though she'd been expecting a visitor.

Full makeup. Another designer suit. Motown oldies on the stereo. A large coffee urn set up with a dozen cups waiting on a tray.

Sorry, honey, but I'm it, thought Annie.

Susan covered her disappointment adequately enough. "Oh . . . hello. We met yesterday. Anne Shannon . . . right?"

Annie nodded. Beyond the cursory introduction they hadn't exchanged a word. "Paul DeVries asked me to drop this off for you," she said. "It's all we've got at this point. I imagine you've already seen most of it, though." Annie glanced around the room. It was the closest thing Lockport had to a posh suite. Susan had converted the sitting room into a makeshift office, a folding table and chairs in the centre of the floor served as a desk. A laptop computer. Printer. A mini-bar. A room-service tray with the remains of a light breakfast.

There were also three storage boxes stacked at the side of the desk. The one on top was filled with carefully labelled files. *Someone* had been working hard . . .

"So, Paul DeVries sent you. And you're, what—the public relations coordinator?"

"Communications officer. A lieutenant, actually," Annie replied. She realized she was already on the defensive. "I'm still attached to the department."

Susan glanced at the small folder of material Annie was passing to her. "Well, that must be very uncomfortable for you," she said wryly, then set the file aside without opening it.

Annie noticed that she'd automatically squared the folder with the edge of the table.

It was an annoying habit she'd often seen in people she didn't like. She noticed something else too: the tics of a reformed smoker. It was in the way Susan slid her pen repeatedly between two fingers to tap the tip of it on the desktop impatiently. The unconscious movement of one hand towards her lips when she paused, the not exactly knowing what to do with the gesture otherwise.

But even without that there was a tense, almost highstrung quality about her. Behind the flawless smile, a kind of expectation. Annie had seen it in a few other women, the ones who'd spent most of their lives being judged on appearance alone, as though they had to redefine themselves every morning when they looked into a mirror. Susan Shaw had undoubtedly been very pretty at one point; still was, in fact. But, perhaps, it had bred in her the habit of being far too self-aware, too sensitive to the reaction, the approval, of others. That's usually what remains when looks fail to do the job any more, Annie thought. The craving. It made some women edgy.

For now, though, she appeared only to be waiting for Annie to leave. She'd obviously decided that her guest was nothing more than a courier—lieutenant or not.

Trying to sound more friendly, Annie again indicated the thin file. "The commissioner asked me to check if there was anything else you needed. I know there's not that much there—"

Susan just shook her head, occupying herself with the laptop opened on the desk. The screen glowed more brightly as the daylight began to fall off in the room. She hit a few computer keys impatiently. "Well, maybe you could arrange a high-speed hookup. The phone system in this damn place is like trying to draw sludge through a straw." The screen suddenly filled with vivid bar graphs. Over and over again she brought up different versions. Dazzling, though none of it meant anything to Annie. Finally, Susan shrugged and let the screen saver take over—a series of scenic photos from state parks, one blending into the other in a hypnotic rhythm. From the looks of it, regulation government issue.

But for the first time Annie questioned her own assumptions. Maybe this *was* intended as nothing more than a state-sponsored fishing expedition. Yet it appeared that Susan Shaw had already managed to gather more information than the entire Lockport police department. And if this was connected in any way to the Mallicks, she'd started long before Monday.

"I'm sure you didn't come to Lockport to hole up in a hotel room and surf the Internet." Annie looked again at the stacked boxes of catalogued files. What was in all of them? "Maybe there's someone you'd like to meet?"

Susan sounded distracted. "No. Thank you." As though she'd almost forgotten that someone else was still standing in the room.

Annie picked up one of the business cards from the small stack carefully aligned on the coffee table: *Susan Shaw. Director, Department of Business and Professional Regulation.* Underneath that, *Diplomate American Board of Forensic Examiners.* She certainly didn't seem much of a diplomat right now.

"Well, think about it. I happen to know everyone in town." Annie attempted a small laugh, appropriately self-deprecating. "I do a little local television."

"Yeah. So I've seen." Susan glanced at the silent TV in the far corner of the room. She'd just watched Anne Shannon's most recent announcement on the noon news—something about a charity competition between the police and the firemen's local. "You run the chili cook-offs . . ." Susan raised an eyebrow.

Annie's eyes narrowed. *OK, let's compare how each of us got here.* "Right. But let me ask you, then—what do you believe happened?" *Here's your opportunity for spin, lady. On a silver platter.*

"Well, I don't know what makes you think I'd know anything . . . but I certainly don't accept that it's all an unpredictable chaos." Susan's voice was perfectly even. "I think there *is* a point. A reason. In the end, I believe, patterns meet their promises."

It was more the style than the substance of the remark that caught Annie by surprise. She didn't expect to hear anything like that right now—a cool perspective, a note of disinterested curiosity. Especially from someone representing the governor.

Annie nodded slowly. "OK, let's say I agree with you. But you have to realize that there's a reasonable limit on what any local department can be expected to work up in an investigation. It's sometimes enough that we cover the basics adequately. We have the victim and we have the killer. And it's difficult to rationalize any additional expenditures, if there's nothing . . ." She could practically hear DeVries whispering in her ear. "The truth is, we're not really equipped to do the kind of thing you seem to want. We usually have to go at these things in a more . . . prosaic way."

"Well, I don't know that it's a particularly helpful technique in sensitive investigations." Susan turned away and bit her lip slightly. There it was. She heard it herself—that familiar condescending tone. Emerging whenever she was stressed. Always there, lurking just beneath the surface.

Annie gave her a level stare and took a long, careful moment before responding. The other option was to tell her to fuck off and slam the door on the way out. "OK, enlighten me. What makes this one so particularly 'sensitive'? I mean, aside from the obvious . . . um, political concerns for you?" It was her turn to be snide now.

Susan ignored the question. Instead, she opened the file folder that Annie had delivered and made a show of reading it. "What about the toxicology reports—was he on something? Were there any previous reports of domestic abuse?" It sounded more like an imitation of words she might have overheard elsewhere.

Why bother driving all the way up here for that? Annie thought. “I can tell you that there was cum all over the sheets, if that helps at all.”

Susan blanched slightly. “Meaning what?”

“Page eight of the medical examiner’s report. You don’t have to wait til Friday. I’ve included an advance copy in your file. There was no indication that they’d had sex that night. But, apparently, he got himself off. Maybe that speaks to marital breakdown.” Annie knew it could mean a thousand other things, but she couldn’t resist the impulse. She resented the feeling that Susan Shaw was simply playing some role to an audience of one. “Would you happen to know anything about that?”

Susan went to one of her file boxes and pulled out another slim folder, opened it and slid it across the table towards Annie. “Look for yourself. That’s everything we have.” Her manner became more matter-of-fact. “We didn’t take our internal investigation very far. It wasn’t a particularly important appointment.”

Annie studied the page. A couple of handwritten notations. Leah Sanders. Graduated from Stanford medical school. Class of 1984. Married Tim Mallick in 1988. Did a psychiatric residency at Johns Hopkins. Their only child, a boy, born in 1995. All in all, a rather modest c.v. in a profession noted more for its compulsive overachievers.

“There’s nothing here to particularly recommend her sitting on a state board, either,” Annie said, looking up. “*Someone* must have met with her.” *There’s something missing . . .*

Susan looked startled. “Why?”

"Well, don't all nominations have to go through the Office of the Attorney General before confirmation? Some vetting process? An interview, at least?"

Susan fingered her phantom cigarette. "Well, I suppose *I* did once. At some dinner party or fundraiser or something. She was involved in establishing a research program for palliative care in California. Apparently, it showed some early promise," Susan said. "I think we talked about that."

"Palliative—you mean for cancer patients?" Regina Welles had said she'd met Leah in a experimental program. "Is that a new initiative for this state?"

"For other types of things too, not just cancer. I suppose you could actually call it a general growth industry, with all the baby boomers coming up." Susan allowed herself the trace of a smile now. "There are probably any number of proposals floating around."

Jesus. Could anyone possibly be *that* dry, Annie thought. She handed her back the file.

Susan immediately slipped it out of sight. "And you have nothing else?" she asked.

The two of them stood facing each other, empty-handed.

"Nope," Annie responded.

"I see. Then maybe you could tell me—what's the possibility of your arranging a meeting for us with an investigator more directly involved, perhaps someone from Operations?"

Her transparent attempt at a kind of professional courtesy appeared to have lost a little something in the translation, Annie thought. She decided not to answer. Instead, she summoned the semblance of a polite smile as she headed for the door. "Please go through what I've included there. If there's anything else I can do, you know how to reach me. But I'm fairly confident there won't be any more information." She reached for the door handle.

"If there were, would you tell me?" Susan spoke from behind her.

Annie turned and looked at her.

Susan had dropped all pretence. She was fuming now and didn't care if it showed. "Maybe you haven't figured it out yet, but I'm trying to do you a favour, Ms. Shannon. These were important people. What happened to them matters to other important people. I don't believe that it was just a domestic tragedy. And despite the line you're putting out there, I don't think you buy that either. There is something going on here and you may want to think about that before you say much more. Because I will find out what it is. I'm an experienced pol. And I can tell you, you're better working with me than against me."

How many times was she going to pull *that* one out of the holster? But Susan had let something slip. She'd said "I" this time. It wasn't "we" or "us" any more. Not "he" . . . Susan Shaw was the one doing the asking.

OK, Annie thought. She drew a package out of her briefcase. "You want to know what's going on, Ms. Shaw? Why don't you start with these. Let us know if you see anything there you think we should be investigating." She threw the manila envelope on to the coffee table.

The door clicked shut.

It took Susan a full minute to realize that she'd been holding herself stiffly the entire time Anne Shannon had been in the room. Enough that her muscles actually ached for a few moments when she finally relaxed.

But it was only too true—she hadn't left this room since she'd arrived, except for that one useless and ineffectual presentation they'd allowed her to make. She'd spent all the rest of her time here, staring at the computer screen and ordering up room service that she never bothered to eat. Waiting for an answer.

Well, now she had one. She was being palmed off on a middle-aged PR flack. They were going to try to "handle" her. Get it gone and get her out.

Susan stalked about the room for a minute. At least she could still depend on Georgia to do what she'd asked her—create a credible cover for her unexpected absence at the office without invoking some clumsy version of "executive privilege." It left her free for a few more days. And no one else needed to know where she was.

Susan unwrapped one of the cheap hotel glasses and poured herself a short Scotch. She didn't bother with ice from the machine out in the hall, just added a splash of chemical-smelling water from the bathroom tap.

Out of sheer boredom she'd already read every tourist brochure in the room, all of them describing Lockport's last days of glory—the late Industrial Age, to all appearances. The story was that one of the great giants of architecture had been brought in to design the city's principal manufacturing plant. Structural steel. Forging the colossal pylons and beams for soaring buildings all across the country, the monstrous steel supports for bridges spanning each of the ten great rivers of the continent. The renowned architect, known more for egomania and leaking houses than for great factories, had deemed this place his highest achievement in human engineering.

Lockport had set out to create another heart beating in "the middle of the middle" of the country. And when it was completed, Palladian Steel stood at the centre of everything. The length of a dozen airplane hangars. So high that it developed its own rain. Generations of workers saw their source of pride and permanence in its sheer size.

Now it was nothing but a leviathan run aground. Those were its last breaths, burning the sky red in the slowly setting sun. And she watched the last light of the day fall across the face of the buildings across the river.

Why did Leah ever choose *this*? Susan asked herself. Why had the state's next Secretary of Health and Human Services put herself here, in this failing place?

Almost absently, Susan picked up the other package the lieutenant had left. She opened the manila envelope. It took her a moment to realize that she was looking at a set of crime-scene photographs.

A large, darkly panelled bedroom, expensive furnishings, luxurious fabrics. The setting was flatly rendered in the light from the photographer's flash.

Tim Mallick's face was serene beneath the space where the top of his head had been sheared away. The gun was still visible at the edge of one photograph, his hands curled around it as though sheltering a treasure.

The first one of Leah was in profile. White-blonde hair spread back off a high, clear forehead. The lips were slightly parted. Strong chin. Long, elegant neck. Susan was stunned to see that the blue eyes were open. She knew that it happened sometimes—part of the early state of rigor mortis. Later coaxed into a closed position by others charged with ministering to the bodies.

Even in death, Leah Mallick's beauty was startling.

Susan laid the stack of pictures in the middle of the coffee table and went into the bathroom to throw up.

∿∿∿

April Vaughan was smoothly narrating the slowly dissolving images of a smiling, breathtakingly beautiful couple. April Vaughan, creating the fable of record: *They Were Golden, The Story of Tim and Leah Mallick.*

Annie sat with an ice pack on each knee, watching Thursday evening's *BackPage.* She recognized that she still had the unvarnished truth on her side—all the science and technology that could be pressed into the service of the facts, everything neatly compiled and accurately measured, every intimate detail of biology and blood chemistry catalogued and available. She could have told them what the Mallicks had eaten for dinner the night they died. A fresh copy of the medical examiner's formal report was now sitting on her coffee table if she wanted to look it up.

But none of that could begin to compete with these pictures. For the gifted and the lucky, it seemed, there was the real possibility of an afterlife. Because onscreen, at least, Leah and Tim Mallick had become themselves again, and completely alive. Worthy, still, of admiration and envy. So alive that you could still afford to love—or hate—them.

The TV screen showed the family in some backyard somewhere. It didn't look like Lockport, the sun too high and strong in the sky.

In part, Vaughan had conjured them up in the simplest chronology: schools, marriage, child, death. Her approach fed off the brilliant surfaces. A sense of the hyperbolic permeated it all—everything was unfailingly described in terms of "the best" or "the most." Unerringly, Vaughan captured a sense of vivid intimacy, dropping the eager viewer right inside the walls.

She had found a way to develop solid definition at the centre too. The Mallicks were each described as only children of now deceased parents, Tim Mallick as the scion of a once wealthy family. Yes, Vaughan said, he had attended his father's Ivy League alma mater, but on academic scholarship. Her implication was clear: in a less enlightened time, Mallick's father had probably suffered the same dangerous and debilitating symptoms, finally losing the fortune built by generations before him. Leah's origins were more clouded—an itinerant family who'd slowly emerged into modest wealth out of California's early aerospace industry.

Through a kind of alchemy, a rather ordinary history was transformed into a modern pioneer journey of gritty survival—one costumed in designer labels—towards triumph, then to an achingly inevitable and altogether satisfyingly tragic end.

Annie thought only that the story the program celebrated was backwards, the perspective far too limited. It insistently viewed the Mallicks through the banal prism of middle-class striving. What it missed was that, by birth or by gift of grace, these people already *were* what everyone else could only ever dream of becoming. Something in nature and the circumstances of fate had wrapped them, from the very beginning, in a sense of entitlement. The world and its advantages flowed freely towards them. Whatever they reached for, they grasped. They'd never had to claw their way up in that hard-scrabble way. They'd never had to *acquire;* they already possessed.

As Annie saw it, the truth was closer to the old joke: "He was born on third base, but he'd convinced himself he'd hit a triple."

At the end Vaughan offered the supporting testimony of "real people." Little more than a collection of sentimental comments from those Annie would have bet had hardly met the Mallicks but who, nonetheless, had an opinion to express. Neighbours in the Belford area, other mothers who tearfully recalled seeing Leah Mallick every morning at the school bus stop. Not one of them, Annie knew, were among those who'd thought to alert police that there might be a problem in that house.

They related similar vignettes. How she'd blended in "just like a regular person." Described her as "a loving mother." That she'd talked about "the usual things." She was "beautiful" and "absolutely glowed." "Very gracious and friendly." Et cetera. Et cetera. Et cetera. How reassuring, Annie thought.

Maybe it hadn't really sunk in yet, that for all her gifts and advantages Leah Mallick was nothing but a cold-blooded murderer and Vaughan's piece itself a complete and utter misrepresentation. The only "normal" thing about the

Mallicks was that a gunshot, in forcibly removing a sufficient quantity of vital organ material, could kill them too—or that carbon monoxide, mixed with Nardan at twenty-five parts per million could stop any beating heart.

Then came Vaughan's deliberate editorial swipe: "Despite several invitations, the spokeswoman for the Lockport police has refused to appear," voiced over a segment of Annie flapping away in some two-year-old archival material. April's famous face looked almost sorrowful, hurt. Great technique, Annie thought with grudging admiration. She wanted to throw an ice pack at the screen.

At the end, elegant in a stark studio spotlight, April Vaughan performed a brief dramatic reading. The picture dissolved over documentary news shots of fragile, bedridden patients. ALS. Cerebral palsy. Cancer. Dementia. AIDS. Huntington's chorea. The latter stages of Alzheimer's. Confused, hollow-eyed. Trapped. Terminal. Hopeless.

"There all the rest of his good company was lost,
but it came to pass that the wind bare
and the wave brought him hither.
And him have I loved and cherished,
and I said that I would make him
to know not death and age for ever."

5

The conference room was almost empty this time. Only a few had bothered to show up for what promised to be an anticlimax. Department officials were standing together at the back: Roy Warren and the several senior officers attached to the Mallick file, including Bill Williamson Dan Hewitt. DeVries himself was nowhere in sight.

As Annie walked in, Bill turned and gave her a guarded smile.

Bobby Canon was already at the front, ready to read his formal statement. It was Annie's own suggestion that he deliver it from police headquarters.

"The preliminary conclusion of the medical examiner's report relating to the deaths of Tim and Leah Mallick will state that Leah Mallick was solely responsible for the incident in the Belford area of Lockport five days ago. Timothy Mallick died of severe head trauma, as a result of a single shot fired at close range from a 9 millimetre Walther handgun. It is further concluded that Leah Mallick fired the gun. Mr. Mallick's death has been determined to be murder. Leah Mallick expired from asphyxiation due to toxic levels of carbon monoxide present from a vehicle left running in the garage of the family residence. Further, this caused permanent injury to the couple's son, Kyle, aged eight. Dr. Mallick's death is ruled a suicide. Unless a formal inquest is convened, the coroner's final report will be released by the end of the month, confirming all remaining details."

Bobby Canon stepped back from the podium. There were no questions because there was no news. She'd managed to pre-empt everything in his report.

Annie took her position at the microphone and waited. A few comments were made, all focusing on Leah Mallick's role as perpetrator.

Only one reporter still tried to make any issue of the discrepancy between the initial leaks from the scene and the ME's conclusions. "Who do *you* hold responsible for this apparent 'rush to judgment,' then, Lieutenant Shannon?"

She recognized the reference; it was a direct quote from the buried report. She saw Bobby Canon wince. Those notes must have gone out to a few *other* people as well, she surmised. It didn't matter any more. It was already a dead issue.

Still, she felt a sudden surge of anger. *You* are, she wanted to say. With information, wrong or right, moving at the speed of light. With speculation made to sound like fact. What time was ever available for sober second thought any more? It would happen again, but there was more than enough blame to go around right now.

"We're not responsible for spreading unfounded rumours," she said tersely. She carefully avoided looking in Bill's direction. "This report accurately reflects our professional judgment. While we can't testify to Dr. Mallick's exact mental state at the time of the incident, we can say that, whatever her reasons, she intended to create the impression that it was her husband who'd committed these acts. And, despite considerable evidence to suggest that that might be the case, our own investigation continued. In fact, at this time, I would like to specifically commend the efforts of all officers involved. Yes, it took time, but they pursued it, appropriately, to its proper conclusion."

Annie knew that no TV viewers watching this play later tonight would think to compare it to anything that might have been suggested a few days ago. Instead, they'd see a calm and credible Anne Shannon, issuing a mild *mea culpa*—a "maybe we weren't fast enough." And it looked like the truth. That everything was being looked after by people they trusted.

She accepted the ritual last question from Jan Brackage, senior member of the media corps. By tradition it was a planted one, the generally accepted signal to wrap up the proceedings. "In view of all these new revelations about Tim Mallick's medical condition, will the investigation continue any further, Anne?"

Everyone knew it had to be asked. They'd all watched April Vaughan's *BackPage* last night. And it was really all they wanted to talk about this morning.

But Annie cleared her throat, taking her time as she looked around the room now. She needed to frame her response in the most effective way. This press conference was for show. As far as the Lockport police were concerned, it served as the cut-off point in this investigation. There was no one here who wasn't expecting that. So when she spoke, it was in a voice composed, calm and dispassionate. "We're not in an appropriate position to comment upon private medical matters. My understanding is that patient records in this country still remain privileged information. All I can say is that the final report of the coroner's office is due in thirty days and we have no reason to believe that anything in it will materially affect these conclusions."

She saw a few smirks exchanged, some eye-rolling accompanying quiet snickers.

"However, we *will* be keeping this file open until we have a formal determination in hand, at which point we'll assess what further action may be necessary." Those still in the room looked almost shocked.

Annie knew that, when he heard about it, DeVries would go through the roof. He didn't want to leave even the suggestion of a crack in the door. She was pushing it. But he's not the one standing here, she told herself.

Whatever else Leah Mallick had been, she wasn't capricious or impetuous. She was a skilled doctor. And she'd done this purposefully, with great precision. In some unknown way it had to have fit with her view of the world. Maybe it *was* only what April Vaughan was touting—that Leah had discovered her husband was suffering in the terminal stage of a debilitating neurological disease and she couldn't cope with a negative diagnosis. On the other hand, in a world so ready to ascribe everything to an elaborate conspiracy, and amidst widespread down-market paranoia, there were those who would yet find a way to connect this to the Trilateral Commission, the Illuminati and UFOs, if they were of a mind to. It was difficult to accept that a beautiful, troubled woman, acting alone, was the Destroyer of Worlds.

But there was the boy and, either way, no one could really believe *that* didn't matter.

∿∿∿

It was a damp, dark Saturday morning. Ben followed her quietly down into the kitchen. Annie opened the fridge. No milk. No coffee. No eggs. Apparently, no food. Obviously, she'd have to hit the market at some point. But there was still time for a run. Maybe that new cappuccino place over on Becker was open. Then she noticed it was still only a quarter of eight. Well, Ben needed to go out anyway.

At a slow run, Annie headed off along Portman Street. No one else around yet, on a morning that clearly threatened rain. No one else, at least, with her obvious ambition and inspiring persistence.

Halfway down the block, she stopped. She couldn't come up with a sensible excuse, but she wanted to see the house again. There was an explanation there, something perhaps tied to that place alone.

Annie called the dog back. Clumsily, Ben half crawled, half jumped into the back seat of the car and they headed across the bridge into Belford.

As she crossed the road to approach the Mallicks' house, she could see that nothing about it had really changed. It looked strangely, impressively tranquil, its windows opaque, reflecting only the rainy, grey skies.

She still found it hard to think of it as anything other than Fred James's old place. A vision frozen in deeper ice.

There were kids out on Rollerblades, playing road hockey in front. They swooped past her—an old woman and her fat dog standing in their way. She heard the familiar shout, "He shoots. He scores!" and noticed that the goalie thumping the stick on the pavement in frustration was a little girl stuffed into foot-thick padding.

Annie and her brothers had finally met Fred James, after all those dark winter afternoons hanging out in front of this same house.

She could remember it as a moment preceded by blood.

One of her brothers had been showing off, playing the puck while simultaneously riding his bicycle, and jammed the end of the stick into his mouth trying to make too tight a turn on a pickup. Was it Harry? Or Jack? No, it was Harry.

Annie's mittens had been dangling from the ends of a string run through her sleeves. She had to take them both off to use one now, reaching towards Harry. In the midst of all his crying, snot ran down from his nose and mixed with the blood on his face. She was mortified. She didn't want Fred James to see it and think they were just some poor kids. She tried to wipe the mess off. Harry yowled and pushed her away.

There was Harry, writhing on the ground, crying, blood pouring from his mouth. Then a big, strangely familiar man was there. "Just relax, buddy. Let's see what you done to yourself." The man gently pulled Harry's bloody glove away from his mouth and looked close. "Hey. A coupla stitches, maybe. It's gonna look damn good on ya." Fred James carried Harry, already a large ten-year-old, to his brand new Thunderbird. Harry loved that drive to the hospital.

Fred James had the nurse call their parents and waited with them until the doctor finally came out to examine Harry. By the time the stitches were done, their parents had arrived. Jack stared up at Fred James, almost comatose from the excitement of seeing his one true god stepped down from Madison Square Garden. "Can I have one of your old sticks, Mr. James?" he said. Her parents were embarrassed and tried to shush him.

Fred James wore his fame with the genial grace of a Roy Rogers. He looked down at them and all but tipped his white hat. "When you come and get your brother's bike, I'll see what I can do for ya."

The whole next week was torture. Their parents refused to let them go over until the weekend; they weren't to bother Mr. James again so soon. And even then they weren't allowed to take all their friends along.

When they finally knocked at the door, a woman, presumably Mrs. Fred James, answered. Fred James was away with the team, she said, a three-game series with the Toronto Maple Leafs. Harry almost starting blubbering again through his swollen mouth. But, yes, she assured them quickly, the bike was safe at the side of the house and Fred James had left three brand new hockey sticks for them. In the dim light from the entry hall, they stared, transfixed by the scrawl of his autograph, in indelible ink, on the blade of each one. An official NHL puck too.

Harry held bragging rights for the rest of the fifth grade, showing his scar throughout the long weeks of Stanley Cup playoffs. It was a seminal event for all of them. But by the time Fred James finally left the Rangers and disappeared—already an old thirty-four-year-old—into one of the early expansion teams, the scar had lost its lustre and Harry had been forced to look for another means to impress the world.

Fred James, it turned out, was the type of old-style athlete contemporary sports writers still liked to point to as a "real" hero. They meant one who never made millions. Fred James's time was long before skate deals, when no one wore advertising logos on their sweaters like breathing billboards. And when he died in a car crash a few years later—supposedly from falling asleep at the wheel on the way to an assistant coaching job at a small community college—no one was paying too much attention to men like Fred James any more.

On the sidewalk in front of the house now, Annie felt Ben suddenly leap to the end of his leash, issuing his other, squealing bark—the inheritance from generations of hunting ancestors. It meant he'd spotted something. A squirrel or chipmunk, maybe a raccoon or fox, coming up from the ravine in back. Probably just a cat. Annie saw nothing. Only the dead eyes of a house no longer lived in.

She felt ill at ease, even foolish, being here. Too much like one of those tourists flocking to a gravesite, looking for something to take away from the experience. The wilted bouquets on the front steps had left their colours permanently imprinted on the antique-style bricks. Hues and tones had run into the clay crevices with the rain, baked in the sun. The new owners would have to dig them up and replace them before the bright red stain would finally disappear.

The house couldn't tell her anything. It was nothing more now than a warehouse for unused furniture. Everything inside it would soon be moved out, and new lives would replace the ones who'd once been here. There was already a For Sale sign on the front lawn.

Annie started the car and pulled away from the curb into the street. The kids were still at it. It was true—rich ones played street hockey exactly the same way poor ones did. She heard the familiar wail, coming down to her through the years. "Car!" This time, she realized, they meant her.

At the back door, out of sight, the cat sat on the expansive stone step, futilely working to clean away the raindrops as they fell on her. She gave up, and entered the house through the all-weather door. It was two days since she'd escaped from the ASPCA shelter, but no one had bothered to look for her. She would have been easy enough to find—here, where she waited for the next people to arrive. Knowing that each family in turn changed everything, ordering their world, in part, to understand who they wanted to be—to create their own version of the right way to live. To exert some primacy over it all, when in fact, it was the shadows who would always own it. Emma could have told them that.

She was here, where one day soon yet another family would be surprised to find a friendly cat at their feet one morning in the kitchen, waiting impatiently for breakfast. It was one way to break the ice. People usually felt flattered when an animal appeared to like them for no reason.

They just didn't understand how easy it was. All you had to do was feed her.

~~~

Susan let the phone ring a half-dozen times. She knew it was late, but Georgia was usually still up, watching the last news with her husband. And she'd guess who was calling.

Georgia didn't even bother with hello. "Hi, sweetie. How're you doing?"

"OK. Just a little tired."

"Things winding down?"

Susan laughed a bit. "They never really wound *up,* that I can see. These people don't even seem curious about what Leah Mallick was doing here." Superficial tabloid interest aside, Leah Mallick had never attracted the kind of questions she should have. *After all, someone like that doesn't land in your backyard every day.* "Why *don't* they know anything about her up here, Georgia?" It was a question she should have asked long before now.

There was a long silence. "Maybe she'd just decided to play it low-key until the formal announcement."

Maybe, Susan thought, but it still didn't feel right. They might have intended Leah to be a surprise to the public, but they didn't play it that way inside. Inside, a great deal of time and effort was always put into softening the ground for something this big. The last thing your friends and supporters ever appreciated was a surprise. Normally, Dr. Mallick's name should have been carefully positioned on the tip of everyone's tongue by the time any formal announcement was made. "But if she was supposed to be the next poster girl for upstate economic development . . . They're all dismissing her as just some soccer mom gone postal."
~~~

"It's *good* that they think that. Now we know—we've got nothing to worry about."

"Georgia, I . . ." Susan hesitated. "I think I'm going to stay on a couple more days. Can you cover for me for a little while longer?"

Georgia paused this time. "Don't you think you might be making too much of this, Susan? Aren't you the one who always said her husband was tied up in something odd? So, maybe she was just trying to distance herself from *that* first. The announcement was still a month off."

Georgia was right. Tim Mallick might have given her one reason to exercise some discretion. Susan heard Georgia yawn now.

"Maybe you should just come home, sweetie. We'll sort all this out."

Home? Susan almost smiled to herself. The concept didn't really seem to apply. It was the right address, high above the city, a perfect view, beautifully decorated. But it was no Hallmark card . . . "No. Not yet."

She wanted Georgia to say it was all right, but all she heard was a small sigh at the other end. "Sweetheart, sometimes you have to know when it's time to go." Then the phone went dead.

Early Monday morning, Annie sat at her desk with the office door closed. It couldn't hurt to make a phone call or two. Easy enough to find out if money was a real issue . . .

After only a moment's hesitation she dialed the number.

Someone answered, brightly. "Mountain View Realty." There isn't a mountain within a thousand miles of here, she thought.

She'd noted the name on the sign. Annie asked for the listing agent, someone named Steve.

"That would be Steve Barker. And may I have *your* name, please?"

Annie sighed. "Anne Shannon." She waited for the usual reaction.

"*The* Lieutenant Shannon—the one on TV?"

Too late to hang up. No matter what she did, it was going to be broadcast throughout the city. Maybe she could just pretend she was thinking about buying a house.

Barker came on the line almost immediately. "Steve Barker. How can I help you, Anne?"

"I wonder if you could provide me with some information on a new listing?"

"Sure, Anne. You're looking for something specific?" His voice was friendly, almost believably so.

"It's 2247 Scott Boulevard."

She heard him shuffling through some papers, then tapping a computer keyboard.

"That's the—oh, yeah. Yes. Well, obviously, it's just come on the market. But I guess you'd know that—better than anyone else, eh? Anyway, I've already had a number of calls on it. I got the listing here for . . . it looks like $825,000."

Annie smiled to herself. Fred James might have paid $50,000. If that. Maybe she could just rent it for a day or two.

"But I think I can get that closer to 800—maybe even 775. So, Anne, what are we looking at in terms of a down?"

Right. A "down." Even on the highest debt-ratio mortgage the down payment alone would exceed her annual income by a substantial percentage, and her savings by light years. "Actually, I'm just making an inquiry about the vendor."

"Ah, I see." He sounded only slightly disappointed. "Well, of course, it's an estate sale. Too bad what happened there. Should be pretty uncomplicated, though. And what is it you want to know?"

"Who currently holds the mortgage."

She heard him shuffling through papers. When he spoke again, a few seconds later, his voice had become more wary. "It doesn't look like there is one. It's an assigned sale."

"Assigned?"

"Yeah. Out of a testamentary trust, as far as I can tell. It's not an institutional mortgage."

"What's the name of the trust?"

There was a short pause. "Ah, listen, Lieutenant Shannon, this sort of stuff probably should be going through our head office anyway. I can provide you with their number and maybe you all could sit down and talk about it. I'm a little uncomfortable here. You know, I could say something I'm not supposed to. In fact, now I'm looking at this—we mighta actually acted a little out of turn on this one. It's still really in the hands of the court. We shouldn't even be listing it out there yet, I guess. I don't know how that happened." Then his voice sounded muffled. He'd covered the phone with his hand to speak to someone else.

"Maybe you can just tell me who holds title in the property now?" That, at least, was public information, available to anyone who walked into a land registry.

"Why do you want that?" he said.

Well, *this* isn't going to work, she thought.

Steve Barker remained silent on the other end. She could hear a dozen phones ringing behind him.

"I know you're busy. Thanks for taking the time, Mr. Barker."

"No problem, Anne. I've got a lot of listings in the Belford area, right now—you know, that whole 'dot com' thing . . ."

Maybe in another lifetime, she thought. And only if I start saving in *this* one, right now.

So it was a trust. Tax lawyers and accountants had a regular field day with projects like that—sheltered income, depreciation allowances, corporate and family trusts. Probably nothing that could be identified as "personal" in the end. Almost certainly the Mallicks' assets were tied up in complex structures that would take years to unwind.

Annie swung her chair around and faced her computer. She was fairly comfortable, if not actually adept, in using it for her own minimal requirements: letters, reports, e-mails, spreadsheets, press materials—regular stuff—on a daily basis.

This is just another form of research, she reassured herself.

Annie went into city records. Who really owned the property?

Access denied.

Motor vehicles registrations?

Access denied.

Credit bureau?

Access denied. Denied. Denied.

She opened her door and called out, "Tina."

After a moment Tina arrived in the doorway. "Yeah?"

Annie realized she'd have to trust her. She indicated the computer screen. "I'm trying to do a little looking on my own . . . about something." She hated to admit it—she really didn't know where to start any more.

Tina was diplomatic. "And you don't mean just your regular, everyday stuff?"

"No. The research databases. Which ones are we using now?" This was ridiculous. Here she was, a twenty-year veteran, having to relearn the basics of investigation, from someone less than half her age.

Tina ran quickly through an extended list of acronyms.

Annie carefully wrote them all down. Maybe you should have been paying more attention for the last ten years, she chided herself. She turned back to the computer, clicked over and logged on. Aside from regular e-mail, she rarely bothered with the Internet. Mostly it seemed an impressive waste of time, hours spent finding some esoteric fact you could look up in an encyclopedia in thirty seconds. And she wasn't involved in casework any more, so there was little incentive. She stopped herself. She knew she was just trying to come up with every excuse in the book.

She quickly entered one of the names on the list. The search engine indicated there were thirty-two possibilities. Annie stared at the screen, forgetting for a moment that Tina was still standing there, watching her.

Suddenly, Annie felt herself being pushed aside. "Jeez, just let me do it," Tina said from behind her, nudging her out of the chair and sliding into her place. "You really *haven't* done this for a while, have you? There are some shortcuts, you know . . . nowadays." With just a few strokes she was already inside one of the larger databases. "There you go. OK, what do you need?"

Annie hesitated. "Um . . . Well, I was looking for something on a doctor."

Tina raised a pierced eyebrow high, immediately guessing which. "Ohhh, I see. That one. OK, what?"

Annie stared at the screen for a moment, then raised her hands in a gesture of helplessness. "I just want a general picture . . ." There were too many possibilities.

Tina looked at her doubtfully. "You know, the guys downstairs can do this stuff in their sleep. Why don't you just get one of them up here to help you?"

As unconventional as she looked, Tina was better at this kind of thing than any of the IT guys the city kept sending them. Annie decided on some version of the truth. "I can't push this into more overtime. Unless I want to go back to DeVries, I've kind of got to do it on my own."

Tina thought about it for a moment. "Oka-a-ay. Let me try something else." Then she turned back and starting entering keystrokes rapidly again. "They want to know who I am." she said to Annie.

"Who?"

"Premcom. It's an open site for the most recent medical research. Abstracts, that kind of thing. At least we can see if she's in the literature."

Annie hesitated for moment. "Tell them you're from a university. Would that work?"

"Sure. They're just tracking user demographics. Which one?"

Annie glared impatiently.

Tina typed in *Princeton. Masters Program.* User name *Kilts.* Then, beside Search—*Leah Mallick Psychiatrist.*

It took a few seconds. There were two matches. According to the abstracts, only two short articles published in the last three years. "Do you want me to print them out?" Tina asked.

Annie nodded. "Please." Then, "What about the secured sites?" This thing could take her all the way up to Interpol now, apparently.

"Doing your little Jessica Fletcher thing, eh?" She winked at Annie. "You already have clearance for most of them, Lieutenant. You just never asked to use it before."

Annie gritted her teeth. "All right, how do I get in?"

"Just type in your name and badge number. It'll ask you to create a password. But do me a favour, please, and make up something you can't forget. I won't be able to help you if you do. Even the system operator can't get you back in without it. Just follow the menu. It's already coded for entry on our network."

Annie took back her chair and flapped her hand in Tina's direction. "Go away now."

Tina smiled slyly. "Think you're ready to explore the dark side on your own, young Skywalker?"

"I'm a cop. I do this for a living. Get out." There just hasn't been a good reason to do it for a very long time, she admitted to herself. *What do they expect, anyway? I'm just a dumb TV star. Or maybe just the stupidest person on the face of the planet.*

"You still know how to get into all the regular sites, right?" Tina was enjoying this a little too much.

"Ye-e-s-s, I do it every day," Annie glared ferociously again. "And, hey . . . just between us. Right?"

Tina grinned back at her. "No prob."

As a kind of warm-up she decided to hit her regular news sites first. Local papers and TV stations offered small, fairly unsophisticated operations. The few that mentioned the Mallicks included them in lists of attendees at charity and arts events. There was one photograph, so low in resolution that it hid Leah Mallick in a blur of other faces; only the caption identified her. But there was nothing recent, not even the mention of the name, in the last six months.

Annie finally moved over to the major dailies in southern California, then Santa Barbara—and there began to find the Mallicks again . . .

Most of what turned up was only what she'd expected to find: a few of the articles that Bill had included in his package, some of the same pictures April Vaughan had used.

As a couple, Tim and Leah Mallick had shone brightly. Even knowing how it ended, Annie understood how others could so easily romanticize them. It was almost impossible not to. Here they were, front and centre. In photos taken at dozens of parties, in attractively arranged gatherings at golf and tennis clubs. Thoroughly modern, they seemed to evoke, as well, the qualities of another period—the ambience of icy martinis in silver shakers, MG Roadsters, summers on sandy islands. Sparkling, sly wit. A time out of time.

Annie expanded her search, eventually finding two personal interviews. One was in a small lifestyle publication, an article telling how Leah Mallick, a busy doctor, seemed able to balance the professional demands of her practice with her family life, her high-powered marriage to an equally successful, driven man.

The other was a feature story in an alternative weekly from the Bay area. The writer's theme was evident within the first two lines: national health care and all the conspiratorial forces ranged against it. But Dr. Mallick thoughtfully, patiently, described the particular challenges facing public systems, and the efforts necessary to reframe the questions. She explained how all the issues went well beyond just the contemporary practice of medicine. Were people aware, for example, that more than twelve percent of the country's GDP was already going directly to health care? More than anywhere in the world. Where was the balance? That was the dilemma posed to every concerned medical practitioner, she said, on a daily basis.

Annie studied the photograph that ran alongside the piece. It showed Leah in a simple denim work shirt, jeans, expensive sunglasses casually pushed up into her blonde hair. It had caught her in a lighter moment, her head thrown back in an easy laugh.

Annie began another search. What was that old exhortation—"publish or perish?" Yet Leah Mallick had collaborated on a total of only five minor papers, including the two already found. This, in a high-profile medical career that had spanned almost fifteen years. Surely below an acceptable minimum, if she really expected to advance.

Annie stopped herself. That was an assumption she couldn't make. To advance to *what?* Maybe Leah herself had wanted nothing other than to sparkle in all those photographs, to summer on islands. Perhaps it was only everyone else who saw her as something more.

Annie logged on to the state medical association and entered the name again: *Leah Mallick, MD + Psychiatry.* There had to be—The cursor blinked. It required additional information to access the next level.

Annie brought up the dialogue box to create the password as Tina had shown her. Random but memorable. Here was the real key to the kingdom, she knew. People inevitably chose words and numbers that meant something to them, usually in a fairly obvious pattern. It was hard to create something truly random. And when you knew enough about someone's life, it was often a simple process of elimination to discover their passwords. She thought for a moment, then entered a series of numbers and, at the prompt, re-entered the same sequence.

She tried her new password. Nothing happened.

Authorization required. This server does not recognize . . .

Access denied.

∿∿∿

Annie sat in her living room alone, reading. The cardboard remains of a hurried late supper lay abandoned on the floor. Unfortunately, "pizza" wasn't only a euphemism any more. She could feel her backside spreading out in whole new directions on the couch.

The television news was on, as usual. And everything she'd assembled on the Mallick case was arranged in a careful semi-circle around her again. For the last hour she'd been forced to work with Ben stretched, sleeping, across her lap.

She'd hauled out absolutely everything this time. Even with the perspective of a couple of days, it hadn't changed. It was still a typical inventory: computer records, copies of bank statements and Daytimers, phone logs, a catalogue of letters, notes from more than twenty personal interviews, a transcript of the incoming messages on the Mallicks' answering machine.

She recalled only one interesting item among it all, and found that again: a notebook, filled with parts of poems written in Tim Mallick's own hand. It wasn't immediately clear whether they were original. Many of them didn't qualify as poems anyway—just sentences, linked with arrows, words underlined. Some even decorated with bright colours. Mostly red.

And we,
And you,
And I. My tender fingers clutching your heart,
Joined hands, we two earthly ministers
Fly above the heavens
Beyond the jealous gods.

Only one unusual pattern emerged from all of it, she realized. Nothing here went back more than two years. Nothing found in the house preceded the actual date of the Mallicks' move to Lockport. It was like some cliché straight out of a witness protection program.

And by now all too organized for her taste, every piece of

it overly familiar. It meant that her presumptions were being locked in and she could no longer entirely trust her own objectivity. From time to time Ben shifted uneasily. Her irritation, apparently, was creeping into his dreams too.

Without thinking, she picked up the phone and dialed Bill Williamson. Unexpectedly, a woman's sleepy voice answered on the other end.

A quick glance at the clock. Shit—after midnight. Maybe she could just hang up. "I'm sorry to disturb you. I was looking for Bill Williamson . . . ?" The woman said nothing, but a moment later Bill himself came on.

"Williamson." He was using his cop voice—the one that said *No. You didn't wake me, asshole. What the fuck do you want?* When she said nothing, Bill repeated "Williamson" again.

"Bill, it's Annie."

She heard him relax immediately. "Sure, Annie. What can I do for you?"

"I'm sorry to wake you, but—"

"No. It's OK. What's happening?"

She hesitated now. How could she tell him that she'd gone through everything again, for what must have been the tenth time. But there was nothing in what she read or looked at. Nothing except an uncertain dissatisfaction.

"It's this Mallick stuff." Annie heard what sounded like a sigh in response. "With everything that's here, you'd think we would have found something. At least a suggestion of—"

"—of why she did it?" Bill completed her thought. Since they'd known each other, they had always been able to do that. "I don't know either, babe."

Babe. He must still be half asleep. Annie smiled, wondering how *that* would go down with the other woman, the one presumably lying beside him in bed. And why did every man in her life call her babe anyway?

He chuckled then. "You're thinking the doctor should have had the courtesy to leave us a letter, at least?"

Annie wavered for a moment. "But she planned everything *else* to the nth degree. Why would she deliberately leave a loose end like this?" If Leah Mallick had been fully prepared to indict her husband, why not at least provide a plausible motive for *his* crime?

In everything she undertook, Leah exceeded the standard definition of "intelligent." Everyone she'd ever met said she was absolutely brilliant. They spoke of the potent combination—the dazzling looks, the striking presence, a sophisticated and discerning sensibility. A blend like that could be expected to engender a certain amount of envy among acquaintances. And there was some of that, of course. But most of those who really knew her—or claimed they had—struggled to find new words adequate to describe how very impressive she really was. Her unusual empathy, her capacity for an almost instantaneous emotional connection—people weren't used to finding those qualities in any woman who looked like Leah Mallick. It was what made her most surprising.

Yet no one denied that she knew her own value. There was no indication that she had suffered from any kind of false modesty. So maybe she'd really been nothing more than an unrepentant egomaniac—one of truly epic proportions, Annie thought. Someone like that *might* have found a rationale for martyrdom. Paul DeVries had suggested as much: " . . . worried she's losing her looks, or her husband . . ." The loss, for her, would have been so much worse than for the rest of us mere mortals, thought Annie.

Bill was starting to mumble, drifting back into sleep. Annie saw him, lying on his side, the phone cradled to his ear. "You'd need a psychiatrist to tell you that." He adopted a pedantic tone. "A personality disorder with paranoid, narcissistic, passive-aggressive, histrionic and borderline features, unable to distinguish her needs from her husband's or—"

He was in the middle of his sentence when the line abruptly went dead.

Annie could picture the unknown other woman in his bed, fed up, finally reaching over and disconnecting them. Bill had never mentioned to her that he was even involved with someone.

Annie lay back against the couch again. "Her son's?" That's what he'd been about to say: "Unable to distinguish her own needs from her husband's—or her son's."

Maybe they were all still looking in the wrong direction.

Then Annie glanced idly up at the television, just in time to see Callie Christie being interviewed on CNN. Callie was reporting that Kyle Mallick had just been removed from life support.

~~~

Annie exited the elevator on the fifth floor. The sign read: *Devan Palliative Care Unit.* The nursing station was
~~~

halfway down the hall, and the several staff working tonight were far too busy to pay her much attention. There were knots of worried-looking doctors and medical technicians everywhere. Annie put her head down and walked quickly in the direction of Kyle Mallick's room.

"Just a minute." It was a loud voice right behind her. Almost a shout, and completely unnecessary at barely twenty feet.

Annie turned to see someone vaguely familiar separating herself from one of the groups.

"You're going to need a warrant, Lieutenant Shannon," the woman said.

A warrant for what? "I'm not here officially," Annie answered quietly. It was easier. "I'm sorry. You're . . . ?"

The woman raised one eyebrow high. She managed to look both insulted and dangerously on edge. "Yes, well . . . we have met before. Several times, in fact. I'm Laurelle Stepton, chief administrator of this hospital. I understand you think you should be able to walk through here any time you like. Well, unless you have some official reason to be here, our visiting hours are over."

Annie remembered her now. Laurelle Stepton had just received the "Executive of the Year" award from the Lockport Renaissance Committee. To Annie it had been just another long dinner.

They were both startled when a new voice intruded on them from the side. "But if you *don't* let her in, Laurelle, someone might have to start asking the really tough questions."

Annie's stomach clutched automatically. She saw Callie

Christie, standing in the doorway of the waiting area just a few steps down the hall. Not the ally she might have wished for right now.

Callie approached. "You *could* call security, Laurelle, but don't you think it might look bad—throwing a homicide detective out just after you've pulled the plug on an eight-year-old kid? Doing it in the dark of night. . . ? People might think that you were trying to pull a fast one. I'd be reporting it anyway." Callie's tone was pleasant and professional, and though what she was saying was patently ridiculous, she'd certainly delivered it with impressive style, Annie thought.

Stepton stared back at Callie in shock. "Homicide! She's not even a real policewoman." The administrator snorted. "You must be joking. We followed every hospital procedure to the letter." It was anger showing now.

Callie didn't blink. "Then I suppose some people might start thinking there's something wrong with your procedures."

"*That's* what you're going with on this thing? My God, you types really do stick together when it suits you, don't you?" After a moment, and only reluctantly, she stepped aside, glaring at Annie. "I don't know what you expect to find here, Lieutenant. Maybe higher profile. But it's your last time, I can guarantee you that."

Callie edged past her. "Yeah, well, thanks, Laurelle. And don't forget that hospital auxiliary silent auction on Tuesday. Maybe we can all carpool together." Callie had already stuck her arm through Annie's and was pulling her towards Kyle Mallick's room at the far end of the hall.

Callie snickered under her breath as they walked away. "They're way more afraid of me than you now."

Annie looked at her. So am I, she thought.

The old Callie had already disappeared inside a larger persona. Annie had needed almost half an hour to get a call to her, routed through three assistants. "Ms. Christie's on the air . . . Could I help you?" And when she'd finally taken the call, Callie herself sounded like a hyperactive five-year-old. It was her second national exclusive in five days. In another month she'd probably be guest-hosting *Saturday Night Live.*

Together they entered the darkened room. It was empty of anyone but the boy, still, on the bed. Only one low light, shining straight down on him.

Callie's news reports hadn't told her what to expect, only that after a week they'd discontinued life-support.

Callie looked around quickly. Annie knew that she was filing all the details somewhere for later use herself. A description of the pipes suspended just under the cracked ceiling, the tapping of the old radiator, the two tall windows—black mirrors on this late night—reaching up practically into the shadows. The array of shiny machinery still organized around the bed. Annie stood to one side while Callie circled the room for a moment. How would anyone really colour this in the end? She knew that Callie was watching her too, just out of the corner of her eye, hoping as always for some kind of unguarded reaction.

But now that she was really here, she was at a complete loss. What was appropriate? What was she meant to do or to feel? She observed it all. A chart, several monitors attached to various machines. Most surprising, the overriding sense of serenity.

Without a ventilator pumping air in and out, the silence was nearly complete.

Quiet now, but for the soft sound of Kyle Mallick's own slow breath—his little boy's chest rising and falling with the effort to continue living. Some base impulse had replaced technology, and he continued in spite of them all and what they'd tried to do.

Annie finally looked down at the sleeping boy. She was close enough to reach out and touch him. She saw that he was pale, with an almost translucent quality to his skin. Somewhat longish, straight dark-blonde hair, darker eyebrows. Lashes long and thick, casting shadows on his cheeks in the flat light. His small fingers were curled slightly in towards the palm of each hand, both arms laid straight at his sides, on top of the sheet. She knew it wasn't appropriate to picture him awakening, to imagine his eyes opening to look into hers. Blue eyes, so much like her own. Knew not to, but couldn't stop herself. It was too easy. And too late.

The crowd of medical personnel out in the hallway was making enough noise now to tell her that yet another argument was breaking out. Obviously, no one had expected this particular turn of events. Things had gone very wrong. There'd been a miracle, and no one wanted to be held responsible for it.

Who was Kyle Mallick now? The figure who lay here, still and white and obviously more dead than alive, evoked little. He looked like a parody of an eight-year-old boy.

She'd expected to recognize something more of him, struggled to remember what that might have been by reminding herself of the family photograph she'd seen displayed on the antique side table in the blood-painted master bedroom.

A reluctant child—that was what Annie could recall now. Kyle had been pushing himself away from the camera at the moment the shutter opened—back tight against his mother, her cheek settling on his blond head. Leah's hand holding his high, lightly, in her own. Was that an attempt to keep him still? to reassure him? to protect him? Tim Mallick positioned slightly behind her. They hadn't been touching, Annie remembered. And Leah in the centre, looking, above all, like she belonged there—in that moment, at that time. Careless and vivid simultaneously, suffused with sunlight, her extraordinary blue eyes sparkling.

But that photograph, whatever it might seem to suggest now, *that* was the big lie. For in it they were all completely alive and happy.

Callie spoke suddenly. "Did you know that Riverview has already instituted a claim against the Mallick estate?" Her voice sounded coarse and unnatural in this setting—a trick of the acoustics, perhaps.

Annie looked up at her in a daze. "What—?"

"I mean, how likely is it that a couple like that wouldn't have a valid will? No one named as guardian?"

"You know that for a fact?"

"Nothing's been filed. Nothing here, nothing even in California. They died intestate, apparently. The hospital just wants to get its foot in the door, I guess."

"What about provision for—" Annie glanced down again at Kyle, lying between them.

Callie looked impassively at the child, then raised her eyes to Annie's. "He isn't supposed to be here," she said quietly. Callie spent another minute or so studying the room before indicating that she'd be outside, finally leaving Annie alone with him.

Callie was right: Kyle wasn't meant to survive. Then what could explain the wide-open window in the boy's bedroom? When all was said and done, it was the one image that had never really left her mind. The rain coming in. The fresh movement of air, fragrant with grass and trees and sweet spring. The telescope . . .

And it always led her to a simple question she would have asked Leah: why the silent gas? Why not simply two more bullets?

There was a nurse in the room now. She'd come in so quietly that Annie hadn't heard her enter. This time it was someone she didn't know, someone who didn't appear to know her either. Someone new, who actually bothered to apologize for interrupting her visit. A young woman, there only to change the bed. And she did so, expertly, laying the folded sheet in such a way that it could be opened and spread under the length of the boy's body with the slightest movement.

"Usually, we have to have two of us for this. But this little fella is easy enough for me by myself," she said cheerfully. Once, twice, she rolled him from one side to the other, without a wasted gesture. A silent procedure, aside from her own "ums" and chirps of "there we go" or "good,

good." As she was about to pull the fresh top sheet close up under his chin, there was a jerking motion in one of his arms and his hand fell off the edge of the bed towards Annie. The nurse paused in what she was doing.

Annie stared fixedly as the hand floated away from the body, the one alive thing. If she were to touch it—smooth and cold, the small fingers curled stiffly against the palm . . . She was, she realized, actually repulsed by the thought, something in her refusing to reach out now.

The nurse made a soft clucking noise, then came around the other side to lift the arm gently back into place, tucking it under the sheet and out of sight. "That happens sometimes—a kind of muscle spasm, sort of an involuntary reaction. They say it doesn't hurt. Another little miracle."

What the hell am I doing here, anyway? Annie asked herself. This has nothing to do with me. In the next moment she found herself back out in the hallway, pushing herself hard against the wall, trying to calm her frantic breathing. A nurse leaned out beyond the counter to look, then disappeared again. Annie could hear them talking, followed by a burst of far-off laughter.

Callie Christie was still there. "You look like you're ready to pass out."

Annie waved her off impatiently and turned to leave. Just go, she told herself. It was a mistake to have come at all.

Callie caught up with her at the other end of the hall. Then they stood together, waiting for the elevator.

It was Annie who spoke first. "Can you not say anything about this for a while? I mean about me—my being here?" She sounded almost hostile, she knew. It was dangerous to ask for any favours right now. Callie was completely full of herself, puffed up and probably prepping another nationally syndicated feature. Maybe something more—a book deal, a movie of the week. Public interest in the Mallicks had simply entered the next phase. As she'd predicted.

Surprisingly, Callie didn't respond to her immediately. "You know, even you might be shocked at some of the secrets I do manage to keep," she said at last. Her expression was carefully veiled for the first time.

The elevator arrived. As they rode down together, Callie leaned back, appraising Annie openly now. "Why do you—of *all* people—have such a hard time with the media being interested in this?"

The media? That modern confection of incident intertwined with conjecture. Committed to nothing more than the idea that any truth was simple enough to be understood in a single, iconic image. It had become ludicrous. And Annie knew she'd made herself a part of it.

"I don't. I'm not in any position to," Annie said abruptly. The hospital was making mistakes. That much should be obvious to anyone.

Callie shrugged, saying nothing. Only continued watching her.

Annie closed her eyes for a moment, resting wearily against the wall. "I think that maybe what you really want, Callie—it just ends up making people betray some better part of themselves. It's like a game show to all of you. Winners and losers. Who's up, who's down. It's becoming a daily competition for best atrocity." She knew she should shut up, knew she was too tired to have this particular conversation right now, to even care whom she might insult any more.

"You would deny the power of the press, Lieutenant Shannon?" Callie smiled briefly, though her voice had gone colder.

Annie shook her head. She was all too aware of what it had taken to get in the door this time. "No, Callie. I can only acknowledge it."

6

Annie had arranged the meeting for the very end of the school day, a quiet opportunity to stockpile a little information of her own.

Kyle Mallick's fourth-grade teacher, a Mrs. Kiehl, was initially reluctant. Maybe the police should be seeking permission from someone "higher up" first. . . ?

It's really nothing, Annie told her—nothing more than an informal chat.

Still, the teacher hesitated.

"Maybe you've seen me on TV," Annie added, as casually as possible. She couldn't believe she was resorting to it. "I host those little Crime Stoppers segments?"

"You're *that* Anne Shannon? The one on the news all the time?"

Annie felt herself blushing slightly. "Uh-huh . . . anyway, would it be possible, say, six o'clock? I realize it's late, but . . ." She waited.

A short pause. Then, "No, that would be fine, Lieutenant Shannon. I'll look forward to it."

And for my next trick, Annie thought, I'll start demanding a better table in restaurants.

On the stroke of six she was sitting in a school classroom, facing Mrs. Kiehl. At least it wasn't one of the tiny chairs arranged throughout the room; the teacher had looked around and found a "big girl" one for her.

Mrs. Kiehl seemed uneasy. She'd never been interviewed by the police before, she admitted with a nervous laugh.

This wasn't an official visit, Annie repeated again. It was completely off the record. A little background information. Just for the file.

But it was the teacher who asked the first question. What was really going on with Kyle Mallick? "The hospital reports tell us one thing, but . . ." She appeared disappointed that Annie could offer no new "insider-type information." And within moments she'd tearfully described her own reaction to the tragedy. The most difficult thing, she said, was knowing that the children were suffering from "a lack of closure." "With little Kyle in a coma, I confess I'm in a real pickle as to how much to tell them."

A pickle. That was one way to describe it all, Annie thought. But Mrs. Kiehl had raised an unnerving possibility. "Do you mean to say that the children haven't been told what's happened yet?" Every one of them could turn on a TV—what was she waiting for?

The teacher blew her nose again. "Oh, I'm sure some of their parents have mentioned it to them, but I felt it was inappropriate to take it up as a classroom discussion. They seem to have accepted that Kyle's parents have gone away—though there was even trouble with that in the beginning, I can tell you. It tends to trigger unresolved abandonment issues. But I certainly can't, in all honesty, tell them that Kyle is *with* his mommy and daddy. You understand. So, of course, they can't mourn properly. After all, he's not—" She looked at Annie. "And how do you explain to a room of eight-year-olds what some parents are capable of doing to their own children?"

Annie shook her head. She had no suggestions, except that maybe it was impossible. She gently steered the conversation back towards Kyle.

Mrs. Kiehl proceeded to describe him in glowing terms—inventive, creative, sensitive. Despite the fact, she added, that he was often away from school. It made him "present" as a bit delicate, almost fragile, she said.

"What do you think was the reason?" Annie asked. "All these absences?"

"I really don't know. His mother went out of her way to make it clear there was nothing actually *wrong* with him—in any way, you know, where we'd have to be concerned about his having contact with the other children. And he kept up with the work . . ." She looked at Annie and smiled reassuringly.

"But when he was there, did you find him in any way . . . troublesome . . . in class?"

"No, not at all. He was very bright. Not a surprise, of course, given his parents. A little bit of a loner, I'd have to say. But never what I'd call disruptive."

"Then you met with them—the Mallicks?"

The teacher became appropriately sombre. "Never with *him*. Never Mr. Mallick." She appeared puzzled for a moment, as though that hadn't occurred to her before. "No, it was she, Dr. Mallick, who'd come every time we scheduled a parent-teacher conference. She always made a point of attending them. Though she didn't choose to participate in regular school activities that I can remember. Most of the mothers try to pitch in a bit. I'm just speculating, mind you—but it seemed she couldn't find much in the way of spare time for us. A very busy woman."

Annie heard the faint thrum of resentment towards Leah Mallick. Mrs. Kiehl seemed to want to focus on the doctor. "Was there any suggestion of family troubles?" Broad enough to open the discussion up to a wider spectrum, she hoped.

Mrs. Kiehl was thoughtful for a moment. "It's rather like that Tolstoy quote," she said finally. "You know—'Happy families are all alike; every unhappy family is unhappy in its own way.'" She smiled at Annie. "*War and Peace.*"

Well, actually, no, it wasn't, Annie thought, it was *Anna Karenina.* Nonetheless . . .

Mrs. Kiehl continued. "Dr. Mallick never implied anything of the sort, of course. But women like that can sometimes create their own worst problems. She tended to interfere quite a bit whenever I had a discipline issue with Kyle, for example."

Discipline? She'd just described the child as a quiet loner—though maybe that wasn't the best impression to leave either. At least she'd clearly said that Kyle wasn't "disruptive."

"Actually, I found him to be quite . . . manipulative," Mrs. Kiehl said now, in an intense whisper, leaning towards Annie.

Annie offered no response. That didn't make him any different from every frustrated eight-year-old. It's how they got what they wanted. Or what they needed.

Mrs. Kiehl noticed Annie's subtle recoil. She looked at her now with a cool, more appraising smile. "Make no mistake, Ms. Shannon. Children can be extraordinarily manipulative, even at that age—I like to say *especially* at that age. As I'm sure you know. You have children of your own. . . ?"

Annie shook her head. "Was Dr. Mallick receptive when you brought up your concerns?"

"She certainly *appeared* to be—at first. Each time I spoke to her, she seemed completely approachable. We even spent some quiet time together, discussing personal things—talking about our favourite books and such. Dr. Mallick was extremely well read, you know. And my own graduate degree is in English literature, of course.

"But then I found out that she was making secret arrangements to have Kyle transferred to a private school. Apparently, he wasn't being given the appropriate opportunity to *develop* fully here." Her face took on a slightly pinched look. Obviously, Mrs. Kiehl had taken the judgment personally. Secret arrangements and all.

"And I can certainly see now that she was trying to control the situation, in effect. Quite obvious about it, really. In retrospect. She *was* a psychiatrist, after all. But I think it was more that she was the kind of woman who expects that her charm and looks will get her exactly what she wants. It doesn't always." Mrs. Kiehl tried to hide the bitter edge in her voice. Then she looked down at a pencil she was rolling between her fingers, lost in thought for a moment. "In fact, Kyle was a lot like her," she added quietly.

"Would you actually describe *him* as charming?" Annie said.

The teacher looked surprised for a moment. "Well, not in that same way, of course. She was very sophisticated. Worldly. Very polished. Kyle was a more fragmented, excitable personality type. Expressive. We see it a lot in boys of that age and temperament—certain borderline cases. Then the Ritalin comes out. But when he really wanted something, he had that same look of intense concentration. Even I found it a little disconcerting at times. When he chose to, he could always convince the other children to go along with just about anything he wanted. Some of them seemed to absolutely crave his attention." Suddenly the class angel had become the devil.

Annie wondered how much of this was really just about the boy any more.

The teacher was silent again. When she looked up, her eyes were harder. "I found him to be quite insolent, actually. And obstreperous." Mrs. Kiehl said nothing further. It was quite enough.

Maybe there was someone else here in need of closure, Annie thought. Or a nap.

~~~

Leah Mallick had entered the schoolroom quietly. It was late afternoon, getting dark already. Sharon Kiehl was busy putting chairs back into their nice straight, regular rows. She didn't hear the knock at first, a soft rap on the door frame.
~~~

When she did look up finally, she saw a quite extraordinary woman standing there, watching her. White-blonde, medium-length hair. Startling blue eyes. Slim. What seemed a light gold tan, though it was winter. A camel-hair polo coat, loosely draped over her shoulders.

"Hi. I'm sorry to disturb you. Mrs. Kiehl? I'm Leah Mallick—Kyle's mother."

The teacher closed her mouth, then said, "Oh. Mrs. Mallick. I didn't hear you." She shook her head. "Sorry. How do you do. It's so nice to meet you, at last. We've been hearing a lot about you."

Leah smiled. "I just wanted to stop in. By myself, I mean. After all the kids . . . after Kyle left." Her accompanying gesture was offhand, even a little nervous. In a woman who looked like that? Mrs. Kiehl thought.

Then Leah laughed, apparently amused at her own slight awkwardness. "I have to be honest—I didn't want him to see me here. I always think it's better if he takes the bus with the other kids anyway. You know. They always get a little embarrassed at this age when they see their mothers hanging around." She widened her eyes slightly.

Mrs. Kiehl found herself smiling in return. She watched as Leah moved around the classroom, studying with interest all the artwork displayed on the walls. In the next moment Mrs. Kiehl had invited her to sit down. "I suppose we could talk about Kyle a bit—while you're here," she suggested.

"Oh, I don't want to hold you up. I know it's late. I just wanted to come and say hello, at last. And to thank you, so much, for doing everything to make Kyle feel comfortable here. It's hard to switch in the middle of a school year. Both his father and I are fairly busy. I know you've made a special effort for him."

The words she was saying were polite, even friendly. But it was her voice that Sharon Kiehl noticed now: warm, rich, a certain casual intimacy. If there'd really been any suggestion of awkwardness, it was long gone. Leah Mallick sat down opposite her now, comfortable and easy in the standard-issue office chair she'd been offered, making it look almost luxurious. Chic, Mrs. Kiehl had to admit. She'd never met anyone to whom that word actually applied before.

"Well, what can I say?" she began. "Kyle's a wonderful boy, of course. Bright. Very well mannered. Considerate. Generous with the other children, I've noticed. He seems to make a real effort to always include the shy, less socially developed ones. They chatter away to him quite easily. And they usually don't want to interact with *anyone,* especially the more aggressive boys. Kyle—I don't know, he seems able to reach out to them in a way that's—well, that's unusual. Certainly gratifying for a teacher to see something like that *these* days."

Leah Mallick listened attentively.

By the time she'd gone through most of the details of Kyle's first few months in her class, Mrs. Kiehl was surprised to notice that it was pitch-black outside. The glass reflected only the two of them, still talking.

She'd already moved well past her pet theories about teaching and was discussing her own plans to return to college for a doctorate. Maybe it didn't make sense, really, for a primary school teacher in this employment market. But she had other ambitions, she confessed.

At that, Leah Mallick drew something out of her pocket and presented it to her. "Then perhaps this'll inspire you."

For a moment Sharon Kiehl didn't understand what she was looking at. Then she did. It was a pristine, signed first edition of F. Scott Fitzgerald's *Tender is the Night.*

"It's just a little thank you. For everything you've done. I would have sent it over earlier, but I wanted to come and meet you myself."

Mrs. Kiehl was dumbfounded. It was probably worth hundreds. She stared at the book in her hands. "This is extraordinary . . . my thesis is on . . . But I can't accept this."

Leah Mallick was already standing above her, her hand extended. "Please do. I very much want you to. And I hope we can talk again soon."

In many moments of idle reflection over the next few months, the teacher found herself going back to that meeting, wondering what it was about Leah that made her intriguing. It was a distraction she came to appreciate. Though after a while she came to the uncomfortable realization that she was paying far too much attention to Kyle Mallick in class, helping him with what he should be handling on his own. And in time she had to admit that she might even be shortchanging the other children and backed away. Just a little.

But when she *did* draw back, well, that was when she—Leah—started making all those noises about sending her son to some fancy private school. Supposedly it was because "the standard of teaching was higher." Bitch.

~~~

Holly's Bar & Grill was a semi-regular hangout for most of the cops in the division. It had tried to revamp itself as an upscale bistro, but ended up offering only the same old deep-fried pub fare. Smoky, smelly, but convenient. Annie arrived shortly after six. Coming out of the bright sunlight, she had trouble spotting Bill for the first few moments. Then she saw a large table at the back, and around it, seven or eight other cops.

Bill automatically pulled out the chair next to him as she approached. She ignored him and took the empty seat beside John Bartlett instead.

Susan Shaw was seated directly opposite, apparently too deep in conversation with Marty Watson even to acknowledge her arrival. But when the next round of drinks came, she looked over at Annie and nodded slightly.

Annie snarled under her breath, "What is *she* doing here?"

Bartlett grinned back at her, cocking one eyebrow. "R-r-r-r-r-r."

"Oh, Christ," she said, "don't give me that. I just wanted to know why. This doesn't really seem like her kind of place, does it?"

Bartlett leered across the table at Susan. "I don't know—I think she could fit in pretty well anywhere she wanted to."

Annie turned away impatiently and ordered herself a club soda.

The table was already full of platters: pizza, potato skins, buffalo wings, mozzarella sticks—every arterial threat on the menu. Large pitchers of beer. The kitchen couldn't do
~~~

too much damage to any of it. After a while even Annie began to relax. It felt almost like old times. A group of cops just shooting the breeze for an evening, taking apart the same cases, burying themselves in the same esoteric details, laughing at the same things. They ate, and talked about everything in between.

Everyone shifted and regrouped around a dozen different conversations. Annie noticed that Susan had already switched her seat a couple of times, giving her ample opportunity to extend her long legs languorously. It looked like she'd subtly turned everything else up a notch, too, and a few cops were already beginning to jostle each other for position. She certainly had their attention anyway. And now she was listening, nodding at something John Bartlett had just said. Bartlett, Annie saw, was getting ready to make a move of his own. His hand carelessly brushed Susan's arm a couple of times. She seemed to be considering his suggestion. A few more words—then she shook her head, still smiling, and straightened away from him. Poor John, shot down again—

Bill slid into the empty chair beside Annie. "I thought you might wanna know that she showed up. What are we supposed to be telling her *this* week?" He said it half seriously.

Annie glanced over at Susan Shaw and shrugged. "I don't know. This is her idea. Just answer her questions."

"You reckon *we* can handle that?" Bill laughed. Then he cleared his throat and leaned towards her, more serious. "Listen, Annie, about the other night—"

"How did she *get* here, anyway?" she asked.

Bill looked at her, then hung his head for a moment with a resigned sigh and a half-smile on his face. "She just dropped in. I don't even know she's there, then I hear someone giving out one of these real old-fashioned wolf whistles, eh? I look up, and she's standing right in front of me."

"Every good boy's dream," Annie drawled. She could just picture the unfortunate whistler laid out with one icy glare. Susan Shaw was a walking mixed message, resentment wrapped inside a tight skirt.

"Yeah, well, anyway, she said she just wanted to talk with a few of us. She offered to buy dinner. So I thought, what the hell, eh? Turns out she just wanted us to go through a couple of things in the report with her. Basic stuff. How could we be so sure she'd been the one to fire it? I guess everyone has trouble with that one—"

"Why?" Annie said sharply. "Are you saying there's any doubt?"

"Whoa, nelly—not from *us*. That's for sure." Bill grinned at her genially. "Aren't we all just trying to get out of the way here? Drop it in front of DeVries's door and run? It's not our fight." For twenty years he'd been telling her the same thing: "choose your battles."

Another hour passed as they ordered a round of drinks. Then someone noticed it was after nine. One by one each rose to say goodnight until only the three of them were left.

Finally, Bill yawned and stretched too. He was ready to leave. Neither Annie nor Susan moved. He waited a few seconds. "So . . . uh . . . can I walk you to your cars?" he said at last.

It was Susan who spoke first. "Thanks, Bill. I think I'll just sit here and nurse this one for a while."

Annie didn't look up at him, just shook her head.

Bill glanced uncertainly from one to the other. Then he shrugged. "Well, then . . . *Susan,* thank you for dinner." He lightly massaged Annie's shoulders as he passed behind her chair. "And *you,* Lieutenant—I guess we'll see you tomorrow." He seemed unsure about leaving them alone together. Neither spoke. "Well, OK, then. Good night."

After he left, they remained unmoving, each studying the drink in front of her. The silence stretched to an uncomfortable length.

"I take it you're good friends?" Susan said at last.

"Bill, you mean? Yeah. We started out together twenty years ago, in training. Then we became partners, out on the street. Eventually, lead team in homicide."

Susan raised one eyebrow. She found it hard to picture Anne Shannon piloting a patrol car through Lockport's downtown streets, let alone attending murder scenes.

"And how about you—have you always been in accounting?" Annie barely stifled a yawn.

"My undergrad degree's in architectural history."

"Really?" How do you get here from there? Annie wondered. Like choosing to be bored in advance. "So, what kind of accountant are you? Chartered? Management?" This was painful.

"Forensic."

"So you do tax returns for—"

"Yeah. Dead guys. Heard it." Susan had given up all pretence of this being social. "It's an accounting perspective applied to relevant legal issues. Determining criminal intent. Preparation for court testimony. The paper trail. As you well know."

Ooh—fascinating *and* defensive. "So . . . you're more like an auditor—"

Susan interrupted. "No, I'm not. Listen, you don't want to talk about accounting. And right now, neither do I. Ask me what it is you really want to ask me."

Annie looked straight at her for a few seconds. "OK. What are you really doing here? In Lockport."

"I'm investigating a file that—"

"A file that you should have closed by now. Leah Mallick's certainly not going to rise from the dead and take her place on your *commission* any more. If that's all it really was . . ." But it wasn't, she suspected. Not by a long shot.

"As far as I know—"

"Come on, Ms. Shaw. That doesn't explain all those boxes I saw in your hotel room. Why are you still so interested in this? In her?"

"Don't try to bully me, Lieutenant. I *will* admit that I believe there's more to it—I've already said that. But I haven't uncovered any big secret. There's nothing in my *boxes* that would interest you."

"Perhaps it's about something more than a minor committee appointment?" Annie said evenly. "Of course, I'm just guessing . . ."

Susan stared back at her in cold anger now. "That Tim Mallick was up to his ass in some local fraud you're all scrambling to cover up. And I'm *not* guessing." Tit for tat.

Susan's lips were pressed so tightly together they were white.

OK, so they'd both held something back.

Susan finished the last of her drink and swirled the remaining ice in her glass.

The waiter returned to their table. Susan ordered another vodka on the rocks. Annie waved him off impatiently. They sat, silent again.

The moment it arrived, Susan took a generous swallow of her drink. "You're sure?" she said after another minute, motioning to Annie's empty glass. Only club soda all night, she'd noticed. It was the kind of detail that jumped out in a crowd like this.

Annie shook her head.

Finally, Susan spoke. "You have to understand that there are very few secrets left, Lieutenant. But, believe it or not, I'm not particularly interested in watching all of you run around this place like a bunch of second-rate G. Gordon Liddys. Leah Mallick was a prominent consultant on health care policy and what I really want to know is why she left California and ended up here."

Annie stared back at her, stunned. "You're saying this is all about *Leah?*"

Susan hesitated, then nodded slightly as she finished her drink. "Um-hmm."

Annie sat back, to catch her breath. *That* was the other shoe—despite all appearances, she wasn't really here for Tim Mallick or what he'd been up to. Not Island Boys and deputy mayors and all the things they did. A convenient diversion. It was only Leah she cared about.

Well, if nothing else, DeVries could stop worrying that Thomas Acton was planning to have their phones tapped—if Annie ever remembered to tell him.

But there was another, more significant implication. Susan Shaw wanted to know *why*. And for her own reasons, not Acton's.

Annie felt a rush of unexpected excitement. Maybe here was the chance to do something more than just bury it all. If Susan Shaw had better information . . . Annie pressed her elbows into the table hard now, forcing herself to remain calm. Just because they wanted the same thing, it didn't mean . . . "Then, how would you propose we do this—"

"I don't think we do, Lieutenant." Susan's words were bitten off, through a rigidly polite smile. "You were right—it *doesn't* make any sense for me to sit up here. I think I can do better on my own. So I'm going back tomorrow. Tell everyone they can 'stand down.' You're all off the hook." Susan picked up her briefcase and pushed the chair back. "Thanks for the assistance. Please convey my appreciation to the commissioner. You have my number." She extended her hand.

Annie took it numbly. That was it?

Susan was gone out the door before she thought to go after her. She threw some money on the table and hurried out in to the street.

"You haven't even tried to make sense of what you already have," she said loudly.

Startled, Susan turned at the sound.

"You don't really care what happened, or you wouldn't stop asking questions. This little charade—what's that all about? One minute you make it clear you don't want any questions about her. The next minute you're blaming us for not going after her. I think you know a lot more than you've said. I think you've been at this for a very long time—long before Leah Mallick killed herself. What's really in those files of yours? Some protection? I'd understand that. Given the sharks you swim with, I wouldn't be a bit surprised. But I would have thought you'd have better taste than to look for it in a place like this."

They were standing close together now.

Susan's brittle veneer cracked, and underneath it was real anger. "Taste? Please. That stunt with the pictures . . . ? I know what death looks like. And from everything I've heard, I certainly don't need a life lesson from you."

Annie's face paled.

Susan had never raised her voice to anyone on a public street before, and now she heard herself yelling. No one passing by even looked in their direction. "How would you know what I should care about? Your job's to stop this investigation . . ." Susan started to walk away again.

From behind her, Annie spoke. "There *is* no investigation. Don't you get that yet? No one wants to have anything to do with it. Everyone just wants both of them dead and forgotten." Annie stopped to catch her breath. They were supposed to be grown-ups here. She wasn't going to chase anyone down the street, and Susan was already a good twenty feet ahead. "Why didn't you say *you* were the one who interviewed her?"

Susan felt her stomach lurch unexpectedly. She stopped, turned, came back. "I believe I did mention it." There it was, she heard it herself—that *tone* again.

They stood only a few feet apart now.

"No, what you *said* was you *might* have met her. Some dinner party wasn't it? What strikes me is that you didn't even bother to make a note of it. Hardly worth remembering, apparently. But, you know, nothing I've read or heard since the night she died says anyone could ever forget every minute detail about a woman like Leah Mallick. In fact, people can't fucking stop talking about her—what she looked like, what she said, what they thought of her, what they wanted her to think of them—how *effective* she was, after nothing more than a few minutes of conversation. Certainly not an entire evening spent in her company. So were you the only one oblivious to her charms, or did you just decide not to notice for some reason?"

"I'm not the story here, Ms. Shannon."

"Maybe not, Susan. But you know a lot more of it than I do." It was hard to admit: she had the body of fact, but only Susan could provide the real context.

Susan still glared at her with suspicion. "Why does this matter to you, anyway? The tabloids have it now. And they go after anything that crawls—until the next movie star overdoses, anyway. What do you want me to say?"

"So you're going to leave this to *them*—to the April Vaughans of the world? How much truth is going to be found in that? Maybe you don't believe me, but *I* want to know what really happened too. I want to. Me. I don't give a damn what everyone else around here might be saying. You know something I don't. Start by showing me what's in those files of yours, then maybe we can start asking real questions. I can't do it alone. I've tried. But every time I make a move around here, everybody in town knows it."

Susan made a small sound. It was a laugh. "One of the misfortunes of celebrity, I've heard."

In spite of herself, Annie smiled too. "Well, it'll get you a good table at Holly's."

"Until the health department shuts them down," Susan said. And for a moment she seemed to be considering the offer. Then she shook her head. "I'm sorry. I can't help you," she said. "There's nothing here for me, aside from the crime scene. And I assume you've given me everything from that . . ." Back to smug.

"You have what we found," Annie said more sharply. "But that's not all—and you know it. We could at least take a look around. Lockport's more than just a 'crime scene' in this. Their house—"

"Unless it can tell me why they were here, I don't think it means very much either."

They were standing stiffly, each with arms folded protectively in front of her. They would have looked, to any casual observer, like perfectly reasonable people having a perfectly reasonable, if tense, discussion.

Annie, frustrated, pressed. "And you're really willing to go back there now, with nothing? How does that serve your purpose?" Or maybe, she reminded herself, it had already had its intended effect. Maybe that *was* the point after all—that she was here only to prove she could still rattle someone's chain at will. Whoever's it might be.

Susan's tone was deliberate. "My 'purpose' is to determine the threat Dr. Mallick might have posed to this state—had she become the Secretary of Health and Human Services, as planned."

Annie actually gasped. It was certainly more than a minor commission—and far beyond anything she'd really expected. *This* would have put Leah Mallick in the cabinet. This was the larger truth they were worried about—that the governor had been about to appoint a beautifully designed certifiable wing nut to head the most high-profile and influential department in the state.

Leah, then, had been on the verge of a stunning new political career.

"What does that mean now?" Annie asked cautiously. Obviously, no one in Lockport knew this yet, or everything would already have been so very different.

Susan became cryptic once more. "If there was something else going on, then there have to be others still involved. If there's a connection, I can make it." Another faint smile. "As I said, patterns meet their promises."

But maybe that was the other threat here, Annie thought. If you look for patterns long enough, you begin to see conspiracy around every corner.

"So, I agree that Leah Mallick is important. I just don't know if it matters that she's dead," Susan added coolly, her face a polite mask again.

In the next moment they both heard the sound of a long, high-pitched scream nearby. It continued for some seconds. On the street just ahead, an elderly woman was resisting an attack, her shouts frightened and indignant.

Then Annie saw a small figure, a young boy, breaking away from the woman's flapping arms, her old purse, minus its strap, clutched under his arm. "Little bastard." She knew she could catch him; it was only a kid, making a break for it. And there was no way she could just stand here and watch. Annie shouted at Susan over her shoulder, "You . . . stay here."

She took off across the street, the victim screaming still for the police. At Broadway Avenue, Annie caught sight of the boy ducking into the laneway behind a block of commercial buildings.

In the same moment that she rounded the corner, she saw the gun in his hand, waving in her direction. A .380 semi-automatic.

"Shit." One leg collapsed beneath her and she found herself sprawled face down on the pavement. Her only thought was that she'd somehow managed to step into a pothole. There'd been no noise; the gun hadn't fired, at least that she could remember. Then she sat up and saw the blood running along her left leg in thin stripes from a small wound just above the knee. There was even a wisp of smoke rising from the surface. It had to have been a fragment from a wild bounce. At this range, she judged, a direct hit with anything bigger than a .22 would have taken her leg off. Time stretched out, and a low thudding sound she recognized as her own heartbeat began to drown out everything else.

Then, somehow, Susan was beside her, supporting her with one arm while frantically trying to staunch the blood flow with a handful of Kleenex. "Oh, God," was all she kept saying.

How did *you* get here? Annie thought. How much time has passed?

They stayed low, crouched behind a large garbage bin. Annie moved just enough to peer along the length of the alley. She could see nothing moving in the darkness, but she knew that he was still waiting out there, and that they were completely vulnerable. She'd managed to chase him into a dead end.

She, who'd once known these streets better than her own neighbourhood, had allowed herself to become drawn into a blind alley by a child with a gun. And for what? A five-dollar purse? Her mid-life identity crisis? More like her fear of the embarrassment if she—the most famous police officer in the city—hadn't tried to do something. "I don't actually carry a gun any more," Annie admitted aloud. She sounded unnaturally calm.

Susan hesitated, then pulled a small Beretta out of her purse and held it out. "I do." She saw Annie's bemused expression. "I have a permit for it," she said somewhat defensively.

"And just what were you planning to *do* with it?"

"I've been trained, by the governor's security detail." Susan checked the ammunition clip, her hand shaking slightly. She'd never fired it outside a shooting range.

The state troopers must have had a field day with this one, Annie said to herself. "And you think you're going to—Je-*sus*. Just wait a second here . . ." She was stuttering slightly. It was hard to grasp all the really bad possibilities in the situation. What she knew for certain, though, was that it was utterly inappropriate to involve *any* civilian, let alone the governor's girlfriend.

Above all else, she needed to remain focused. Her leg

was completely numb except for an uncomfortable burning sensation. It was her throbbing head that really hurt. That, and the fact she couldn't see very well out of one eye any more. "Well, you're not the Girl from U.N.C.L.E. either. Give it to me. It was just some kid. He's probably long gone. There's no reason to risk—"

In that exact moment, another shot was fired, the sound trapped by the buildings and ricocheting around them. Bits of the concrete pavement flew up, less than two feet in front of them. Susan let out a small explosion of breath. "*Shit.*" As the echo died away, they heard a child giggling in the dark. It was nothing more than a game to him. And he was moving.

Susan refused to acknowledge her rising panic. "And what are you planning? There's nowhere else for him to go. He's just going to keep taking potshots at us until he runs out of bullets, or something worse happens. And even *I* can tell he's got a fucking cannon there. Use my cell and call for help, dammit." *Which,* she wanted to say, you should have done in the first place, *Lieutenant.* She handed her phone to Annie.

One of those fancy new chrome models, Annie noticed, studying it with mild interest.

Susan crept to the corner of the bin and looked out into the laneway. The alley ended in a three-storey brick wall. It was dark enough to provide reasonable cover for her in the shadows if he wasn't paying too much attention for the next few minutes.

Annie was looking at her almost amiably now. "You actually took security training?" Her voice was eerily normal.

"It was only a couple of sessions. The basics . . ."

And isn't that just who you want carrying a deadly weapon? Annie thought. "Very reassuring." This was pleasant. Maybe they could just sit here and snipe at each other all night long. She tried to focus again. "Look, this is insane. I can't let you go out there. I don't want—"

"I really don't need your permission, Anne." Susan removed her high heels and moved to the corner of the dumpster. "What do you suggest we do? Wait until he finds a better position to keep shooting at us? Just phone someone."

From behind her she heard Annie's voice again, more faint, a different, tighter sound. "The safety . . ." she was saying now.

Susan glanced back. Annie's face had taken on a grey pallor. She was struggling to hide persistent tremors. Shock. But she was also trying to point out something to her, reaching for the gun. "You have to take off the—" Annie's hand closed around hers on the grip and flicked off the safety catch, leaving an outline of blood smeared across the back of her hand, the sight of it like a slap. This is very, very real, Susan told herself.

"He's moving. Somewhere on the left now—"

"Call," Susan said again, and crept out from behind the bin. Low, quiet. *Control.*

Annie closed her eyes just long enough to take a deep breath. When she opened them again, she was alone. Susan's shoes were lined up amidst the trash, the left standing tidily beside the right. And she was holding a Nokia in her hand. The keypad lit up instantly; at least she'd remembered to charge it. She worked to slow her breathing, more afraid now of passing out.

The 911 operator picked up after five rings. "Emergency. Which service please?"

"Police. Officer down." She couldn't stop a new wave of shivering. She wasn't absolutely sure she could be heard clearly through her chattering teeth.

"Can you identify the officer?"

Annie heard the tapping keyboard entering information into the computer on the other end.

"It's me, you idiot. I'm the one down. Give me dispatch, Division Seven. I can't get to my own radio." Everything was coming out in the wrong order. And far too aggressively.

The same even voice, someone she didn't recognize. "Your name and location, please."

"This is Lieutenant Anne Shannon. I'm in the alley behind Darrell's department store, between Fifth and Nolet Street. We're being fired upon by a grab-and-run suspect. I think it's just the one, but I can't tell where he is now."

"Are you in a safe position? Do you have someone there with you?"

Annie couldn't remember the name for a moment . . . It was Susan. Susan Shaw. "There's another officer . . . no, I mean an accountant. Gone in pursuit." She hoped that the high-pitched sound in her head was the siren of a police car already on its way towards them. Annie could taste oily gravel in her mouth. She touched her lip and found it bleeding. One eye was swollen almost shut. She must have hit her face pretty hard at some point. "Tell them she's got a weapon but is not in uniform."

She heard the dispatcher entering that into the computer too. However this ended, at least they'd have a nice, orderly incident report.

"Stay on the line," the dispatcher was saying. "Keep talking to me . . ."

Annie lay back against the garbage bin. This all proved just how easy it was to lose your place in the rule book. After a while it was inevitable: the edge—whatever that was—got blunted. You allowed yourself to become careless and complacent. And every safe, sunny day conspired to lead you on, letting you convince yourself that it would always be the same. When really it was only ever a matter of inches and seconds . . .

Dear God, what have I got us into? She let her eyes fall closed again.

Susan crept silently alongside the brick wall, hiding herself as much as possible in the deeper shadows. Mouldy garbage grew in piles everywhere, old mattresses and torn plastic bags, the smells of it all peculiarly sharp and vivid. There were more than enough hiding places for a smart boy here, she knew, but if he didn't think he had to stay out of sight . . . *We're just playing war.*

She spotted him first, under the ledge of an old, abandoned loading dock. Betrayed by nothing more than a small movement. He could easily have run by now. Instead, he'd occupied himself in cataloguing the sundry contents of the purse he'd stolen, setting everything out neatly in front of him. The gun lay carelessly across his knees. He looked up only when she was already in a formal firing position.

"Huh . . . ?" It was a grunt of surprise, and it rolled out of his mouth like an old hiccup.

"Hi there," Susan said with a faint smile. So, this is what real, unadorned power felt like, she thought. *This* was why Nancy Reagan had bragged about having "a tiny little one" of her own.

She watched, with unexpected satisfaction, as genuine terror developed in the kid's eyes. For just a moment she wanted to reward it by actually pulling the trigger, willing the gun to explode in her shaking hand. It didn't. Instead, a deadly calm voice issued from her mouth. "Don't move an inch. I will kill you if you do, after which I will read you your rights."

The eleven-year-old in her sights summoned as much of the street as he could. "No way, man."

That's the best you can do? she thought. That's the eloquent appeal for your life? "Oh, yeah. Really. Way," she said. *Now I'm resorting to repartee from a sitcom.* She shifted a bit in her stance. It was a tough position to hold; those inner thigh muscles so rarely got a good workout, sitting behind a desk.

Instinctively, he flinched with her slight movement. It occurred to her then that he really expected to be blown away—just like that. It was time to end this. She wasn't here to terrorize children, even the ones who shot at her.

"Lay face down on the ground. Put your hands behind your head. And don't move a muscle."

He obeyed immediately, and the barrel of her gun followed him down. I'll bet if his mother'd had one of these things, she thought, we wouldn't be here right now.

The flashing lights of the arriving police and paramedics lit the scene from fifty yards away. A young officer in a Kevlar vest was suddenly at her side. "Can I help you here, ma'am?" He glanced at her gun nervously. It wasn't regulation issue, that much he could see.

Susan indicated the eleven-year-old prone at her feet. "This is the one who was trying to kill us."

The cop glanced down then shouted behind him, "It's OK. We got him."

Before he could say more, Susan found herself running, flat out, back down the alley, towards the garbage bin where she'd left Annie.

It was like being swept up into a travelling carnival. People were coming out of nowhere, grabbing at her, trying to ask or tell her something. The whole area seemed filled with noise and light now, everyone moving with restrained urgency, though the sense of danger was already retreating. Maybe this was normal for them. Inexplicably, she felt her own anxiety growing, thickening into dread. She didn't see anyone she knew. She couldn't find Annie. Finally, someone pointed her in the direction of an ambulance.

Annie was waiting there, already propped up on a stretcher and surrounded by what looked like half the cops and paramedics in town. She welcomed Susan with a kind of drunken half-smile, shaking her head in awed wonder as she watched her cutting through the crowd. "What the hell kind of accountant *are* you again? Jesus. Un-fucking-believable," she said. Then she held out her hand. "OK? We're going to deal for real this time? From here on . . . ?"

As they lifted the stretcher into the back, Susan leaned over and slapped Annie's upraised palm lightly, grinning. "Not sure why I need *you,* though—I already got myself a gun."

7

Bill was the first person Annie saw as she awoke. She spent a long time trying to describe to him what had happened, that her brothers, in full hockey gear, had slammed her repeatedly into the boards. That was why everything hurt, she explained. Bill smiled, and disappeared.

Flowers, cards, too many people. Then Bill was there again.

This time he was showing her a newspaper, a photograph of herself on the front page that she didn't remember being taken. In it she looked dazed but cheerful, propped up in her hospital bed, her fingers held in some limp version of a thumbs-up.

Less than thirty-six hours later she was discharged, with a collection of pills, a crutch and a photocopied sheet of new exercises to perform. Nothing more than a temporary glitch in a working woman's week.

Someone had left a homemade casserole on her front step with a note attached: "When you're finish eating please return to Theresa (across street, two houses down)." Another name to meet. Well, there'd be time to introduce herself to all the neighbours now.

She'd checked herself out of the hospital early, taking a cab home alone. The last thing she needed was a ride from yet another cop razzing her about being rescued by "an accountant." Everyone had heard the dispatcher's tape; they were already passing copies of it around. It sounded to her like someone else's pissed-off voice: "It's *me,* you idiot . . ."

Susan Shaw would probably get a medal. Whereas I, thought Annie, will be lucky to end up as a school crossing guard. Time to slide the career aspirations into the delete bin.

It was getting a bit easier to relax, at least. After a restless sleep, she'd wallowed in a late, lazy morning, and now faced an entire afternoon comfortably ensconced on a battered old chaise lounge she'd wrangled out from under the back deck. The only thing above her was a blue sky and a warm summer sun. She'd pulled on an outsized pair of baggy shorts, exposing a swollen knee and a godawful bruise spreading up her thigh. Maybe it would all look better with a tan.

She'd just closed her eyes when she heard the sound of the front doorbell bouncing through the house. *Shit.* Ben roused himself out of a nap only long enough to bark from where he lay near her, on the flagstone patio. "I'm out back," she yelled. A run up the steps was far too labour-intensive right now.

A minute or two later the side-gate latch was lifted and Susan Shaw was standing there.

Not much of a surprise. They hadn't had a chance to talk since that night. And Annie hadn't properly thanked her yet.

Susan was holding a large box out in front of her. "Hi. I hope you don't mind having company so soon. This came for you while you were in the hospital. They thought you might get a kick out of it . . ." She was smiling, somewhat uncertainly. "So I offered to bring it over."

Annie pulled herself up to a sitting position, shading her eyes with her hand. "You were at my office . . . ?" That was fast work, she thought. She felt a quick flare of jealousy, then firmly rejected it. She knew it was unwarranted. Unseemly. Petty. Every cop in the city knew the same thing she did—that Susan had probably saved her life.

"Yeah, they needed me to give a formal statement. About what happened."

"Sorry. Right. Of course. Good. Thanks. Please . . ." In a few seconds of confusion Annie tried to take the box and point out a nearby chair at the same time. Susan sat down and Ben went over to throw himself at her feet, asleep again almost immediately. "So, how did that go?"

"OK, I guess." But after a moment Susan made a comic grimace. "Do they always have ten guys sitting in on those things?"

Annie laughed. "The cost of celebrity, I've heard." And she knew they liked to look. She could picture all of them around the interview table, panting like puppies every time Susan crossed her legs or wet her lips. Be honest, she scolded herself again. She's got more practice at that than you'll ever have. But Jesus, what must it be like to always be so—and the word escaped her for a moment. Poured into a vessel not of your own making. So easily pigeonholed, if not by the world, then by yourself. *Objectified.*

"And, so, how are we feeling?" Susan asked, mimicking a cheery nurse.

Annie tugged self-consciously at the bandage. It looked huge right now. "What, you mean this? It's mostly for show." She laughed again. "Really, it's fine. A couple days, at most . . ."

"Good," Susan said. She was polite and interested, though distracted. One foot swung constantly in a small, constricted circle.

"And how are you?" Annie said, more seriously. After what had happened, she should probably find someone to talk to.

Susan blinked, surprised by the question. "Me? I'm fine."

"No trouble sleeping?"

She frowned. "Why? Is that usual?"

"Some version of it. I had pills."

"Yeah, well . . . I had a large Scotch." She laughed uncomfortably. "That always leaves me feeling like a bit of a lush, though. All the travelling I do. You know, lining up all those little bottles that someone's going to be counting the next day."

Annie nodded slowly. "It's a good idea to be patient with yourself right now, however you're feeling." She stood up. "Anyway, I was just going to make up some cold lemonade. You OK here for a minute?"

Susan began to rise. "I'll give you a hand . . ."

"No, it's fine thanks. I'm supposed to be exercising. You stay. I'll be right back."

Susan settled into the chair again.

While she ran the cold water in the sink, Annie looked back out through the kitchen window. Susan was leaning down now to stroke Ben's belly. He'd rolled over and given it up to her immediately. *Boy slut.* At least dogs liked her.

Annie saw that she was dressed casually for the first time—designer jeans, an expensive leather jacket. Her shoulder-length blonde hair down. Lighter makeup than usual. A different person when she wasn't "on." Still, a little fancy for the room . . . Annie stopped herself again.

She was the one who wasn't used to polite company any more. And it showed. The house remained unfinished after ten years. And from here the backyard looked like the disaster it was: flower beds buried under weeds, overgrown paths, a pile of junk she'd always intended to send to the dump, burned patches of grass from all the times she'd been too lazy to take Ben out for a walk. One "good" chair, rocking on a bent leg.

Framed by the window, Susan sat waiting patiently, clutching a thick envelope on her lap.

They both knew why she was really here; the parcel from work was nothing but an excuse. What was I thinking, Annie said to herself, even to suggest this? I don't need a partner. I don't want one. It'll only make my life more complicated, and I'm finished doing that.

And maybe it's time I accepted that I can't always understand everything that happens. Even Nancy Drew has to grow up eventually.

Annie returned to the backyard and tried to summon up some interest in the large carton, expecting nothing more than a few jokes from some of the guys at headquarters. Instead, she unwrapped packages of cookies and chocolates, gift certificates from area businesses, dozens of greeting cards and handwritten notes from people all over the city—many of the "our prayers are with you" variety. Dozens of names familiar from the old neighbourhood. There was even a pair of jeans from the Levis store at the mall. Size four.

She held them up in front of her now. Never in a million years. "I'm that one person in the world who looks thinner on television," she said. She set them aside with a grin. "I don't know why—sometimes they just *give* you things . . ."

It was another uncomfortable reminder of her place in the public consciousness. In Lockport she'd become a genuine low-rent phenomenon. And from her first media appearance, strangers had been sending her gifts out of the blue. She usually returned them with a note of thanks, or passed them on to local charities. But *this*—this was more like Christmas. For a twisted ankle and a boo-boo on her knee. She decided to keep the cookies and cards anyway. "They'll probably send you something too," she said to Susan.

In response, Susan smiled broadly and extended her long legs, showing off a pair of blinding white Nikes. "Actually, these are new. Your guys in homicide gave them to me. They suggested I wear them the next time I go anywhere with you."

The next time. Just the idea of starting over, when people might begin to expect something of you again. Annie lay back in the chaise and studied the empty sky.

She heard Susan's voice, firm now. "Look, I know what you're thinking. I don't have the whole picture. Neither do you. We can at least admit that much now. But, there are worse reasons to work together, Annie."

It was the first time Susan had called her that. Annie looked at her again. She still wanted to team up, even after what had happened? She'd had to *rescue* her, for God's sake.

"When do you have to go back?"

It wasn't meant as an innocent question. Neither of them could afford to be naïve about what they were doing. She needed to know—who else was interested? Who was watching them now? She saw the tension form again around Susan's eyes.

In the hard light Susan Shaw looked every minute of her years. There were deep lines there. A mature face, with few illusions left. She stared at the ground for a long moment, then back at Annie. "I don't have to," she said.

There *was* no one watching. Something had come to an end for her too.

Annie nodded again. "OK." She knew it was always hardest to accept what used to be, when there was nothing else to take its place.

As if to confirm Annie's thoughts, Susan squinted up into the sun. "I guess you'd have to call me a rogue accountant now," she said with a hollow laugh. She glanced at Annie, unsure of what she should expect to find there—disapproval, perhaps. Even a certain subtle malice. She saw nothing more or less than sympathy.

"Sounds like we could use a few of those nowadays," Annie said. It wasn't hard to imagine what had happened down there at the capital. Susan Shaw had simply run out of time.

Annie slid the gift box aside and pointed to the thick envelope Susan still held. "So, what do you have there?"

Susan took a deep breath, then untied the flap. "Well, I already had a few things—"

O-o-o-hh, *really. . .* ?

"Leads, I guess you'd call them," Susan said. She pulled the material from the package and handed it to Annie. "But it really *doesn't* have anything to do with Lockport."

Annie saw a three-page-long list of companies, neatly presented in alphabetical order; and, as a half-inch-thick attachment, a comprehensive analysis of a series of business deals going back almost six years. Percentages, estimated dollar values, industry sectors. Offshore, onshore. All around the circle.

Annie realized this was a summary of everything contained in all the files in Susan's hotel room. She leafed through the report more slowly, specific names and dates jumping out. It was a massive amount of data, along with careful flow charts linking past partners and their substantial inside connections to major corporations, travelling well beyond the borders of any one state, to places as high as it went. Annie looked up.

Susan was sitting quietly. She'd put on a pair of Serengetis against the bright sun, and her expression was unreadable.

"This looks amazing," Annie said, "but you know I have no real idea what most of it means." Someone would have had to walk her, *very* slowly, through most of it.

Even so, there were dozens of formerly high-flying companies even she recognized—names from *Forbes* and the *Wall Street Journal* and the *New York Times.* There were CEOs who'd been cover features on scores of important magazines, most of them now headline stories on the evening news, she noted with wry amusement. It just proved that if you looked hard enough . . . But why would anyone have made such an effort to detail this now? Federal prosecutors were already lining up in teams, three deep, to take turns at the perpetrators. How could it relate. . . ?

"It's what you've been hearing about for the last two years or so, of course," Susan said. She seemed to be expecting some reaction.

Annie continued leafing through it, puzzled. "You mean all that 'off-book' stuff?"

"And wash-sales. And butterfly spreads. And virtual loops and death-spiral financing."

Annie's only reaction was keen disappointment. It looked like maybe they'd *both* been wasting a lot of time. "So you mean you've been following all this—" Talk about *obsessive.*

"Not 'following' . . ." Susan replied coolly and with one slender finger pointed at the date printed under the large red *Confidential* stamped across the front cover. Three years ago—long before the first story had broken on the greatest series of business scandals in decades. "There's even a few in there they don't know about yet."

She hadn't just documented broad corporate malfeasance; she'd anticipated it. Annie was incredulous. "You mean you knew about them before everyone. . . ? Then, why didn't you say—?" Annie felt her heart pounding in her throat. It didn't seem to fit in her chest any more.

Susan leaned back in her chair, silent for a moment. "Maybe because it had nothing to do with state regulation. It certainly didn't fall within my specific jurisdiction. And some of what was going on was—*is,* in fact—completely legal under existing practices. Unexpensed options aren't a crime. And it's never been my personal ambition to rewrite the securities laws." She glanced quickly away before looking at Annie again. "And I'm pretty certain I would have been facing censure at the end for a number of disclosure violations. Whistle-blowers enjoy a very short professional lifespan." She raised an eyebrow with a faint smirk. "Or maybe it was just because of my *own* limited local resources." Susan reached for the glass of icy lemonade, beaded with cold moisture, and shivered slightly. "Anyone'll tell you—it's almost impossible to indict U.S. corporate culture in the middle of a bull market. And you want to be very, *very* sure before you take down the entire Dow Jones."

Annie nodded again, more warily. Susan had already taken this matter a long way past her job description. And this exceeded, exponentially, any issue related to Governor Acton's run for re-election. Annie corrected herself: *this* run—but maybe not his next. Acton's name was being floated for the presidential primaries as the state's "favourite son." Information like this could have afforded real protection to someone. She knew she was still missing something. "What does it have to do with Leah?"

Wordlessly, Susan pointed to a name halfway down the second page. Timothy Edwin Mallick.

Stunned now, Annie sat back and let out a low whistle.

"They call it 'gaming the system.' Hundreds of people playing various discrete parts. When it touches on broad areas of governance and oversight, you can't always—" Susan stopped herself. "Anyway, I just put it all together, in one place." She took the report from Annie's hand. "And, *that,* Lieutenant," she said with a self-satisfied smile, "is what a forensic accountant does."

Annie shook her head, then lay down to stare at the sky again, thinking. "You do know what they're saying now? About him?"

Susan had pushed her sunglasses up to enjoy the unaccustomed feeling of warmth on her face. "That he was in the advanced stages of dementia," she said distantly.

"Right. So, you'd have to assume certain people might have started thinking that he couldn't be trusted with his part of a broad-based scheme like this any more. It presented a risk that he could expose something." A rogue. And as a partner, far less predictable, far more reckless.

Susan opened one eye to look at her. "Maybe . . ."

"I think there's a reason this happened in Lockport," Annie said.

She knew there couldn't be two people less likely to care what happened next—the two of them sitting here in an ill-kempt garden, in a burned-out industrial has-been of a town that meant nothing to anyone beyond its city limits. Lockport wasn't the centre of *anything* any more. But it mattered now. The truth didn't always grow somewhere else.

Annie sighed and pulled herself upright again. "Look. There's this group of local businessmen . . ." She began to scrawl out a name and a phone number. "They call them the

Island Boys. I know I can't touch them, but you could. You could say you'd like to have a little chat about Tim Mallick. They were involved with him, and I think they might know something more about *this* too." And they'd squeal like weasels if they got a call like that right now—especially from someone they believed was connected to the governor.

Susan took the scrap of paper from her and looked at it with a small frown. She made a quick gesture of impatience. "But this isn't about some pissant local land scheme—"

Annie interrupted. "I know that. But let me ask you something—what was the first thing you thought when you got here?"

Susan coloured a bit. She hesitated.

"No, be honest." Annie was leaning forward.

"Well, I guess it was how the hell did they ever end up in *this* hole." Susan blushed self-consciously. "Sorry. But—"

Annie laughed heartily. "No. That's exactly what I mean. Listen, I know it's conventional wisdom . . . to 'follow the money.' And maybe Tim Mallick was entangled in everything from conflict-of-interest regulations to violations of federal securities laws. For a long time. But *he* didn't commit murder that night. *She* did. You said it yourself—why did it end here? If you were someone looking at it from the outside, what's missing?"

Not the pattern, but the pattern broken. The anomaly.

Annie could feel it: Susan was still holding something back. There'd been another connection to Leah Mallick—something more than a single, accidental encounter at a dinner party.

Susan's frown deepened. "OK," she said finally. "It wasn't *what* they were doing, but that they both stopped doing it. They pulled back from everything and came here." Suddenly, without reason or explanation. Something else had happened—or ceased to happen. Something more specific, which finally drove Leah Mallick to destroy them all.

"How did she really strike you?" Annie said. "What did she talk about? Leah Mallick."

But Susan couldn't hear her now. She'd drifted away to another place.

It was an afternoon in the country. A long, unseasonably warm day when she'd confessed for the first time to anyone—apart from Georgia, anyway—the cost of a brief, troubled and spectacularly ill-fated love affair with the governor of the state. And Leah Mallick had seemed to be the one person to whom she could have told almost anything at that moment.

Leah was beautiful enough that everyone seated in the restaurant had turned, almost in unison, at their arrival. The maitre d' immediately agreed to open the outdoor area for them alone, at Leah's mild request. Yes, it was an early spring, he agreed—a lovely day—of course it was no problem. And Susan felt every eye following them as they moved through the main dining room to the terrace beyond.

All her life she'd been told she was the prettiest girl in her group. She'd grown accustomed to the kind of attention that came with beauty. But as time went on, it made her feel more like a target or a trophy, more the victim than the beneficiary of some unearned privilege.

Leah must have heard the same thing, probably a thousand times. But that awareness had given her instead another kind of power, which she dared to hold at a careless, ironic distance. She appeared almost indifferent to it.

Susan was cynical enough to know that that was far from the truth—that no one is ever entirely unaware of the power they hold, in any given situation, and in whatever measure they hold it. But Leah seemed completely at ease in herself. She offered so much more than physical attractiveness: an incisive wit, a formidable intelligence, a finely tuned sensitivity. There was a kind of equanimity about her too. Susan felt it—a stillness—for just a moment, envied her that self-possession above all. And in almost complete contradiction to what was so gleaming on the surface, Leah possessed a surprisingly, fundamentally down-to-earth quality. Though even that was, in some way, a heightened, more amplified version.

It had taken only a few minutes before Susan realized it was as though they'd been exchanging confidences for years. Leah described everything so easily, and with such wry good humour. All the regular, rote intimacies: schools and family and first jobs and favourite vacation spots. And even when asked, Leah didn't dwell on her own considerable accomplishments, but instead subtly turned the attention back.

Even now Susan couldn't conceive exactly how it happened that her own cautious reserve had folded out of the way in the very moment that Leah asked her a few simple questions. In retrospect she tried to chalk it up to Leah's profession, her expertise and experience. Leah had probably listened to the same dull, pathetic story, told a hundred times by a hundred other hurt women.

At one point Susan had even reminded herself that the woman sitting across the table from her was a highly trained psychiatrist. People like Leah Mallick did exactly this sort of thing for a living; it wasn't personal.

That was why, it was such a surprise when in the next moment—when Leah had so easily announced that she would not be able to accept Susan's offer to chair the committee—it had felt like such a deliberate and unnecessary betrayal. She'd made a simple statement. No histrionics. It was delivered, as was everything else that day, both elegantly and unpretentiously.

She'd certainly considered the opportunity, she said. Very seriously. But perhaps the time had passed for her to make that kind of contribution. She didn't need or want a public profile, she said. Her family was her only priority now, she said.

Her response was so unexpected that Susan knew she must have made some small, involuntary gesture that revealed her dismay and disappointment.

Leah Mallick, watching her, had seen it and smiled. "Thank you. I'm very flattered," she said, "but you'll be fine. I happen to know the administration has several excellent candidates under consideration." It didn't seem to be a negotiating ploy. "I want a quiet life," Leah had said after another moment. "I hope you can understand."

Then they remained, talking of other things. More glasses of wine. The warmth of the sun fading away until there was no question that it was still a winter day. And no, she didn't understand—that, or what came after.

~~~

Susan looked up now, startled to see that it was only another hot, humid summer afternoon and she was sitting in a suburban backyard, facing someone a little less ethereal than Leah Mallick, a fat dog asleep at her feet. But despite the heat, she'd wrapped her slender arms tightly around herself, as if for warmth. And Annie Shannon was observing her far too closely.

Susan roused herself after a moment and shrugged. "Nothing, really. We didn't talk about much at all," she said. "Music. Mozart."

Annie didn't believe her, but the door had already shut. She indicated the thick report now rolled tightly in Susan's hand. "So why didn't you try to use that?" Careers were made, or saved, with less. At some point a smart and desperate woman could have bought *herself* a lot of protection too. But she'd let the clock run out.

Susan disappeared behind her sunglasses again. "You'll have to leave my reasons to me, Lieutenant."

Then the only sound was a light summer wind, high in the trees. And Ben, lightly snoring.

~~~

It was shortly before the full blast of noontime heat. Susan drove towards the gatehouse at the edge of the slow-moving river. Nothing but a tin-roofed shack, with some minor attempt made at landscaping. The sign read: *The Yarmouth Yacht Club.* The gravel road leading down to it had been winding and wet, bordered on either side by alders and brush. A few deep holes had forced her off to the side a couple of times. There were no other visitors that she could see. No reason to be so nervous.

She half expected a cartoon-like troll to emerge from the shack. Instead, the gatekeeper approaching her car now was a sharply uniformed security guard. He carefully checked her identification against the short printed list he carried on a clipboard. She could hear the sound of his radio coming from inside the shack. Motown oldies. She was instructed to nose her car up to the line painted on a short section of asphalt and wait for his signal.

Then, with the push of a button, the complicated bulk of machinery out in the river began to round itself into place. It was an old-fashioned swing bridge—the only access to the island—and it slowly pivoted and ground its gears in a long bellow of frustrated iron. Another remnant of the infamously abandoned lock system, and the only part of it still working.

Here, the Stoney River met the Albion and widened into an almost magisterial vista. The water, though brown and murky, still gave rise to a fresh breeze at this time of day. In the convergence of the two streams, an antediluvian delta of an island had developed, land fertile enough to grow anything. Now it was being cultivated in Kentucky bluegrass and Bermuda bent grass, artificially coddled into the unnatural requirements of a proposed eighteen-hole golf course. The sprinklers rotating in the sunlight made it seem mysterious from the short distance offshore, the misty air above the brilliant green turf shot through with rainbows in every direction.

A hundred tons of steel slammed into final position with a monumental sense of ceremony. Susan could feel the thud come through the ground towards her. The gatekeeper motioned her car forward.

When she reached the other side, the bridge immediately broke its tenuous connection with the shore. She saw someone she judged to be Lewis Stephens, waving at her from the curve in the road up ahead. She parked where he pointed—right at the foot of the broad stairs leading up to an expansive porch that ran the entire front of the building. The structure itself presented a strangely familiar outline. It was a carbon copy of The Pines at Augusta, scaled to about half size. She could imagine them all sitting out here on a summer night, mint juleps in hand, swatting mosquitoes and complaining about the heat.

She began to relax. Crowds like this had always been her bread and butter. Country-club contributors. At the start of each campaign her job had been to empty their polyester pants. Is that a big cheque in your pocket, or are you just happy . . ?

Stephens wasn't waiting alone. Behind him stood five other men—all at least eighty, and all of whom looked ready to play a round at a moment's notice. It would have to be a short one, obviously. From where she stood, she could see that only a small portion of the course was developed so far—only the section showing to the Lockport side of the river. One of the men swung a putter, a cross between a cane and a pointer.

Lewis Stephens helped her from her car. He was imposing and well-groomed, plump pink cheeks freshly shaven. His faded ginger-coloured hair rose in a stiff pompadour. "Welcome, Ms. Shaw. We were delighted to hear from you. The governor, as you know, was our honoured guest here only last year. For our official reopening." He introduced the others.

She hadn't mentioned Thomas Acton to him, made reference only to her department. But it was a small state, and people liked to talk.

"Thank you, Mr. Stephens. It's a lovely setting." From here, she saw, that's *all* it was.

Stephens swelled. "Ah, just wait, Ms. Shaw. Wait till Jack works his special magic on this place." Stephens looked at her, rubbing his hands, pushing up both eyebrows meaningfully. He meant her to be impressed—though with what, she wasn't sure.

One of the other men leaned towards her. "You know Jack Nicklaus? He's redesigning the executive course for us. Lew's an old pal of his from way back. Got him to come in on it for a percentage."

She smiled thinly. This was their turf, so to speak. "Is there a place we could sit down to talk?"

Stephens looked pained. "Oh, we'll come to that. But allow us to be hospitable and give you a bit of a tour first, at least. At our age we don't often get the chance to show off for a beautiful young woman." He affected a kind of genteel courtliness that probably worked for him most of the time. It was entirely lost on her.

Her fingers fluttering briefly at her side, felt for a

phantom cigarette. This was already beginning to resemble one of those interminable white-wine fundraisers—the ones that took the campaign on a swing through three or four towns in a single day, in addition to the formal schedule of breakfasts, lunches and dinners. Give it some breathing room, she reminded herself. Maybe it had been a couple of years, but she'd been one of the best at carrying these things off; everyone always said so. She forced another, more sociable smile to her face. "Thank you. That'd be very nice, Mr. Stephens."

They began a stroll along the gravel path, an ungainly mob moving towards the first of three tees. A couple of times Stephens touched her elbow to emphasize a point or view. Near the conclusion of their walk he reached out his hand politely as they came to the slight, final rise. But his own breathing was already slightly laboured and she was actually forced to help him up the last few feet.

From where they now stood, she could see the giant swing bridge in the middle distance turning again on its central axis. Teenage boys were clinging to its sides. They were using the momentum of it to hurl themselves far out into the river, then they swam back to shore.

The entire group gazed with unbridled satisfaction across the flat expanse of the island. They obviously saw something in it she couldn't. In every direction the small greens were tapping out splashes where water from the sprinkler's arc struck them. She could envision every square inch of the place simply floating away in the next rain. "And I see that every hole already has its own water hazard," Susan said.

They all froze for a moment, until one of them chuckled. Then the rest joined in.

"That's pretty good," Stephens said. "I'll have to tell Jack that one when we're talking. He likes a good marketing hook."

After a few more minutes Stephens finally suggested they head back for lunch.

The clubhouse was casually appointed, old-fashioned, pleasant enough—unlike the faux exterior, not notably ostentatious. The newly redecorated lobby area was large and open. Its reception desk served as a small pro shop. The young man behind the counter, all tanned cheeks and thick black hair, glanced up with a full white smile at the sound of their arrival. He looked like Donnie Osmond wearing a Tommy Hilfiger costume. "Morning, fellas. Did you all happen to catch Jack on TV over the weekend—the Seniors? Still looking pretty good out there. Had Greg Norman on the run for a while."

Stephens smiled with paternal pride. "That's our boy. Seems to have licked that back problem for now. Maybe I can get him to give you a few pointers on that shank you're working on." Stephens guffawed loudly.

The young man's smile didn't change one iota. "I'm looking forward to it, Mr. Stephens," he said.

Then, tightening in a circle around her, they moved in unison towards the dining room. It was like being guarded by a cadre of ancient Secret Service agents, she thought.

Without a word, they took the largest table, in the exact middle of the room, and quickly settled into what were obviously their regular seats. A finger-snap from one of them brought two servers to the table at a quick run.

One waiter filled water glasses while the other presented the oversized menus. "Afternoon, gentlemen. Ma'am."

They all urged Susan to try the special—a terrine of ocean perch, a carpaccio of vegetables—shaved mushrooms, artichoke, red pepper, topped with Parmesan and balsamic reduction. Then they watched her place her order, pleased that she seemed impressed. They meant it to be a civilized place. The rest of them passed their menus back to the waiter without looking and chorused "The usual."

Susan sipped her drink as she listened to the small talk build around her. They were arguing about timing the rollout on the share offering, sources of possible bridge financing if it fell through. The atmosphere was cordial. She could easily follow the conversation without exertion. How clearly they loved the sound of their own words.

Then someone finally thought to turn to her and ask her first impression of "our little hideaway here." Susan had noticed that, of a total of perhaps twenty, twenty-five people seated for lunch, she was the only woman.

She paused to look pointedly around the room. "It's like all you boys, you've got yourselves your own little tree house here. With the secret handshake and the password and everything . . ." She smiled, well aware that the men around this table probably wanted to let out a collective groan right about now. What have we got ourselves here, every expression said—a feminist, or worse, a liberal? "I'm very flattered you included me today."

At that very moment the explosion of a twenty-gauge shotgun right outside the window rattled the entire dining room. Everyone jumped.

"Goddamn skeet again. Sonofabitch. I told them to move that away, far away, to somewhere else, where I wasn't," one of the men said. "There's a bylaw, goddamn it. And if there ain't, I'm writing one myself." Obviously a city councilor, Susan noted.

A second volley came in the next second.

"Je-*sus.*" Stephens slapped his hand down.

The man who'd been introduced as Doug Korshak was leaning towards her, trying to talk over all the noise. "You know, we were way ahead of every other city in this part of the state, I mean, for things like you're saying now. Letting in women and all. The president of the Lockport Chamber of Commerce is a woman." His earnestness was at odds with the rest of the ritual old-boy repartee surrounding them.

"But wasn't your congressional district one of those that voted to suspend the federal affirmative action bill?" Susan found she was beginning to enjoy playing with them. It kept her from being bored.

Barnett Sloan jumped in. "That's just that goddamn Harris. We didn't tell him to do that. It was all *his* bright idea—going all independent on us. Sonofabitch." Harris was the senior congressman for the district.

Korshak continued, oblivious. "Lots of women come in here all the time, now." He looked around. "Well, maybe none here today. But going on a good couple of years, now, eh, Phil? They got their committees and their fashion shows and all their benefit things. It's never been a problem for any of us. And heck, the food's sure gotten better, hasn't it, Phil?"

Phil, sleepy in front of his half-gone double gin, nodded agreement. He rocked forward in his seat with some gravity. "We are prepared to welcome anyone who can put up twenty-five a year for membership. Blacks. Natives. Vietnamese." He paused. "Of course, they damn well better be from *South* Vietnam—" He laughed loudly, the others joining in. "Yep. Bring your mega-millions to town, baby, and you can run the goddamn place." He mumbled back into a half-sleep.

The servers returned. Each man now faced the same large blood-rare steak, baked potato and green string beans, heavy on the butter. All discussion was suspended as if by tacit agreement. For five minutes they ate like it was their last meal, without interruption or breath. Susan sampled hers while she waited for them to finish. She had to admit that the food was surprisingly good. She just wasn't very hungry.

Then, Lewis Stephens loudly cleared his throat in the silence, calling them to attention. "Now, Ms. Shaw here has some questions for us about our friend Tim Mallick. I figured we might as well do this all together. All at once." Everyone looked away uneasily.

She'd expected they'd want a more private discussion, not while there were still other guests in the dining room. But Stephens seemed comfortable enough to lay everything out for her here and now. Then, why not? He owned the room.

Susan dropped her guise of easy sociability. "Well, as I've already told you, Mr. Stephens, my department would like some idea about what Tim Mallick was *really* involved in up here at the time of his death. It's my understanding you may be able to help us with that." From memory she could still trace the lines interconnecting the complex hierarchies of corporate officers and boards—lines that ended abruptly here, as though an eraser had been swept across the chalk marks on a blackboard.

She almost jumped when Stephens began to hoot in response, loud and long. After a minute he wiped his eyes and coughed roughly into a folded napkin. "Well, I can tell you, he wasn't involved in *nothing* by then. Not with any of us, anyway. Maybe it's left up to me to be the one who has to say it—that Tim Mallick was possibly the biggest fool who ever came to town. The only bigger fool, I guess, was the rest of us who let him at our money after the first six weeks." He looked around the table at the others.

They all nodded solemnly in agreement.

Stephens settled back in his chair. "Look, we're the ones who're *really* gonna have to bite that bullet in the end—no pun intended. We coulda owned a piece of the moon by the time we understood what was really going on. Only one good thing come out of it—I don't expect I'm gonna have to pay one red cent to your government for quite a few years. Some of my own friendly associates, if they even suspected anything about this, they'd be calling me up today just to offer to take the tax losses off my hands at pennies on the dollar. While they laughed up their sleeves at us, left sitting here like buggered rabbits.

"I'll admit we weren't born yesterday, but I'm damned if I . . . Well, I guess we can tell you now that we're just ordinary small-town businessmen. And none of us can afford for this all to get made too much of in our regular places of commerce, not that we got ourselves outsmarted by a slick carpetbagger like that."

Stephens surveyed his circle again. "So, a few months back, we all just come to an agreement between ourselves that we weren't ever gonna file formal complaints. And you can inform anyone else who still cares that any more discussion about it stops here and now. 'Cause not *one* of us'll admit a thing about any of it outside this room. Any problems we mighta had with the man were completely eliminated when he . . . suffered his unfortunate tragedy, and that's what we'll say."

"Saved us from shooting the son of a bitch ourselves," Phil Schmidt added in a sleepy growl.

It was anger she was hearing, but it was tinged with real trepidation. She paused, deciding the best direction. "Complaints aren't the issue, Mr. Stephens. I'll agree to go off the record with you, right now. But what was Tim Mallick selling?"

Stephens looked with extravagant surprise around the table. Then a slow, sly grin spread across his face. "OK, Ms. Shaw. We can do it your way. It's probably nothing more than you've already seen a hundred times anyway at close range down there at the capital. I'd say he was selling some kind of influence, if I had to put a name on it—greasing those same ol' wheels we all like to drive on."

Susan narrowed her eyes. "Political influence? At the state level, you mean?"

"For starters. Mallick was holding on to what he told us was some kind of 'futures options.' Excess dump-site capacity, effluent rights, emissions allowances—that sort of thing. He wanted to broker any unused quotas we could find. It was supposed to start with Palladian Steel, right here in town. Then we were gonna pick up more sites, all over the country, and hold the spread. Syndicate the fund. It looked real good on paper. Turned out that paper shoulda been used for something else, like the outhouse.

"The other side—they bought themselves some serious influence too, as it were. Big oil, private utilities, expensive lobbyists—I don't know. They got the EPA bar lowered all over the fucking country. That set the regulation standards to dropping like rocks—even got a five-year moratorium on some of 'em. Mallick, though, he keeps on talking about some kind of a environmental 'bubble.' Guess we were outside any bubble that really counted. Bubble? Fuck. Maybe *that's* what blew his head off."

Stephens sighed deeply, his rheumy eyes looking towards the vista outside the big windows. "Millions, he said. I can remember him saying it just like that. 'Millions!'" Stephens stared fixedly at the cliffs, on the other side of the river. Susan noticed that he was pale and perspiring now, and there was a faint bluish tinge about his mouth.

"But there's Timmy—still going on and on about Kee-oto standards. I didn't know what the hell he was talking about half the time. And at the last there, he's almost crying." Stephens pursed his lips and mewed in a weak, soft voice, "'Oh, please don't pull the paper now. We can't c-c-cover our c-calls—'" Stephens did a bad imitation of a stutter. "It was disgusting, I can tell you that.

"We all got taken. But as I stood to lose the most in this whole mess, I figured I got to call the tune. So we walked—

got enough out to cover about half our margins. I guess it teaches ya not to play in the schoolyard if you can't afford to lose. We're all big boys here . . ."

Susan saw that a couple of others around the table looked slightly pale now too. Perhaps they could afford to play just a little less than Lewis Stephens.

Stephens thumped the table. "And I can tell you, I don't care if there *is* an election coming up. If our governor thinks I'm going to just let him flog it in the media like he does everything else he gets his Harvard hands on—and make us all look like goddamn fools into the bargain—then I guess *you* can be the one to inform His Excellency that he's gonna get his nuts cracked this time." Stephens laughed roughly. "And he won't be getting a cent of support from this part of the state from here on in, if he tries." Stephens stopped, spent, still daring anyone to challenge him.

Susan knew it wasn't going to be her. Not this time, anyway.

They were talking about supplemental emission reductions: environmental offsets. The difference between surplus emission allowances and operating reductions. And anyone Stephens might have asked could have told him the same thing—that there would never be any available for trading in this town. No chance of them, ever. No company would be prepared to invest the millions necessary to exceed even minimum regulatory requirements—especially in the state's ruined resource sector. No incentive, short-term, long-term. Not in Lockport any more. And beyond filling potholes on the Interstate flying by the outskirts, no federal infrastructure program was going to put one red cent in here until the bridges themselves fell down.

Mallick's strategies had always created the appearance of simplicity. But this one—it was more like a sprawling, absurd spectacle. It created exposure on every side, was highly susceptible to the slightest change in the political winds. It required too many partners to make it happen—in the hundreds possibly. There was no downside protection; and given the margins, no real upside potential. They were all lucky, in fact, that they hadn't lost everything they'd put on the table. Luckier still that they hadn't gone in far deeper.

But Susan now understood two things about Tim Mallick's plan that they couldn't: that Mallick had set himself up for a cosmic throw of the dice, and that it was brilliant.

She looked at the ancient, lined faces turned towards her. There was legal recourse open to them, of course; they could still launch a claim against Mallick's estate. But any civil proceedings would probably take more time than any of them had left.

And they'd already said it themselves: they'd rather lose money than lose face. Shame, humiliation. It was a powerful disincentive to a public lawsuit. Others—rivals, competitors—would say that they'd deserved it. It was what professional con-artists had always preyed upon—the threat of public embarrassment. To them, Tim Mallick had been nothing more than an elegant, upscale grifter . . .

"OK, then. Let's say, just between us, gentlemen . . ." Susan leaned in towards the table and lowered her voice dramatically. She felt like playing it up a little now, like one of those smart-talking cookies in an old forties movie. Jean Arthur or Myrna Loy. "I'll see to it that you aren't bothered any further. There's no real reason why anything we've discussed here has to leave this room. You don't tell anyone I was here—and neither will I. Deal?" Favours earned.

Their relief was palpable. Phil Schmidt summed it up for everyone at the table. "Well, good to see we're all pitching up to the same green. And who the hell knows, eh? From what's going on nowadays, we got off pretty light, anyway. Thanks to Lew here."

Stephens, she saw, was taking in the expansive view through the big picture window—his born-again golf course, the Stoney River and the cliffs beyond.

By the time their bill was delivered to the table, Stephens had already recovered something of his sanguine composure. "I think young Mallick mighta just been trying to play catch-up with that fancy wife of his." Another chorus of agreement around the table.

Stephens reached across Susan and slid the cheque out of the imitation leather folder. "And I'm thinking too, gentlemen, since this kind of thing has such a high symbolic value to all these pretty young ladies today, we're going to force ourselves to set aside our natural good manners and let Ms. Shaw here pay the cheque. I figure the governor can afford it better'n we can, anyway." He placed it directly in front of her, smiling slyly, back to form.

Susan opened her billfold and set her personal Platinum Card on the table with a loud snap. "I'm sure the governor would be delighted—but this one's on me, boys."

That was pure Barbara Stanwyck.

They chuckled appreciatively. She downed the remaining Scotch in her glass. "And if no one seriously objects, I'd like to buy another round for the table."

No one did.

She declined their offer of an escort to her car, saying her goodbyes before excusing herself to the ladies' powder room. She wanted an opportunity to look around a bit on her own. She came upon a small room done up as a kind of library, its walls lined with glass trophy cases, and stepped just inside the doorway to study a collection of framed photographs hung on one wall.

One of them was of a large gathering, in front of another clubhouse a long way from here. Pillars and porches and southern flowering bougainvillea. It looked like it might have been taken in the early sixties. At the centre of the group, there was someone who resembled a boyish Jack Nicklaus. Beside him, a taller man stood with his arm thrown across Nicklaus's shoulder. She moved closer. Perhaps it *was* Lewis Stephens, forty years ago.

"Ah, you've found it too." A greeting coming from someone half hidden in a large leather wing chair near the window. A youngish, well-dressed man. He smiled at her now.

They seemed to be the only two people left in the place. "Found . . . ?" she said.

"Surely you must have noticed the same thing—that even in the most exclusive of places, you can *always* find at least one more private room, reserved for those who know just where to look. Whereas people like that"—the man casually indicated the faces in the photographs watching them from the wall—"they'd rather spend their time looking at images in the rear-view mirror and trying to convince themselves that they're still driving forward." He tipped his head to the side like a bright schoolboy with the only right answer. "As they say, nostalgia ain't what it used to be."

Susan offered him a neutral smile. "Lovely traditions, though . . ." She edged carefully towards the door. Whoever he was, he was making her uneasy.

"More *illusions,* Ms. Shaw," he said. "All of this, in fact—nothing more than an abandoned stage set, isn't it? A museum of leftovers. Bricks and mortar. Like bridges and highways, yards and rails. A pleasant deception, at best. Just look around you here, for example. It's a theme park. An historical re-creation. They still want to celebrate something else that came and went a long time ago. But surely not the future—yours *or* mine I hope."

His singsong patter was becoming grating. And he obviously knew who she was. She could feel a new kind of apprehension.

"It *is* far better to be inside, though, isn't it?" he said, gazing around the small library again. "Safe in our own little tree house, I mean."

It was exactly the phrase she'd thrown off at lunch. She quickly tried to recall those dining at the other tables. Had he been there?

His quiet voice floated to her again. "I understand that Dr. Mallick's recent passing might have some serious implications for you."

It was the name and the casual way he said it that really shook her. "And what would those be, Mr. . . . ?" She knew she was holding her breath now. It was her old childhood response to dread.

He waited another moment, looking at her without saying anything, then shrugged. "Well, then—perhaps only for me. For Cross Corp. I'm sure you've heard about their offer to create a little start-up here in town? This sceptred isle, this other Eden, demi-paradise. This blessed plot, this earth, this realm. This . . . Lockport." And he was smiling at her again.

Georgia had only mentioned something about medical research. So, this was the connection. "Frankly, I don't see any particular 'implications,' as you put it—at least, from my perspective," she answered crisply. Her mind was already processing a million bits of information. "Though, of course, I'd understand it if the company found the option less than attractive, after what's happened. Dr. Mallick's involvement provided a significant incentive."

She was making it up as she went along. Cross Corp's name had never been raised, at least not in any meeting she'd attended. And certainly not in relation to Leah Mallick. But an important link was starting to make sense . . .

Inexplicably, he looked pleased. "And as we know, Dr. Mallick is, unfortunately, no longer involved." He drummed his thin fingers on the arm of his chair, still looking at her. The room was quiet enough that she could clearly hear his manicured nails striking the leather.

She finally took a deep breath. The slight dizziness seemed to go away. "Be that as it may, I'm unlikely to have much to say about it, Mr. . . . ?"

"Starr," he replied. "Michael Starr."

"Mr. Starr . . ." She hesitated before continuing. "From what I understand, Cross Corp already owns several of the largest health-services companies in America. Lockport would be fortunate to get it—or any *part* of it."

"You're right, Ms. Shaw. You *do* have very little to say about it." His smile was really more like an involuntary contraction, she saw now. "But you could. I mean, if together we want to *encourage* the continued economic health of this city, this state . . .

"Cross Corp, as I expect you're well aware, is a company with combined assets exceeding twenty-five percent of the world's national economies. It is very able to negotiate the complexities of modern global markets, well beyond the reach of any *one* jurisdiction—local, state *or* national. Nothing so mundane as bricks and mortar to worry about *there.* It can go anywhere. Anywhere in the world. But I will tell you, they're here now. And I think they'd like to stay here."

Starr looked up at her from his wingback chair. His eyes were hidden by a reflection cast across his glasses from the low sun streaming through the library's window.

"I remember reading something very interesting once," he said, "about a kind of plant organism—it was called mycorrhizae. A species of symbiotic growth that both lives off and feeds living material. The term actually describes the interdependent relationship between the two—what they call 'mutualism.' All these threads of fungal hyphae spreading outward, underground. Someone once measured a single specimen—it covered almost two square miles. Imagine that. Two square miles . . ."

He took a sip from the short cut-crystal glass. "And in the end, it turns out that it's absolutely essential to the functioning and feeding of at least three-quarters of the seed plant species on the surface of the earth—virtually everything that we see and touch. Completely essential, and completely invisible at the same time. Irreplaceable. And if that special relationship were to be severed, if that *specific* mutualism were to be disturbed or compromised, maybe through ignorance or malice, all the other things that so completely depend upon it, all the things that we can actually *see* and most care about, would simply fade away too. No matter how solid they might once have appeared to us.

"Each requires the other, you see. Most people don't even know it's there, yet it's what makes all the rest of this possible." He seemed taken again by the idea, a dreamlike quality in his voice. Then, a shade more darkly, "*We're* the big thing you can't see. And if we're disturbed—through ignorance or malice—everything that depends on *us* can certainly be made to disappear too. Is that maybe a little clearer?"

At that moment, as if on cue, both of them heard the whistle from Palladian Steel, faint, almost three miles from where they were now. Illusion or not, it still sounded solid and real to her—like the cry of a dying giant. And when it finally stopped forever, Lockport would become completely vulnerable.

"Leah Mallick was beautiful and intelligent. Few would choose to resist her attractions. I'm sure several people will be talking about her for years." He indicated the ancient photographs on the wall again. "But we both know that nostalgia can be fatal. And so very much depends upon the invisible . . ." His face was open and bland. "Let her go. You already have exactly what you need here, Susan. Another chance. Take what you know and *use* it this time. Let that be enough. You'll be inside again. And these boys won't know what hit them."

She stood still for a long moment, her eyes scanning the vast display of yellowing framed photos. Her mind drifted only to one irrelevant thought. "It's funny, though. They still believe that Jack Nicklaus is going to come." She said it almost to herself.

"Sounds like that old Beckett play, doesn't it—'Waiting for Jack'?" He gave her a sly smile. "Well, he might . . . if *I* asked him," Starr said.

Susan took the long way around. She pulled off the swing bridge and turned towards the sun, finding the old highway that went twenty miles away down the valley. After a while she saw signs for the freeway interchange coming up ahead.

It would take only a couple of hours and she'd be back in the capital, able to forget all this. Lay out a better, brighter future. Make the necessary phone calls. Start by sending a carefully worded message to Acton's new campaign director: "Cross Corp looks like a very interesting idea. I've got some thoughts on it . . ."

Then every one of her calls would be returned. And invitations would flow again. And she'd never be left out of another meeting. Susan glanced at herself critically in the rear-view mirror. She still had options . . .

The entrance to the interstate was a quarter-mile ahead now. She flicked on her right-hand turn signal.

In only a couple of hours she would be walking back into her expensively furnished, tastefully appointed apartment, the glow from the capital dome still shining brightly through the window. And start calling people. And promise to leave the ground undisturbed beneath their feet.

She steered the car over the line and moved smoothly into the exit lane.

If Leah were still alive, things might be different. It wouldn't even be a question; all Cross Corp would have to do was wait in the shadows, while Leah subtly swayed the political will towards some new plan for public policy. They'd already given her Health and Human Services.

Susan yanked the steering wheel hard to the left, her tires spinning in the low verge of grass. The driver following too close behind had to swerve sharply on to the rough shoulder to avoid her. He flipped her the finger as he flew by.

Her own car skidded a few feet, then gripped pavement again, back on the main highway, looping gracefully up and over the cloverleaf, curving around to take her back towards Lockport instead.

Someone else could water her plants for a little while longer.

Yes, Leah Mallick was dead. But little else had changed. In fact, maybe it was all going exactly according to plan.

8

They'd agreed to meet back at the hotel.

"Pour yourself a drink. There's some wine . . ." Susan excused herself to change in the bedroom.

Annie looked around. While the suite itself still looked shabby, she saw that Susan had added a few distinctive touches of her own: fresh flowers, a set of wineglasses, a portable stereo playing a Gershwin CD. Obviously used to travelling first-class.

A moment later Susan returned, now wearing plain linen slacks and a black turtleneck, glove-soft leather flats.

It's always so simple for women like that, Annie thought. Throw on any old thing . . ."I gather that's what cashmere is supposed to look like," she said.

Susan picked at her sweater with a small, self-conscious smile. "To tell you the truth, I've got five just like it. It's easier that way—I don't even think about it." She noticed that Annie had ignored the bar. "So, can I get you something? Evian?"

Annie nodded. "Thanks. Sure."

Susan began to describe her impressions of the meeting—Lewis Stephens, Island Boys et al. It was a typically dry presentation: time, place, those in attendance, a complete and accurate summary of what was said. It was only when she got to their tangled involvement with Tim Mallick, when she actually slowed enough to become aware of it, she saw that Annie had started to grin.

Then, surprising herself, she began to play to it: the golf course sinking beneath the waves, the shooting range blasting away right outside the window. The ritual of the swing bridge. Waiting for Jack. She even came out with a decent imitation of Lewis Stephens issuing his threat against the governor and illustrated it with a thump on the coffee table hard enough to make the glasses jump.

At that, Annie finally collapsed sideways on the couch, doubled over with laughter. It was a minute before she could speak. "I'm sorry—but you have to understand how funny this is. These are the same people who've been running this town since I was a kid. Who ran the entire *world,* as far as I knew. Lording over it all from their little thrones on that Xanadu they built themselves. And they end up getting taken by a guy who was selling air."

"I guess it *was* fairly weird," Susan said, laughing as well.

Annie shook her head and took a deep breath as she wandered to the window. From here she could see all the way to the lake, fifty miles distant. This was a view she'd always envied, at a time when the "penthouse suite" at the Creighton Hotel meant something. No more. "For more years than I can even remember," she said, "it was always some version of 'what do the boys say?' You couldn't move around here without asking yourself that. Now it turns out there's nothing on that island that even matters any more.

It's nothing but *The Wizard of Oz,* and Lew Stephens is just 'The Little Man Behind the Curtain.'" She turned to look at Susan. "It was a bad idea to send you there. DeVries was right. It has nothing to do with Leah Mallick."

Susan could hear under the disappointment in Annie's voice. This wasn't just about a dead lead. She understood. Illusions—even the treacherous ones—were hard to let go. At least the Island Boys were something you could see. Susan turned away, concentrating on the arrangement of the few items set out on her desk.

"But it's the only way I could've confirmed what I suspected," Susan said quietly.

Annie didn't react at first, just rubbed her eyes wearily. The pain pill was starting to wear off and she knew there were no more at home. "Oh, yeah? And what's that?"

"That it isn't true what they're saying about him now. Tim Mallick hadn't 'lost his mind,' or whatever it is they claim happened," she said quietly.

"How do you know that?"

"Mallick committed fraud—more than once." Susan poured herself another glass of wine. "But for each of the plays he ran, it was always the same series of steps, never varying. First one, then the next. A strategy. Essentially, an execution menu . . ."

Patterns again. Returning always to the comfort of that same place. Abruptly, Annie grabbed a pen from the desk and held it out to her. "Show me."

Susan hesitated, then took the pen and began to sketch out a series of intersecting circles. "OK. Part of it's what you call a Perpetual Loop—you set things up so that you're selling and buying simultaneously, without providing underlying assets to support the trade. Just a modern version of cheque kiting, right? But in this case it serves to create an illusion of rising revenues so you can juice the quarterly reports and meet financial projections in support of increased stock prices."

She filled in the circles with a few names, arrows leading back to the centre and punched it with the tip of her pen. "Some of it's simple arbitrage—taking advantage of a spread in buy and sell prices. But in this case, they create counterparties to serve as both customers and suppliers . . . to themselves. That's the 'Loop' part. They created a phantom problem, then solved it by manipulating emissions reduction schedules. Gaming the system.

"With open-market trading, they arrange payments in advance on emissions reductions schedules, then buy CO_2 credits later from companies operating offshore in developing countries—with minimal verification processes or regulatory review. Without quantification protocols, they could take, say, Russia's 'hot air' credits—the billions in surplus that were created when their own economy collapsed in the early nineties—convert them into Euro credits and trade them on the open market for something else, like high-value benzene emissions in non-attainment areas in this country. Apples for oranges. The legal right to pollute. Traded for the allowance schedule on a facility that was never going to be built in the first place—"

"Whoa!" Annie looked shell-shocked. "I don't have a clue what you're talking about. Where does Tim Mallick come in?"

"They create these off-book companies with nothing but paper going back and forth. Taking a small percentage with each trade—but remember we're talking billions. And with each exchange they can show new revenues on the books. Then they launch it as an IPO, allocating offering shares to friends or family, various of the fund managers involved, before they come on market, and take the spread when the price goes up. Pump and dump. That's usually where the biggest profit is realized. At least, it would have been—before the sector crash."

She saw Annie looking almost fearfully at the diagram she'd drawn. She set it aside with a faint smile. "Look, what's important is that he did it the same way each time. Same parameters, same procedures, right down to the computer software systems entries. Every transaction, every play. What he'd presented to those guys was no different. He was going to use one of these 'phantom companies,' then, basically 'franchise' it back to them, after taking out various management expenses and 'nuisance fees' by working both sides of the transaction. As long as no one along the way called the paper . . . the whole thing was built on a virtual commodity, manufactured out of thin air. It didn't exist. But his real problem came with the crash—because IPOs on the NASDAQ were suddenly being suspended left and right. It pushed their own payout too far downstream. They were going to have to trade on the actual value of the ERCs—the Emission Reduction Credits. And only after someone *else* made a lot of money. And if the ratification of the Kyoto Accord is further delayed—"

"But you're that sure of all this?"

"About him? Annie, it would hold up in court."

Annie studied all the lines and arrows, the circles drawn around names, a list made up of code words. "What you're saying is that this is what he *always* did."

"Well, your Mr. Stephens actually provided the one new piece—that Tim Mallick was 'trying to play catch-up' with his wife. I think maybe that's true. If she was on her way up, he got worried she might leave him behind. So maybe he was looking for a way to make a quick killing this time. Everyone got greedy. The important thing is, I don't see 'diminished capacity' in any of this."

"But you're also telling me that what he put together—fraud or not—should have worked eventually. So how did they lose all that money?"

Susan got up from the desk and walked to the window. She stared out, watching the sun set over the river, Palladian Steel outlined in fiery red.

"I don't think they did." She set her glass of wine aside and broke open a bottle of twenty-year-old Scotch, automatically filling two tumblers with ice. She poured a heavy shot into each, setting one in front of Annie, sipping on the other as she paced about the room for a moment.

Annie eyed the glass carefully but left it untouched.

"Do you remember that old game of pick-up sticks kids play? You remove one. Then another. Until . . ." She seemed lost in thought, then shook her head firmly and turned back to Annie. "When things started turning down, they were left holding something that wouldn't pay off for maybe twenty years. Well, I think someone found out just how long it was really going to be to turn a profit.

And wanted the deal to collapse." Susan remembered the faces of old men who couldn't afford to wait forever. "There *was* one way to make quick money from that deal."

"How?"

Susan stood completely still. "If they knew that *that* was going to be closed," she said quietly.

Annie glanced in the direction she was pointing, confused. "What? What do you mean?"

Susan turned away from the window and looked at her. "They intend to shut down the plant. Permanently."

Annie paled. "Palladian Steel?" She couldn't be serious . . . "*Who* is?"

"It's been in the works for almost a year. Replace outmoded manufacturing with a new technology hub. Supposedly, no one knew about it. But it's the only thing that would make a new play work. If you can close down a traditionally high source of environmental pollution, you get not only the capital losses, but high-quality ERCs. Emission Reduction Credits. Which you *can* sell on the domestic energy market. For cash."

"So, if someone found out about that—"

"Then worthless options could suddenly be worth a great deal." Especially purchased with someone else's money. Susan noticed that Annie hadn't picked up her glass. "Not your brand?"

Annie glanced aside for a moment. "Actually, I don't drink much any more."

Susan said nothing, raised an eyebrow slightly.

"I used to . . . a long time ago. In fact, I developed a bit of a problem with it."

Susan removed the glass and set it on the bar. "Sorry. Could I get you something else, then? Some more water? A soda?"

Annie shook her head, nervously running her fingers through her hair several times. "Turns out I'm statistically susceptible." She forced a laugh. "One of the Big Three—cops, stockbrokers, doctors."

Susan sat down again, saying nothing. She set the diagram aside.

"It wasn't that hard to quit after all. Like anything, I guess—if you have the right motivation." Annie sighed and smiled at her. "You know how it is. You gave up smoking, right?"

"Frequently," Susan replied dryly.

"Yeah. Well, then you understand." Annie stood and picked up her briefcase, "Anyway, I should probably get going." She picked up the page of notes. "Mind if I keep this?"

"Sure." Susan smiled. "It's completely illegal but you could make a killing in the stock market with something like that. Sell Palladian short on insider information."

"Then I guess I'm lucky I don't even know what that means . . ." Annie laughed again. But Susan sensed a cloud of tragedy was sweeping past her.

The drinking problem wasn't the only issue, Susan knew; it just explained a few things. "We could . . . talk . . . if you like. I've got nothing to do tonight. We could discuss what to do next. Have dinner . . . ?"

Annie stood with her hand on the door. She couldn't even remember the last time she'd done that—just sat and talked with someone. "Thanks. Not tonight. I've got a lot to try to absorb. With all this." The sun had already set and Palladian was nothing but a silhouette now. "That place, you know—it's what put Lockport on the map. For five generations. And they're going to shut it down, just like that."

Susan nodded, her throat tightening unexpectedly. "Yeah, they are."

Annie pulled the door open. She spoke without looking at her. "You know, you can ask *me* what it is you really want to ask too." Then the door closed.

Susan sat and finished the glass of Scotch, then poured herself another. After a few minutes she went into the bedroom for a separate portfolio, pulling out an unmarked file. She opened it, and a pile of copied newspaper pages slid into her lap and spilled out on to the couch.

Anne Shannon as a young patrol officer in a twenty-year-old photo. Annie named as the Lockport police department's first communications director. Others, from times in between—detailing high-profile arrests and homicide convictions. There was more. Notice of a commendation—several of them. A recent ceremony honouring her regional Communicator of the Year award.

One large photograph showed Annie at a funeral, surrounded by a circle of officials, adrift in a sea of cops. Her hand was bandaged, and the city's mayor of ten years ago was holding it carefully as he comforted her for the loss of her only child.

The personnel record told a different story. A series of short suspensions. Mandatory counselling following several minor traffic accidents. The record of it eventually expunged.

But nothing ever really disappeared, Susan knew—not if you knew where to look. "Deleted" didn't mean "gone" any more.

If Annie Shannon really wanted to rewrite the past or create a more palatable truth for herself, she'd already forfeited that possibility. It was too late. What drove her forward had also led her back. And Susan felt nothing but sympathy.

Sitting in front of the TV, Annie felt comfortable enough to pour herself a glass of chilled white wine for supper. And another glass or two, maybe, since.

The only hard part had been to find an open liquor store in a part of town where the clerk wouldn't automatically check her out when she entered, wouldn't bother looking up as she paid for it, didn't watch the news but wanted her gone so he could get back to the demolition derby on the small TV under the counter.

She was busy now, studying the performance of her replacement. They'd put in a staff sergeant, Stan Kendra, who looked completely terrified as he gave the details of some convenience store holdup.

Too military and *way* too intense, in her opinion. No one had been hurt. It wasn't a big deal. But his brief appearance on the broadcast was filled with the kind of jargon and circular statements that made them all sound like bureaucrats with guns—an impression she'd worked hard to change over the last year and a half. She hoped the media missed her.

Stan Kendra. Jesus Christ. What are they thinking?

It was obvious, too, that he was taking specific direction from the top. At least once or twice, Annie heard a DeVries-style remark coming out of his mouth. He'd find that wouldn't work for long. Temporary substitute at best, she told herself.

She knew she had nothing to worry about. Three generations of cops—both grandfathers, several uncles, cousins, brothers. That was a guarantee of permanent employment in this town. Short of shooting the president, or some member of the country club.

Well, she reminded herself with a laugh, *that* was still an option . . .

Annie poured herself another glass, surprised to find that the bottle of wine was already three-quarters empty. But at least it's still one-quarter full, she thought. Ever the optimist.

~~~

After more than four hours, Susan had found next to nothing. No matter how far she dug, she could establish no substantial financial connections between Cross Corp and the Mallicks. A few insignificant details one could point to, a couple of instances where they held a minor position in one of Cross Corp's subsidiary companies. Easily dismissed as nothing more than coincidence. But anything tracked
~~~

directly to either of them was effectively irrelevant in any case; the percentages involved were infinitesimal. These people, these golden people, weren't what anyone would ever have called players. At least on the surface.

Quite the contrary. Over the last two years the Mallicks' personal wealth had neatly evaporated, declining by the time of their deaths to nothing more than a registered family trust holding ownership in the home and a conservative portfolio of blue-chip investments—barely over a million dollars in total. Nowhere near what anyone might have been led to expect, looking from the outside. Neither Mallick, husband *or* wife, appeared to have benefited, at least in the short term, from any particular ties to Cross Corp.

But that wasn't the whole truth, Susan was sure of it. The potential of real wealth was wrapped up somewhere else; she would have bet on stock options. Leah Mallick would have been uniquely well-positioned to negotiate a big piece of any high-tech start-up built around new state program proposals. And, as Secretary of Health and Human Resources . . .

Abruptly, the Internet connection failed, the fourth time in the last hour. Damn hotel phone system. Probably happened every time more than one person called out for pizza . . . *Fuck.*

She waited impatiently for the dial-up again. Infuriatingly long beeps and clicks and bubbles of noise.

Throughout the rest of the night Susan followed search strings to a variety of Web sites. The most frequent links were those taking her to universities, particularly the ones attached to medical schools. A few independent political coalitions.

She tried every word and phrase she could think of: "HMOs", "palliative care." "End-stage medicine." The legal definitions of "terminal" and "informed consent," the difference between "active" and "passive." Nothing drawing a connection between Cross Corp and revived efforts to develop a national health-care policy. Sure, maybe the Senate Majority leader derived most of his own fortune from stock held in one of Cross Corp's for-profit health-management organizations, but . . .

As she'd expected, Cross Corp's own site was completely irrelevant. Pure, unadulterated PR. "We offer integrated support to the patient in an ongoing partnership with the most advanced state-of-art technology . . . it's like a family." If you wanted something more, something *substantive,* you found yourself directed to a 1-800 number. Which, of course, would be tracked. There was a section marked "Restricted Area." Given some time, of course, it wasn't impossible . . . But there was no mention of any Michael Starr in the corporate profiles, board of directors, company officers, or anywhere else she looked.

Susan finished her seventh cup of coffee in two hours. That probably explained the slight buzz—and the unusual appearance of the words lined up across the screen, all slanting to the left.

She stood up and stepped away from the desk. What did I really expect? she thought. That they would lay it all out, like a prospectus?

She ran through the list again in her head: Cross Corp is a major world-class corporation, used to aggressive lobbying. Instead, they offer a start-up research facility in a place far away from every major centre. Deliberately, very quietly, *very* low-key. Where they can be the sole saviour of a whole city in danger of fading away. I'm the last bureaucratic level, and they've made it this far without attracting attention . . .

Cross Corp owned not only several of the largest HMOs in the country, it was also one of the biggest medical services companies in the world. Manufacturers of medical equipment and supplies, pharmaceuticals, research, laboratory testing, information technologies—everything. Complete vertical integration.

A prospectus. *Dammit, that's exactly what they* would *do.*

If they really wanted to propose a large-scale change in the delivery of health care services, they would start by getting the corporate line in place. Memos, videos, political backgrounders, academic forums, surveys, economic reports ready to leak out of hand-picked or newly assembled think-tanks—whatever it took to package the essential talking points, however they chose to frame them. They would talk about the good of the many . . .

They'd look for someone to design a broad process to manufacture consent, and find a way to do it with mathematical certainty.

The sun was starting to come up when Susan began posting innocuous messages in various chat rooms.

It was almost impossible for her to reconcile the image of the dead woman in the autopsy photograph with the same person who'd spoken so easily of Aaron Copland's music or Robert Stern's architecture or Arthur Laffer's infamous economic bell curve, the night of that dinner party.

There'd been only ten of them at the table for the evening. By coincidence, Leah Mallick's husband, Tim, had been Susan's dinner partner. With his slightly affected stutter and prep-school drawl, he'd reminded her of Tony Blair. His left leg jumped under the table in constant motion, his face perpetually bright and animated. He'd continually used his fingers to stuff bits of food into his mouth—pieces of bread or meat—all the while setting out an impressive analysis of the UN's failures in Kosovo and Rwanda.

Leah on the other hand, had reminded Susan of no one. Brilliant white-blue eyes, a strong jawline, what one would characterize as classic northern European features. A natural ash blonde. She'd seemed tall too. The post-mortem put her at barely five foot four.

The biggest surprise, though, was her disarming modesty. Obviously accomplished and well off, certainly beautiful, Leah Mallick was particularly gracious, thoughtful and soft-spoken, even in the few comments Susan overheard at dinner. There was nothing of the noblesse oblige one might have expected in looking at her.

As the evening progressed, the atmosphere became less formal, more convivial, if somewhat competitive. Conversation ranged freely in all directions. Far from accepting the conventional etiquette to avoid religion and politics, most dinner guests, that night, could barely wait until the main course was served to get at it. The publisher of the *Tribune,* a known provocateur according to his own wife, began the debate by casually scorning the governor's proposed balanced budget initiative. He glanced deliberately in Susan's direction as he spoke. Like most others in the room, he was well aware of her rumoured liaison with Thomas Acton.

Susan had prepared herself. These evenings, she'd quickly discovered, were rarely "social" in the narrow sense of the word. In the salons of the capital, politics was all anyone ever wanted to talk about. Most times, she thought, they were like a bunch of Iowa farmers discussing commodity prices and the weather every time they met up at the local feed store.

"If the governor were really committed to a balanced budget act, he wouldn't have allowed that 'Buckthorn Bob' amendment, for one thing." Everyone who was listening chuckled.

Robert Fiedler Johnston was a nursery grower isolated on the northern fringes of the state, always out and about promoting the next cash crop. Despite, or maybe because of, his crackpot reputation, Johnston had somehow managed to champion a populist amendment adding the cultivation of cannabis intended for medical use to the omnibus budget bill before the state legislature. It was all the press had been focusing on for more than a week.

"From what I hear, there's a whole bunch of those folks running around up there in the north woods, creating real businesses worth more than all the legitimate potato farmers put together. I don't want 'em arrested—I just want to *tax* 'em. Eliminate some of these damn loopholes, at least." The publisher looked lazily at her again.

"Though I'm sure you must have been relieved there were still enough loopholes to drive your fifty thousand tons of Japanese newsprint through," Susan said, more sharply, in response. These people never wanted the law to apply to *them*.

The publisher's smile became somewhat strained. Then his own wife leaned across him to laugh loudly, and a little drunkenly, with someone on his other side.

Susan watched his eyes as the expression in them toughened.

He pushed his chair back slightly. "OK. You're projecting the debt to go to what—fifty-one percent against GDP? It's an accounting sleight of hand. No matter what you're trying to tell us. You're just waiting for some phantom expansion to reduce the debt ratio and float yourselves to Fantasy Island, and it ain't gonna happen. Most of the cutting you're taking credit for is coming from program downloads, anyway, to county and urban councils. Where's the real tax cut? Net spending has gone up at least three and a half every year since you guys took office. You're blowing smoke up *all* our asses. It's just electioneering, like everything else conceived by this weak-kneed administration. If you'd put the money out there in the market when Morgan Stanley first *told* you to, the debt'd be a thing of the past."

Normally, at this point, Susan would have been perfectly willing to concede that it wasn't her area of specialty. In another ten seconds she knew she'd be swimming well out of her depth. Then she'd have to remind them how the Secretary of Commerce so *rarely* consulted with her before releasing the annual state budget . . .

At that very moment, though, Leah Mallick caught Susan's eye and gave her a slow smile before turning to address the publisher.

"As a strategy, that can be fairly risky. Orange County tried it," Leah said casually. "Bonds. Actually, options on the foreign markets. And they got so completely addicted to all the rising revenues that they couldn't stop, even when they were warned. They just kept cheering from the sidelines. Until they were so exposed, they couldn't hold their position. Someone working all alone—"

The publisher stopped in confusion. "Someone working—?"

"The county treasurer, I think. He had them wholly vested with a highly leveraged position in reverse purchase agreements, inverse floaters—derivatives. When the inevitable downturn hit—nothing more than a temporary glitch, as it turned out—when that happened, they panicked, and locked in a loss of somewhere in the neighbourhood of $1.7 billion. And with that, of course, went several years of school renovations and kids' immunization programs and community centre staffing. I understand they still can't borrow on the short-term market."

"But my point is, they got over it," the publisher said. "There's a big boom going on out there now."

Leah Mallick nodded agreeably. "True. For now. But what I found much more interesting about it all was that, even when they asked everyone involved—the county CFO, the administrative officer, everyone right up to the Board of Supervisors, even the auditors—how could you let that happen? how could you give one bureaucrat—one person—carte blanche to risk public confidence on a throw of the dice? Do you know what they said?" She paused for a split second. "'We just thought he was smarter than all of us. He seemed to understand everything so much above and beyond what we did, that we didn't feel that we could question him.'"

There were a few glances exchanged around the table. Then the publisher leaned towards her. "OK. So, Doctor, gun to *your* head, then—what's the expert diagnosis?" His grin was wolfish. You've given us the lead, his look said, you owe us the wrap.

"I'd see it as the wilful isolation of one individual—someone who was encouraged, even supported, to construct a separate, almost completely self-perpetuating reality. It isn't particularly unusual at that level. Maybe a cliché, but I'd say it's as simple as he ended up believing his own press. Always dangerous. But this one happened to be holding 'the red handle.'" She smiled at him directly.

The publisher looked around at the other guests. "So, it sounds like we should be insisting that all government officials meet with a good psychiatrist before they're appointed," he said in an acid tone.

Leah Mallick responded evenly. "You don't have to *meet* someone to know them," she said. She matched his self-satisfied smile with a small upward curve of her lip. "They could have considered something else—maybe a series of international equity index-linked notes for net performance on a couple of the exchanges, without any direct foreign currency exposure. But a ten-point spread on the Swiss franc? Come on! I'm a psychiatrist—I know 'crazy' when I see it." A pause. Then she laughed lightly and after another moment everyone joined in, delighted. And impressed.

Later, when they'd all removed to the living room, Susan found herself seated beside Leah Mallick. The newspaper publisher, now making a concerted effort to charm, approached and presented a cognac to each of them with a practised flourish. Then he settled himself into an armchair placed at an easy angle to the sofa, eager to continue the debate.

"I think you stand alone on this balanced budget initiative, Doctor. After all, it was opposed, in its original form, by members on both sides of the House."

Susan couldn't recall that Leah had come out either in support of or in opposition to the budget proposition. In fact, she'd deliberately moved the discussion away from that question. It didn't seem to matter to the publisher, however. As Susan watched now, she fully expected Leah to once again steer the conversation to something less contentious. She could well-afford to "make nice" after all. Clearly, the man was already wrapped around her finger. Anyone else would have called it a draw, accepting that as an appropriate social strategy.

For a moment that's what it looked like she was going to do. Leah Mallick tilted her head slightly, the light blue eyes sparkling at him with some subtle amusement, a shared understanding.

But apparently she'd been taking it easy till now.

Leah began to review the last three years of the state's budgetary process. Her knowledge was wide-ranging and exhaustive. With effortless assurance she led him through the key details, including the voting records of each of the legislators involved in the Ways and Means Committee.

Then, with another bright smile, she wrapped it up. "And anyway, from what I understand, this state already has a lower ratio of public-capital expenditures to GDP than any of its major industrial competitors," she said. "That doesn't tend to encourage much confidence in the money markets either."

The publisher found himself wanting to counter, but suddenly aware that he couldn't. He was comfortable, even assured, dealing in the easily accessible tales of who owed whom what favours, who was getting screwed, who was doing the screwing. That's what do's like this were meant for, he knew; he wasn't invited for what was in his newspaper, but for what was left out.

In a matter of minutes Leah had presented him with a damning indictment of his own paper's position—and done it in a way to lend the discussion a certain ironic twist, appearing to include him in the joke. It was only a game. He could decide to play or not.

Susan watched him pause, silent for a moment. She'd met him several times before and at every gathering he liked to trot out his favourite quote from Henry Adams, that practical politics consisted in ignoring facts. Leah Mallick hadn't ignored the facts, but she'd certainly beaten him at the politics. Maybe later, the publisher would be able to refer to their one encounter as a "conversation"—even a "stimulating" one. But he'd never admit that he himself had said nothing for most of it. Not aloud, anyway.

On that winter night, as the publisher drifted away again, the two women remained seated on the small couch.

Leah moved slightly to face Susan. "We're so new to town, I don't know whom to offend first."

"Him? Oh, I don't think he was," Susan said.

Leah merely smiled, shrugged.

Then they had the usual discussion about movies and art and fashion. Or perhaps it had been epic poetry and quantum mechanics and the Protestant Reformation. Afterwards, Susan couldn't quite remember everything. The wine, the warmth, the perfume.

But once, she found herself glancing over Leah's shoulder. And she saw that Tim Mallick was all alone for just a moment, pressing himself tightly against the far wall. He looked utterly confused, almost terrified. Leah followed her gaze, and in an instant had left her seat and stepped to his side.

Leah attempted to draw him into a small alcove beside the bookcase. Her bare back was to the room, her pink silk gown glowing in the corner. Tim was unsteady, his expression a kind of snarl as he leaned down to her and said something. It was obvious he was drunk. Then he reached out with one hand and roughly grabbed Leah's breast through the bodice of her gown as he sloppily kissed her. She seemed to accept it. In fact, it was he who straightened away from her first, separating from the aspect of couple they had formed, and moved out from behind her protection.

Susan stared, shocked—the sole witness to the incident. Still, she expected to see some indication of distress when Leah turned around—some slight embarrassment, discomfort, even annoyance, perhaps. Instead, she watched as Leah moved quietly through the room towards their hostess, her face clear and untroubled.

"It's been a wonderful evening," she said. "But we've both got a very early day tomorrow, so we'll say our good-byes now." The hostess leaned over for the requisite social peck, genuinely regretting that her trophy couple was leaving already. Leah cast her smile in the general direction of the room. "Good night everyone. It was a pleasure meeting all of you." The other guests murmured a soft chorus of farewells after them. Leah Mallick didn't look at Susan as she passed.

When they had left, one man commented that it was as though a light had gone from the room, then laughed self-consciously at his own hyperbole.

Half an hour later, Susan's escort, Peter Donovan, signalled that it was time for them to make their exit as well. After a few minutes he approached, her coat over his arm. The hostess protested. "But no," she wailed. "You can't all leave so soon. We're having such a lovely time." That was the generally understood hint for everyone to begin making their way to the door. A flurry of hugs and handshakes, backslaps, the discreet exchange of a few business cards.

Evenings like this, as someone once said, should be viewed as scientific exercises in plant grafting, measured by the number of connections that "took." Their hostess's batting average was considered high. One or two marriages of convenience invariably emerged from any single evening spent here, to be developed to further advantage somewhere down the road. Even tonight.

Peter's car was parked a half-block away, a brisk five-minute walk. It was a cold night, only a couple of days before Christmas, and the snow fell heavy and wet.

"Drink?" he suggested when they were inside the freezing car. The Four Seasons was just around the corner.

Susan shook her head. His interest wasn't something she chose to encourage. These things had a way of becoming complicated. He frowned slightly, conveying his disappointment by making a forceful U-turn in the middle of the empty street, then headed back towards her apartment. She gazed out at the swirl of white beyond the car's steam-covered windows.

"Did you have a chance to talk with Leah Mallick?" she asked casually. She could tell Peter was annoyed, but he was always ready to talk about work.

After a moment he responded. "The blonde? No. Interesting, though."

She smiled indulgently. "So why was *I* supposed to meet her tonight?" The invitation had come out of the blue—but it hadn't fooled her.

He grinned. "What an ego. You weren't the only two people there, you know."

"Perhaps. But I'd have to say it rather closely resembles one of your signature plays, Pete."

Donovan was Thomas Acton's chief of staff. He glanced over at her more fondly. "Sure I can't buy you that drink?" Susan smiled back. He sighed loudly. "OK. You know your health care commission? Well, some guy in the office who knows someone—blah, blah, blah—he suggested that we throw her name in the ring. Nothing much more than that. I just thought it was a good opportunity to take a look."

"Connections?"

"Her? Yeah, some. She got a lot of good local press a couple years ago in southern California. No grandstanding or anything, but she headed up a consolidation feasibility study on the delivery of long-term medical services for a LAFCO—a Local Agency Formation Commission—in Santa Barbara. The stats were pretty impressive. Possible consultant for us, if we hook up."

"Why are we looking for outside medical consultants?" Susan asked.

He hesitated before answering. "I guess I can tell you. We're thinking about trying to pull in some federal funding to support a new managed-care initiative. Instead of letting it all flow out of state in dividends."

She reacted with undisguised surprise. "A public non-profit?"

He shrugged. "At first. So far, we're calling it a co-venture. I mean, I don't think we're going to be able to build on the existing numbers for single-payer," he said, referring to the state senate vote, "not after that Clinton fuck-up. Yet."

She held herself very still, her voice even. "But next term—?" And why was this the first she was hearing about it? She'd always been in the room whenever they'd had these discussions in the past.

"Yeah. That's the thinking." He kept his eyes straight ahead, on the slushy street in front of them.

She was quiet long enough that Peter finally glanced over at her.

The windshield wipers could barely keep up with the thickly-falling snow. "What's her area, anyway? Her specialty?" she asked finally, if only to fill the silence.

"Mallick? Palliative care, I think."

"Does she know about it—the opening on the commission?" That sterling performance, then, was probably nothing more than a conscious attempt to woo some inside support.

"I don't think so. The recommendation actually came from one of the HMOs we're talking to."

Contrary what he'd just said about "some guy in the office," she thought. They neared her apartment. Susan stared hard into the darkness.

"Their numbers are really good. It could be important for us," Peter added after another moment.

"How serious are we about this, then—*her*, I mean?"

"Take a good look. Let me know what you think," he said finally. Clearly, they wanted her. "But it'll wait until after Christmas. Give yourself some time. Have a good holiday." He parked in front of her building, letting the car idle. The heater had finally warmed the interior.

It was already apparent, to her as it would have been to anyone, that Leah Mallick was perfect for a high-profile policy role. Comprehensive grasp of esoteric detail. Impressive in person without coming off as condescending—in fact, she seemed gracious and warm. Witty, in a detached, ironic sort of way. Even slightly reserved, which was most certainly to her benefit. She'd be completely irresistible to the major players in boardrooms. The display tonight assured Susan of that, if nothing else.

"I don't see why she'd be very interested in a one-time community committee," Susan said. "She *is* gorgeous, though, isn't she?"

Peter became serious for a moment. "I hardly noticed. You know I can never see anyone else when you're in the room." Then he tried to bury the remark in a short laugh.

She almost believed him this time. So used to rote compliments, she was sometimes overtaken by the rare one that had any semblance of sincerity. Peter's were infrequent enough to suggest that he meant what he was saying, at least in part. How anyone ever really got together in this town remained a mystery to both of them.

"Don't mind me. I'm just fishing," she said, laughing too, as she got out of the car. "Thanks."

Once inside, out of the storm, she poured herself another brandy and put on a CD—Dawn Upshaw performing Barber's "Knoxville: Summer of 1915." Delicate, searing, elegiac . . .

She realized, only then, that she had no idea what Leah Mallick thought—about balanced budget amendments or investments in suspect derivatives, let alone health care programs. But she'd witnessed her encyclopedic range of interests, the calm assurance, the complete willingness to dominate a room. Perhaps that had been the only point that needed to be made tonight. Or implied.

Though, long afterwards, there were two other things she remembered as well: that the blizzard shut down the capital for almost two full days that time. And it was the last social event the Mallicks ever attended.

~~~~

Annie had broken the only promise she'd made to herself in many years, and was again standing at Kyle's bedside. Maybe it was a dream. Then in that dream at least he was meant to open his eyes and look at her.

She forced herself to think objectively, to go as far as she could go—if necessary, to the very end of the road this time. What was the exact measure of his worth here? Was it only that either he would eventually wake up or he would eventually die? What of this time, of him, here and now? What value did that hold? And if he did awaken—and the dream began again with his return—what was he? A suicide's child, a murderer's second victim. No relatives or friends. Emotional problems, physical disabilities, mental incapacity. At best—a child growing to a man, but one left angry about loss and fate, survivor's guilt, nightmares and buried memories. The costs of hospitalization or incarceration, drugs to handle depression or just to dull the voice of the world. Treatment for the treatments, a drain on the system, on the psyche, driving drunk or pulling a gun during a robbery. Everyone would then agree that it would have been better if he'd never come back. If he'd just gone on.

In a time of miracles, he awakened. Annie watched him slowly open his eyes. They were blue, like her own, but so brilliant, they seemed almost white.

There, in that future, he was a bigot and an idealist, a repentant fundamentalist and an unrepentant atheist, a Republican demagogue and a Marxist revolutionary—both
~~~~

a cynic and a romantic, both light and darkness. Every child is already that and everything else, she thought. A mass of expectations and disappointments and limitations and countless scenarios. All doom and destiny wrapped up in being.

9

Annie sat on the edge of the examination table, watching her knee being forcibly manipulated by a physical therapist. There wasn't much she could do to resist him. He had the hands of a mechanic. She presumed he could have twisted iron bars with them. He moved the joint sideways, in a way she didn't think knees were intended to go. Then up and down. The cracking noises were deafening. "I think it always sounds like that," she said timidly.

"Uh-huh. Well, maybe you can actually start to do a few of those exercises I showed you. You know, the ones with the belt?"

Obviously, he meant that stretchy rubber thing she was supposed to attach to a doorknob somewhere and pull on until either it snapped or she did. How could he tell, just by looking, that she hadn't started yet?

In the next moment Annie let out a small shriek. She knew her knee wasn't supposed to go *that* way.

"Sorry," he said blandly. He didn't seem to be.

After another minute he picked up the form and signed it. It was her disability record, listing the only two incidents in her career; the other was pregnancy. He passed the form back for her initials. She was now officially cleared for a return to active service. *Not bloody likely.*

As she dressed, she checked her watch. Still early enough that she could probably blend in with the other visitors. The long-term care ward was on the far side of the hospital, four floors up, at the end of the longest corridor. As good a time as any to get some exercise.

Annie took the stairs. The knee wasn't the problem this time; it was that she had to stop for breath at every landing. She couldn't have done a 5 K now if they were all chasing her with a knife. You know you're middle-aged, she thought, when you can get out of shape in only five days.

She slipped past the desk on the ward, then stood outside Kyle's room, looking in, preparing to cross the threshold again. There was an orderly washing the floor, sliding his mop in a circular motion through a new tangle of cords and metal stands. He was completely unaware, it seemed, of the boy in the bed only a foot or two away.

The man was singing nonsense syllables to the tune of "Jesu, Joy of Man's Desiring." He dragged the bucket out behind him and set a sign in the doorway: *Caution. Wet Floor.* It was enough to stop her. But what was she really expecting to see, anyway?

Staff pushed lunch carts along the hallway. She knew they wouldn't come here. Three times a day, they could pass by this door without giving it a second glance. What was the point? Annie shook her head impatiently—as usual, she was asking too many questions of herself. Others were supposed to have answers too. She walked back to the counter. *Get used to this mug. You're going to see a lot more of it.*

A nurse looked up. "Can I help you?"

"Who do I talk to about Kyle Mallick? He's the one—"

The nurse stopped her with a look. "Don't you think you should leave well enough alone, Lieutenant Shannon."

"You know who I am." No surprise there, but it made the situation a little more complicated.

The nurse smiled tightly. "Oh, I think we *all* do by now. But then, we're not really used to celebrities in here." The sarcasm was intentional, the hostility perhaps less so.

Annie waited, one eyebrow raised. *And you can stick it straight up yer—*

The nurse was tense, trying to appear blasé. "Everyone gets the same treatment, no matter *who* they are. Or even who their mother might have been." Unusually brusque. Or maybe it was usual for her. How would Leah Mallick have handled someone like this?

"An interesting woman, I've heard," Annie said casually. Everyone seemed eager enough to talk about Leah Mallick, given half a chance. Here's yours, she thought. Please. Tell me about your own brush with greatness. "So you knew Dr. Mallick too?"

"No, actually I *didn't* know her, Lieutenant. She came here once or twice. Swanning through the ward like Lady Bountiful. Smiling in that oh so mysterious way of hers. Acting like she owned the place. She certainly didn't have the time of day for people like *us.* So, maybe I just happen to think that it's kind of ironic, him ending up in here, like that. And *her* being the one who did it to him." The nurse looked up at Annie again, her lips pursed. "And I know it's inappropriate to say anything, but maybe it serves her right. Arrogant . . ." She didn't have to finish the sentence.

But how the hell do you get to "serves her right"? Annie wondered. That wasn't Leah Mallick lying in that room. And what had happened to him was not some form of otherworldly justice; it was all too earthbound. And Leah herself well beyond the reach of such righteous indignation.

Annie glanced to the side. The other nurse was eavesdropping on them, her face a mask of careful indifference—except for the eyes. She didn't appear to agree with what was being said, but she turned away without adding anything of her own.

Annie knew there would be a shift change in another hour. Maybe that would offer a better opportunity. The hospital cafeteria was three floors down. She jammed herself into an elevator filled with a noisy gaggle of high-school candy stripers. All of them looking about thirteen, with the makeup and manner of jaded thirty-year-olds. One whined: "But if I want to get into Bennington, my mom says I've got to have some charity thing on my transcripts. How long do they make you stay here before you can use it?" Annie squeezed out past them at the next stop.

She could hear the sharp, ringing clatter of the cafeteria ahead of her, the only alive sound in the entire place. She threw something on the tray that looked like vegetable rice casserole and found a table by herself, along the line of windows at the side of the large, open room.

In the next minute, without warning, her temperature soared to a thousand degrees. She knew she was only moments away from spontaneous combustion—a nuclear reaction inside her cells, in five . . . four . . . three . . .

Through the blur Annie saw that the nurse—the silent one of the two from upstairs—had arrived in the cafeteria and was waiting in the cashier's lineup. And every few seconds she glanced over in Annie's direction.

Annie was fully occupied just trying to breathe. She could feel the heat rising in slow waves now, imagining the air currents above her head, like ripples from a hot street on a midsummer day. At a distance she probably looked like a desert mirage.

She didn't think of the nurse again until she heard her speak. "I just wanted to tell you—don't mind Scarlett, eh? Up on the floor? They told *all* of us not to talk to the police."

Annie read the name tag: *Florence Schellenberg*. Florence had pulled out a chair on the other side of the table and was already sitting down.

Annie wondered how widespread an order that was—

The nurse smirked. "I guess more specifically *you* . . ."

So, not all that widespread. Annie shrugged indifferently. "I'm just here for a checkup. The orthopaedics lab." The one that was practically a city block away, on another floor, on the opposite side of the building. Florence had to be kidding, anyway.

"Oh, yeah, I saw it on the news. How's that doing now? The leg."

"It's fine. I'll be back at work full-time next week." Annie could feel the heat radiating from every pore of her skin; everyone within ten feet of her should have been singed by it. She dipped a paper napkin in her ice water and blotted her upper lip.

The nurse tilted her head and squinted at her. "So, right in the middle of that happy time, eh? You're about, what . . . fifty-one, fifty-two? Try some black cohosh. It's an old herb, supposed to help regulate hot flashes. Here." She took a handful of napkins and poured half the glass of water over it. "Put this on the back of your neck."

Annie did, and it seemed to help a little.

Florence took her in wholly, with a practised eye. "You're kind of a mess, aren't you?" she said, not unkindly.

Annie laughed a little. "I'm a bit off my game right now. I just need to get back on a more regular schedule. Or something."

Florence looked unconvinced. Or maybe only uninterested. "Well, it happens, I guess." She busied herself with the plate of lasagne in front of her. A few bites, then she stopped again. "I have to admit it, you know. I didn't really think much about it till you came around, just now. But it *is* a weird coincidence, isn't it? Her own son ending up in the same place, like this? The same department? Eight years old. I guess no one would have ever predicted that one, eh?" The question seemed casual enough.

"What do you mean, the same department? She never *worked* here, did she?"

"No, but they brought her in a few times, as a consultant or something. A coupla days here and there. About a year ago. I think they were looking at maybe making some changes. Like, what else is new, eh? They're always futzin' around like that. Somehow it's never for the benefit of us worker bees, though, is it?

"But it's funny—it was right around that same time we were going through a bit of a rough patch ourselves. The last thing you need at that point is someone looking over your shoulder at everything with a fine-tooth comb, eh? I don't mean that she got in our way or anything. But one of our patients was in pretty bad shape—well, most of 'em are, I guess." She laughed a little at that. "And then he dies and all quiet hell breaks loose."

"There were concerns?"

"Oh, yeah, sure. At the time. They had their usual M&M behind closed doors—what they call a Morbidity and Mortality conference. But everyone must've answered all the questions right. Then it was just . . . over. Like." Florence left the sentence hanging in the air.

"Was she ever questioned?" Annie asked, as she suspected she was meant to.

Florence tried to look surprised. "Dr. Mallick? No, of course not. She wasn't on staff. She was nowhere in sight when it happened. There was no reason they had to speak to her. None at all."

No reason to speak *now* either, Annie thought, except perhaps to hear a private thought spoken aloud—to seek the comfort that came from that. "But you're thinking now that she might have been involved in some way?" Annie said.

Florence paused for a long moment. "I saw it happening." A short shrug.

"Saw what? What was there to see?"

Annie watched Florence steer the food around on her plate for a few more seconds. Then she peered up at Annie. "I gotta ask—how far is this going to go?" Something in her voice had slid underneath the flat, uninflected tone. Uneasiness?

"Go?"

Florence looked at her deliberately. "You're a police officer, Lieutenant. In case you haven't noticed."

Annie waved her hand impatiently. "I'm not here for that. I mean, I'm not even *involved* in investigations any more. Just a PR flack now, Florence." It was true.

The nurse glanced up at her with a trace of a smile.

"I'm a little curious about Leah Mallick, that's all." Annie added.

"Well, *she's* dead. But there might still be some people around who could be affected by this." She was watching Annie closely now.

Annie looked her straight in the eye, then shook her head slightly.

It seemed enough to satisfy Florence. She visibly relaxed, adopted what Annie had always thought of as a "pull up the chair, dearie" posture, the moment when you usually heard what you'd really come for, though it often took quite a while. "Well, I can confirm she was certainly 'interesting.' I only got to talk to her myself, oh, maybe four or five times. But you could always tell when she was on the floor."

"How?"

"There was a real different feel about it. Not that people were intimidated by her exactly. But they became too aware of themselves. In that way. You know how some folks get around a celebrity or something—a little edgy, kind of? Talking a bit louder or arranging to stand in the one place where they know she's going to be passing by, just so they can happen to be there.

"But then, after she got killed, it felt like maybe I'd been imagining it all—you know, that she'd even been up here. No one on any of the other floors had ever said a word about her. Even on my ward we stopped talking about her after a day or so. It just seemed too eerie, like we were going on about . . . a spook or something. There's enough living ghosts in that place, not to have to start making them up."

Florence leaned a little closer and her voice dropped. "But two weeks ago, I was on alone, just for an hour or so—it must have been right around the time when she . . . when it happened to her, and—I don't know why—I just started looking through everything again. You know, going back through the records. There was nothing."

"What do you mean, 'nothing'?"

"I can't even swear for sure that she was here, officially. The first time, she came through talking to some other doctors—I don't remember who right now—but, you know, wearing the coat and all. I couldn't find anything of her anywhere. No orders. No schedules, no initials on anything. Not even a pass signed out for her. I checked myself."

"Why would you bother to look?"

Florence pushed herself back from the table. "I don't know. I guess I just found her pretty interesting. Everything seemed real focused when she was around. You got to see everything clearer. Like you finally knew what you'd been thinking all along . . ."

"You still feel that?" Next, she'd probably be reporting sightings of Princess Di in the O.R.

"It's the timing, as much as anything. Stuff like that always is. It was nothing that she ever *did.* She just said it to me when I brought her in a coffee that it was time to go. Casual, just like that. I thought she meant, like, leaving—herself—at first. She'd been there for at least six hours, most of it just sitting in a chair, watching Mr. Clarke breathe on the ventilator. I'd never seen any doctor do that. Then she said: 'It's time to go.'

"She got up and left right after that. The very next morning. Dr. Somerville decided to administer a dose of morphine so Mr. Clarke could finally get some rest. They disconnected the ventilator. Then it was over. By the book, as far as anyone could see. Everyone knew the morphine would probably kill him at that stage, combined with everything else that was already going into him. They talked about it, what they call the 'double effect.' But it's still an accepted protocol for regulation of pain in some cases like that—terminal cancer and . . . Well, it's a call. At least he wasn't crying any more." Quick tears had sprung up unexpectedly in the old woman's eyes, too. "It had to be better . . ."

"Then what were the concerns?"

"They had permission from the son. But then the sister flies in, expecting to have some 'quality time' with her dying brother, as she puts it, and we get to tell her he's already gone."

"She didn't know?"

"Well, it just happened. But I heard they were all at odds with each other, anyway. For a lot of years, one of the daughters told me. Her permission wasn't needed, so no one bothered informing her in advance. She was just royally pissed off, I guess.

"She was screaming on about lawyers and threatening to sue everyone involved. Even her own family told us to ignore her. The hospital had covered itself. I know they went through everything. The records were perfect. I don't even know where half of them come from—these computer-type things I've never seen before. *I* never used them."

"But there's no doubt in your mind that Mr. Clarke was terminal?"

"Oh, God, yeah. Three-quarters of his oesophagus had already been removed, everything like that—throat cancer, metastasized—he was in absolute agony. *None* of us liked going in there."

"How long would he have lived without the morphine?"

"That's the thing, you know. It might have been as much as a month, six weeks. Hell on earth, I grant you. But his vitals were still functioning adequately. The ventilator was just to make it easier for him—went in through a trach tube."

"So you're saying that *particular* dose killed him?" Annie felt a growing apprehension.

"Looks like. But it was only a matter of time, Lieutenant. In my career, I've seen it too much. And there's very few who wouldn't believe it was for the best if they had to watch something like that, too, day after day. I think she just gave him the gumption to finally do his damn job. Dr. Somerville. None of them get enough training in pain management. Maybe six hours in all the time they're in medical school. So that kind of thing usually gets left to us nurses. And he wasn't much of a go-getter anyways. I don't believe he would have gone ahead, right then, on his own like that, if she hadn't already spent a lot of time talking with him."

"She talked to Dr. Somerville?" Florence hadn't mentioned that until now. "So you think Leah Mallick just . . ." Annie tried to find a neutral word, "clarified it for him?"

"Yeah. I guess what I mean is that she gave him someone to talk to, so he could work it out for himself. Any time I saw them together the day before, in fact, she was the one doing all the listening. She never had to say that much. He's just that kind, you know, who always has to hear what he thinks from someone else. Anyway, she was someone he trusted."

After only a couple of hallway conversations . . . ? "He felt he could trust her?"

"Maybe it was more than that, if I really think about it now. It was like," Florence hesitated, "like, after you finished talking to her, you could trust *yourself* better. You knew you were on the right track." It sounded like a question.

Annie noticed that Florence had unconsciously laid her open hand on her chest, just above her heart.

"We're professionals. We do this stuff day after day. But you get so much crap descending from on high that . . . Well, everyone's second-guessing you every minute of the day, and the people you work for are always trying to pawn their own mistakes off on you. So, when you get someone who really *understands* what you're trying to do here . . .

"Listen, Lieutenant, I work palliative because I believe in it. To me, it's the last place of caring in the world. And if you don't happen to believe that there's something else that comes after this, then I have to think it's the last place of mercy too. Not everyone can do it. Some get too involved, they can't handle the job. Others become so cold and go into themselves that they might as well be piling cordwood for all the feeling they have for it any more. I'm not saying it's not tough sometimes. Real tough. I've found myself sitting out there, in that parking lot, in my car, just praying I didn't have to walk back in through those doors at the start of another shift. Because I know, maybe, it's going to be a particularly difficult day. But I never find it hard to help someone let go when it is time. Maybe that's why she only said it to me." Florence was pale but calm. "'Time to go.' I know it helped me."

"Did anyone else hear her that night?" Annie said quietly.

Florence shook her head. "She was alone in that room when I went in. I was being real careful not to disturb her, but she started talking to me, you know, like I was more of an equal, kind of. She asked me about my work with the other cases on the floor, how I got into palliative in the first place. I couldn't believe she was even bothering to take an interest in anything *I* had to say."

"But was your patient actually . . . in crisis that night?"

"Any more than the day before? Probably not. But if you were there every day, Lieutenant Shannon—" She returned again to Mallick. She couldn't help herself. "I know some people found her . . . like, stuck-up. She *was,* a bit." Florence smiled briefly. "Typical doctor. But somehow we got along pretty good. She asked me what I really thought about his care. Mr. Clarke's. I got to talking about that, and how I believed there's an honest limit to what people should have to endure." Florence was quiet, her uneaten lunch pushed aside.

"Why Dr. Somerville? Why do you think it was him, specifically?"

Florence made a quick gesture of irritation. "It wasn't like *that.* He was just the one on call that night, that's all. He arrived, looking like he'd just rolled out of bed. You know, bits of hair sticking up and all. If it's quiet, they can usually find a place to kip down somewhere."

"But *you* didn't call him?"

"No. He just showed up."

Out of a dead sleep. "Did he mention Dr. Mallick?"

"No. She'd already been gone for hours by then, anyway. I presume home. It was about six in the morning. Eddie had just come in. He usually took the first shift with his father. Nice man—the easiest of them all to get along with. The mother was a real piece of work sometimes. But Eddie was this big, gentle guy, sitting there hour after hour, holding his dad's hand."

"And Mr. Clarke?"

"The same. Exactly the same. Moaning—a kind of choked sobbing that never stopped." She shook her head at the memory before she continued. "Then Eddie, he asks for Dr. Mallick. I remember—it was funny—he couldn't think of her name. Getting pretty worn out by then. But he managed to describe her. Dead accurately, I might add." Florence smiled and shrugged. *Guys.*

"She *was* very good-looking, wasn't she?" Annie said.

"Lieutenant, those pictures don't begin to do her justice. She was gorgeous. And it wasn't just the makeup, or expensive clothes, or anything like that. I can tell you—I actually saw people's jaws drop when she walked through here. I even made a joke to her once, that maybe we should send her into the morgue so she could raise the dead." Florence blushed. "After I said it, I worried maybe I was a bit out of turn. But it was late and she seemed like she was someone you could joke around with, a little."

"How did she respond?"

Florence smiled. "She kinda laughed. Then—" Florence stopped, suddenly remembering something else. "Then she—she reached out and . . . Like this." Florence extended her own hand and briefly brushed it against Annie's face. "And I'm a good five or ten years older than her."

Annie guessed it was closer to twenty-five.

"But it was just like something a mother does for a child. I can tell you, it's been many a year for me, my dear. But, you know, sometimes I find myself doing it for patients, that same way. Like when it's quiet and they're having some trouble sleeping, or it's been a particularly difficult day. Just maternal instinct, I guess."

Did Mallick know it was "a particularly difficult day"? Florence had used the same phrase twice.

"It was that same night, I think." She'd left most of her lasagne special combo plate untouched, half-heartedly rearranged the wilted green salad. "Maybe we could never have been real friends or anything—I would never've presumed—but I got a feeling that she really respected my work. She knew all about it. She even wanted me to tell her what changes I'd make in the department. No doctor had ever even *asked* me something like that before. Most of them don't think too much of practical nurses these days."

"Did you suggest any?" Twice, too, that Mallick had used that same technique.

"Just that, well, I said that no one should ever be left to die alone. We hold their hand until God takes it in His own." Florence looked up at Annie. "Shannon—Catholic?"

Annie shook her head. "Once. Not any more."

"I thought that was one of those things you can't quit." Florence smiled.

"More of an undeclared armistice, then."

Florence checked her watch. "Well, I gotta skedaddle. I'm on again in ten. A double. So, you OK now?"

Annie had squeezed the napkins into a sodden ball in her hand, but her hot flash had subsided. She nodded. One more question. "Leah Mallick had already left the hospital the night before. So, as far as anyone knew, it was Dr. Somerville's decision alone that morning?"

Florence sat very still for a moment. "And I prepared the shot," she said matter-of-factly.

The look they exchanged now was unequivocal. Both knew what had just been said. It was an appropriate time to stop. Or maybe recommend a good lawyer. Annie said nothing.

Florence piled the leftovers back on her tray. "I know what they say she did—to her husband and her little boy. And I got no doubt she'll be damned for that unto eternity.

But she had a kind of aura around her. That probably sounds pretty funny to someone like you—kind of wingy, like. I've seen it before, once or twice, in my line of work. It isn't just technical skills or dedication—they're all workaholics anyway. But you'd only have to look at her to see the best of what there really was about it. Some bigger idea . . ." Florence was lost in thought for a moment, gazing around the cafeteria. Then her glance was caught by something on the other side of the room. She lifted her chin now to point. "Looks like you attracted us some attention here too, Lieutenant."

Annie turned and saw a woman she recognized immediately, staring now in their direction. It was Laurelle Stepton, recently crowned Executive of the Year.

"So, maybe you could just try and limp a little when you leave the table." Florence gave Annie a conspiratorial wink, but she didn't seem overly concerned for herself.

Annie could feel an aura of her own building now. Shit! A migraine on top of everything else. And those eyes drilling into the back of her head. She could sense them. Screw Laurelle, anyway. "Florence, tell me something. Did you have any doubts, when it happened? Mr. Clarke?"

Florence shook her head, standing up slowly. "No. None. I'd had that chance to talk to Dr. Mallick. I felt pretty clear about everything. I know what things matter most to me, Lieutenant. You just don't often get the chance to act on it. It's an art, you know—end-stage medicine." Florence's eyes were tired. Hours more to go. "I was envious of her. She had a real talent for it."

When the loud knock came on the door, Susan leapt about three feet. She was in the middle of several simultaneous on-line chats.

She opened the door to find Annie standing there, smiling. "I tried to call."

"I was just—"

"Yeah, I figured."

Annie looked renewed, revived, excited, as she swung a bag of takeout food and her car keys. "I brought us lunch. How do you feel about going for a drive? I'd like to talk to a guy named Eddie."

Susan laughed. "OK. I'll bite. Who's Eddie?"

"Eddie Clarke. His father, Brian, died about a year ago, up at Riverview Hospital. On the palliative care ward. Mr. Clarke was in there dying for several weeks." Annie paused. "I've just learned that every single attenuated minute of it was a complete and utter agony for him. And Eddie was there for the whole Technicolour show."

Susan's smile faded. She'd never really understood cops and their gallows humour. "That's very pleasant. But what's it got to do with this?"

"Ah, Ms. Shaw, you're an experienced pol . . . If you wanted to make changes to the system, wouldn't you look for the 'hard case'? Offer an example of the nastiest possible outcome when someone proposes to stop you? Set up one thing you can point to, in order to rationalize the direction you really want to go?" She twirled her keys around her finger. "Don't you think Mr. Clarke would make the perfect hard case? Especially if his grieving son was Leah Mallick's last patient."

~~~

"I recognize you. You're the one on TV, right?" Eddie Clarke stood aside in the doorway to let them in, his big belly making it a squeeze for them to pass. "Everyone's always telling my mother she looks just like you."

Annie smiled pleasantly. That would be his mother in one of those photographs on the upright piano? About eighty—and about three hundred pounds?

"I guess you're probably on duty, but can I get you a beer or something?" Eddie asked.

Annie refused automatically. Susan, surprisingly, accepted.

Eddie returned from the kitchen with a full six-pack. He passed one bottle to Susan and took another himself. Half gone in one gulp. "You wanted to ask me about Dad?"

Annie had seated herself on a flimsy French Provincial sofa. It didn't seem like furnishings any guy would have chosen for himself—the gilt lamps, the dusty glass fruit on the spindly-looking coffee table. She turned to look at Eddie.

He sat, polite, nervous. "Like I was saying on the phone to you, I guess I don't find it that easy to talk about. I know it's been more than a year, but . . . you know—" He made a face. "It was pretty rough."

This guy looked like a frightened deer, Annie thought. "I understand you were with your dad most of the time," she said.

"Yeah. Practically every minute, when I wasn't at work. I changed to the night shift so I could be there all day with him, as much as possible."
~~~

"How did the hospital staff treat you?"

Eddie looked bewildered. "OK. Fine. I mean, they were always dropping in to do something for him and I didn't interfere with that. I was just there so when he woke up or something, there'd always be someone he knew. They were pretty good to us."

"But I understand your family had some questions, after he . . . passed away."

Eddie took the remaining half-bottle of beer into his mouth and swallowed it. "Yeah, but, well, that didn't really mean anything. It was only my aunt—my father's sister. She got all nuts about it. She has a problem with my mom, anyway. They've always been at loggerheads."

"Did you ever have any reason to question the medical care your father was receiving?" Susan said.

Annie winced. It was too soon.

Eddie reddened slightly, his breathing shallow. "No, I never did. Not really. But there was so much going on. Look at it from my side, eh. It's been more than a year. I can't remember everyone I talked to. I don't know if any of you have ever gone through anything like that, but you end up dealing with all kinds of different people. You got doctors and nurses, lab people, all these specialists. There were lawyers everywhere by the end. Veteran's Administration. There was a phony kind of counsellor, with all that 'do you have issues' stuff. Everyone has something to tell you that you're supposed to understand. I'm not dumb, but they'd all get going on it and I'd feel like I *was* the village idiot, half the time."

Susan looked thoughtful and took a small sip of beer before she spoke. "That part's the hardest, I know. Every choice they give you looks worse than the last. There's no single right way. What treatment options did your dad's doctor offer you?"

"He wasn't available that much. At least not when I could talk to him alone. My mother was always in the room, or my younger sisters. I mean, there were always other people around, and everyone at the hospital was real busy. But what they were telling me *sounded* right. That's all I know. I just listened mostly. Everyone's got an opinion, eh? I don't know what that's supposed to mean, anyway—'options.'"

"Did the hospital ever suggest something to you, Ed, that made you . . . maybe a little uncomfortable?" she asked. Susan's eyes were locked on his now. He stared back.

Annie glanced back and forth between the two of them. *Shit.*

"Why are you asking me about this now—after all this time?" A flush was climbing up his neck.

"Just . . . did the hospital ever approach you with the idea of a change in protocols?" Annie said.

It was Susan who glanced at her now. Please shut up, her look said. Distinctly.

Eddie didn't notice the exchange.

"Yeah, OK, they did put a DNR—what's that? 'Do not resuscitate'—on his chart. I only saw it when they left the file open on the dispensing counter. An accident. We probably weren't supposed to see it, but I was just there to get an aspirin for a headache I had."

Susan persisted. "Did you or any member of your family request it? Or agree to that?"

"I didn't. I don't think any one in the family did."

"Did your father?"

Eddie refused to look at her now. He stared at the floor, the empty beer bottle in his hand. "The hospital never said anything about that kind of stuff to me. I was always afraid they were going to. It's not something I would've been too comfortable talking about, just like that. My dad never said anything about it to me. Then it was too late to ask him any more."

"But if they had asked you, before—earlier—what would you have said, Eddie?"

He looked back out the window, eyes watering slightly. "I probably would have said, 'OK. But just not yet.'" He glanced quickly at Susan, then away again. "You know what I mean? I know they did everything they could, but if I thought it was his time, and there was going to be so much more pain—I would have said yes. For sure." He got up and paced a couple of feet. "I was so fuckin' tired. And by the end, I guess, I did tell someone what I really felt like. Someone else at the hospital."

Susan caught Annie's eye.

"What did you tell them?" she continued quietly.

"That—you know—just like what I was saying now. That if it was for the best, maybe it was the right thing. But I didn't say it out like that to any of the regular doctors there."

He sat down again. His hands were clenched together and he was obsessively rubbing his thumbs back and forth against each other. "I recognized it was her from those pictures—the ones in the paper two weeks ago? All that stuff, you know, when she was murdered? That was when I saw it was the same person. Pretty sad. Until then I didn't even know that she was a doctor from around here. When we were up there at the hospital, they all were acting like she was some big shot who'd just dropped in. You could see they were being pretty careful around her. But she never come off that way to me—you know, all important or anything. She was real warm, quiet, real level-headed. Kind of a regular person . . . except that she was the most gorgeous goddamn woman I've ever seen. Man! I didn't know they *made* 'em like that any more . . ." He shook his head in remembered awe.

"I don't even know how we got started talking. But she was the only one who ever took the time to really listen to me. No jargon, or medical this and that. I had a lot of questions and she always answered them straight out. I probably ended up talking more than she did. When you're in the middle of something like that, it's really hard to see your way through. It helped to talk it out. A lot." A faintly defensive tone.

"Would it have made a difference to you if you'd known she was paid by the HMO to talk to you?" Susan asked.

The look on his face confirmed that he'd been guarding his own suspicion for a long time. "The HMO pays everybody anyway, doesn't it? It was a decision I knew she wanted me to make on my own. That seemed really important to her." He had become darkly flushed again and turned away from them.

"But maybe it was one you hadn't made quite yet?" Susan said.

"No, you're wrong. When I heard it, I knew it was *exactly* the right thing." His expression was more defiant now. "I thought those patient records were supposed to be confidential?"

"But maybe after it happened, you wished it hadn't? Something you regretted?" Susan's face conveyed only compassion.

The air slowly seeped out of him. "I don't know much about regret. I know I was real glad it was over, for him. Maybe that sounds bad for me to say it, but—" He glanced quickly at Annie now, worried. Did this amount to a confession?

Susan, too, looked meaningfully at Annie. *Your turn now, Lieutenant.*

Annie sighed inwardly, then recited the litany. "We're not here to blame you for anything. This isn't a formal investigation. No one's going to come and make you go over it all again." She leaned a bit towards him now. "You and your family, you've all been through enough. And you did absolutely nothing wrong, Eddie." From the look on his face, she doubted that he would ever believe that again.

He spoke again in a rush. "But I did ask her, you know, if there was going to be an autopsy. I know maybe that sounds bad too. But I don't think my mother could have taken that, especially if, well, if there was anything that was—"

"What did Dr. Mallick tell you?"

"She told me there didn't have to be if . . . if I didn't want one. Dad was in the last stages of it. There was cancer everywhere. She said they would give him something for the pain when they removed the ventilator. The rest would be left to—I think she said fate."

Fate. Annie knew now it was anything but that.

Eddie's attention wandered to what was playing on the muted television. Some afternoon talk show. It made no sense at all without the sound. He walked over to it. Then he laid his hand against the TV screen and slowly spread his fingers open across it. The images divided into separate parts of faces, the pieces continuing to argue their salient, silent points. There was a faint crackle of static electricity under his hand.

"I remember the exact moment. I couldn't look at him. I just stood beside this thing—the monitor—and watched the picture. It seemed more real than my father was to me any more, right? You know how those machines are, with the line? And I put my hand over it, like this, and I could see it jumping like sparks from my fingers. And then it stopped—the line was just straight flat, hidden under my hand. I heard the buzzer. Other people came into the room. And I went and phoned my mother."

He turned away from the television and mechanically passed another beer to Susan. She set it aside without saying anything. Annie noticed she'd taken only one small sip of the first one.

"When it was all happening, I was doing sleeping pills. I'd be getting through the day on these antidepressant things. A real numbo, all the time. As soon as everything was over, I stopped 'em—it wasn't doing any good. But then, right away, I start having these dreams about it, every night. That went on for a long time. You know, my dad, family things—I was, like, five years old and the hospital was going through all this stuff with us, and I just wanted to go and play ball, that kind of thing." He smiled wanly. "Just like a kid, eh?

"Then, right after I heard about what happened to her, I had one of those dreams again. There was me, and my dad was lying on the bed all hooked up to everything. And Doctor, uh—" He stumbled and looked at Annie questioningly.

"Mallick," she completed. The same woman whom people like Eddie Clarke preferred to speak of as murdered, rather than a murderer.

"In this dream, Dr. Mallick was there. She was holding my dad's hand. She told me to talk to him, even if he couldn't hear me. Then she said, 'Watch this.' And the room gets dark, and everything around my father starts shining. The air—all of it. The white sheets were just glowing and everything. But Dad had this yellow light, like honey covering all over him. It was sort of swirling around.

"And she told me to feel it. She took my hand and put it in the middle of all this light. It was like a flowing stream. Like when you're a kid and you pull against a fast current? That strong. But it was warm, and it started moving straight up. Fast. My hand went up with it a little and then it was gone. I woke up and my arm was all like pins and needles. You know, asleep. But I could still feel that river pulling on it."

Susan nodded. "Did you ever ask her for help to come to terms with your . . . decision?"

"Only once. I mean, I was completely losing it. Dad was in real pain. That last night—" Eddie looked ashamed. "I knew Mom wanted to leave it up to me. And I just . . .

maybe it's because it was the first big thing I've ever done in my life that I didn't check out with my dad. I know it's what he would have wanted. But I asked her if it had to be now. When push came to shove, I kind of caved, there at the end, I guess, and I asked her that . . ."

"What did she say?" Susan asked. Her voice was dead calm.

"'Yes.' That's it—real simple. That's all she said."

~~~

They drove back towards the city, on a road that followed the river, overlooking the town below. In the distance, the Stoney River flowed past Palladian Steel. Nearer was the island, with its half-finished vision of paradise and the swing bridge making contact with it nearly impossible.

"I was just thinking how many times in the past two weeks I've had to tell people I'm not a real cop," Annie said.

"At least you get to play one on TV," said Susan.

Annie studied the scenery for another moment. "You look a bit like her, you know," she said. She made it sound almost like a joke, but Eddie Clarke's reaction had confirmed her own impression.

Susan seemed to withdraw for a moment. "I don't see it . . ." she said quietly.

"Well, he certainly preferred talking to you. Usually, *I* get to be the good cop." All the trees sweeping by them were leafing out in light, bright green. They came to a crossroad and Annie turned down towards Lockport. "Must be just because you're a leggy blonde."
~~~

Susan smiled. "Maybe I'm Woodward and you're Bernstein," she said after a minute.

"Or we're just playing them."

"Then I'm Redford . . ."

"I know . . . and I get to be Dustin Hoffman." Annie laughed easily enough. But she knew they were both thinking about the same thing: Brian Clarke. And how sometimes death wasn't the worst choice. There was mercy in it. And how it forced you to look at all the aspects of Quality of Life. Annie knew every question Eddie Clarke would have asked himself, every thought that went through your mind when you were finally forced to face that impossible decision. The difference was, *this* time, they hadn't asked. Leah Mallick had made the decision as surely as if she'd put the syringe in Eddie's hand herself.

"So, play accountant for me. How much would they have saved?" she said.

Susan stared vacantly at the countryside passing the window. "A quarter-million dollars. Give or take," she said finally.

By the time they got back to town, the hot sun had turned to red along the line of the land, and the first street lamps were coming on. Lockport looked different at dusk, settled and permanent.

They drove around almost aimlessly for a while, listening to the radio, saying little. On impulse, Annie pulled into the old city works yard. It was a site adjacent to a large abandoned section of downtown riverfront property, with an unobstructed view of the water.

Susan slowly stepped from the car, looking around her now with growing interest. "Now, *this* is interesting . . ." The steel factory just visible in the distance through the gaps between the surrounding buildings. "An industrial milieu. Turn-of-the-century brick construction. Heritage registration, right?" She became more excited. "It's exactly what they're looking for now, all these new businesses. Boutiques, galleries, design firms, restaurants, brew pubs. They look for places like this."

"I thought you might appreciate it. These were all working factories, right up to the late fifties." Annie adopted a rough Irish accent. "Ah, darlin', but you should have seen it in the old days. Lockport was really something then . . ."

There were old warehouses, laneways going off in a dozen directions, classical architectural motifs everywhere she looked. Even in its derelict state, one could see potential for commercial development around here, Susan thought, something substantive and solid.

"You know, we have a new state urban improvement initiative—" she began. Then she stopped herself. "Milieu"? The word didn't belong here. That took some imagination. In any other city this would already have become the next trendy area—the SoHo, the SoBe, the SoMa of vibrant urban renewal. In a place like Lockport it was only something else on its way to being condemned, and the real reason why any deal with Cross Corp could be made to look like the only game in town. "We" wasn't an option any more.

They made their way further along the riverbank, on a tarred service road bordered on the water side by rusting railway tracks. From this vantage Palladian Steel looked as massive as a mountain laid upon its side. Its vanishing point seemed to sit on the horizon. Susan could hear the thunderous pounding of machinery coming from somewhere deep inside—mile-long belts and lines, metal on metal. Arcs of pure light formed in the dark interior, exploding as sparks and heat from a multitude of mysterious openings, to reflect like fireworks on the expanse of slick water in front of them.

Turning back, she saw that Annie was now lost in some private reverie, settled on a low concrete wall, watching the river flow. She was still favouring the injured leg, still waving off any suggestion that it bothered her.

Susan went and sat beside Annie on the wall. She stared at the water too. After a moment she said, "How did you know it was about saving money and not just . . ." Her voice quavered slightly.

"Mercy killing?"Annie glanced towards her. "It was actually something *you* mentioned." Annie leaned back to look at the darkening sky. "Palliative care. You told me that it was the one thing you and Leah Mallick had discussed." Annie's expression hardened. "What else did you two talk about?"

"I know. I—"

"Oh, that's right—I remember now. It was Mozart . . ." she said sarcastically.

Susan put up her hand. "OK. Just listen to me. You're right. There's a major corporation called Cross Corp that I've already started looking into."

Annie waited.

Susan was holding herself stiffly now. She felt as cold as ice. "I once held a briefing for Tom Acton. I gave him the numbers that they could use to justify something like this—" Susan stood up and walked a few steps away. "Ninety percent of hospital costs are incurred in those last three weeks. If you can just move someone out of intensive care . . ." *Or if you can just shave it by a few days . . .*

She continued to stare across the water at the factory. "I didn't know about Cross Corp then. And I didn't know that Leah Mallick was supposed to become the Secretary of Health and Human Services. I'm fairly sure that Cross Corp put her here. And whatever they really did to Brian Clarke, it's nothing compared to what I suspect they're *about* to propose."

In the silence, Susan thought back to that conversation with Michael Starr. Starr and his "mutualism" . . . For some reason, she'd never mentioned her meeting with him to Annie. She knew why now. "I think they chose me too. From the very beginning. They're probably going to considerable trouble to ensure that all the right people are in the right places. Everywhere." *Beneath the surface, everything invisibly interconnected.* "We just can't see them yet."

Annie felt a sudden chill of her own now. Her heart thumped uncomfortably. What exactly was Susan confessing to her? "So, were they wrong?" Annie asked quietly.

"About me? No," Susan said, shaking her head with a rueful smile, "they weren't." She turned away. "They had to know that some part of me *would* agree with it. At least in theory. After all, my thing's numbers, the alpha and omega of contemporary political policy. Personally? Given a decision made by a fully informed, rational adult, I have no profound moral or religious objections to it. It appeals to my sense of logic. I'm pro-choice. I can comfortably throw around phrases, like 'rationalization' and 'capitation' and 'limits of compassion' without embarrassment." One after the other, she'd ticked off each point on her fingers. Then she threw her hands up angrily and walked a short distance away. "And it wouldn't be hard to convince *me* . . . I'm as afraid as anyone of suffering. Loss of control. Dying alone. In some parts of the world, they *are* legalizing it . . ."

Susan didn't speak about the other truth she knew—that almost two-thirds of physician-assisted suicide cases weren't being reported in some jurisdictions now and one in five weren't even agreed to. And that was before things *really* got started.

"So you're saying that Cross Corp actually selected you?" Annie sounded more sad than angry.

Susan was lost in shadows, only a voice. "No, Leah Mallick did. I think *I* was the one being interviewed when I spoke with her . . ." The sound had a detached, almost abstract quality.

"But if it's anything like I think you're suggesting, if everything could be made so completely predictable to her, then how did she misjudge *this* situation—you, right here, right now, telling *me.*"

Susan responded with a short laugh. "Because she *didn't* know she was going to kill herself. It's the very first rule of politics I ever learned from Tom Acton—the Law of Unintended Consequences. It was the one thing she hadn't planned for."

"But Cross Corp—or whoever it is—they haven't tried to stop you."

Yes, they have, Susan thought. And came very close to succeeding. It would have been so easy just to drive away. "Maybe they're still thinking that I won't want to rock the boat. Or that I'll probably use any information I find quietly, for my own purposes. Just like you thought I would . . . They deal in probabilities, actuarial tables. The timing's in their favour. I mean, who in their right mind expects to confront a principled ethical position in the middle of a campaign?" She glanced over at Annie now. "And they wouldn't have anticipated that I might join forces with someone up here. They would have been pretty sure that you weren't my type, for example."

Annie raised an eyebrow sardonically. "And just how would you define *that?*"

Susan smiled again. "But, it's true, isn't it? You were the last person I'd ever have chosen to work with, under normal circumstances. It was the same for you."

She was right, of course. Annie remembered her own instant, almost irrational dislike of Susan Shaw. "I don't know—*I* felt an instant rapport," she said evenly.

Susan laughed, more easily now. She leaned back against a metal railing. "For God's sake, you drive a Volvo."

"So?"

Susan snorted. "Well, I wouldn't be caught dead driving one. And any freshman stat student would be able to categorize you pretty effectively with that one piece of information alone—how you see yourself, what your priorities are. Or maybe just that you used to like ABBA

. . . Then there's your job, your age, your salary range. But think about that for a minute. What value would it have—all the data you could gather on people—if you also controlled information technology, dominated the market in health care management software, private administrative services, held the purse strings on insurance underwriting? What happened here wasn't an isolated incident—it was a proposed business service."

It was evening now. Susan stood up straight, her arms wrapped tightly around herself. It was too cold down here, by the water. "The law is a blunt instrument. And there are *always* loopholes—political pressure from lobbyists, corporations that have the necessary resources to plan that around every technicality you can put in their way. They'll follow the letter of the law—but are perfectly prepared to circumvent the spirit. You can't control attitudes with legislation, but you can control legislation if you find a way to define attitudes. They've already got us wearing two-hundred-dollar running shoes, and drinking five-dollar coffees. If people want something—or can be *convinced* to want it—no law on earth will ever be able to stop it . . .

"For a while we'll continue to debate the 'slippery slope.' And we'll still put a fraud like Kevorkian in jail, but not until he's already killed dozens—and then thumbed his nose at us on prime-time television. Because no one thinks of it as 'unspeakable' any more. Soon, we'll be calling it patients' rights. Or saying they're already doing it anyway, so wouldn't it be better to just legislate it? Or, better, yet—tweak the existing regulations and avoid any political fight. The White House does it all the time. Look at what's going on with environmental policy. Do you know how flexible the definition of 'terminal' really is?

"You can make people choose anything if you know exactly how to skew the message the right way. It's marketing. And I promise you, they'll be holding a national referendum on it within a year."

Annie spoke, her mouth dry as dust. "But if this *is* all Cross Corp—it's still a public company, isn't it? They've got to have boards, directors, shareholder representation, information filings, annual meetings, regulatory hearings. People ask questions. What about negative PR?"

In answer, Susan gave her a look of comic disdain. "You mean from an investor's perspective? So, Cross Corp's got a piece of a local research start-up—so what? The largest proportion of investment now is through major institutional vehicles—pension funds, mutual funds. How do you think big corporations got away with everything they *have* in the last couple of years?

"And how many people do you know who bother to read—let alone understand—the fine print of every annual report for each company they might be holding a few shares in? If they did, maybe there wouldn't be a need to create a separate category called ethical funds. People will continue to put money into everything—from tobacco companies to arms manufacturers, strip mine producers, blood diamonds—despite any and all negative publicity attached to them. You don't define moral character by the market."

Annie felt weary and uncomfortable. Her leg was stiffening up. She stood, this time with some difficulty, and walked down closer to the river. Suddenly, it was all too overwhelming.

Susan spoke again. "Annie, for the last couple days I've been working a contact on the Internet. I didn't want to tell you until I knew more. But it's in a medical chat room—someone inside who may be willing to provide me with real information . . . who already *has,* in fact."

Annie looked startled. "Who?"

Susan shook her head. "I don't know yet. But whoever it is is close enough to be worried about personal risk . . . And it's credible information. Among other things—that almost every physician associated with Cross Corp has higher than usual death stats. That there was another test case exactly the same, in California. I don't know if Leah Mallick was involved. And now this . . ."

Christ, Annie thought. Whatever was happening, it wasn't anything like chasing down some random eleven-year-old with a gun. "You're playing with fire, you know. It's so much bigger than either of us can handle alone. Take it to someone you trust, then, one of your own contacts. This isn't some kids' game going on here."

Susan, looking at her, laughed shortly now, the sound bitter. "And Leah wasn't just some garden-variety psychiatrist. She could make anyone do almost anything. Who else did she get to? Who do you propose I take it to, *this* time? Who do I know that I can still trust?" Susan was barely outlined in the twilight now. "But I've found a way to get inside her head. To the fundamental. *That's* where all this started. I'm willing to be there. And if you can't go that far, then I need you to at least stay out of my way."

Annie cast her eyes over the water again. Even in the dark, nothing was ever really black and white, only infinite, infinite shades of grey. She sank back down, almost unwillingly, on the low wall. "Jesus, Susan. You're telling me that you are—that you've *been* in some way a part of this all along. Whatever 'this' is. And now you think you've found Deep Throat or whatever. What am I supposed to do with that?"

"I guess you're supposed to trust me, Bernstein." Susan took a deep breath. "Annie, what's hard to accept is that someone is really prepared to make this state the charnel house of the nation. But Cross Corp holds the mortgage on this city. There's no way to keep them out. And what's about to happen here—I think it's only a dress rehearsal for the rest of the country." Susan sighed. Then she came back and sat beside Annie. "Look, you're thinking the same thing I am. Because you know as well as I do what we saw back there," she said. "It was a demonstration. It was nothing but a fucking demo . . ."

10

"To some extent, it's a family of symptoms indistinguishable from schizophrenia. But usually late-onset."

As disturbing as it was, as impatient as she'd become, Annie found herself seated in front of another doctor—a specialist this time, prepared to address the sins of the brain. A neurologist.

She raised one eyebrow in a question now.

"Mid-forties. Fifties. Even sixties—some, maybe," he explained. "It's degenerative, of course, but the brain tends to cope better with a loss of this type when it can still very actively displace function to other parts. Like recovery from a stroke. I doubt most physicians would be able to diagnose the symptoms until it was quite a long way in. Intermittant short-term memory loss. Various inappropriate social behaviours, increased consumption of alcohol or sugar. A tendency to repeat certain phrases or words. Low-grade paranoia. And I've seen some *incredible* coping strategies. People hide it for years—it's almost as if whatever they were before, they just become more *that.*"

"And by then it's too late."

"Well, there is no cure. So, early or late—it doesn't make much difference. It's not like we can do anything about it anyway. They're trying various drug therapies, but it's palliative, at best."

"But there would be nothing apparently wrong with him at this point? Nothing that showed? At eight?"

"Well, it would be difficult for any child to deal with a dysfunctional parent, of course—"

Jesus Christ. "Doctor, please, I can't talk about 'dysfunctional' right now. In fact, I am sick and tired of all the complicated words people use to say that a kid's home life is probably the shits. If his father was a lunatic most of the time . . ."

The doctor registered little reaction to her outburst, except for the slight narrowing of his eyes, the deepening of two furrows on the bridge of his nose. "Lieutenant, I don't find that particularly appropriate language. There's still a place for some *sensitivity* in all this. What I mean is it wouldn't have to be a congenital disease. He—any young child—could have exhibited various affects, simply in response to constant proximity to anyone suffering advanced symptoms. Children can even integrate such behaviours as a way to normalize them. Particularly if the other parent wasn't particularly forthcoming—if denial was an ongoing issue, for example. It would be, quite naturally, very confusing to him. Some psychoses can certainly mirror actual symptoms."

Very briefly, Annie found herself longing for someone like Leah Mallick—what a relief it might have been to come upon that one person who seemed so open and accessible.

The profession, as a whole, was utterly incapable of ordinary speech.

"How old did you say this boy was again?" he asked.

"Eight, almost nine," she said curtly.

"No, I very much doubt there would have been *any* observable symptoms. Not for years, anyway. Then a rapidly developing manifestation of everything I've already described—defects in memory, aphasia, apraxia, agnosia, loss of executive functioning. Once it begins, of course, the progress of the disease is inexorable."

Like waiting for a time-bomb to go off if you knew one was there. How would you live with the knowing? "Is it inevitable? Inherited from a parent—"

"Among genetically determined diseases, Huntington's chorea provides a similar example. A male child has a fifty-fifty chance in that case. But you certainly wouldn't know he had it for sure until symptoms started appearing. The difficulty with this one is that it's very late showing—most people have already had their families before they've reached those ages. And then, well, it's rather too late, isn't it?"

"Unless you went looking for it . . . ?"

"Unless, of course, you went looking for it," he agreed. "You mean in identifying the presence of the chromosome, I gather?"

Chromosomes. Good genes. The lucky sperm club. In the past, people sometimes used it to explain why others had and got and kept, and not they. Maybe it helped to clarify the unfairness, the imbalance, the injustice, of fate. Here too, a simple accident of birth *had* given Kyle Mallick everything the world could offer—all the advantages of looks and money and access to power and resources. Everything for and about this child was already perfect: exactly the right schools, the right nutrition, the right music and sports training, the right clothes and friends. His life was going to be flawless. What child could have sustained those expectations? Apparently, not even Leah Mallick's.

Then how difficult it must have been to accept that such a failure had been born to *her.* Where was the fairness in that? Fate itself was mocking her.

For a moment Annie experienced Leah's pure panic. Life should have been anything but this . . . profound disappointment.

She looked around her. They were in some kind of restaurant, a Howard Johnson's or a Bob's Big Boy—it didn't matter. She'd suggested they meet at whichever one was standing at Exit 84. Every city, town and village had one or the other, adjacent to the Interstate. She'd made the trip in under four hours—hopefully, far enough from Lockport to provide anonymity, if not a broader perspective.

The waitress set two club sandwiches down, the thick plates ringing loudly on the table. A side of fries for each.

"Why *would* a wife kill her husband—" Annie began.

The waitress pulled a bottle of ketchup from under one elbow and cutlery from the band of her apron. "Well, *I* can tell ya," she said. "There's exactly a hundred reasons why *any* woman would *want* to kill her husband. And vicie-versie, probably. So can I get you guys anything else?"

Annie shook her head, biting her lip. "Not right now, thanks." This time she waited for the waitress to move away before speaking again. It was outside a neurologist's realm of expertise, but she asked anyway. "Would she have wanted to kill him just because he carried the gene that indicated a susceptibility? I mean her motive . . . psychologically."

"Are you asking me as a *doctor?*"

As opposed to *what,* she thought. A garage mechanic?

"Look. This disease is certainly rare enough that anyone—even a good psychiatrist—could be forgiven for misinterpreting those same symptoms. Present in the father, I mean." He consumed his sandwich with enthusiasm. "You could easily believe it was something else for quite a long time. Masked as any number of other disorders. Severe depression, for one.

"Years ago, before the specific genetic identification, it would have been possible to misdiagnose this kind of thing forever, in fact. And families, even the best ones, would just hide it. You know, crazy old Cousin Gertie in the attic . . ." The doctor smiled faintly. "But if she felt that she'd missed it—or been in some way deceived—as a professional, anger, humiliation, maybe even self-loathing is attached to that too. Like someone had made a fool of her. It's an extreme case—I'd say you'd have to have pretty well given up on everything in order to commit murder and then suicide yourself."

He'd made it a verb—a redundant one at that. You couldn't very well "suicide" someone else, she thought.

His eyes glittered now in a kind of detached amusement. "This is that *BackPage* thing, right?"

Annie nodded. Even illustrious physicians watched tabloid TV these days. "So, in effect, you think she might have been punishing him for passing this on?"

"Actually, I think the husband was just collateral damage."

It wasn't what she'd expected. But she was more taken aback by his casual use of the term than his conclusion.

He noticed, and laughed slightly. "Sorry. But yes. That's what I'd call it. A little hold-over, I guess, from my time in the war."

She looked at him, judging him to be in his mid to late fifties. Vietnam. "You were a doctor—over there?"

He sighed. "Just barely. I got out of medical school about six months before they called me up. I thought my medical degree would buy me a deferment, but the war went on just a little too long and I guess they thought they needed me. I interned in a military hospital, far enough away from the front that I wasn't getting shot at. But I certainly saw the results. I even went up a couple of times, to the line—just to say I'd been there."

He swallowed the last of his sandwich. "You know, I saw a lot going on over there . . . people who'd kill their own children rather than let them fall into the hands of the enemy. Things you never thought really happened in the modern world any more."

He shook his head slowly. "But, then, look at Jonestown. Waco. That's *us.* Not some backward, third-world, myth-riven, agrarian dictatorship," he said, wiping a dot of mayonnaise off the tip of one finger.

If you were Leah Mallick, Annie wondered, who would you come to think of as your enemy? Maybe one you knew intimately, from the inside. Or one you'd helped to create.

By mine own hand rather than unto theirs . . .

"We doctors don't fool ourselves that we're immune to the vicissitudes of life, but we do think we're supposed to *know.* We don't much like to be on the receiving end of surprises. And denial's still the most powerful coping strategy of them all."

Annie saw an image of a child hiding his eyes and saying "You can't see me . . ."

She waved the waitress over for the check, then glanced back at the doctor. "One more question. How do *you* think April Vaughan got that medical report?"

He looked at Annie now with a kind of pitying condescension. "Somebody gave it to her, of course," he said.

Annie picked up Tim Mallick's notebook again. One of a collection of five. Hundreds of pages altogether. This was the last of them, according to a few dated entries she'd found. It was a large amount of material to generate in a two-year period.

Annie found the poem, the one that had caught her attention the first time through. She remembered that it had made some reference to "envious gods" and quickly scanned the lines until she found it. The word he'd used was actually *jealous.* "Beyond the reach of jealous gods . . ."

Annie pulled an old anthology off the shelf and began searching first lines, indexes. Then a book of quotations. There were references in a few places. But one evoked something familiar.

April Vaughan had concluded her documentary—her overcooked hagiography on the Mallicks—with a dramatic reading. Annie remembered thinking it sounded vaguely reminiscent of a pompous old professor she'd once had, from some time back in the dark ages of her own grad degree in English lit.

The videotape was still in the machine. Annie rewound it, zipping through a couple of samples of Stan Kendra at the podium—*God,* he was bad—to find the last few minutes of Vaughan's piece again.

" . . . and him have I loved and cherished, and I said that I would make him to know not death and age for ever . . ." If it was a Trivial Pursuit question, Annie would have guessed one of the standard translations of the *Iliad.* But it was without metre and even Vaughan had resisted the singsong sound people automatically adopted when something screams "poetry." The kind of thing someone like Dan Rather reaches for when he's trying to load weight on a subject.

Then it jumped out at her: "Hard are ye gods and jealous exceeding, who ever grudge goddesses openly to mate with men . . ." Milton. The bane of her undergrad existence, and the subject of one of her earliest papers. *Paradise Lost.* She quickly found the passage. April Vaughan had quoted the last section of it: "*There all the rest of his good company was lost, but it came to pass that the wind bare and the wave brought him hither. And him have I loved and cherished, and I said that I would make him to know not death and age for ever.*"

Annie ran her finger up the page, quickly reading what immediately preceded it. "*Even so when rosy-fingered Dawn took Orion for her lover, ye gods that live at ease were jealous thereof. So again ye gods now grudge that a mortal man should dwell with me. Him I saved as he went all alone bestriding the keel of a bark, for that Zeus had crushed and cleft his swift ship with a white bolt in the midst of the wine-dark deep. . . ."*

Leah, too, had sailed the wine-dark deep. A goddess brought down by a mere mortal. And the jealous gods had wreaked their revenge: that she couldn't save him, or herself. Was Tim Mallick's allusion a prediction?

Annie found another, more unexpected occurrence of the phrase. In Buddhism, of all places. It represented a lower state of consciousness, the realm of power-seeking. The entry she read even made some crack about Washington, DC, being filled with asuras—jealous gods, obsessing after power and self-aggrandizement. The dominance of ego and self-importance. The titans. The exact opposite of ascendance into the light. *Diabola est Deus Inversus.*

Perhaps, then, it was meant as a condemnation. Perhaps Tim Mallick wanted only to warn her of her own fate.

Annie closed the book now, a headache beginning to build behind her eyes. Because what really mattered was that someone had given April Vaughan *this* as well.

~~~

Susan found the newest message waiting for her at the hotel.

For several days she'd been hovering just outside a number of on-line discussions. Watching, waiting. She was, in the parlance, "lurking." The first forums she found were
~~~

simple chat rooms, usually promoting alternative medicine. A few were grassroots political coalitions. She left postings in most of them. But one in particular, she noticed, seemed to attract a disproportionate share of health care professionals, or at least those who claimed to be. Most of them appeared to be reasonably knowledgeable about budget debates, cautious about the political climate in various jurisdictions.

She'd carefully created an identity: doctor, a psychiatrist, with a special interest in palliative care and the development of health care policy, and a particular focus on HMOs. And she'd woven all the details she could remember of Leah's life into the persona, exploiting everything with a casual familiarity. Specific seminars and conferences Leah had attended, people with whom she'd associated. Lexicon. Syntax, accurately rendered. Sense of humour intact. Susan played the percentages: there had to be someone out there who'd recognize her. And see the lie.

After a couple of days a few respondents had proposed a private exchange of information. She'd approached each cautiously—offering little more than implication and ambiguity. Most of them quickly dropped out when she made her questions more pointed and specific. It was a problem. Cross Corp's reach was a long one.

One correspondent in particular, though, had stayed, one who seemed conversant with the arguments and comfortable with the jargon. Surprisingly, too, almost playful. And just as carefully feeling *her* out, she knew, in a kind of virtual dance. But whoever it was, they'd sent just enough material to prove that they knew what they were talking about. Malpractice suits settled, stats, references to certain in-house documents.

The latest message had been left for her in the last couple of hours. They'd probably signed off by now.

BAK, she typed. Back at keyboard. She calculated the possible time differences, east or west. Two, three hours earlier or later. Lunch or dinner. She waited.

She'd almost given up when it appeared suddenly on the screen: *Hi again. Good day?* The anonymity made banal socializing almost enjoyable. You could be a different person.

Yes. Glad it's Friday. Too much paperwork.

No paper, no pay.

True. Thanks for conference transcripts. Question about additional OTR session, with insurers. Can you provide? It was something she'd read about. At one of the last conferences Leah had attended, an unscheduled event had been added to the program; someone had made a reference to another session. Off the record, likely off-site and strictly for invited participants.

Her contact was more circumspect this time. *Don't think so.*

Come on . . . professional courtesy : -) *Lost my notes.* Leah Mallick had been booked into a symposium at Whittier College: advanced demographic profiling in standardized psychological testing procedures.

No response.

She tried again. *But we talked about it when I was there. Remember?* Susan knew this was a more provocative suggestion. If they remembered *meeting* someone like Leah, what were the chances they wouldn't also know that she was supposed to be dead?

But not her, are you? . . . Not LM? :–[Despondency.

Susan's heart pounded against her ribs. They knew she was not Leah Mallick. Obviously, this was someone who'd been playing her all the way along too. Susan stared at the screen, waiting for more. There was nothing.

She answered. *OK. But talking about the same thing?*

Yes. yr interested in Company. Confirm?

She didn't enter a response.

RUST? Are you still there?

Yes

Need F2F. Face to face.

She paused, more nervous now. *Where?*

How about there?

It was impossible. She'd been too careful—there was no way to tell who or where she was. And she had no intention now of revealing her identity. *No. PAW.* People are watching.

Your loss.

She thought carefully for a moment. *Interested in trade?*

=>$ Show me the money.

LM wanted out.

: - /. I have trouble believing that.

Sceptical son-of a bitch, she thought. *OK. You give me something.* She waited but there was no response. She tried again. *I hear company looking for office space.*

Yes. I hear 2.

How *would* you, she thought. *Where?*

U know routine ;-) *Confirm or deny.*

It was a chance to find out how far this had gone. *Inside the Beltway?* Might as well ask, she thought. They could dance later. Unless *this* was Cross Corp.

The cursor blinked. Nothing happened for several seconds. She'd bet and lost . . .

The answer came. *Deny.*

They were saying not in Washington. Not yet. *Where?* she typed again.

Nothing.

She waited for a moment, the cursor blinking on a blank line. She wrote *Then what?* No response. Apparently, it wasn't going to happen this time either. She'd been following another dead end. Like the rest of them, this was someone just trying to stir up problems, looking for an anonymous way to vent. Or someone frightened off the moment it got too close to Cross Corp.

She sighed and began to sign off. *Thanks anyway. I need specifics. Don't think you can help me—*

Her screen filled with the photograph of a state park she'd seen hundreds of times. She half laughed to herself; she'd been sitting so long that her screen saver had kicked in. But instead of dissolving to the next picture, it froze. She tried to move the mouse and found her cursor locked out.

Then the image grew into a series of dots, enlarged pixels, spreading out from the centre like flames licking the page towards the edges. Someone was using a public key, the encryption software installed on her hard drive. And what was left, when it finished, was a screen full of gibberish. Letters, numbers—none of which meant anything, she knew, until a second key was issued, then a third created by the sender's own random keystrokes and cursor movements. It was the state's new security up-grade.

A complete message was buried in the photograph itself. *Steganography.*

Before she had the chance to respond, there was another message. *Use private key to retrieve session. Counting 15 seconds . . .*

She scrambled. She had one chance, after which, she knew, the temporary "session key" needed to decrypt would expire. Fifteen seconds wasn't enough—She grabbed the key, used it. Then it opened up, a momentary breech, and she had the entire document in front of her. And quickly, she began reading it, stunned now, her heart accelerating, her fingers clenched above the keyboard . . .

"The solution is to make Cross Corp's arrangement exclusive to our participants, unable to provide any other entity the tools/capabilities you will have . . . we could not even divulge or apply our knowledge of the unique and state-specific protocols (nor their tactical implications) to any other entity . . . 'gaming' may be a dirty word to HHS, but the sooner the market clears out the distortions . . . large range of opportunities between what is ethically viable (profitable) and ethically dangerous (illegal) . . . reduces congestion and relieves constraint . . ."

Another message jumped on to her screen, obscuring the document. *Verify cert.*

She'd been leaning close, to read. And the interruption was like a shout in the silent room. With trembling fingers, Susan immediately tapped in a string of new numbers that enabled her to authenticate the digital certificate. It was as clear as a signature would have been. She stared at the identification. Why didn't I even begin to guess who it was, she thought. *RUST?* she typed. Are you still there. *RU safe?*

In answer, the page of information itself began to break up, before her eyes. Frantically, she tried to save something, anything, but the words dissolved away until all that was left was a photograph of a nearby lake.

Yes or no? F2F.

A meeting. *Yes. Of course.* She paused before adding one more word: *Why?*

Tnt. Yr. Another few seconds, then *TGIF.* Tonight. At your place . . . Thank God it's Friday. A happy face icon popped up on the screen.

Susan pushed the laptop away. Leah Mallick wasn't the only person who knew too much.

She poured herself a drink and put on a new CD. "Figlio perduto." She half-listened to it while she watched the sun set and finished her Scotch. Then she went into the bedroom to lay out another outfit, selecting business-casual—it seemed the most appropriate. Finally, she dialed Annie's number. No answer. Dammit, how far could anyone get using a cane? The machine picked up after six rings. Impatiently, Susan waited for the three beeps, picturing Annie lounging in the backyard, screening her calls.

"I can't tell you everything right now, but I think I've finally got what I needed . . ." She cleared her throat nervously. "I'm about to introduce you to the concepts of modern encryption. It'll give you something to do while I'm solving the case." She could imagine the look on Annie's face when she finally picked up her messages. Susan smiled. "Listen, I *know* you're probably going to have trouble with this . . ."

~~~

The restaurant was at the end of a long raked-gravel driveway that followed a serpentine course until it found the view of a lake and a building—a large conservatory—set on a slight rise. Even in winter Susan could tell she was very near water. Moist air touched the skin of the face and neck with a chill that was unexpected but not unpleasant. There was the smell of earth beneath patches of wet snow, the leaves from last year solidly matted together and richly rotted. The sense that, at any moment, the day could be broken with an early spring thunderstorm. The premonition of an event nearly upon you.

They had driven out together in Susan's car, Leah offering directions once or twice during the trip. But Susan seemed to find it as if by instinct. Leah had described it, its physical setting, so specifically that Susan could imagine she might have been there in the past. Only after they arrived did she realize she had seen something like this before.

It was an architecture, Susan recognized, intentionally modelled on an old structure called an orangerie. Wealthy European landowners—and later, their colonial cousins—had created prominent outbuildings, the progenitors of modern-day greenhouses, which allowed them to demonstrate particular horticultural prowess in the growing of oranges and other citrus and exotics in the middle of a gloomy northern winter. All it really served to demonstrate
~~~

was the advantage of money. Expensive glazing and hordes of gardeners could turn *anyone's* thumb green.

They entered, and weak, watery sunlight was translated into a soft, warm ambience. Still, Leah requested—in her polite, direct way—could they possibly open the patio for lunch? It was a perfect day. And certainly warm enough to enjoy spending an hour or two outside, under the winter-bare pergola. Would it be too much trouble . . . ?

The manager himself waved off any concern. Of course the ladies were to be given a table outside, if that's what they desired. Of course the wine selected was one brought up from the owner's private cellar. Of *course* the hot white-truffle oil trickled over the house salad was the same variation she'd so enjoyed on her last visit. "Dr. Mallick has excellent taste . . . and an excellent memory."

The service was as unobtrusive as it was impeccable, and they were left alone, the only ones seated on the terrace. A low stone wall separated it from the open land around them. Susan saw that they were posed at the top of a gentle summit. Beyond the wall, fields sloped down to distant hedgerows, set out in regular and orderly fashion. Cattle grazing in the pasture, blue hills beyond covered with maple forests. From where they were, Susan could imagine they sat at the centre of a great country estate, that these fences and furrows and vistas were theirs . . .

She made constant minute adjustments to the silverware arranged in front of her and was surprised each time at its cold burn to the touch. It was still winter all around them and yet here, they sat outside in complete comfort. The day itself was bracketed by storms; both the Tuesday before and the Thursday that followed recorded unexpected late winter disturbances. But in the middle of it all, this . . .

Leah had mentioned, earlier, having attended the Washington Cathedral School. Susan could observe the results of that training herself. It wasn't that Leah was particularly "refined," not in a obvious way. Not in the least. But it still showed, of course, conveyed in every gesture. Everything done for her—for them—was appreciated. All the small attentions acknowledged yet not dwelt upon. Leah's manners were flawless—practical, effortless. The waiter appeared throughout the afternoon, always when most appropriate, like a kind of punctuation, with an unerring sense of timing: in between stories, at the end of punchlines, even as they made shifts in their conversational direction. No secret signal that Susan could detect, just a rhythm that seemed as natural as the Arcadian setting.

Then lunch was over. Leah had already remarked that she wanted "a quiet life"—a phrase that unexpectedly evoked a deeper yearning in Susan too, at the moment she heard it. Right along with the disappointment. So, no, Leah had said, unfortunately she would not be able to serve on the governor's health care commission . . .

Then Leah did something extraordinary. She made it clear that she had time, that she wasn't in a particular hurry to leave this place. That they could easily linger over another glass of wine if Susan wanted to. And did she?

Susan realized how infrequently she'd been asked that in recent years. Or had asked it herself. How few times anyone took the opportunity to change course in the middle of a day in which, inevitably, every minute was accounted for. *These* three lines in the Daytimer on *that* day. Then, "we must do this again sometime."

Instead, inexplicably, Leah had suggested that they "linger." And it was then that Susan chose to discuss, completely dispassionately, her unfortunate affair with the current governor of the state. She had already sustained the judgment of every possible cliché, every stereotype, even the sophomoric jokes. She was determined to bring every ounce of strength and discipline to bear, and would not be driven—from—to—

Leah said little.

At some point, the waiter had delivered another bottle of wine, a rich, velvety Merlot. Susan began to calculate how many glasses she could safely allow herself. Over the interval of time, given her specific body weight . . . Then she remembered that she'd lost quite a bit during the past few weeks and realized that she was probably already a little drunk.

In making some point, her hand brushed lazily against the wineglass and sent it over. It had been recently filled, she guessed, judging by the sheer size of the red stain that spread slowly across the white linen towards Leah Mallick. And it meant, of course, that she'd been exposed. That she lacked all manners, any sophistication. Lacked essential control.

Leah looked at it without expression for a moment, then began to speak in a precise German accent. "Ah. I see a butterfly. Its wings are spread wide—" She pronounced it as vings and vide and her eyes grew larger as she spoke. She was smiling. "Nein. It is more a very impressive, very fat cat, which fills its stomach every night with songbirds. Here, zis iz—" She hesitated. "Zis iz its tail wrapped around the last one killed before the morning. It iz a bru-u-utal cat. But a very schm-a-art one, I zink . . .

"And these," she continued in a normal voice, her finger outlining the shapes, "are the gypsies, who all gather below the old city walls on market day. See the woman's scarf? It's flying out as she twirls, helplessly, in a wild dance of utter abandon. There's the fiddle and bow, held by the man she calls husband—but who is, in reality, her brother, the notorious pickpocket! The townspeople, crowding all around them, gather to watch and be entertained, even though they know they will leave this place lighter of their purses."

Leah paused and looked up at her expectantly.

Susan felt sleepy and relaxed. She studied the stain for a few moments. "It looks like spilt blood," she said finally.

Leah appeared surprised, even a little disappointed. "Why? Just because of the colour?"

Susan smiled as she shook her head. "No. Because it leads to the victim."

She tilted her hand slightly to show that a few drops of wine had fallen on the back of it and lay there still, small red beads on her pale skin. With her gesture they fell down and spotted the white tablecloth anew. Leah looked at the marks made, then leaned across the table and used her own napkin to blot the remains on Susan's hand. Susan sat, unmoving, being ministered to.

Then they were on their way back to the capital, only an hour away. Navy blue light. Dampness had turned to harder frost, and Susan ran the heater at full for the first several miles. She turned it off finally, and in the quiet Leah suggested they take the next turn off the highway. There was a small hotel not far from here, she said. They could easily stay over, if Susan wanted to . . . Susan glanced over and, in the darkness, caught the small upwards curve of a faint smile.

They were only thirty minutes from town. The roads were clear. There was no reason not to continue straight on to the capital, say goodnight. Something polite, sincere, simple, unweighted. *It was a pleasure to meet you. I'm sorry we won't be working together . . .*

And Susan was driving. It was her car. She was free to take it anywhere she chose. The decision, it was clear, was hers alone to make. But she knew it was what she'd wanted, probably from the first, confirmed for her in the moment she heard Leah Mallick suggest it.

She slowed to take the off-ramp and glided down to the two-lane. Neither of them said anything. The smaller highway followed several large, lazy bends, back and forth, as they drove across the countryside, only another ten miles or so. The frosty cold had left a crystalline sky and, away from the peculiar orange glare of the freeway, the only light here was provided by their headlights, defining the shadows of large trees alongside the road. They could pick out the stars easily.

After a while Susan grew uncomfortable with the silence. She was afraid Leah Mallick could hear each heartbeat, could see the taut stretch of every muscle as she fought to control her slight trembling. She flexed her fingers on the steering wheel.

"I was surfing one night, on the Net, and I found this funny little quiz kind of thing," she said into the dark. Then stopped dead. How pathetic that sounded, she realized. So many nights wasted looking for simple, summary answers. According to the onscreen counter, she'd been the 357,000th visitor since last July. WhoamI.com.

"Like a personality test," Leah prompted. Naturally, she'd guessed. It sounded profoundly trite.

"Supposedly, though, it's one based on Japanese archetypes," Susan said. She hoped that made it seem more credible in some way, less like a tabloid horoscope.

What had possessed her, she later wondered, even to bring that up? She'd suddenly remembered, with a sick thud, that she was actually addressing a widely respected, eminent expert—someone for whom this sort of thing was ridiculous child's play, cheap navel-gazing. "I know they're silly—all these amateur self-help—"

"No, it's fine. Tell me about it."

Susan cleared her throat nervously. "It starts out with—well, you're crossing a desert. You're accompanied by five different animals, but you have very little food and water. Definitely not enough for all of you. If you don't leave one of them behind, it's certain that none of you will survive. There's a lion, a sheep, a monkey, a horse and a cow. You have to decide—which one do you choose to sacrifice first? Then, next—each one after that—in turn . . ."

Leah said nothing for a moment.

"Sorry. I know it's really stupid. Just forget it," Susan said.

Leah held up her hand very briefly. "No . . . I'm just thinking."

Obviously, Leah was indulging her now.

"Let me see. Umm, first, the sheep, of course. Just the name, all those 'sheeplike' qualities associated with it . . ." She thought for another moment. "Then the cow. Not much use for one out there in the desert. What were the others again?"

"Horse, monkey, lion."

"Ah, yes. Well, the lion's got to go, I guess. Beautiful and brave, but, with deepest regrets . . . So just the last two. The horse, then. It's taken me *this* far, but I guess it'll have to be just me and the monkey from here on." She smiled gently. "So, interpret all that for me—what does it mean?"

Susan held her eyes on the road in front of the car, blushing now. This was a foolish exercise, she knew, more like tarot cards or tea leaves. Who was she to tell Leah Mallick about archetypes?

Leah prodded her, laughing. "C'mon . . ."

"Well, the sheep is friendship," Susan said in a tentative voice. Then she glanced at her passenger, trying to gauge a reaction.

Leah raised her eyebrow. "First to go—hmmm." She smiled again, encouraging Susan to continue.

"The next one was the cow, which supposedly refers to basic needs."

Leah nodded wordlessly.

"Then, the lion. Representing pride."

"Hmm. It *is* dangerous to hold on to that one for too long. The horse?"

"The horse stands for passion."

Again the eyebrow. Then Leah made a comic-sad face. "Oh, well. But at least I still have my monkey. What does that mean?"

"The monkey . . . it represents a child. The one thing to which you will cling, at the expense of all others."

Leah was thoughtful for a moment. Then she laughed merrily. "And that's what remains, eh? My passion and my child."

"Actually, you did abandon your passion. In the end," Susan pointed out.

Leah looked at her, nodded again. "But I still have my child. Just me and my little monkey . . . " Everything else gone but that one thing she would not sacrifice, until life itself ran out across the desert sand. "And we make it safely to the oasis, I presume. Unless, of course, it's only a mirage . . ."

Afterwards, when Susan replayed the scene back in her mind, she wondered the same thing. A mirage? Had there really been a slight rise in Leah's voice at the very end of that comment? Making of it yet another question?

She could only wonder, hopelessly, now—as she knew she always would—about everything that had happened that night.

As they'd pulled up under the portico of the hotel, she heard Leah Mallick's warm, rich voice beside her in the dark. "So, which one did *you* decide to keep in the end?"

It was the moment before they stepped out of the car and she relinquished her keys to the waiting valet, Susan looked over to Leah with a smile at last. "I sacrificed them all—and embraced the desert."

There's a small hotel, Leah had said. How would you feel about stopping . . . ?

~~~

Annie counted down in her head. Five minutes . . . four . . . three . . . It wasn't the distance, she'd been told, it was the time. No matter what, a full thirty minutes. This time she'd managed a complete circuit of two neighbourhood blocks, at the pace of a sedate ninety-year-old. People with walkers were passing her. At this rate, Annie thought, I can watch the gardens grow. Literally.

And they were. Everything around her was out, lush and full. Plants she'd never really noticed before—flowering trees and large displays of ornamental grasses, vines winding around new trellises. Perhaps they'd always been here. The neighbours working outside, stripped of their bulky winter clothes looked as small and frail as new birds. Maybe they'd always been here too. A couple of them, apparently recognizing her, waved as she passed. Very slowly.

She was sweating now, soaking through the thin layers. It was, what, maybe a quarter-mile? she asked herself. You know you're middle-aged when you finally accept that you're never going to qualify for the Olympics. You're middle-aged when you realize you're closer to being an *éminence grise* than an *enfant terrible.*

She saw a car waiting out front of her house. It took her a moment to recognize it as Bill's. He hadn't been by for years. And his being here didn't fit now. It was never a good thing to find a cop at your front door, she thought.
~~~

Bill had seen her. He rose now from the porch swing and came to stand at the top of the stairs, watching her approach.

It gave her a chance to show off. Annie quickened her pace into the semblance of a run for the last ten yards, raising her arms in an imitation of victory as she turned in to her front walk.

But his reaction wasn't what she expected. He didn't smile. This time his face was deadly serious. *Never* a good thing to see a cop at your front door.

Annie pushed the shadow away. "Hey, that had to be worth at least *one* attaboy."

She stopped at the bottom of the steps, out of breath and chilled. It was almost dark. The house looked lifeless and empty behind him. She hadn't thought to leave a light on before going out.

It was more his voice than his expression that made her heart start hammering again.

"Annie—"

He wasn't moving. As though frozen in place.

"Something's happened," he said. "To Susan . . ."

As they drove in, the small crowd parted just enough to let each vehicle squeeze through. They had to walk down to the water. Annie got out of her car and a flash from somewhere nearby went off. Another picture for the local newspaper. This time they would see her dressed in a badly fitting, sweat-stained jogging outfit, her face no longer the mask of reason. Someone in the group of sightseers called out her name loudly and a small ripple of excitement spread, then died out just as fast.

She followed Bill through the confusion of official cars and an ambulance, towards whatever was being protected from public view. A couple of tarps had already been hung up. The body was partially in and partially out of the water, almost hidden under an abandoned wrecked car covered with spray-painted graffiti: Mutherfuker.

John Bartlett was crouched down close, at the water's edge, his shoes buried in the soft mud. He was talking to a uniformed police officer.

He stood up, looking tense and subdued, as she came towards him. "Hey, Annie . . ." He was shaking his head. "Hey, I'm really sorry about all this. It doesn't look like much more than a mugging, though. Small contusion on her forehead, broken heel on one of her shoes. Might have tripped, or been knocked down. I don't know, but I'd say it looks like she probably drowned. She wasn't—" He hesitated. "I mean, there's no signs of any sexual assault. We found her purse down there a ways, about two hundred yards. No money left in it, of course—just everything scattered around, like." He gave a little laugh. "But after getting caught out last time like we did, I guess we'd better wait for the ME to give us the final—"

In the next moment Annie struck him. He had only the time to lift his arm weakly before she slapped him again.

Then Annie felt herself being lifted and shoved roughly off to one side. It was Bill, pushing her out of the lights, away from the crowd, nearer to the water. The sour-metal smell of iron. The greasy flow of the river.

She didn't see the whole picture at once, only pieces of it—the thin sludge already coating everything that had been so clean, a cigarette package caught in the current against partly submerged rocks, a flash of white in a foot of black water. Susan was so fastidious.

"This filthy place . . ." At last Annie caught her breath and pushed back hard against him. "You—none of you . . . All you want to do is cover your fucking asses."

He held on. The smell of his jacket, her own drying sweat, a warm summer night.

And he was taking her blows. OK, OK.

Everyone had stopped and was now looking at each other in a kind of innocent surprise. The crowd, held back fifty feet or so, craned to see what was happening.

Annie tore out of Bill's arms and plunged back towards them. John Bartlett looked pale and shaken. He didn't even try to defend himself.

Annie got within a few of feet of him. "I don't want to hear any more of your shit, John. You don't want to get *caught?* You think anyone is going to believe *any* of you after what happened? You all got caught out on *that* one, too, didn't you? A bunch of goddamned geniuses—"

Another cop, a new second lieutenant let out a braying laugh. "Aaall-riiight. Now, the big TV star is gonna tell us how to do the job." In the next instant, Bill had grabbed him, half swinging him off his feet, to put a fist within inches of his face. In the damp night air coming off the river, their breaths billowed up and mixed under the bright lights, two bulls blindly charging. A couple of others were already stepping in between them. Everyone looked shell-shocked.

In the sudden silence, another voice came out of the darkness. "Get her out of here, Williamson." It was Dan

Hewitt, squinting now in the lights as he made his way through the stunned group towards her.

Annie didn't care what she said now or who heard. She whirled on him, ready. "Go ahead, Dan. Get it off your chest. You've been wanting to say it to me for a long time—"

"I'd say the same to *any* cop who's doing what you're doing right now. You're losing it, Lieutenant. Leave. You're no use to anyone here." His voice didn't rise. And he continued to look at her. But something seemed to change in his face. He wasn't trying to punish her this time.

Then it was the old Dan Hewitt, the one she remembered from too many years ago—from every Saturday morning during childhood's long summers. The best cop in the department, who'd made her want to be one too. The man she'd once thought of as a better father than her own.

And he spoke only to her. "Annie, darlin', go home. I'll make sure everything's done right."

"Someone has to identify her, Dan."

"*I* will," Hewitt said quietly. He reached out and clumsily squeezed her hand, then turned and slid down the slippery bank, to the body buried in the water.

Annie stood far back in the darkness, outside the ring of the working lights, waiting on the abandoned railway tracks that ran along the river's edge. Across the river, the sparks of Palladian Steel, glittered like stars in the water.

She could see that Susan was wearing a summer-weight crème white suit, perfectly matching shoes. Her hair had fallen down and was now swept over her face in the slow flow of the water.

Annie stared until she couldn't, until she felt her stomach rolling hard. "Christ, Bill. Don't let them leave her there. Like that." Then she turned and walked away.

11

For hours, she'd searched in the dark for sleep, then gave up and went back downstairs, back to replaying the same phrases of the phone message, over and over again.

"*Listen. I know you're probably going to have trouble with this . . . posed as her . . . an anonymous account.*" The short pause. "*. . . I'll explain what I can when I figure out why . . .*" Then the change in tone, more upbeat, "*. . . really need now is a high-speed hookup. You claim to know everyone in town. Come on, pull a few strings for me, Lieutenant. You must have a guy . . .*"

Yeah, I got a guy, Annie thought, answering her the same way each time. I got a guy—one who can accurately describe the trajectory and force of the blow. Another who can tell me the direction of the body's entry into the water. How far the current had carried, in the given interval of time . . . A bunch of guys, in fact, who are all running around, tripping over each other's feet, trying their damnedest to find out who hurt you.

And then Susan, laughing again. "*This stuff can't be so hard. If two old broads like us can do it.*"

Annie took another swallow of the indifferent wine she'd found at the back of a pantry shelf. How had it survived there for so long? Eight, nine years. It had to be the disguise—a light coating of dust that made it look like expensive vinegar or olive oil, the kind she'd once bought on impulse after reading some magazine article about Tuscany. She'd never had a bottle of wine long enough to find out if it aged well or not. This one? Basic plonk, she concluded. But by the time you got to the bottom, it didn't really matter.

She let the kitchen door swing closed behind her and climbed the stairs unsteadily. The end of the phone message rolled away into the darkness below. The voice always contemplative as it approached this part, "*. . . it's more complicated than I can even say.*" Then the longest pause. Annie had timed it out at three to four seconds. *"Anyway, you can be Woodward tomorrow. 'Night."* Susan said again, the final sound of it more faint this time.

Right now, Annie wanted nothing more than to phone someone too. Almost anyone. She tripped slightly on the step, and a bit of the overfull glass splashed on to her bare foot. Where does that impulse come from? she wondered. That the minute you got a little loaded, you wanted to call everyone you'd ever known. Instead, she just stood in front of the long mirror and watched herself finish the last of the wine.

Right now, what she wanted most was to reach out and lay her hand over Susan's again. "The safety . . ." she'd say. "Here, this is how you turn it on." Not off.

Because she knew that safety wasn't in having a weapon which couldn't fire any more, but one that could.

She dreamed again. And whenever she dreamed, it was that he was taken, still missing, yet to be found. Sometimes swept from her arms in rising flood waters, and she came out of that water choking and gasping for air. Or frozen, in a sudden blizzard. Always the last touch was of cold skin.

In all these years she'd never had one of those movie moments where the protagonist is jolted up to an impossible sitting-at-attention position in bed, surrounded by phantom flames, wild-eyed and sweating, breathing heavily enough to awaken the sleeping partner beside her, who dutifully whispers, "Are you OK?" The hero sliding back down, heart still pounding, mumbling, "Nothing. Just a bad dream. Go back to sleep."

No. Instead, in the beginning, it was always some sunny late afternoon, when they bought banana Popsicles on the way home from the ballpark and argued about who was or wasn't going to eat supper after three hot dogs. It was the homework not done, or the room not cleaned, or the best video game ever made, the whine of "you never buy me anything." But it was never about the fire.

She never viewed the child through a red-angry blur or the merciless rock of a headache. The day was always a warm, shiny, blue-sky wonder, the boy was still all right and she hadn't yet turned the key in the lock for that one single hour apart. A fifteen-minute walk away. A group of semi-regulars who didn't pay enough attention to anything beyond the immediate reach of their own arms, to know where she should or shouldn't be at this time of night, with a kid at home, pouring the third straight scotch, with a beer chaser.

While she remained awake through most of the next thousand nights, the simple vision of a doorway was what she looked at much of the time. A big, wooden, cracked, varnish frame of maddened light at the end of the hallway. She saw that the top two panels of the door were in splinters. The brass-plated number twenty-three, was resting amidst thick grey canvas hoses, floating in milky water. Yellow slickers and helmets outlined faces of nothing but soot-rimmed, bloodshot eyes. And black rain ran down the beige-painted walls.

But when she slept, she swept him up in her arms and carried him into the clear night air. She watched the colour seep back into his face, the purplish cast warming into a little boy's late summer tan.

She could see the old apartment in the evening, the antique lamp, bought at a garage sale, on the sideboard, the window slightly ajar, the curtain bending to the air. It was warm that night, warm enough not to need a jacket when she left. He had already gone to sleep under a cotton Star Wars sheet, the old quilt hanging down over the end of the bed in case he got cold in the night. On an ordinary night she would have checked on him as soon as she got back. Probably two or three times after that. Made sure he hadn't kicked off his covers, that he was still breathing, that his lunch was packed for school the next day. She was a good mother.

She usually ended her dreams—the ones she could remember, anyway—with a flight over the city, a triumphant coda tacked on to the end of the night's silent symphony of screaming. She saw herself flying over the familiar skyline, dimly aware that the experts claimed it was an image representing something hidden, buried. But sometimes flying was just flying.

~~~

Annie squeezed between the two vans pulled up to the Creighton Hotel's loading dock. They were shipping stacks of kitchen supplies, boxes of frozen foods, fresh fruit and vegetables through the propped-open double doors. She could see the kitchen staff working inside amidst a cloud of heat from the stoves and smelled the fragrance of fresh baking. A couple of busboys were sitting on upended milk crates to grab a cigarette break before the morning rush really began, talking in Spanish to each other. After an uninterested glance, they ignored her.

As though I'd planned it, she thought. Lank, wet hair from the shower. Wrinkled clothes. Hell, wrinkled *everything.* Not looking like much of a TV star any more, she knew. And an hour of sleep wasn't the cure-all it used to be.

She followed a narrow cinder-block corridor to the service elevator. She'd worked this hotel often enough—once as part of the security detail for a presidential candidate—to know every possible route in or out. There were a number of ways to avoid the main lobby.

"Security" was a misnomer, anyway. If you'd ever provided security, you knew there was none; it was an illusion. And nothing had changed. Annie easily slipped the lock to the fifth-floor suite. Technically, it didn't constitute an illegal search; she wasn't on the formal duty-roster till Monday. This was simple break and enter.
~~~

She closed the door silently behind her and stood with her back against it. As though from a great distance she surveyed the whole scene, this time not knowing what to look at or how to feel about looking at it at all. Ten seconds and then ten minutes. The sun hadn't yet worked its way around to this side of the building, leaving everything a sturdy, monochromatic brown.

Susan had left here expecting to return. And the relics of those last moments sat frozen in place. A half-eaten sandwich, an almost full cup of coffee. An expensive leather jacket thrown over the back of a chair. A pair of jeans crumpled on the bed. A sweater. The new Reeboks tossed on the floor nearby. She had probably changed into the white business suit just before going out.

Going out and, for some reason, heading down to the river, a place of old warehouses and abandoned rail sidings. But nothing, Annie suspected, *nothing* in the world would have made her go into that area alone. She'd gone with someone. Or to meet someone.

She didn't seem to know anyone in Lockport. Yet Annie remembered watching the other detectives circling around her during that one evening at Holly's, making their moves, their clumsy pitches, which, on the surface anyway, Susan had ignored. She'd even turned down a couple point-blank, John Bartlett for one. But maybe she'd later agreed to drinks or dinner?

Another cop? Abruptly, Annie stopped herself. But even the thought of that was almost more acceptable than this dark hole she was facing.

She forced herself to the details again. The contusion on

the forehead. Absence of any defensive wounds, not on the hands or the arms. She'd had no time even to try . . .

Annie gripped the back of the chair, digging in until her fingers hurt. *Jesus Christ.* The indifferent room swung around her like a mechanical ride. If someone was meting out punishment, they could do worse than these few minutes, she thought.

And all I can do is make myself stand here and take it, and know that it won't ever really go away. Not with *these* images flickering past. It's not about "being out of practice." You can never get used to this, no matter what you try to tell yourself.

She waited until the room slowed then stopped. The boxes of files in front of her became straight and orderly again. Susan's briefcase had been left unlatched, flat on the makeshift desk. Annie lifted the lid. The contents were carefully arranged, as she'd expected. She let it fall closed. The other papers, all the ones laid out on the table, were lined up with their edges squared as usual. Nothing in the least disturbed here.

Annie heard a shout in the hallway directly outside. She remembered that she'd closed the door behind her but forgot to lock it.

"Hey! Georgie. Ya got the supplies cart there? Room 429 wants more TP. Some guy called down to the front desk. He's stuck in the john." George must have replied. There was more laughter, moving a little further away now. "I don't know, man. Probably had a cellphone with him. Probably in there doing the crossword . . ." A few more unintelligible words, then they came back in her direction and went right by, the service cart rattling in front of them.

She recognized the voice, picturing the big familiar grin, so like his father's. James S., Trainee Assistant Manager and future cop.

Annie waited until they'd passed, then listened for the distant, whistling sound of the elevator descending. She edged the door open. The hallway was empty again.

She looked back over the sullen, quiet room she was leaving. Once housekeeping had passed through, it would quickly return to its absolute, peaceful anonymity. The same old-fashioned flocked wallpaper and stained upholstery, the same view of the river and Palladian Steel. And it would always be exactly as ugly as it was in this moment.

Soon they would all admit that Susan's death was more than just a matter of being in the wrong place at the wrong time. So, it was still essential to check for fingerprints here, to examine the contents of the files stored in this room. There were enough people named in those records, Annie knew, to provide for a hundred motives, if someone wanted to spend the months and the money to put it all together. It was still necessary to scrutinize the record of the phone calls that had come in and gone out of this room. Interview the staff at the front desk. Inch by inch, examine the victim's car left abandoned in the parking garage. Begin the odyssey of another criminal investigation.

But they wouldn't find anything that mattered, Annie knew. The truth was in here, somewhere. As Susan would have said, it was in the pattern broken, the subtle anomaly; maybe the one thing on which they'd always agreed.

Annie hesitated for only a moment, then quickly crossed the room to the desk. She snapped the laptop shut and pulled the plug, shoving everything into the carrying case. Then she picked it up and slung the strap over her shoulder. *Now, this—this,* bunkie—*is theft* . . .

And before she drove all the way back across the Stoney River, back to her own home again, she placed a call to the division dispatcher, casually inquiring if anyone had thought to put a cop on the door of Susan Shaw's hotel room.

∿∿∿

On Monday morning, Annie found herself circling the block, waiting for a sign to tell her that it was OK to go in. She was already expecting a "particularly difficult day," trying to set aside doubts that weighed more than her best intentions. Either go forward, she told herself again, or give up, right now.

As she crossed the lobby, a couple of people waved. Some came close enough to reach out and pat her arm. "Welcome back."

And some took a moment to add, "Listen, I heard about what happened over the weekend. I'm sorry . . ."

How do you ever reply to that, she thought. Etiquette books always tell you that a simple thank you sufficed. "I didn't . . . I didn't really know her very well—" Annie began at one point. Then her voice caught and she stopped even trying to respond. *Thank you.*

And from the beginning it was nothing like a regular day. There was no mountain of paper facing her when she finally made it into her office. She felt vague disappointment. That, at least, would have provided *some* distraction.

But Stan Kendra had turned out to be a frighteningly effective choice as her replacement: he'd so thoroughly bored everyone and discouraged any inquiries that there were very few messages left for her to return. Only a couple of memos lay neglected at the bottom of her in-box, outlining arrangements for various upcoming community events. An invitation to join an anti-racism conference, judge a poster contest.

More than anything, it felt like a too quiet morning. Like waiting for the other shoe to drop, she thought. Everyone too carefully soft-shoeing around her. After a couple of hours, nervous and on edge, she looked up to see Tina standing in the doorway, holding out a cup of coffee.

"Hi. I thought maybe you could use this. Cream and sugar OK?"

Annie preferred it black but smiled as she reached for it. "Sure. That's great. Thanks." She noticed a small change: Tina had removed her nose stud. "What happened to the . . ." She tapped the side of her own nose.

Tina felt for it absently. "Oh, yeah, that. I gave it to my boyfriend, Jazz. We trade stuff like that all the time. Like, this is *his,* eh . . ." She held up a heavy silver bracelet, twice the size of her thin wrist.

"You can type with that thing on?"

Tina giggled, the sound a welcome surprise to both of them.

Annie had to remind herself that Tina was still little more than a girl under all that black-painted attitude. She raised the cup again. "Anyway . . . thanks."

Tina glanced around, seeming reluctant to leave. "No problem. Anything else I can do for you, Lieutenant?"

Unexpectedly, Annie's eyes stung for a moment. Just say thank you, she told herself. Thank you, and let it go. She stared down at the almost empty surface of her desk.

But after a moment she looked up at Tina again. "I would like to ask you a question. You can just answer yes or no."

Tina's eyes grew larger, but she said nothing.

"Is it possible to tell if something's been deleted . . . I mean, on a computer? And maybe when?"

Annie could see Tina constructing a hundred possibilities in her mind. Then, "Yes."

OK, try another one. "Is it ever possible . . . to recover it?"

Tina looked out the window for an easy explanation, considering her words, making them simple. "It depends. You have to be really careful. Like, you can't just screw around with it. Jazz always says it's like looking for a footprint in the sand. You know, you could just end up blowing it all away. And he's a really excellent hacker."

Annie raised an eyebrow briefly. *I'll just bet he is.* OK, then, one more question. "Could you teach me something about encryption?"

This time, Tina simply nodded.

And Annie let out one long, slow breath. O-*kay.*

Over the next hour it was as though a clock had wound itself up again. The day actually took on some semblance of normalcy. It was the noise Annie noticed first, a phone going off somewhere every ten seconds. Every time she looked up, someone had their head stuck in her doorway, wanting a favour. "Sorry, I know you're just back, but could you . . . ?" "Would you mind if . . . ?" How does anyone ever get real work done in an office? she wondered.

Every request for information was more trite than the last. She could have sent out year-old press releases for all the difference it made. Who actually read this shit, anyway?

Late in the morning, there was a small scratching noise at her door and Stan Kendra crept in. She saw what his problem was: he was far too diffident. Not the kind of guy to whom she'd ever been attracted. Or could trust. You got to take it like you own it, m'man, she thought. Find it or fake it. Otherwise, they're going to kill you.

Stan cleared his throat. "I thought I should debrief you on these files. For the regular Friday media conference. You know, because you're going to be taking over again . . ."

He spread everything out across her desk: the plans for a school visit, a car rally, a skateboard freestyle competition at the new city facility, a legal conference on the efficacy of the Miranda Decision in the wake of proposed federal search-and-seizure legislation, a preschool safety exercise, a little race in the park with decorated baskets . . .

She stopped him. "Didn't we already do one of those? At Easter?"

"Well, yeah. But that was chocolate *eggs,* and this is—more like . . . marshmallows." The difference seemed significant to him.

Annie studied him for a moment. He glanced up nervously. Setting her own taste in men aside, she decided he was probably capable enough. "You know what you have to do, Kendra? You have to tell them to fuck off sometimes. And you're going to have to learn how to relax. At least try and pretend not to care so much."

He looked back at her, uncomprehending. If he didn't already have an attitude, she thought, he was going to have to *acquire* one pretty fast. Maybe Tina could teach him.

"Look . . . um, Stan, you know I just got back. I've got a lot of catching up to do. Do you think you'd mind carrying this part of it for a little while? Until I find my feet, at least. I'm actually pretty swamped here."

The delight dawning on his face was almost poignant, she thought. God, had she ever wanted it *that* much?

He practically vibrated. "Sure. No problem. I'd be happy to help out. Anything else? I mean, I've got some good ideas for the Crime Stoppers segments—"

She put her head in her hands. Christ. Did *everyone* want to be in show business? "Just do the Friday chat thing for now, please. We can talk about the rest of it later." This is turning into *All About Eve,* she thought—and *I'm* Margo Channing.

They spent the next half-hour going over details. Kendra finally left, after making pages of notes—backing out and scraping all the way, she presumed.

After he was gone, Annie sat for a long time, staring at the non-existent view out her window. Then, from half inside a daydream, she overheard voices, the tail end of a conversation, convened just outside her door. The governor was making a private visit to Lockport, mid-afternoon. No publicity. No police escort.

The three cops standing there stumbled into silence, too late, when they finally looked up to see Annie was standing in the doorway.

Everyone knew why he was coming.

An hour later, she was waiting in her car across the street from the Cedars of Lebanon Funeral Home. At a few minutes past two, the gunmetal grey hearse drove up from the basement garage and positioned itself in the curve of the wide driveway, right in front of the stairs.

A group of people emerged from the building. The governor, even more handsome in person, was solemn in a navy suit. Three men followed close behind him. An older woman, sturdy-looking and plain, with a blotchy-red complexion, wiped her eyes. There were handshakes all round. Each said something to the funeral home director before descending the steps into the waiting limo. The mortician stood at formal attention as they left, a model of propriety.

The hearse pulled out slowly and turned on to the main street, trailed by the limo. It was a two-hour trip back to the capital. Annie watched as they drove past her.

The windows of the limousine were heavily tinted; there was no way to see who was inside. Nor were there any external markings, except for the almost invisible holder on each front fender normally used to display the official state flag. The procession grew smaller and finally disappeared in her rear-view mirror.

This time Annie stayed for close to forty-five minutes, ignoring several broad hints from one of the nurses on duty. In general, though, the hospital staff seemed less willing to confront her, despite the administration's threats.

She'd tried to focus exclusively on the boy but found her attention constantly being drawn to all the things outside him that more concretely defined his presence here. Everything he was was entirely externalized now. Even his heart beat elsewhere, beyond the limits of his own body. She heard the amplified electronic sound of it. For only a few moments that sound seemed to pulse in the same rhythm as her own. Then it travelled away again, increasingly out of step with hers, until it was in diametric opposition. Then it returned, waxing and waning throughout the whole of the time she noticed it.

It was probably the right time to leave. Annie leaned closer to him, and whispered aloud what she'd only been thinking: "Good night, Kyle."

Here was the real broken promise. To say good night once more. To brush his hair back from his forehead and allow her hand to rest there forever . . .

Annie could hear the shift change on the ward. The greetings exchanged, someone bragging about a parking spot they'd lucked into, complaints about a husband who forgot to get the right kind of cream cheese when he even bothered to pick up the groceries. The thought of being confined in an elevator with any of them—people who would just look at her in that way they all seemed to now—was less than appealing. Leaving the room, she turned to the stairs instead.

Somewhere, in the thin silence, Annie heard whistling, a light, familiar melody she recognized but couldn't remember. She hummed along, trying to identify it.

She didn't notice the man approaching from behind until he was walking right beside her.

"You're Lieutenant Shannon, aren't you?" The tone was friendly. It didn't match the face.

She gave him a quick glance. No one she recognized. *Another fan.* The lights in the hallway were too bright after the darkened room, but what she'd seen was a man of indeterminate age and height, one so nondescript that any eyewitness would have had trouble picking him out of a lineup. "What can I do for you?" She walked a little faster. Probably a reporter. Or maybe just another dedicated, one-note bureaucrat from hospital administration, lying in wait to inform her that she wasn't welcome here.

"Could we talk for a moment?" he said.

"I've had kind of a long day. What is it?" Annie replied shortly. She felt him pressing too close to her now. She could smell the egg salad sandwich he'd just eaten. It made her want to gag.

"OK, I'm more than happy to make this fast. It's come time for you to end this little game you're playing. This so-called 'unofficial' scavenger hunt you're on. Shit or get off the pot, lady. You're about to miss the main chance."

She stopped dead to stare at him. At least he wasn't from the hospital. No clip-on security pass, no identification. And no beating around the bush.

Then his tone altered abruptly. "Was that more like what you were expecting, Lieutenant?" He smiled at her perplexed expression. "No, seriously. I'm here to tell you that you've successfully attracted our interest. You should already understand, of course, that we're completely within our rights to protect a wide range of significant, proprietary technologies developed for substantive commercial investment potential. And we're more than prepared to do so."

"That's quite a mouthful. Some HMO, I presume?" A strike at the fly, she thought dryly. It meant Cross Corp was now coming for her.

"You're certainly not *that* naïve, Ms. Shannon. I don't work for just 'some HMO.' But that's not why I'm here."

Like Susan had said, it was so much *more* than that. "But you'd say that you currently represent their best interests." *If you insist on splitting hairs.*

"No. What I *want* to say is that we've already become the victims of unfounded and thoroughly irresponsible speculation, clearly bordering on libel. And that pursuing it will compromise any credibility you might ever be able to claim—either within the medical community or in any significant court of law. And I *would* say that any person who chooses to ignore that—to continue along a demonstrably more reckless course—does so at the risk of revealing herself to be nothing more than just another irrational, bitter and incompetent fuck-up." He looked positively ingenuous now.

Her blood pressure rose dangerously, but she matched his faint smile. "Uh, uh . . . careful there. Libel laws work both ways. We incompetent fuck-ups might take exception to that."

"I believe I'm on fairly solid ground." Again the smirk, more disturbing this time.

Annie turned and started to walk away again. "And *I'd* have to say, we're looking in several different directions," she said dismissively.

"So I understand," he said, very quietly. Something in his voice made her stop and look back at him. Even in the brilliant glare of the hospital corridor his features seemed blurred and indistinct. "But then it's not really 'we' any more, is it, Lieutenant?" he said.

In one moment, all the blood drained from her face.

"You didn't *really* think we would sit still for it, did you? Your little secret investigation? Where our legitimate interests are involved, we're prepared to engage in legal proceedings that will extend to the *next* millennium, I promise you. We can already make a case for something closely approximating illegal search, harassment, perhaps even malicious prosecution. *Ad nauseam* . . . *Ad infinitum* . . ."

She listened. You've picked the wrong person this time, she thought. She could have said that it was a waste of time to threaten her, because she had nothing left to lose. Instead, she gave him a look of clear disdain, then edged past him.

He faded back to let her go. "But legal niceties aside—I believe there is something else you do care about." Then, in a mocking, singsong voice, he said, "Good ni-i-ight, Kyle."

She felt a violent trembling in her legs. Despite it, she spun back around and stepped as close to him as she could stomach. "Don't even *think* about trying to intimidate me, you bastard."

He didn't flinch. "No. You misunderstand me. I'm the one who's actually going to help you. You're starting to dream again. When you're ready, I'll get you the answers you can't find. I'll answer the questions you've always had. And I will ensure that it all falls into its proper place." He moved his hands in a cheap version of a magician's gesture. *Abracadabra.* "I can turn back time for you. You want to start over? Ten years?" He snapped his fingers. "But don't think you'll be allowed to go where you're not meant to go."

More rage than any fear now. "You're seriously threatening me? A police officer?"

"Oh, I wouldn't emphasize *that* point too much right now, if I were you . . . *Lieutenant.*" His ironic emphasis was perfectly played. "That's the *easiest* part to undo . . ." he said. He gave her another penetrating look. And there was mild satisfaction on his face when it was she who finally backed away a few inches. Then he walked down the hall, unhurriedly, and disappeared around the corner, whistling.

He hadn't introduced himself. But then he really didn't *have* to, she thought. "His name is Legion—" she said to herself. They still needed her to understand that they were everywhere.

Annie hurried by the nursing station on the way to the elevator. Forget the damn stairs; she'd suddenly noticed that her leg was throbbing painfully. Another nurse on duty watched her pass. Annie smiled grimly at her. "It's time to go," she said aloud. Deliberately. Distinctly.

The nurse stared back, uncomprehending. No sign of any particular understanding on her face, that Annie could see.

Almost unconsciously, Annie began to hum the same tune she'd heard in the echoing corridor. Then, it came to her: "Lili Marlene." Not Wagner or Beethoven, or even

Bach, in the end. Just a familiar music-hall ditty. Sung by millions, for a hundred years. A bit of nostalgic flotsam. Someone singing *that*—in a place like this.

Annie half-sang it too as she drove along the darkening, empty streets, taking the bridge into Belford. She vaguely remembered Marlene Dietrich's Teutonic growl. Then it was all around her again, the evergreen promise of Belford. One promise broken, she said to herself. A new one to make.

Annie pulled up to the curb. The curtains and blinds were closed. The yellow plastic tape had long ago been removed, but the front door was still sealed under order. The house had finally been released by the court. And tomorrow, she knew, a county-contracted moving van would empty it, carrying the contents to a large industrial warehouse on the flat outskirts of town, near the municipal airport. The court-appointed executor of the estate had already arranged for the inventory, in its entirety, to be disposed of through a liquidator.

She imagined the usual boxes of family photographs, school records, old tax returns. Books and CDs, paperweights and pen sets, found shells and stones, shirts missing a button, too many plastic containers stacked up in a kitchen cupboard. The incalculable weight of evidence that three lives had been cataclysmically interrupted. Personal effects of little value. What remained would be cleanly divided into assets or liabilities. Legal notices would have to be published: "Those having claims . . ." Something could yet come out of the woodwork, but no one would ever conceive of the meticulous Dr. Mallick as having been careless.

So why had she tried to frame her husband? What purpose did that serve? Maybe because she did believe it was his fault. His weakness. His failure. That he had to be held responsible in the eyes of the world for the lost dreams, the ruined child. Biology offered its own unequivocal evidence. He'd condemned himself as surely as if he'd pulled the trigger . . .

Annie walked slowly up the driveway. It was as if the house had been holding its breath, waiting for her to return to it. In that moment, she knew what "haunted" really meant.

All roads led back to Leah Mallick, and she to this place. Something endured here. Annie walked around to the backyard, studying the vacant house from another perspective. A telescope, an opened window . . .

It took her a moment to register it in her mind. The open window on the second floor—Kyle's room. The flash of white curtain floating on the breeze. Then, while she watched, someone ducking quickly out of sight.

She heard a fading, dry-papery voice beside her. Susan. "Isn't this where I came in, Lieutenant? Don't even *think* about going in there. Call a real cop, for God's sake . . ."

Annie ignored her. Most break-ins were over, their perpetrators long gone, in less than ninety seconds. Someone was in there now, inside this particular house. The lock on the garage side-door was at least twenty-five years old, and Annie easily slipped it with a pocket-sized shiv. A million-dollar home protected with something that cost less than fifty, giving it up to a thin piece of metal worth about two bucks. She walked through the empty garage. The pricey cars had been removed days ago.

She moved carefully into the house, bathed in pale light from the street lamps outside, the final remains of sunset.

Annie reached the top of the staircase on the second floor. Almost three weeks since she'd been here, but she turned to the right automatically, and found herself standing once again in the doorway of Kyle Mallick's bedroom.

Annie saw the boy immediately. He was kneeling beside the telescope, the pale, lank hair falling down as he bent his head near the eyepiece to adjust the focus. Whatever the modern complexity of lens and mirrors, this telescope was aimed at all the same astounding sights that had once intrigued Leonardo da Vinci and Copernicus and Ptolemy. Yet even after all the centuries of such observation, she thought, we still remain convinced the cosmos revolves around us . . .

Without intending to, Annie made a soft sound, no more than an intake of breath. And without warning, the boy threw himself violently sideways, staring towards the door in terror as he scrambled into a dark corner. From where she stood, though the room was buried in dusk, she could see his widened eyes and open mouth. The next sound, she knew, would be a scream.

She flicked the switch. The light was flat and hard and white. The boy's strangled shout was immediately suspended and they were left looking at each other. He could tell that he was probably in trouble, but not in any danger.

Annie saw a skinny kid, clean and well dressed, about eight or nine. Clear, smooth complexion, already a light summer tan. This was no runaway—he belonged in this neighbourhood. Anyone else would have been out the window before she'd taken two steps inside the room. She noticed that he had a raw scrape down the whole length of his forearm.

"How'd you hurt yourself?" She pointed to his elbow.

He pulled his arm up to see for himself, as if aware of it for the first time. He looked back at her, still silent. She motioned him towards her. "C'mere," she said quietly.

He held his arm up to her to be examined. Dark pink, a bit of blood, a pretty good surface abrasion that would heal into a spectacular showpiece for the other kids at school by tomorrow.

"I came in through that little door in the kitchen," he said in a subdued voice. She knew that he meant the pet entrance cut out of the back door—the one thing the sheriff's department hadn't thought to seal against intruders.

"It's pretty small. That how you did this?"

He studied the wound again. "Yeah. I guess I'm too big for it."

Annie laughed softly. "Well, you're certainly getting there. Just a second." She gestured for him to wait. She turned and went into the large bathroom, counting on being able to find what she needed easily—the disinfectant, some cotton swabs, a Band-Aid. Everything was precisely where she expected it to be. No matter how insane these people had been, they still stored their things in the usual places.

Annie walked back into the bedroom. The kid was amusing himself with a toy car he'd found up on a bookshelf.

Annie reached down and gently bent his arm towards her. He winced when the disinfectant touched the opened skin. "Do you want me to blow on it for you?" He nodded and lifted his elbow higher, up towards her. She put her mouth close and blew carefully, up and down his arm, as she remembered doing a hundred times. Little boys were always being wounded.

He let his arm drop and stepped away, the sting fading.

"I guess you'll live," she said, setting aside the first-aid supplies. "So, tell me what you were doing here, anyway—in Kyle's room?"

He offered no reaction to the name.

"I guess you and Kyle hung out together, eh?"

He shook his head vehemently.

"He wasn't your friend?"

"My mom doesn't want me coming over here. She doesn't like them."

Didn't, anyway. "But you still visited him sometimes?"

He nodded, looking worried. "But don't tell her, OK?" He seemed more concerned that his mother would find out where he'd been, than anything he might have been doing.

"What did you guys do, when you came over?"

He pointed towards the ceiling. Annie looked up and saw that it was covered with dozens of white stick-ons in the shape of stars. Their placement looked disordered and entirely random. He came and stood close to her again. "There's Jupiter and Saturn. There's one I don't remember—you can't see it except for a little time in the year, just in the summer. That one over there is cheating. It's only in the southern hemisphere."

The Southern Cross. She nodded solemnly. "Australia."

"Yeah. And that one's Sirius. The dog star," he continued. He stared straight up at the ceiling above him, swaying a little in concentration.

She walked over to the telescope and leaned down to look through the eyepiece. Nothing. "So what were you trying to find tonight?"

"The constellation Orion. It's the same one they named me after," he said eagerly. "It's my birthday sign too. You're not doing it right." Orion came up beside her and carefully positioned the telescope. "You're supposed to look through here—like this," he said, demonstrating. "But probably it's still too light out. I don't know about it as much as Kyle and his dad."

"So it's your birthday soon," she said.

"On Saturday. We're going go-karting."

"And you must be, what—about ten? Eleven?"

He grinned now, pleased. "I'm just going to be nine. But I'm already a year ahead in school."

"That's pretty good. So you like astronomy?"

"It's OK," he admitted, reluctantly. Then, more excited, "But I *really* like *WWF SmackDown*! All the really big guys." He modelled a wrestler's exaggerated promotional pose. In the next moment he became self-conscious and suspicious. "Who are you, anyway?" he asked suddenly.

"I'm a police officer. I saw that someone was inside the house."

That scared him. "I didn't touch anything, honest, except for the telescope a little bit." He began to pull on the window, stuck in its frame in the summer humidity. "I can put it right back down."

"No. No, it's OK. I know," Annie said. She reached across him and struggled with it briefly, then locked it closed. "So you never got to see your own constellation?"

"I can find it for myself, later," he said, almost angry now. He'd picked up the car again and wouldn't look at her any more as he repeatedly pushed the model racer fast, back and forth across the surface of Kyle's desk, making loud, explosive car noises.

Suddenly the toy flew out of his hand and up into the air, then bounced once, twice, on the floor, shattering into a hundred pieces. He was stunned, immediately horrified at what he'd done. "Sorry. Sorry. Sorry. Sorry. It was an accident," he whirled around to her, frantic.

Then she saw his eyes fill up. Immediately, he tried to turn away so she couldn't see him. He slid down the wall, crouching at her feet with his thin arms wrapped around his knees, and hid his face. She saw his shoulders heaving, and the simple sound of his crying was both unbearably young and uncommonly familiar. It could have been her own as well, this night.

She closed her eyes. *No matter how much I want it all undone . . .*

Finally, Annie reached over and turned off the light. In the sudden darkness the summer night air regained substance, blue and scented, filling the shadows. She sank down beside the boy named Orion and put her arms around him. She waited.

His louder sobs broke over them both. And with that, her own tears came, and the sure knowledge that the old dreams would return and stay for a while. Orion slipped his small, light hand into hers. She felt it like a bird among her fingers, the sudden warmth as it settled there, trembling.

Annie finally allowed herself to imagine Kyle in this room, awakened by a dull bang from the other side of the house, muffled through the two closed doors at opposite ends of the long hallway. Not recognizing what woke him, he would have called out. The faraway sound might have brought Leah to herself for a moment. Perhaps she wrapped the kimono-style silk gown around her quickly and went into the hallway, leaning close to his door, listening. She heard him restless inside. She ran a glass of cold water in the bathroom and brought it to him. He asked if she'd heard that loud sound too. Perhaps she dismissed it as just a passing car.

He would have been reassured, sliding down under the covers that she settled around him, ready to go back to sleep. Leah closed the door behind her. And after she left, he drifted into a half-dream. But perhaps he kept thinking that there was supposed to be something special happening tonight. He would have lain there for a while until finally he remembered. Maybe it was the constellation of Taurus, his own birth sign, rising to show just above the western horizon, starting this week. He climbed out of bed, dressed in only the bottom half of his Star Wars pajamas.

He would have been very careful not to make any sound. Tomorrow was a school day and his mother would get mad if she knew he was still up. He moved the telescope into position, aiming it a few degrees above the line of the trees. Then slowly inched the window up. Up, and out of the way, about two feet. A completely unobstructed view of the heavens.

Kyle used the side-scope, as his father had taught him, trying to locate the right piece of the sky. He knew he couldn't turn on the light to look it up in one of his books without her catching him. From memory, then. To the left of Venus—below the Pleiades, the Seven Sisters.

There, perhaps he saw a part of it. Tomorrow night he could get his dad to help him again. His dad, who'd always had trouble rotating the gear-head in two directions simultaneously, necessary in order to set up the correct line of sight. It was like trying to rub your stomach and pat your head at the same time, he always said, every time he tried it himself. But Kyle could always do that part without thinking, from the very first time. Thankfully, he had inherited his mother's physical grace, along with her blonde colouring and honeyed complexion.

From his father, though, came an early love of secret puzzles and cryptic word games and ancient mythology—and the telescope that had once been Tim Mallick's own, as a young boy, something he was now passing down to his son.

But Leah was moving around again in the hallway. Hearing her, Kyle froze, waiting. Her footsteps faded away down the stairs. He quickly climbed back into bed, not wanting her to catch him up if she checked again. The air coming in the open window was early-spring cold and damp. He pulled the blankets right up to his chin and burrowed deep into them.

At approximately 2:30 a.m.—give or take thirty minutes, according to the medical examiner's report—and after attaching a twenty-foot hose to the exhaust with more than seven layers of duct tape, Leah Mallick started the 1999 silver Porsche in the double-car garage. The other end of the hose fit snugly into the outlet for the central vacuum system, and thereafter began to circulate carbon monoxide throughout the huge house.

Kyle must have listened for Leah's return, planning to get up and close his window as soon as he heard her come back and shut her own door. But she didn't, at least for a very long time. So he forgot, and went to sleep instead.

Annie opened her eyes again and the images died too. Until this moment, in spite of all the evidence against hope, she'd wanted to believe that Leah Mallick had never really intended her child to die with her that night. That the window left open was her sign to whoever could interpret it. Whatever atrocity was being played out between two troubled parents, the child had been meant to continue.

But it wasn't true. The child, left alone in the solid dark that arrives only after midnight, perhaps sensing now that something had changed in the whole of the world that surrounded him. His mother promising it was nothing extraordinary, as she brought him a glass of water with blood on it. Then, lying awake, at an unaccustomed and mysterious hour, knowing only that Taurus rose in the western sky on this night, unobscured by a new moon with no light in it.

And the use of gas. Why a death so disinterested? Leah's child would easily have accepted murder from her own hand. Any child *would* from his mother. Crushed pills swirled into a glass of bedtime milk, a cup of poisoned Kool-Aid held to his lips.

Instead, Leah Mallick had offered up a corpse as a murderer, the delusion of another's hand.

Further evidence of Leah Mallick as a bad mother: that she didn't check on her sleeping son before finally retiring for the night, before she laid herself down beside the shattered body of her dead husband. She didn't even take the time to confirm, for one last time, on such a cold night, that he was covered, that his window was closed.

Annie knew now that Kyle had probably been her intended victim from the beginning.

She rested her head back against the wall and wished her heart to quieten. The stars on the ceiling, the constellations, almost three-dimensional, now glowed with their stored phosphorescence. Idly, she began to pick out the designs of a divinely ordered universe.

She was back—thirty-five, maybe forty years ago—lying on the wet grass, as the sky oh so slowly darkened to a royal blue. School was done and they'd started having their campouts in the backyard again. This, the longest day of the year. Summer solstice. Harry and Jack seemed oblivious to the tragedy she found implicit in that. That from this night on the days would keep shortening, until it was winter again. *They* didn't care. Hockey season couldn't come fast enough for them. It was more ominous to her. It meant that none of them could afford to get too attached to this night.

There was Ursa Major. Polaris. Annie began reciting the names again slowly to him, in a whisper. The boy inside her encircling arms stirred at last. He looked up, following her finger as she hesitantly pointed them out. "Andromeda. Aldebaran. Cassiopeia. Castor and Pollux. That one. . . ?"

"That's Orion. *My* star. Betelgeuse on top and Rigel underneath," he said proudly. He had calmed beside her. "Kyle did it for me especially—so I'd know it when I saw it for real." He sighed heavily. "But you can only see some stars when it's really dark out."

Orion. She recalled, from the stories of ancient gods and myths, that Orion meant "hunter." This Orion was forever destined to a quest too—to find and lay forever the stars upon the sky in a pattern that might explain everything. The hunter, with a ghost for a quarry.

Emma, the cat, sat on a distant stone wall, deep in the shadows on the faraway, fading perimeter as the light inside the house was extinguished.

It was easier now to hunt and catch and hide, waiting there. The garden was slowly, slowly returning to itself. Nature had enough of whatever was needed. The delicate and expensive imported plant materials were already wound 'round with opportunistic weeds, the strong again asserting their right to flourish and dominate. Emma watched the car leaving, its headlights turning aside. Now to dark peace, pursuit and sovereignty over it all. *Et in Arcadia ego* . . . And I too in Arcadia.

~~~

Orion's mother was astounded when Anne Shannon appeared at her front door. Apologetic when she saw her child emerge from the darkness, to wander sullenly into the lighted front hallway. Apoplectic when she found out where he'd been.
~~~

Annie tried to calm her down. It was really nothing, Annie repeated. Just that he'd been out and it was getting dark. She wanted to make sure he got home all right. No problem.

Orion's mother glared at him now as he stood silent and defiant. "Why would you go *there?*" The very idea of it seemed to make the woman almost hysterical.

"He was telling me that he and Kyle Mallick were friends," Annie interrupted.

"He told you that?" She laughed sharply, a bitter sound. "Well, I don't *think* so. They didn't have much of anything to do with each other."

Annie was careful. "You didn't want them playing together . . . ?"

"She didn't particularly encourage it." The woman went on to describe Leah's standoffish manner, the way she kept herself apart.

Annie raised an eyebrow in question.

"And besides, she used to let them get into anything they wanted to. He'd come back, all wired up, going on about some stuff I didn't know anything about. It didn't sit too good with me. She didn't seem really that . . . involved. I tend to supervise my own kids quite a bit more."

And that would explain how her nine-year-old had been found breaking into a house a block away at nine o'clock at night . . . ?

"Turns out I was right to have my suspicions, I guess." She smiled brightly now at Annie. "You know, she—"

Orion made a small noise. The woman seemed startled that he was still there, listening. "Go into the kitchen," she said. "You get your own juice tonight and then you can go right up to bed."

He walked away from them slowly, dragging his feet and pouting.

She turned back to Annie again, more eagerly. "So, it was pretty bad. Both of them were dead when you got there, I hear."

Annie had no intention of discussing the details. "Well, I don't—"

"I even brought the kids out to watch you that night, when you were doing the TV over there." The mother persisted. "So, how is he doing in hospital? Not going to come out of it, I guess, eh?"

"There's nothing really—" Then Annie saw Orion, still watching them from where he was hiding behind the half-open kitchen door. She knew he shouldn't be hearing this.

Orion's mother followed her glance. She whirled around and spotted him. "I *said* to go upstairs."

He began to go up, then, slamming his feet hard onto each step, pounding the railing each time. "I—told—you—I—wanted—to—see—it . . ."

His mother turned back to Annie, embarrassed. "I don't know what the hell he's talking about half the time." She shrugged. "But, anyway, thank you so much for bringing him back. I'm sorry about all this." Orion's mother waved her hands around almost helplessly.

Annie smiled. "No, it's fine. I know what it's like." She opened the door. "I think he might just be missing Kyle."

The sound followed her as she let herself out, Orion continuing to yell while he climbed—half angry, half crying—to his room. He screamed something else down at his mother, from somewhere near the top of the staircase. Annie heard the woman respond, her voice rising in a shriek of frustration. Loud, now, even through the closed door. "No . . . No, *you're* a poo-head," she was shouting.

∿∿∿

Leah Mallick's Mercedes sedan pulled into the gravel lot adjacent to the playing field. Among all the SUVs and minivans, it stood out.

Orion's mother watched her drive, as usual, to the far end, well away from where everyone else had chosen to park. She saw Leah get out and walk around to the front of the car, resting against the hood to watch the last few minutes of play. She always arranged to arrive like this, just before the end.

Orion's mother decided that, for once, it was up to her to make the first move. It seemed like the only way she was ever going to get to meet her. The Mallicks had already been there a couple of months. She headed over.

Leah was watching her from behind her expensive sunglasses, though the day itself was dull and overcast, spitting rain. She didn't make a move to take them off either, even when Orion's mother got near enough to introduce herself.

"You're Kyle's mom, aren't you? Hi. I'm Jill Davis. I figured it was about time we said hello." Jill managed to sound bright and friendly, though her voice wavered slightly.

There was no sign of recognition. Leah's expression remained fixed, polite. Completely opaque.

Inexplicably, Jill Davis felt nervous. "Orion's mom. . . ? Our sons are good friends." She extended her hand.

Leah Mallick took it, lightly, a faint smile. And watched her.

"I'm glad I finally bumped into you. I've been meaning to give you a shout," Jill said. She settled up against the expensive car, casually, trying to imitate Leah's own posture. "Some of us mothers are getting together to plan the soccer team's trip. We usually try and raise money by selling chocolate bars." She forced a laugh. "You'll probably end up buying most of them yourself. We all do."

Leah Mallick's silence was disconcerting. Jill Davis looked back, almost longingly now, at the others gathered in a friendly group nearer the centre line, waiting for the game to finish. It was almost over. "Though you sure don't look like you eat much chocolate," she said after a moment. She turned back to see Leah still studying her from behind the dark glasses.

"I don't think I can help you," Leah said after a pause. Another distant smile.

Jill Davis found herself growing more uneasy under the steady gaze. Perhaps she'd misunderstood. "Well, maybe later, then," she said, edging away. She always liked to leave the door open. "After you're more settled in . . ."

Leah nodded. Then, without another glance, she returned the whole of her attention to the muddy children dragging up and down the field. The last few minutes of play. The score still zero-zero.

12

DeVries handed her the package of faxed documents. The formal procedure required hard-copy originals, a set of which was already on its way to them via the state police. But this was notice enough. A more colloquial letter over the governor's personal signature didn't mitigate its message. And Acton's attorney general had been on the phone twice in the last hour.

"They don't think we can handle it." Annie laughed bitterly. "Not with the requisite discretion, at least."

"You're taking this too personally. I see no indication of that in here."

"Well, it's not exactly a vote of confidence." And why would this be personal to me, she thought, when *you're* the one who's just had the chief executive cut off your *cojones?*

"As an alternative to a federal—"

"Y'know, maybe having the feds in here on this *isn't* the worst idea right now, Commissioner. We don't know who's responsible, but none of us can claim to be naïve about what's happening. Tom Acton's former mistress is murdered in our jurisdiction, and we're letting him walk in and clean out our evidence locker. In another couple of hours it'll be like Susan Shaw never existed anywhere outside of a dirty joke."

Annie looked at him now as though what she had to say still mattered. But nothing, she knew, had the same power as the simple cost he was already toting up in his head. City services had made itself so dependent upon the largesse of those ruling the state capital, it was like asking him to challenge the Medicis. Declining population, eroding tax base. Whatever they chose to blame as the cause, Lockport required Tom Acton's grace and favour, like a welfare mom at the end of a long month. Even local schools were facing the imminent elimination of programs, increasing class sizes and a new wave of laid-off teachers. The police weren't immune. Unions in all the public services were being pushed to negotiate rollbacks on overtime and benefits.

But whose fault was that? They'd had their hand out for years, and were left coming up empty more often than not these days. She wasn't unsympathetic.

However, this was a profoundly ill-considered move—even for DeVries.

Annie leaned forward on the desk. "It's time that we started acting like a police force, instead of some photo op for every politician and his cronies. If you do this, you're going to have to find some way to spin it for yourself. I can't convince one reporter out there to believe we *asked* for the state police to take over."

For the first time DeVries looked nearly defeated. He tried to laugh. "Then why don't we just extend your disability leave for another couple of weeks? I'll pass this all off to Kendra. He could bury the second gunman in the Kennedy assassination."

Annie's sigh came from somewhere deep inside, expressing nothing more than the sheer exhaustion of a body that simply wanted to numb itself into oblivion. "Paul, you used to be a cop too. You wouldn't have accepted this either, back then. It's not an accident and you know it. Susan Shaw wasn't the type to go prowling the waterfront at night, looking for rough trade. And you should be just as disturbed as I am that *those* are the rumours they want left floating out there. She was set up—"

Is being set up, Annie reminded herself. And about to be disposed of as little more than an embarrassing episode for the charming but undisciplined governor. Discredited in death, in a way she never wanted to be in life. "For God's sake, listen to your *own* gut for once—" Annie stopped, hearing her own voice begin to break. She didn't want to give him the satisfaction.

Because she knew she'd already lost the battle.

Just more proof that they were on the down slide, negotiating for public confidence, toadying to vested interests. But Roy Warren was right about one thing: DeVries wasn't stupid. He wasn't acting out of any kind of innocent ignorance. It was just a different way of processing the world, hard on the side of pragmatism—and *that* defined by a line as clearly delineated in this town as the double-white down the centre of the highway.

"I'm afraid you're about to find out what it's really like to lose," she finished.

Two tiny circles of red burned high on his cheeks. "I don't think you've ever understood the fine art of compromise," he responded.

Spoken like a true courtier, she thought. Not so much Machiavelli's sinuous corruption, as Kissinger's *realpolitik.* But he looked most of all like a kid to her in that moment—a balding, fourteen-year-old kid.

"Well, I know I sure don't understand one damn thing more now than I did when I was twelve," she said.

And you know you're middle aged when it's already too late to die tragically young.

"I'm not going to make you go out there," he said. "It's your choice . . ."

"You're right," she said, "I always have that." She summoned herself to a necessary anger again. "But you know damn well I'll do it."

The wall shook as she slammed the door behind her.

By the time she entered the conference room, Stan Kendra was already standing ramrod straight at the podium, putting his notes in order. She'd completely forgotten that she'd told him to run all the briefings. He was clearing his throat nervously through the speaker system. Apparently, he didn't realize his mike was on. *Idiot.*

Annie approached the front of the room and put her hand over the microphone. "I'll take it for today," she said evenly.

Kendra jumped when she spoke, then began to protest weakly. He was just getting the hang of it, he said. She had visions of having to tear his fingers from the podium. She stared at him until he finally retreated, disappointed. Then she leafed through the materials he'd left behind. Nothing here that couldn't wait for another day. Or another decade.

"Ladies and gentlemen, may we begin. . . ? There's only one item today." Annie could feel them all exchanging glances. Most hadn't been expecting her to show. Few, if any, suspected how difficult it really was.

She refused to look up from the paper in front of her, though she'd already committed the single paragraph to memory. "Lockport police have today agreed to a joint effort in the investigation relating to the death on Friday of Susan Shaw. Local authorities will co-operate with state police, under the direction of Attorney General Albert Gelfant. Given Ms. Shaw's prominence as . . ." She had to consult her notes momentarily, "the director of the Department of Business and Professional Regulation, the Office of the State Attorney General has generously offered our local authorities the fullest extent of its resources, pledging its continued support to a coordinated operation."

Annie's hands, held just below the level of the podium, were shaking now. "The victim was earlier identified as Susan Eleanor Shaw, age forty-six. Ms. Shaw had served with the state regulatory agency for almost twenty years." It was the end of her written statement.

Annie finally looked up. "As you all know, Susan Shaw was found dead in Lockport last Friday night. The medical examiner has already determined the cause to be as a result of drowning. Evidence suggests, however, that the deceased was rendered unconscious at the time of entry into the water, the victim of blunt head trauma. Assault, if not murder. I understand Mr. Gelfant's office will be releasing additional details later this afternoon. In the meantime, if you have any further questions, I'd suggest you contact the governor directly."

After a moment of shocked silence, first one reporter than another: "Why is the state taking over?" "Do you have concerns about jurisdiction?" "Why exactly was Susan Shaw in Lockport?" "Is it true she was consulting with the police on Belford?" "Will that investigation continue?" Annie glanced impassively from one to the next, until the questions died out and everyone was left looking dazed and confused again.

She stepped off the podium, passing Stan Kendra. "It's all yours, Officer," she said.

No one had to tell her that this was her last press conference.

Kendra hesitated, then stepped up and sneezed into the open mike. The cacophoney began again immediately. No one cared who answered their questions, as long as someone did. And as she walked out, she could hear Kendra droning on in the room behind her. "With regards to jurisdiction, I would direct you in the direction of the policy of . . ."

"Annie?" Brad Moore had followed her into the hallway. "Why are they shutting you down? It can't be just because Acton was involved with her. You know yourself that'd probably *boost* his numbers . . ."

He was right, of course. Adultery was no longer the political negative it had once been. It gave the candidate street cred in some places. A touch of the bad boy.

Annie shook her head. "I'm not holding a scrum here, Brad. You've got my statement." He was one of the few local reporters she respected, even trusted. A shambling comfortable gait, a familiar hangdog expression. Too bad that didn't work on television.

"You think this is connected in some way to her too, don't you? To Leah Mallick, I mean?" he said.

Annie's face felt stiff, her skin stretched tight. She pulled her lips back in an imitation of a smile. "If you listen very carefully, you'll be able to hear that Stan Kendra's the one conducting all the news briefings from now on."

Brad approached her, only inches away. "But why are *you* rolling over on it?"

She left him standing in the middle of the corridor.

When she reached her office, she saw the memo waiting for her, a single sheet sitting all alone on the otherwise clear surface. The extension of her disability leave had been approved. Effective immediately.

~~~

Annie entered Holly's alone. It was crowded enough that she considered trying to bounce a couple of junior cops off a good table. She had no problem with the idea of that; she just didn't want the conversation it would entail. She took a seat at the far end of the bar instead, and idly studied the room in the streaky, smoked mirror on the wall.

The last light of the day cut in through the door as it opened from the street. Annie ignored it when someone slid onto the empty stool near her, acknowledging Bill only when he called the bartender over.

"Whatever you got on draft," he said casually.

He waited for her to speak now. "Ginger ale," she said finally. Maybe he *was* watching her, following her, just
~~~

waiting for her to come into a place like this and decide something on her own. Why? He had his own home to go to. With someone else waiting there for him.

Annie's hands were still trembling slightly. She saw him looking at them.

"Too much coffee," she said. "I can't seem to sleep at night, then I have trouble keeping going during the day."

He nodded blandly, then took a swallow of his beer. "So, I hear we've been put on ice again."

What d'ya mean *we,* Kemo sabe? she thought. Certainly not *me* anymore—I'm out of the business. But she nodded. "Yeah, I just released the statement."

"If the AG's coming in, I guess it means we're going to have to hand back everything. We haven't even gotten through most of it yet ourselves." He laughed a bit. "Christ. Not that I understood half of what I saw there."

She smiled slightly. "Yeah, I know. I got a summary you don't want to know about either."

"All that financial shit?"

She nodded.

"But I'm guessing it really doesn't matter, anyway," he said quietly.

She glanced up at him. "Why would you think that?"

He weighed his words carefully. "Because I don't think that's what the two of you were doing."

She hesitated, then shook her head. Quiet for a moment. Bill waited.

"We kind of started there—turned out that it doesn't have much to do with Leah Mallick," she said finally.

He glanced around the bar. There was no one close

enough to hear him. "But something else does. And you and Susan found it."

Annie weighed her options. "I don't know . . . I'm not really sure. But Susan believed there's a major corporation that is trying to develop a new health care model in the state. And that's what Leah Mallick was working on: gathering personal information on patients that could be used to control their choices." Take it slow, she cautioned herself. "Anyway, it's a big multi-national, called Cross Corp. And she got this idea that they were going to start out with a series of cost-cutting measures and if it worked in here, they'd package it for the rest of the country." She paused, wanting to sound completely rational. She remembered Florence Schellenberg's off-hand remark during their talk at the hospital—her reference to some 'computer-type things' she said she'd never seen before . . .

"What do you think they're packaging?" Bill said.

She didn't answer. *It's all about information.* Pure and simple, it was the acquisition, the transfer and the technology of information. The selling of it. Assembling and offering bits and bytes, in the global bazaar. All the information necessary to create new protocols, strategies, perpetual loops. Plays. They never had to get their hands dirty. Just tell others how to do it. The ultimate virtual commodity.

Annie shrugged. "A new way to cut down insurance costs."

"So it might have put her into serious conflict with *him.* If she approached him with it."

"The governor? Yeah maybe. But they'd been over for a while." Annie took a sip of her drink. "She did tell me that

Acton was planning to appoint Leah to his second-term cabinet. Secretary of Health & Human Services."

Bill let out a low whistle of surprise. "And *that's* how it gets back to Mallick. When did she tell you that?"

Annie smiled faintly. "As I recall, it was when we were screaming at each other on the street outside here, that night—" Just before the shooting.

Bill nodded, laughing slightly. "You two were an odd match. Funny how it worked out."

"Partners don't always get along." She spoke lightly enough, but there was an delicate thread of sorrow through it.

He turned and looked at her, more seriously. "But, as it turns out, sometimes they do. You and I were pretty good for a while."

Annie said nothing. She didn't want to open that wound here and now.

He shifted on the bar stool. "So her coming here wasn't idle interest—just looking for another way to help him nail us?"

"No. Acton didn't send her. She was here on her own. At first, I think she saw it as a way to attract some attention inside."

"And maybe a little revenge on the boyo. . . ?"

Annie frowned slightly. "Maybe. But even if Mallick had had ties to Cross Corp, if it became a problem Acton could have washed his hands of it all at almost any time—force Leah to withdraw with some excuse."

"Right up to the time she killed herself anyway," Bill said with a smirk.

Annie held her breath. *And the questions began.*

If Acton had ever had second thoughts, any real opportunity to distance himself from Leah Mallick and her proposals had effectively ended with her death. The manner of it, the whole ugly, unhinged mess of it, made it far too dangerous to admit how close she'd really been to power. Not if he still wanted to win this campaign. But Cross Corp knew. And they could make very sure that anything less than his continued full support to the program lacked the essential political element of 'plausible deniability.' Acton was stuck with her. Dead or alive.

Annie realized she'd been staring at him, unseeing, for several seconds only when Bill waved a hand in front of her face, and repeated his next question. "All that material she brought, there's nothing there on him?"

Annie blinked slightly and shook her head. "On Acton . . . ? No. Tim Mallick appears somewhere on the periphery. It was all about money disappearing on the major markets, not into some local politician's pocket. It might have been a bit embarrassing if they'd gone forward with Leah's nomination." She rested her elbows on the bar. "But they would have had to really twist that stuff to bring it back anywhere near Tom Acton. Unless all that Susan *wanted* was revenge." She'd had the chance, and twice resisted it.

I could have just told her *do* that, Annie told herself. Told her to take all that information, make the markets quiver and quake and correct themselves. Make scandal out of some and celebrities out of the rest. Let her go home and be an accountant. Instead I convinced her to stay. Annie rested uncomfortably on the stool now. Every bone and muscle seemed tired and bruised, and she needed something more than ginger ale to help put *that* away. "She told me she'd made a high-level connection. I think that's why she went down there."

Bill looked intrigued. "Really? Who?"

Annie snapped with sudden irritation. "Someone who could provide her with more information about Cross Corp. Jesus, Bill, I don't know *who.* Maybe 'Deep Throat' . . ." He was ignoring the real point. "You have to understand—we were *this* close to finding something that probably led back to some of those new campaign people surrounding him right now. She didn't know who the good guys were anymore. She didn't know everything that was going on. But she still went looking anyway. Know what I mean? I think she intended to warn Tom Acton. She knew someone was watching. And it didn't stop her from trying to find out what Cross Corp was really trying to shove down everyone's throat."

Bill took another swallow of beer. "The lady had guts. And class."

Annie nodded. Yeah, maybe that's what I was trying to say, she thought. Then she relaxed a bit, giving him a quick grin. "She said something funny to me once. When we were up there, working late. There's piles of paper everywhere. And I'm bitching about how it has nothing to do with real police work. She does this real slow take, looking at me over her glasses and says: 'Fuck right off, Lieutenant. Remember, it took an accountant to get Al Capone.'" Annie recalled the exact moment, at the end of a long, dry session poring endlessly over documents. In the midst of it, an unexpected flash of wit. One of many, as it turned out.

But where do *I* start? Annie thought. How do I get Leah Mallick now?

Bill raised an eyebrow, smiling gently. Then he pushed aside his half-finished glass of beer with a finger. "You get the feeling that some people are still watching, then?" he asked.

"Yeah, actually I do." She looked at him more frankly now. "Starting with you. Are you watching, Bill? Are *you* watching me now? Is that why you followed me in here?" *Tell me why what I'm doing matters so damn much to you any more. And tell me why someone else had to answer your phone that night . . .*

"I think you believe this is your fault."

Her heart made a painful, convulsive leap. She looked at him warningly. "Don't . . ." *Don't you dare try to get inside my head.*

"You know you couldn't have—" He thought better of it. "The point is, you *can* stop, right now. You got the timing on your side—all that financial information. She *handed* it to you. From the sounds of it they don't even know what she was really up to. And what I've seen—hell. It'll take them months to figure it out. I'm just saying you can beat them to the punch. Go around them. Blow the biggest whistle you can find and bring the feds in on it. Blow DeVries right out of the goddamn water, if that's what makes you happy. Be a 'real' cop again, like you're always saying. They'll be tripping over themselves to give you any investigative unit you want after that."

Maybe even the Financial Crimes Unit, she thought. What an irony that would be: her in charge of the accountants. She shook her head. "It doesn't mean anything to me any more."

His expression hardened. "Then what the hell does? What's your exit strategy on *this* one—because you'd better start looking for it right now. Setting them onto the governor? I heard what happened at your press conference today. That's why I'm here. And I knew exactly where to find you. And from where I'm sitting, you look like you're getting ready to turn everything else in your life upside down again. You want to keep going after Leah Mallick now? Because of this Cross Corp thing? Because of what happened to Susan? Even if you're right, what do you think a major company like that is really going to let you find? Some psychiatrist who blew her gaskets. Who couldn't cope with a husband in deep financial trouble, a guy that everyone's prepared to say was a complete nutcase anyway. So what? They'll say it—and so would I: everyone has their breaking point—even those kinds of people. I've seen enough shit going on over there in Belford to write a book. No one's got a corner on it. On happiness, on sadness, on plain fuckin' murderous irritation with the world."

It was a new, more dangerous kind of anger mounting in both of them now, too. She could feel her own careful control beginning to fray. "Then why are we even bothering to discuss it, Bill?" she said. "Haven't we done enough damage to each other yet . . . ?"

"Because you're right—I *am* watching. I see it all. You've never had it so good. And I know that you are so close to blowing it, it breaks my heart."

"Then don't watch anymore," she said dully. She felt cold, almost numb.

He grabbed her by the shoulder, forcing her to look at him. "What do you think they're 'packaging'? What . . . ? Let me help you then."

She shook him off.

He didn't stop. "This is about that boy," he said. "It's something you're forcing yourself to play out again."

"There's no connection."

He laughed bitterly. "Sure, and I heard about your trips up to the hospital, too. And I'm the one who knows, better than anyone else on this earth, what that really means to you. I was there that night too, Annie. When Charlie died. Ten years is long enough. You've got your own life back. Take it, and move on." She knew he wasn't talking about the job any more.

Annie looked hard away from him and stared at nothing in the mirror until she saw him finally, wearily, throw up his hands and leave her alone at last.

"I can protect you." That was what he'd said to her, that long ago night. It was his voice, his eyes looking into hers, his arms in which she'd finally tried to rest. "I can protect you," he had said. If it wasn't the only lie he'd ever told her, it was still the only one she could remember.

She played with an old coaster on the bar, spinning it under her fingertips for a moment. She gazed into the mirror. Posted right in the middle—right under the outdated price list for off-sale—was another sign, a bumper sticker from some joke shop: "E-mail me your troubles. I'll download someone who gives a damn." *Send.*

A few glances came her way. Surreptitious, but she felt them still, like a finger drawn across raw nerve endings, sliding up and over her. Saw one or two staring, baldly, into the same mirror she sat facing. There she was, the most famous police officer in town, big as life. Did it ever become old hat—that kind of buzzing around your head? Multiply it a hundred times: what must it have been like for Leah Mallick simply to walk into a room? Everything seeming to stop for that singular intake of breath she must have heard every time. The eager expectations, a mile high. And look what that had led her to.

Don't look at me don't say I remind you of someone don't offer me another cup of coffee on the house don't say I helped your brother-in-law once don't ask me if we've met before don't tell me the funny joke you heard about a cop and a priest walking into a bar don't ignore me don't whisper and point don't look at me. Don't. Don't . . .

I can retreat, as well, Annie thought. I can start a car. I can use a gun. Or I can keep trying to repair the world. And imagine that it still matters.

The barman tossed Bill's change towards her: six thirty-five. She held up one hand to him silently, showing two fingers sideways, spread slightly apart. A double. And absently dug her thumb into the wooden surface of the bar, scraping a curling thread of brown paste, the combination of old wax polish and beer-soaked veneer, that came up under her fingernail. Hoping no one would notice, she lightly carved her initials into the wood while she waited for the drink.

∿∿∿

From where she was lying on the couch, Annie heard the phone ringing. Twice. Both times had to be well after midnight, judging by the sheer number of infomercials playing around the dial. Obviously, it was someone who didn't really care about her, who didn't care that they'd disturbed her from a good night's sleep. Someone who would probably comment that she sounded "different" if she bothered to pick up right now. The second time he left a message.

It was Bill. She heard his voice through the machine. Quietly. "Sweet dreams, babe. I'll call you tomorrow." Short and to the point. From a guy who wasn't short and didn't get the point. She giggled. That was almost clever. "Leave me alone," she shouted loudly.

She poured another glass of wine. "You have absolutely no idea what I dream," she whispered.

∿∿∿

As she hit the four-lane, Annie noticed only that it was spitting rain.

Then she'd cleared the bridge, and was already moving quickly through the lightly populated outskirts of the city.

She caught a glimpse of caramel-coloured water through the trees. She was travelling parallel to the river and decided to follow it for a while, for no other reason than to give her time to think. The contemplative silence provided by just getting in a car and driving absolutely nowhere. American Zen.

The paved surface gave way to gravel. It grew narrower still and to one side fell away into a dark ravine, a cliffside of trees. She caught sight only of the treetops.

The hills began to rise more steeply here. Her car's tires rumbled violently on the washboard surface. Obviously, heavy traffic travelled this section. Usually lead-footed, she let the accelerator slip back. The speedometer hovered more cautiously around forty-five. Maybe there was a way down to the river from here, a place to sit and think.

Then she saw that a dusty haze left by a line of trucks led off the main road on to a newly constructed service track, and disappeared over the steep embankment. There was a high steel fence guarding the property on either side, hung with signs: Addorée Construction.

Annie pulled over and parked, then climbed to the top of the rise to look over the edge. Hundreds of feet below her was the Stoney River, glinting granite under the overcast sky. She felt the promise of rain building in the air, a welcome relief after this heat.

In the bush all around her, chainsaws whined. An explosive crack echoed through the woods to her left as a tree crashed to the ground, the sound of it dying away very slowly. From here she heard more clearly the low-noted resonances and metallic grinding of the heavy machinery she could see far below. There was a full crew down there, working to carve out an extended plateau about halfway down the slope, cutting and placing an extensive series of terraces that followed closely the contours of the steep hillside. The work carried on out of sight in both directions from the spot where she stood.

One truck had already wound its way down the switchback to the construction site, and was now backing into a storage area to dump the two tandem-trailer loads of gravel. She tried to calculate the scale of what was happening here. An area of four, maybe five acres was being established for a development of some sort.

On land already rough-graded, there were excavations on one side. There they were beginning to pour concrete forms for foundations outlining a number of interconnected structures. It looked like condominiums.

From here, it was absolutely breathtaking. The expanse of the whole valley spread out in front of her. The river wound away to the horizon, coursing towards the great lake beyond. In the middle distance was the island, spotted with the greens of its unfinished golf course. The city, its bridges and highways defining the downtown core in the distance. This view alone had to be worth millions.

∿∿∿

The brochure she studied made it look like Club Med. Regina Welles's office had finally forwarded a small package of information. The program in which Welles had once participated had since grown into a series of nonprofit, community-based hospices, any connection to leading-edge experimentation eradicated by time. Or design. Melded into something entirely commonplace.

Here, empathy itself seemed to have been brought to a peak experience. The photos were plentiful, filled with smart, attractive and obviously caring people.

The words offered every reassurance. *Enlightened sanctuary. Dignity. Humane medical and spiritual support. Advanced pain-control technologies.* Loaded terms like *compassion, choice, patients' rights*. Death, always, described as *a passage* or *a transition*. The essential connotations of faith were there for those who wanted them, with just enough vague double-talk to appeal to all the New Age-y types on the other side.

Annie worked her way through two dozen or so names on the published list of current associates—doctors, therapists, nurse practitioners, a full array of specialists—cross-referencing them to everything else she'd already gathered. Schools, professional organizations, social clubs, medical group practices. No mention of Leah Mallick. No obvious ties. Whatever connections Leah herself had once had with the agency were gone as well.

Yet, nine years later Regina Welles was still talking about her. Had the experience meant as much to Leah Mallick?

If Susan's suspicion's were right, Cross Corp's planning had been underway for several years. By then, Leah had already helped to design several palliative care programs in southern California. It gave her ample opportunity to gain easy access to hundreds, maybe thousands, of psychological and psychiatric profiles of patients undergoing treatment for terminal illness, a mass of demographic detail, additional information relating to family support and caregivers—in short, whatever she'd need to determine what type of person would be most receptive to which specific approach. Education levels, family incomes, religious affiliations. Zip codes.

If the purpose of the whole exercise had been to create a stream of marketable information, then this was the fountainhead.

~~~

"Everything OK on that end?" It was a man's impatient voice, coming through her newly installed speakers.

After a frustrating morning, Annie finally had both video and audio working. "I think so," she replied doubtfully.

She glanced again at the book-jacket photograph in front of her. Alan Wakefield. She'd searched for and found, in a second-hand bookstore, the obscure, out-of-print, dull, academic text he'd authored, then immediately arranged for a conference. He was easy enough to locate—still in exactly the same place he'd been more than twenty years ago, when he became Leah Mallick's first psychology professor.

It was Wakefield who'd insisted on turning a phone conversation into something far more complicated than it needed to be. And for obscure reasons entirely his own. If this was the future, she thought, the technology didn't recommend itself very well. A degraded, grainy image. Stingy, mechanical sound. Colder and less revealing than any simple phone call would have been. But he'd effectively bullied her into "expanding her horizons" as he'd put it. Obviously, he saw himself as some contemporary amalgam of Stewart Brand and Timothy Leary—he certainly looked the part—the kind who never missed an opportunity to proselytize his latest idiosyncrasies and obsessions. Undergrads always seemed to buy it; it was usually sold to them as passion.

But she'd agreed to download the necessary software at his instruction and, as the picture flickered into view, saw that Wakefield was already sitting facing the camera, ready
~~~

to speak with her. It was a peculiar sensation, watching someone like this, outlined as a series of jerky motions, a kind of visual stutter, leaving ghostly images behind whenever he moved.

She'd steadfastly refused to have a web-cam set up at her end, but the exercise wasn't a complete loss, she had to admit. It had finally pushed her to sign up for a broadband Internet service. She'd already found time to download a few of her favourite songs.

The man she saw on her screen now was at least ten years older than his carefully airbrushed publicity photo. About sixty, she guessed. Which would have put him in his late thirties, early forties when he first met Leah Mallick.

"Actually, I flunked her," he was saying now, displaying what looked like a smug grin.

"Did you?" Annie replied. Wakefield, she knew, wasn't the type to need priming. He was interested when she'd first called to ask about one of his former students, positively garrulous when he found out it was Leah Mallick she wanted to discuss.

"Well, an Incomplete at least—I wanted to leave the door open. But as she didn't even bother to hand in her final work on the statistical section . . . It didn't stop her, of course—she was still carrying a full academic load. Ended up in the ninety-eighth percentile anyway. But, ethically, one couldn't just let her slide through."

No, she supposed, one couldn't.

He ran his fingers through long, thinning hair. A James Taylor look-alike, man and boy. "She was the only undergrad I'd ever taken on, to that point. You usually want them to get past that mewling, tequila-party-puking, away-from-home-for-the-first-time stage before you waste real time on them. But she'd heard about my work, I guess, and wanted to hook up." He tried to appear modest. "It all ended up as a major disappointment, of course. And it made me very wary of eager little undergrads for many years."

"Have you . . . *mentored* many others since?"

Before he could reply, he was distracted by someone entering his office. Wakefield turned away from the camera for a moment to greet whoever it was. His whole demeanour changed. Annie saw him smiling in a new way as he answered her now. "Oh, I guess there've been a few."

Annie knew that smile was intended for the other person now in the room with him, an aside to whomever was standing in the doorway, just outside of camera range. "I'll only be a second," he said. And Annie heard a bright, ringing girl's laugh answer. "No problemo."

Annie tried to imagine what she looked like, the girl behind that sound. Someone young, eager, of course, pretty—then she gave up. It was nothing more than idle speculation, anyway. A professional habit. What difference would it really make for her to know? Professors. Giggling undergraduates. Tedious in its predictability. Maybe he'd just found his next Leah Mallick.

He continued, slightly distracted. "As I was about to say . . ." Another snicker off-screen. "In my humble opinion, she could have had an absolutely brilliant academic career."

Probably true, Annie thought, though I very much doubt that's what she was looking for. Over the next couple of years, she might have learned she didn't *want* an academic career. Certainly not the scrutiny that came with it. Or the questions from those she'd eventually come to regard as her inferiors. Or the requirement to publish, the thrust-and-parry of peer review.

Why restrict yourself to exploring a few student psyches when you could be controlling the "coping strategies" of millions?

Annie remembered Bill's remark, a half-asleep throwaway reference to Leah's "narcissistic tendencies." Maybe a lucky guess—he'd meant it as a joke, not a diagnosis. But probably closer to the truth than he realized. Because in every way, Leah neatly fit the clinical definition of narcissism. The tendency to see everyone and everything merely as an extension of oneself. Success as an all-or-nothing construct—accomplishment or annihilation. Omnipotent grandiosity. The compulsive need to dictate the rules and the flow of events.

The clever ones, Annie had read, were usually careful not to allow that face to show. Instead, in public at least, they presented a front of patience, congeniality and confident reasonableness. An attractive mask. But inside, was an unrelenting need to be perfect, an insatiable craving for immediate gratification. The drive to dominate others and govern every aspect of the immediate environment. An unremitting addiction to power. The refusal to accept even the possibility of personal limits: what couldn't be done could easily be faked. Authentic mastery wasn't the issue, after all; only the achievement and acclaim that came with it were. Knowledge was useful as a tool of superiority, merely one more advantage.

Annie had found other, more subtle definitions as well. The true narcissist deliberately cultivates an air of mystery. Uses varying forms of intimidation. In time, inevitably develops a harsh, almost punitive quality in every intimate relationship. For, in the end, others can only disappoint.

Nonetheless, the narcissist becomes entirely dependent upon the image reflected back by those whose sole purpose is to admire, applaud. Even detest. All of it, necessary proof that they exist. Most important, a *true* narcissist is prepared to invest only in those things over which he or she can exercise full, unmitigated control.

The real danger, Annie knew, came when they feared they were losing it—driven to a volatile state of shame, even humiliation, by relatively minor disappointments. All failures, in effect, becoming the narcissist's fault. Everything, an assault upon the fragile veneer. Black and white. Perfect and all-powerful—or nothing. The titan. The "jealous god." Leah Mallick.

"What's your specialty, Doctor?" Annie asked.

"I consult for convenience-food companies. Package design. Product placement."

"Then I don't understand. Why would she—?"

"Oh, I see. No, at that time, I was developing several new systems of clinical assessment. I have to give myself full marks for prescience for *that* much, at least. I was already anticipating the Internet as something more than nerd paradise. And this is twenty, twenty-five years ago, when it was still only used in the defence department and a few university math programs. My proposal was, in fact, to integrate that technology into the diagnostic process.

"Leah and I spent a lot of our downtime talking about it. That's why I ended up offering her the research-assistant gig. There were always dozens of 'em hanging around the department with way more credits than her. At that point, she was still only a sophomore. But she struck me as pretty together for someone that young—eighteen, nineteen, at the time? The only one I saw on the ball enough to get what I called the big picture. It was a real intense opportunity . . . Fun times, though."

Annie let out a snort that she managed to turn into a brief coughing fit.

"I mean, I don't want to make more of it than it was. She had the same stupid infatuation they all have for it in the beginning—you know, the jargon, all the inside jokes. The feeling that they've somehow stumbled on to some secret no one else knows about yet—"

"Like what?"

He stopped, looking puzzled.

"Tell me one now," she said. "An inside joke."

His mouth pouched out dramatically, his brow furrowed. He seemed to be taking forever to come up with something.

Christ, we're not trying to solve Fermat's last theorem here, she thought impatiently. "Sorry. Never mind. It's all—"

He suddenly jumped in his chair as though stung. "No, OK, here's a typical one:

"A patient is in session with his Rogerian therapist: 'Doctor, I'm really depressed.' The therapist responds: 'I see. Yes. You're depressed.' The patient sighs: 'Nothing is going well.' The therapist repeats it: 'Nothing going well.' Then the patient says: 'I feel like killing myself.' The therapist nods: 'Ah. You're thinking of killing yourself.' The patient stands up: 'I'm going to do it NOW.' The therapist answers: 'Yes, you want to do it now.' The patient jumps out the window. At that, the therapist goes to the window, watches for a few seconds, then says 'Whoosh. Splat.'"

Wakefield's grin told her it was done.

"I don't get it," Annie said politely.

"Well, as any psychology undergrad would know, Carl Rogers theorizes that the only valid authority rests in direct experience. The therapist is simply there to provide his client an environment of empathy, unconditional positive regard and complete acceptance. In effect, a mirror."

She considered this for a moment. "I guess it's like one of those *New Yorker* cartoons," she said. She watched him lift his eyebrows almost out of the frame in response, which stimulated an answering giggle from the off-screen girl.

"Anyway, I don't know what happened to her after all that. From what I heard, it was just the same-old same-old—she got involved with some young guy. Who had old money. Not always the best thing for a budding clinical career. Whatever. It seemed to take up all of her time. She dropped our project like a—" He appeared to grope for the familiar cliché.

"A hot potato," Annie said silently. Leah hadn't needed him any more.

Because she was done. Because for someone like Leah Mallick, it was the equivalent of a wine-tasting course. Once you had the terminology down, the essentials of cocktail party chatter, what was left? Psychometrics, split-half reliability, predictive validity, item analysis, deviations from normal distribution curve, cognitive and contextual theories, Wechsler scales, the Minnesota Multiphasic Personality Inventory—comfort food for control freaks. She'd taken just what she needed and Alan Wakefield had exhausted his part.

"It was her research you used though, right?"

Wakefield shifted abruptly in his chair. It showed as a slight jerky motion, leaving a ghostlike image on the left part of the screen. He was immediately defensive. "That's the usual layman's view. But in academe, intellectual credit emerges out of a tradition as old as Aristotle. Leah had no problem with the convention, I can assure you. The work emerged directly out of my thesis. She was appropriately acknowledged." He sat back and gathered himself.

Then he formed a smile and leaned closer to the camera, his suddenly engorged face filling the screen. "OK, here's another one for you. How many narcissistic personality disorders does it take to change a lightbulb?"

"How many?" she obliged.

"Just one—to hold the light bulb. But then you have to wait for the whole world to revolve around you."

The first sight that met her when she finally came back downstairs and walked into the front hallway was Ben's pathetic expression. She'd been up in the spare room, sitting in front of a computer, for close to eight hours now. And he'd piddled beside the door. She noticed it as soon as she stepped in it. Whatever had possessed her to get a dog in the first place?

Maybe nothing more than the need to fill that empty month or two between Ken-something and the next guy.

"I think I might have to get you a little brother, soon, Ben," she said. There were going to be many empty months to come.

His worried brown eyes followed her. He wanted to be sure she wasn't really mad. She reached down to reassure him. "I'm sorry I forgot about you," she said gently. His tail wagged tentatively as he followed her into the kitchen.

She sighed and opened the fridge. Here they were again—another exciting evening all laid out. A long walk. A low-calorie supper, followed by whatever she damn well pleased for dessert. A little more research, and then bed.

Somehow, though, it turned into a sandwich in front of the TV with Ben settled at her feet. She'd just won the *Jeopardy* final round when the bell rang.

Ben obligingly went to the front door and sat, watching it.

She flicked on the outside light. It was Bill, standing alone on her porch. Never a good sign, she said to herself again, to see a cop at your front door . . .

He said nothing past "Hi," smiling. Apparently, there was nothing wrong.

Annie opened the door wider and he stepped into her hallway. They stared at each other for a long time before she noticed that her own heart was starting to thump harder than usual for some reason. "Everything OK?" she said finally.

He nodded as he stepped close enough to take her completely into his arms. "I want to be your boyfriend again," he said simply.

She caught only a glimpse of both of them in the long hallway mirror, before he turned out the light. His thinning grey-blonde hair—her thickening chin in profile. Someone had once remarked that they looked more like brother and sister than partners. It was still true.

They made their way up to the bedroom, and almost in unison, stepped slowly out of their clothes. Ten years had made a noticeable difference in both of them, all the obvious things. The single light was still on—no cover of darkness here. He made no effort to help her, either, just watched silently. Nor did she move towards him. He laid his shirt over the back of the chair between them, on top of her own. She couldn't even hope to gauge her own feelings any more. The trembling throughout her body told her nothing, except that maybe she'd been lonely for a long time. There was no allowance left for self-consciousness; either they could be here together, as they were now, or not at all.

And exactly how big *is* my ass? she asked herself. Would it be better to compare it to agricultural products or to sporting goods? She noticed then that his smile mirrored her own.

"Are you as cold as I am—standing here like this?" he said, his grin growing wider.

In answer, she held out one arm towards him. "Look. Goosebumps."

In the next moment they were scrambling on to the bed, grabbing at the sheets. Bill swept the blanket over their heads and they crouched under it, hiding like two children in the darkness, giggling, so close they could each feel their breaths warming the air between them.

Annie slowly drew one leg up over his thigh. She felt his hand reach behind her and begin to settle her slightly under his length. The movements, the expected shift of weight, gentle and familiar in so many ways. By its own accord, her body stretched out and arched to open.

Annie yelped in sudden pain. "Ouch. Ow! Oh, shit."

He immediately pulled away from her, looking everywhere, quickly, for some sign of injury. "Jesus, I'm sorry. Did I hurt you? I forget it's only been a couple of weeks since you—"

"No." She started laughing. "No, honey, it's OK. I just got a damn cramp in my foot."

He reached under the covers and began to massage her ankle and foot. He mumbled something that she couldn't make out.

"What?"

He came up from under the blanket, flushed and grinning. "I just said that I've never slept with someone who's been shot before."

"That you *know* of, anyway."

He slipped an arm behind her to rest her head on his shoulder. She heard his heart in his chest, maybe a bit fast, but nice and steady. Next she'd be checking his EKG. You know you're middle-aged—

"Do you think about it a lot?" he asked. "The shooting?"

She considered the idea for a moment. "Not really as much as I would have expected. Mostly, just how accidental it all seemed—completely random, in the middle of a million other things that can go wrong. I think about how stupid and meaningless it would have been if something worse had happened. Both for me and that kid—" Random, and it had changed everything.

"You know, that woman had nothing more than five bucks and a Social Security card in her purse, and you take off after him like you're Pepper Anderson."

"Pepper who?"

"You remember her—Angie Dickinson? C'mon . . . that show *Police Woman.* Man! I had such a thing for her. Big time. Maybe I never told you—that's the *real* reason I wanted to be a cop. I thought I was gonna end up with her for my partner."

Annie groaned loudly while he chuckled. They listened to a car go by outside, the sound emphasizing the hush that came after, the leaves rustling like rain.

What else *could* she really think of what had happened that night? she wondered. "Even in the middle of it, you know, it wasn't making any sense to me. And then Susan ran up, and she looks more terrified than I feel. It took me until then to figure out it was deadly serious. I couldn't even get my head around the idea that I'd really been shot. All I could remember was that I'd just been fighting about something with *her.* Then she completely distracts me with that whole . . . you know, about her fling with Acton. I don't think she really meant to . . ." Annie recalled the expression on Susan's face. It wasn't even what she'd said, as much as the way she'd said it.

"So, really, it was just another excuse to gossip—"

She punched him lightly in the ribs, then lay there again, thinking. "And I know if she hadn't been there—" Annie bit her lip. "But I guess I'm just *really* lucky that Leah Mallick wasn't my doctor."

Then they both laughed until tears came.

Eventually, Bill rolled to face her. "Now turn out the light, young lady. I got an early day tomorrow."

"Oh, you're not getting off *that* easily, Lieutenant." Her throaty growl thrilled them both. His eyes widened in appreciation. Old times, maybe, but something new too.

He lowered his voice dramatically. "I only agreed to *sleep* with you—Lieutenant." He reached over her and extinguished the bedside light, kissed her. Another moment of silence as they relaxed back into the dark together. "So, the cramp gone yet?"

She nodded, "Mm-hmm."

"Then maybe I should see if I can give you another one."

She laughed softly and stroked his arm, laid lightly across her breasts. "How do you know this makes any sense—for either of us?" Annie asked. "Nothing's worked out for me for a long time." Even the longest so-called relationship had lasted barely six months. And, obviously, her romantic record wasn't exactly a well-kept secret in the department . . ." Why now, why tonight?"

"I had to wait for you to get to the end of the line."

She could hear the sly smile in his voice. Nicely done, she thought—subtly supportive and mildly insulting at the same time. "Well, I think you should know I'm considering seducing a new contractor. I figure if I play my cards right, I can finally get the house finished this summer."

He yawned. "I'll warn you, too—I'm no better at home repairs than I ever was. And I never was. So you just call up Bob Vila or whoever it is, any time you think you need to."

"Maybe I'll just keep Bob on the side . . ."

In the distance they heard the whistle from the steel mill. Annie couldn't remember ever noticing it before—she hadn't realized it even came this far. A second note, more sustained this time. Dividing all the days and nights for five generations.

She glanced at the clock. Eleven. Probably the earliest she'd been to bed in months. The window was open to the night air. The sweet scent of summer green flowed through the curtains. She loved the warmth of his skin against her cheek, his large hand smoothing her hair back from her forehead. She smiled. Ten years ago they'd have finished by now. All athletic and single-minded. Foreplay only in the time it took to climb the stairs. Both of them tougher, stronger, in those days. Less patient. Higher expectations, lower maintenance. Love, now, covered much more ground. It had to take into account all the things that had gone wrong, the things that would never happen, all the dreams forsaken. And it had to stand up to the invidious comparison with the people they should have been.

They both jumped a bit when the phone rang. Annie considered letting the machine pick up. Instead, she answered it. "Hello?"

The woman's voice on the other end was calm, even poised. "Is Lieutenant Williamson there, please?" Probably someone from work . . . who knew this number.

She passed it across to Bill. "It's for you." And she settled deeper into the pillow, the phone cord still swinging against her arm.

"Williamson." In the dark she heard his voice change, soften. The call wasn't from anyone at work; that much she *could* tell. Annie listened to the cautious monosyllables. Yes. Yes. No. She felt his body tense subtly beside hers. "No," he said finally. "I told you we'll discuss it tomorrow." Then, "You called. You know who it is." Annie knew who *that* was too.

In the next instant she lay on her side, laughing, her fingers splayed across the top of the phone. After a startled moment of recognition, he passed the dead receiver back to her. She replaced it, then felt his hands wrapping around her from behind. It was a moment of indecent, unreasonable, unconscionable triumph.

"Did I happen to mention I was living with someone?" he mumbled into the hair near her ear.

She noticed, for the first time, how really quiet it was at this time of the night. "Is this about sympathy?" she said carefully. She didn't want to begin that way.

He held her closer. "Not any more, kiddo. You used up your quota a long time ago. I want something from you this time."

"There's a limit. . . ?"

He was silent for a long time. "Annie, there's a limit on everything. Even shame," he said finally. Not mourning, or guilt. The real word struck her like a fist. She realized then that it was the right one. More about pain, and disgrace in being held up to the world's eye. Not secret or quiet, but bloodied, and marked forever.

She spoke to the ceiling. "Did I ever tell you the one about the two behavioural psychologists? After they finish making love, one says to the other, 'Darling, that was wonderful for you. How was it for me?'"

He laughed softly in the dark and she turned over to look at him. Everything in shadow but for a glint of light in his eye from the glow of a street lamp outside the window. Why had she never bothered to dream this, amidst all the other things of the world? She took his face in her hands and slipped her legs around him, sliding him inside her effortlessly.

"Hand in glove, babe," she said.

It was already five in the morning. She hadn't come down looking for it, but she found herself sitting in front of a shot of cheap brandy at the island in the kitchen. Waiting for the sun to rise. Or not.

She heard Bill's steps on the staircase. Then, unexpectedly, the sound of the front door being opened. Silence. He'd left it ajar; she could feel the cool cross-breeze drifting through the kitchen. A minute or so later Bill followed it in, barefoot, in jeans, with his unbuttoned shirt flapping loose. He was carrying a black leather case on a shoulder strap.

As he pulled up the opposite stool, he glanced at the glass in front of her. Little point in setting the drink aside now, she knew. But he said nothing about it and simply laid the case on the counter between them.

"I wanted to return this to you," he said after a moment.

Annie glanced at it without making a move.

"It's hers, isn't it? Susan's?" he said.

Annie nodded. She'd given it to Tina at the end of the day, standing out beside her car in the parking lot of a shopping mall. "How did you—?"

"I asked her for it."

Annie reached out and touched the smooth leather. It was cold from sitting out in the car all night.

"The governor's office provided us with a property list. Then I checked with the hotel—you were her only guest. You're the one who knew it was there. And nothing else is missing . . . so I just asked Tina where you'd put it." He could have backed off easily enough if Tina had thought to challenge him. But it was a low-risk strategy, she knew, to imply something in an offhanded way. Bill had the "good cop" thing down pat.

Annie smiled a bit. "Give her another year and that wouldn't have worked, you know."

He shrugged. Part of the game they all played at times.

"Have you looked at any of it?"

He shook his head. "No. But she told me that she'd found part of a memo Susan was writing. It was addressed to you. She must have started it that same night. Tina made me promise I'd give it to you, before . . ." Before they had to hand everything back over to Acton.

Tina must have been expecting the sky to fall in, Annie thought.

"I won't ask why you felt it necessary to involve her. But she's bright. She knows something. I just told her that it was signed out of inventory improperly. A technical violation she need have no part of. It's more than *you* did for her, kiddo."

Annie was tense. "What happens now?"

Bill looked at her steadily. "You'll read it. When you're done, you'll pass it back to me. You have better instincts than anyone I've ever worked with. If there's something there, you'll know where to look. When you're ready, you'll tell me everything. Then, together, we decide what needs doing."

Bill stretched up and opened the kitchen cupboard door just behind her. The bottle of Four Aces, still a quarter full, teetered on the shelf. He grabbed it, poured what remained into her glass and tossed the empty plastic bottle into the recycling bin. "But if you take one more drink after *that* one, I'll turn you in myself."

Then he leaned down and kissed her. "And now . . . I'm going up for another hour of well-deserved sleep. Join me when you're ready."

13

Annie drove down the dirt road to the river's edge. The security installation, toll booth—whatever it was trying to be—was empty, only a radio inside, belting out Motown oldies. If there was a guard, he was nowhere in sight. She got out of her car and wandered the short distance down to the water. The level here had risen at least six inches from all the rain of the last few days. Drowning sedge grasses and a mud-thickened current running at her feet. The island floating just beyond reach, perhaps a hundred and fifty yards away. *I could try to jump it. Cops in movies do it all the time.*

Last night had seen the biggest thunderstorm of the year so far. The air now was clean, almost sharp, the temperatures returning to something closer to normal. She'd never been to the island before, never had reason to. She crouched down and let her hand trail in the water while she looked around.

Her stomach had been heaving precipitously since early morning and she felt lousy and light-headed with it. She remembered now—this was what a hangover felt like.

Boys were swimming out from the small inlets eroded into the banks, a quarter-mile or so upstream. They sunned themselves on sandbars almost equidistant from the shore. Seventeen, maybe eighteen years old. Strong. No, not just strong, immortal. If you could get them this far, she thought, they could be safe.

She smiled slightly, recalling Susan's mocking description of this place. The Island Boys. The big centre table. The endless ritual of Waiting for Jack. Their easy assumption of seigneurial rights. Their temerity in trying to run the world.

Maybe that described the real difference between Susan and her—Susan had dared to call them what they were from the very beginning, unimpressed, unintimidated. Easier for her as an outsider. She'd written them all off in two seconds flat.

But it was also why she'd missed a deeper truth.

"You wanna cross over?" A voice came up behind her now, from the long golden grass. Annie saw that it was a boy, tanned and beautiful, perhaps seventeen. Hard-angled sun cut across his features. He looked like perfection until he opened his mouth. Too many flattened vowels, not enough consonants. One who'd never be allowed to enter through the front door of a place like this.

"No point in waiting for that guy in there, y'know. He always takes a long break at lunchtime. Goes off into town or something. Leaves wrappers from Burger King all over the place. Guess some people are just pigs, eh?" He raised an eyebrow archly and laughed.

Then he shaded his eyes with his hand and looked across the arm of the river to the swing bridge, suspended parallel to the shore. "It makes them nuts," he said. "They can't figure out how it goes round by itself. They're morons anyway. If you know how to boost a car, this is nothin'."

Annie nodded, willing herself into anonymity. "Think you can get me across?"

"Sure, no problem. We whistle it over when we don't want to get wet. Most the time, we don't give a shit—just like driving them crazy. But I as*sume* you don't wanna swim. So . . ." And he motioned her in the direction of her car.

Annie got in and watched as the boy went around to the side of the shed and knelt down on the gravel. Something sparked under his hand, and in that instant, the bridge began wheeling towards them.

He bowed deeply, theatrically—an imitation of an overly obsequious maitre d'—and waved her on to the deck. As she passed him, Annie gave a small salute. His gleaming smile broke her heart.

At the end of a short gravel road, the faux Southern colonial splendour of the clubhouse hove into view. She parked directly in front. There was no one around, none to greet or challenge her as she strode through the empty lobby. She knew exactly where to look.

As she entered the dining room, Lewis Stephens was holding forth as usual. From the defeated appearance of his guests, Annie calculated they were probably going into their second hour.

"Yeah. Yeah. I expect to hear back from him probably to the end of this week. Oh, I'll tell ya, when Jack gets through with this place—the crown jewel, gentlemen—" Stephens stopped abruptly when he saw a woman coming straight towards him. Out of nothing but sheer habit, he actually rose from his chair a couple of inches.

Annie didn't recognize the three other men at his table, but she certainly knew Lewis Stephens on sight. "So, how are your plans for the golf course coming, Mr. Stephens?" she asked casually.

Stephens fell back on his chair. His eyes flicked at Annie nervously, though his outward manner remained jovial. "Well, hello. I'm afraid you have the advantage of me . . . ?" A charade of trying to place her.

You irredeemable old fart, she thought, you know damn well who I am. "Anne Shannon, Mr. Stephens. Lockport police department."

He settled back, eyeing her more comfortably. "Ah, yes. Gentlemen, this is the young lady we all see so often on our television sets. You're becoming quite famous, Miss Shannon."

"As are you, Mr. Stephens."

Stephens' bluff amiability retreated slightly. "Yes. The Lockport police. You're a long way from home, Anne." His tone was bantering, but he stared at her more assessingly. She knew he was trying to measure her against someone in his past.

"Just across the river, Mr. Stephens."

"But still outside your jurisdiction, I believe."

Annie raised one eyebrow, saying nothing. And why would *that* matter?

"Would you care to join us? I was just talking to these fellas about—"

"Yes, I heard. 'Jack.' Actually, what I'd like to discuss with you right now is Addorée Construction."

Stephens's face froze for a moment, his mouth gone slack. Then he cleared his throat roughly. "OK . . . Well, you boys just go ahead and have that drink we were planning on, and I'll be back momentarily." Stephens stood. "Miss Shannon, why don't I give you a little tour of our facilities."

Stephens led her from the dining room, pointedly ignoring the several empty meeting rooms they passed. It wasn't privacy he was seeking, she knew. He was throwing her out. And within moments she found herself standing again on the broad veranda at the front of the building. She looked at him in the strong, slanting sunlight, his arms folded across his sagging chest, facing her angrily now, wanting to bar her way back in. Her or people like her, she assumed.

Far too late to shut *that* particular barn door, she thought. The next generation of Island Boys is already out there, Mr. Stephens. Not your kind, perhaps. But they can come and take this place from you any time they choose . . .

"I'm surprised you don't exercise a little more discretion here, Miss Shannon. I know the police in these parts aren't usually valued for their social graces, but I might have expected something a little better from you. At least you've had some practice. Local girl makes good and all . . ."

His tactic was uninspired, even mechanical. Annie recognized it as little more than a clumsy attempt to provoke her. "You know, Mr. Stephens, it took me about five minutes to determine who was really behind that development across the river," Annie said. "Limited partnerships . . . and all. Because when I heard you recently lost a lot of money, I naturally became quite curious about how you could still proceed with a big expensive project. To what would you credit your apparent change in fortunes?"

Stephens chuckled. "Now, now. I know you don't really expect me to answer your questions just like that. You must be pretty aware that you have no legal standing here." He squinted at her in the sun. "If anything, you're here as my guest—"

"If you don't mind my asking, how much did you really end up losing on that deal with Tim Mallick again?" Annie said. Her mouth felt dry and she wanted nothing so much as another drink right now—these tremors weren't only from nervousness.

At the mention of Tim Mallick, Stephens's entire appearance altered, the phoney gentility replaced by angry indignation. It took more energy than he had to contain it.

"Almost every damn bit of it. I distinctly remember telling that Shaw woman the other day the exact same thing. We barely got fifteen cents out on the dollar, in the end. It was to our advantage to take the tax loss."

Annie rested against the railing and studied the stark white scar of the construction site, easily visible now on the hillside on the other side of the river. Even from here, anyone could see that most of the trees up and down the slope had already been removed in a wide swath, a rough road cut into the cliff face.

She continued as if he hadn't spoken at all. "Because I don't think your friends are as good at acting as you are. I think they did lose their money. And perhaps someone offered to buy *you* out, as long as you did a favour for them."

Annie spoke quietly from a few feet away. "You found a way to collapse that deal with Tim Mallick . . ."

To cover your loss. And remain silent.

There was only one way, and they both knew what that was. "You didn't just discover they were closing Palladian Steel—you made it happen, didn't you?" The Wizard of Oz. "You timed that call on Tim Mallick's paper, when you were sure he couldn't cover it. And you brought his whole pyramid crashing down. Those worthless options . . . ? Not really so worthless anymore. Transferred to another company you own. Your friends got the tax loss. And you only have to hold on until Palladian goes under in the next couple months. It was easy—Cross Corp just had to find someone like you."

His reaction immediately confirmed it. Stephens's broad face coloured alarmingly, helpless agitation in his every movement. "I don't know what Cross Corp has to do with anything. But I remember you now," he said. "Shannon. Yuh. I knew your father, years ago. Little Bud Shannon? Seventh division? Regular beat cop. But a real smart man, as I recall. I know your commissioner over there now, too. He's . . . it's . . ."

"Paul DeVries."

Stephens nodded firmly. "DeVries. That's the fella."

Annie could see that the name, in fact, meant nothing to him; it was just currency. She continued undeterred. "You've used it to secure a majority interest in a private holding company—Stoney River Resorts. What's your piece? Forty, fifty percent? More?" She let the silence build. She hadn't had to look much deeper than that. She could feel an invisible hand now guiding her every step.

"Just a little something for my grandchildren," he said finally. "My legacy . . ."

Annie actually smiled. "Your *legacy,* is it now? Well, I think most of us could understand something like that—family and everything. But just how far were you really prepared to go, to hide this particular 'legacy' from the rest of the town, Lew? From your friends who'll find out you cheated them? From everyone in town who's about to lose their jobs?" she asked. "Then again, maybe you were just hoping no one would begrudge it to you, even if they did find out—you being the only one smart enough and fast enough to grab a good opportunity when it happened along.

"Or maybe, even after you stopped to think about the real implications for a little while, it still mattered more in the end—to build this legacy of yours."

Stephens had turned away from her and was now surveying the construction site on the hills across the river. "Sometimes you have to take the longer view. It was going to close anyway. Maybe I'm just a bit more of a philosopher than most th'other people around here."

Ah, yes. "But maybe there are more things in heaven and earth than are dreamt of in your philosophy . . ." Annie mused aloud.

Yet even as she stood there, his witness, he couldn't quite disguise the swelling pride in what he looked upon. He glanced over at Annie now with a sly grin. "It's just business. I got my finger in a bunch o' pies. A little here, a little there. Like they say—you never put all your eggs in one basket." He'd turned full on to her, leering unpleasantly now.

She nodded slowly. "And after you made your decision to pull the plug, you even managed to look panicky—just enough to convince everyone that you'd really accepted pennies on the dollar. And you kept quiet about the rest of it." And every once in a while took the opportunity for a public rant, guaranteed to be overheard. Susan had described it accurately—a full dining room at lunchtime, the dominating, centre table, with enough people eavesdropping to spread it all the way to the state line.

That one decision had locked in a loss of almost eighty-five percent on the deal. And apparently sent Tim Mallick hurtling into another dimension.

Annie could see the complete outline of it now. Palladian Steel's plant was just too old and too tired to attract substantial investment. And Mallick had put together a portfolio so leveraged as to render the possibility of real profit practically non-existent—at least to them, in their lifetimes. He had made a serious mistake—he'd designed a strategy for privileged men like himself, the ones with luck, and much more time ahead of them.

From Lewis Stephens's perspective, there really *was* only one short-term asset left to exploit . . .

Gamely, Stephens tried again. "In the end, we could have called their bluff. Not tendered. But the stock price would have dropped. We decided to fold our cards because the downside risk short-term was too great relative to any upside. We were on margin . . . they could have called . . ." His voice ground to a halt.

It was just words. And none of it mattered. In the silence, Annie merely stared at him, one eyebrow raised. Oh, *really?*

Then she looked beyond Lewis Stephens into the distance, to the golden boys swimming in the river. Out beyond, where they captured the bridge again and again.

"Well, you fancy yourself a philosopher . . . I hope that's a comfort. Because, just by looking, Mr. Stephens, I can tell time's running out for you. You're going to be left standing alone in that mausoleum you're building for yourself. I hope it's worth it."

Stephens turned away, stung. But even then he couldn't help himself. After only a moment's hesitation he sidled up beside her again and slapped the railing she leaned against, speaking in that practised, cajoling tone she knew so well. It was the very definition of patronizing. He used his finger now to trace an outline of the dreamed-aloud structure in the air. "Those condos are being built over there just because of people like me. Up on those hills, with a nice view over all the world. Would anyone—would you, Lieutenant—still choose to be "down in the valley"—he actually warbled it as the line from the old song—"or would you prefer to be high up there on the mountaintop? Above the bad air and the bad cooking?"

She laughed. "This isn't Dickensian England, Mr. Stephens. We're supposed to be a long way past that by now," Annie said. "And it's no longer 'the company town.'"

He rallied around his own belligerence. "Your shanty Irish is showing, Annie Shannon. In the end—please—tell me what you think I'm really taking from these people. Don't *you* just want to be left alone? Pay your mortgage, go upstate for a couple of long weekends every year? I build things. I'm the one who makes all this happen. Just so you can walk through the front door of *my* private club. That's the kind of progress your people like, isn't it?"

Stephens turned now and poked a finger within an inch of her face. "Maybe I *will* hire you—you and all your friends. And you can protect me from all the bleeding hearts who think they're getting screwed somehow. And I reckon you'll be damn glad of the job, just like your old man was. You got yourself all done up with an Ivy League education—Police Benevolent Society scholarship and all, as I recall—but you're still the kid of a beat cop who put his hand out for a little 'Christmas bonus' every year."

Annie remembered that too. No favour was ever too much for the Island Boys. Discreet car service from late-night drinking parties. Speeding tickets made to disappear. A domestic disturbance quietly smoothed over, behind closed doors.

Annie knew she could afford to let the past flow right over her now. But she felt herself forced, almost imperceptibly, forward. "You don't even *know,* do you? It's not your city any more. It's not yours to give away. Not even *you* can build those castle walls high enough."

"Oh, yeah? Well, don't slam the drawbridge on your way out, little girl." A big, hearty guffaw that ended in red-faced choking.

"And how the hell do you think I got here, Mr. Stephens? The drawbridge . . . is *down.*" Annie said, her voice louder.

Stephens, still gasping for breath, stumbled backwards, away from her.

Surprised, Annie finally stopped herself. What was she intending to do, anyway? Beat up an eighty-year-old asthmatic? Christ!

Stephens finally recovered enough to wheeze something out in her general direction. "I've known everyone who matters for many years, young lady. And all the people who put *them* there. I'm going to be making a few phone calls after this, I'll tell ya." But it was only the jabbing finger that indicated any lasting capacity for anger. His voice had faded to a rasping whisper.

"*Go* to them, Mr. Stephens. Go to the deputy mayor, the city council. To the police commissioner. The governor. The president. The Security Council of the United Nations. Let's just see what *they* all do with this. Because what you do is of no concern to me any more."

Stephens went slowly flat, as though all the air had leaked out of him.

Annie forced herself to speak more calmly. "But even to someone like me—it looks like you've put yourself in a fairly precarious position. I think a man like you is going to let it slip, one day. Very soon. I don't think you are going to be able to just sit there, with your friends, at that big table at the centre of the world, and not say something—watching your legacy go up, big as life, right across the river. Because I think you're going to find it just too hard to keep something like that to yourself. It's such a damn good story. You're going to want to tell *Jack,* at least . . ."

Annie stepped off the porch unhurriedly. She slid her sunglasses down her nose for a moment, looking back over her shoulder at him. It was an almost flirtatious gesture. "In the end, you know that character that everyone's always talking about? He never actually arrives. They end up wasting the rest of their lives—just waiting for him. That's the whole point of the play." Then the ghost of a smile. "You can't take it with you, Mr. Stephens," she said.

Though the only ones who'd really suffer, she knew, were the fifteen hundred or so people who'd put the steel plant at the centre of their life's work. Like the coal mines and the canneries before it. *My sons and my son's sons. My father, and his father before him* . . . That was how cities died—from the inside.

As she drove away from the clubhouse, Annie saw him lift a palsied hand and bring it to his chest unconsciously. It must feel like drowning, she thought. And every day, carried just a little further from the shore . . .

But Annie only wanted to laugh aloud now, like a kid. It felt good to get something right at last.

Cross Corp had planted the seed, probably by offering to introduce Tim Mallick to Stephens a year or so ago. Or, more subtly, to someone else in his same group—Callie had described the Mallicks as "social" when they'd first arrived. Maybe at some country-club barbecue. After that, it required only that Tim do what he'd always done so brilliantly—sweep people up in one of his schemes. But do it here, to a "victim" who wouldn't just lie down. In fact, one who'd be willing to destroy Lockport in the end, if it meant he could save his own hide.

They needed a way to make the city vulnerable and, without Palladian Steel, it would be. The city would come begging for Cross Corp to move in, however controversial it might turn out to be. Cities welcomed toxic dumps and super-prisons, if it meant jobs and revenue—a global high-tech health services corporation would look pretty good.

They'd calculated that Lewis Stephens could be bought with nothing more than the edifice of some ostentatious condo development. At this stage of the game it was a safe assumption; you didn't have to be a Donald Trump to want to leave your name on something. It wasn't even about the money, when you got right down to it. Some people never changed, Annie knew, because some people never had reason to.

But when had Leah Mallick herself finally understood that something was going very wrong? When had she seen her husband become that other person, a man fighting the spectre of failure? Did she ever know that it was Cross Corp who had finally thrown him all the rope he needed to pull himself into the deeper, drowning water?

And timing, as the comedian said, is everything.

Annie drifted off the bridge. The guard scowled and carefully took note of her plate number as she passed his security outpost. She followed the road out on to the main highway, heading back towards town.

"I really thought you were going to hit him," Susan said, the sound more insubstantial than a fading breeze. A light laugh, going away.

"I thought so too," Annie said.

"OK, what am I supposed to be looking for here?" Bill leaned in and studied the screen while the video clip loaded again. Annie had already watched it several times, all the way through, every nuance of expression burned into her memory. "Where'd you find it."

"It was a link on Alan Wakefield's Web-site. He uses it for his seminar in test marketing. Showing how easy it is to skew results. He sells himself as a consultant to food packaging companies."

It started by showing a typical exam room, divided into two separate soundproofed areas. Windowless, flat lighting. A two-way mirror between the observer and the observed. There were two people seated, one on either side, each wearing headphones—a young man and a young woman, both about eighteen or nineteen.

Leah was almost unrecognizable. Bright blonde, soft features. Anyone else would have seen just another pretty girl. Not easy to imagine what lay ahead of her.

The subject of the session, presumably another undergrad, had placed himself firmly on his chair, hands folded on the ledge in front of him, easy and self-assured. Leah sat directly opposite. Each was unseen by the other.

They'd completed whatever preparations were necessary. The test itself began immediately, with a series of questions, the start of each series signalled by an audio tone. The subject was being asked to repeat back a random string of numbers—simple enough, even when letters were interposed. Up to nine items at a time. He had little trouble remembering the sequences. On the surface it seemed impressive; he got almost every one of them right, even appeared to be enjoying himself. And between each series Leah gave him a slight encouragement, usually a "good" or "right," sometimes a brief comment.

Bill glanced at his watch. Going on three or four minutes of the same thing. "What—some kind of test for boredom. . . ?" Bill began.

"Shh . . . wait," Annie said.

They watched as Leah adjusted her chair slightly, placing it at an oblique angle. She leaned on her desk more comfortably, subtly changing the tone of her voice. She was using it like a instrument. "I shouldn't be telling you," she said, "but I guess you've already figured out that there's a pattern. You don't seem to need any help, though—you've nailed every one of them so far." A light laugh.

Bill suddenly looked intrigued. "Hold it—he *did* miss a couple, right?"

Annie nodded. "Yeah, he did."

Leah resumed the test as before. Nothing appeared to have changed. The student continued to recite the sequences back—as far as they could judge, with the same level of accuracy. But now Leah delayed her responses slightly, the pitch lowered. Instead of quick notes of approval, she said little. At most, small, neutral noises. "Hmm" or "uh-huh." Adding now and then what sounded like a little edge of disapproval.

"This is something about flirting . . . or focus . . . something like that?" Bill said.

"The title's 'Contextualization in Causal Structures.' I don't know. But look what she does here."

They watched as Leah excused herself abruptly, cutting off the microphone to her subject. She carefully set a stopwatch, then turned with a grin towards the invisible observing camera. "Pretty low g factor there." And though he'd probably heard her say the same thing a dozen times during these sessions, Annie recognized Alan Wakefield chuckling again, off-screen, from behind the glass.

"What's a g factor?" Bill asked.

Annie's eyes didn't move from the screen. She was still fixed on Leah. "General factor. Comes from Spearman's General Intelligence Theory. It's a starting point. What she was saying was that—"

"—that he wasn't very bright," Bill finished. "Layman's term, of course."

Annie nodded absently.

She didn't notice that Bill was looking at her now, impressed. "When did *you* start learning all this—"

Annie stopped him again with a raised hand. "OK, now. Watch this."

Leah held up the stopwatch again. At the one-minute mark she turned her microphone back on. "Sorry about that," she said crisply. Without further explanation she began the same process. But this time she noted each apparent mistake he made with a "no" or "uh-uh."

Bill narrowed his eyes. "Whoa . . ."

Annie smiled now. "I know. The fourth one in each string. Correct or not."

After only a few series the student began stumbling at precisely the same point each time. It was like tripping on the fourth step every time you climbed a staircase, the one that was out only by an eighth of a inch, until the unconscious took over and made the necessary adjustment. Each time, Leah inevitably approved his second choice with a friendly "yeah" or "good."

Then, with barely a stutter, he began to change every one of his responses, from the correct answer to a wrong one. Perhaps unconsciously. But it was clear, from his gestures, the change in posture, his eye movements. Annie could have guessed it herself. He had it, then he changed it. Even after Leah stopped commenting. And the entire process had taken less than ten minutes.

Annie hit pause.

"So, what am I supposed to get out of that?" Bill said, smiling as he leaned back in the chair, hands clasped behind his head.

She grinned. "You've read Orwell, haven't you, Bill? 'How many fingers am I holding up?' The ultimate control." She waggled her hand in front of his face. "How many fingers? If I can get you to see what I want you to see, I don't have to do anything else. If I can change your belief system, if I can convince you to deny the evidence right in front of your eyes, if I can build you another paradigm, I can create the new truth."

"And you think *this* means all that?"

"She was nineteen years old. Where would you suggest she start . . . Jonestown? She was looking for ways to make something very wrong appear to be entirely acceptable. Even necessary."

They watched the video clip for another minute. Leah gathered up her books and papers, and carefully made sure the chairs were restored to their original positions, as neutral an environment as possible, then left.

Bill waited, looking at the empty room for another couple of seconds. "Is that it?"

Annie nodded as she closed down the on-screen window. "Pretty much."

She wasn't prepared to tell him there was more. For some reason, she didn't want to share everything about Leah Mallick yet. And it was only after Bill left that she replayed the rest of the video for herself again. She watched the door open.

Leah came back into the room and, this time, walked directly up to the two-way mirror, assuming that someone would still be there, still watching her. The effect was striking. Annie found herself looking straight into Leah Mallick's unearthly blue eyes. As though the mirror, the camera and more than twenty years weren't standing between them.

Annie recalled one of Jill Davis's whining complaints, her aggrieved description: "She'd give you that peculiar Arctic-blue stare of hers—like she just expected you to fall into line."

And Leah Mallick was staring at her now. Caught in that gaze for just a moment, Annie felt something of what was to come—the more mature power building behind it. Even the voice had assumed the richer, more provocative tone Annie had heard on the answering-machine tape.

"You and I both know it's going to work," Leah said, smiling at her.

~~~
~~~

Annie had managed to stretch her regular evening walks to a good hour, taking a different route through the neighbourhood each time. Ben, she knew, would happily have accompanied her through the entire night. If neither of them looked any more svelte yet, it was only because there was still such a long way to go.

Cutting through an alley at the back of Grand Avenue, Annie found herself at the end of a short side street, adjacent to what had been, until only very recently, a vacant lot. Over the years a small house on the site had been allowed to tumble into nothing and disappear beneath the weeds and scrub.

But now everything was changed. There were flowers and vegetables, vines climbing over rough-built arbours and trellises, a varied collection of shrubs and small trees in well-balanced arrangements. One bed was filled with plants in a hundred shades of white and grey. In the evening light they seemed almost illuminated from within. Their leaves showed as bright or shiny. Some were a smoky green colour, soft to the touch. There was a small grouping of ornamental grasses, so dark that they appeared black.

After only a few moments Annie could detect the fragrance of herbs, not one separate from another, but blended all together. Something else that might have been evening primrose. Though the lot was small, it now seemed generous and expansive. A trick of perspective. Whoever did this is an artist, she thought.

But there was no one in sight. All the windows in the houses that faced the garden were blank, reflecting only the evening sky, the sharp crescent of the moon. It was as though everything had simply emerged from a dream and grown here spontaneously.

In the next moment Annie saw that it wasn't true. With a slight movement, the small, bent figure of an elderly woman separated itself from the deeper shadows. Annie could just make out that she was busy planting something more in the curve of a bed.

Ben had raised his nose to the ripe smell of compost, and his ears pricked up now at a sound. The woman, working out here all alone, had started to sing an old tune that Annie recognized right away. It was "Lili Marlene," the same song she'd heard in the palliative wing of the hospital.

In surprise, Annie stood watching her for another moment, wondering what to say, not wanting to startle or frighten her.

Then Ben let out a single high-pitched yip. At that, the woman looked over and simply raised her hand in a friendly wave. Annie automatically waved back. The woman bent down to her work again, still singing.

The garden was already wonderful, and growing into something quite stunning. Annie tried to imagine a simple version of it transported into her own backyard, then dismissed the thought out of hand—any garden like this was more than she wanted to take on right now.

It was quiet here, serene. Nothing more than a light breeze. There was no one else around, and it was almost dark. But whether the world would worry or even care, the woman obviously intended to finish her evening's work. Annie waved at her again, though the woman didn't see it, and moved away, pulling Ben firmly to heel.

Given half a chance, she knew, he'd dig up something precious and fragile.

As she walked away, she dared to imagine it already in place—thick lawns and curved flower beds and elegantly arranged groupings of expensive shrubs. Maybe a gazebo . . . ?

Florence Schellenberg's answering machine message had been short and sweet. "I don't much like what's going on up here, Lieutenant. You'd better find an excuse to drop by."

Phone calls to Riverview Hospital were useless. They kept putting her on hold, and each time whoever answered had absolutely no interest in giving out any information. Annie finally drove over.

The parking lot was full, blocked by transmission vehicles. The satellite dish dwarfed two other vans pulled in beside a tractor-trailer providing the main broadcast facility. *BackPage* was back in town. And so was April Vaughan.

Annie could see a crowd emerging now, from the top of the steps. Vaughan was at the centre of it, surrounded by an army of technicians and production people. Her kelly green suit stood out sharply. The others hovering around her, Annie assumed, were publicists. Hurrying behind, wearing a frantically pert smile, was Laurelle Stepton, hospital administrator. Annie could hear her from half a block away. "Miss Vaughan, as we agreed everything will be ready. I'll be making the first statement, then the doctors. Unless there's something you want changed . . ."

April turned to her with a steely smile and took her hand, if only to stop her from following any further. “Mrs. Stepton. Your personal co-operation has made all the difference. We can't thank you enough. Now I want you to promise me that you'll come to our wrap party.” At Stepton's look of confusion, Vaughan said, “I just meant the little get-together at the Holiday Inn we're having, after. Dinner and drinks.”

Stepton shrieked wildly. “Oh, my goodness—I thought for a minute you meant rap—like . . .” She made a couple of awkward gestures, mimicking something she must have seen on television. “You know, like those rap dancers . . .”

April leaned back and looked at her with something bordering on disbelief. “No, just a thank you to everyone for their help. You're . . . absolutely delightful.” She reached out and took Stepton's limp hand again. “So, till Thursday. All these people will do whatever you tell them, and if any of them give you a hard time, you just threaten them with a winter assignment to Butte, Montana . . .”

Stepton laughed. April Vaughan finally pulled her hand free and came down the last few steps, to where Annie was waiting.

April looked up, startled. “Lieutenant.”

“Ms.Vaughan.”

“I think you can afford to call me April—*this* time.” She tried to pass.

“Why are you here?”

“Oh, come on, Lieutenant—we're not going to start playing *that* game again, are we?”

“You're going after him now.”

"I'm not 'going after' anyone. This is where the story is—"

"No, it's not. Kyle Mallick is nothing but a means. A convenience. You're going to create the story." Annie's voice rose slightly. She saw a few staffers approaching with sudden concern. Impatiently, without looking, Vaughan waved them off.

"We're trying to handle this situation with a sense of decency and discretion—"

Annie pointedly looked around them. "*This* isn't, and you know it. But, somehow, you don't see that you're being used as surely as *he* is. They're going to need Kyle Mallick to die a particularly bad death. And they want you around to tell the world about it when it happens."

"What are you talking about?

"You aren't asking *why*—why they've just handed you absolutely everything: a leak from the examiner's office, that confidential medical report, Tim Mallick's private diaries. It's not just goddamn information, it's people lives. Do you know what they're proposing to bring in here?" Annie pulled a crumpled paper from her pocket and shoved it towards April. "*Look* at this, for God's sake."

Vaughan refused to take it. "Stop it. I think you're becoming irrational. For some reason, you've made it personal. That's *your* mistake." Vaughan shook off her hand and brushed past her.

Annie turned. "Why do *you* have to go after him? If you've got that much information, then you already know there's nothing there . . ." She saw again the image of Bill, the gesture he'd made with his hand in that blood-filled bedroom. *Ah, Annie, nothing left to bring back.* "He's not going to come out of it. There's no story for you—not unless you're actually planning to film him dying. Is that what they've promised?"

"For Christ's sake . . ."

Annie began to read the page aloud: "'Unquestioningly, he is reduced to a persistent vegetative state. As a result of a functioning brain stem and a total loss of cerebral cortex functioning, he appears able to breathe spontaneously, but has no self-awareness and is unable to perform voluntary actions. While this condition can continue for an indeterminate period of time, it is apparent that imminent organ failure is likely as a range of infections has already undermined the auto-immune system. He is nearing total renal failure and hemorrhagic toxicity. I noted spastic reaction to sharp stimulus, in addition to intermittent involuntary. I would not say 'pain' as we understand it, but would identify it as extreme and acute distress.'" Annie looked up now from the crumpled sheet clutched in her sweating hand. "That was Kyle Mallick, as of eight o'clock this morning. It's an internal medical report, that normally only five people in total would ever see. And I took it from the Web site of something called the Fortinbras Foundation. You're their featured speaker in a month. You're about to create the 'hard case' they've been looking for."

"Fortinbras is an independent non-profit advocacy group for patients' rights. I've done my own digging on this. I certainly don't deal in rumours—or you'd be the story from what I've heard. At least *I'm* not pulling the plug."

Annie felt the sting of unfamiliar tears in her eyes. She blinked them away.

Vaughan seemed to relish the moment. “Yes, I have found out a few things about you. It *is* personal. And you made an enemy of exactly the wrong person, Anne Shannon.” With a brisk motion she summoned her car now. “I didn’t spend forty years climbing to the top of this business to be stopped by someone like you. I’ve interviewed every president since Johnson—even been propositioned by a couple of them. I’ve got a Peabody, an Emmy and the Pulitzer Prize, and if I wanted to, lady, I could win the fucking Oscar.” She made a loud cackling sound, her grey roots showing in the hot afternoon glare. “You took on the wrong girl, Lieutenant.”

The limo slid into place like a stage prop. April Vaughan angrily waved off the driver and wrenched the door open herself. “And I think we’re still going to be doing that interview all right, but on my terms next time.”

~~~

Annie took the turn off on to a gravel road that would bring her down close to the water, near the spot where he usually set up. The old Cadillac wasn’t in its usual place, and there was no sign of him along the path. She walked at least half a mile before giving up. Dan Hewitt wasn’t here.

She went back to her car and took the long way around, back towards the city, driving further upriver to take the Yale Road cut-off and cross over at the old Portage Bridge.

Here the river was narrower, more like the sepia-toned pictures from the turn of the last century, flowing through the
~~~

steep banks it had cut across the millennia. Dan was leaning on the railing, studying the slow swirls twenty feet below.

Annie parked a short distance away and walked on to the bridge.

The city was already reaching this place too. The signs of it were everywhere around them. On the Belford side, she knew, there were plans in place for gated communities with expensive river views. Below them she could see a section of the new hiking trail built by the local Kiwanis Club, proposed to run almost five miles in either direction eventually. Groups of power walkers were already out on it as the sun burned the morning mist off the water.

Dan watched her approach, his expression guarded.

"Dan, I need your—" she paused, her voice both faint and loud in this silence. She swallowed. She'd almost said "absolution." "Your advice."

The lines along his mouth deepened as he set it hard. "Shoot."

"I'm handing in my resignation." Then she couldn't go on. They stood quietly beside each other until she could speak again. "And I think it's the right time to tell the truth about what happened."

He nodded. After another moment he turned to look down at the water again. "Did anyone tell you? I'm taking early retirement too. Couple more weeks." He squinted into the morning sun. "Though, after thirty-five years, I guess you can't really call it early any more. Maybe more like 'too late,' eh?" Unexpectedly, he smiled at her a little. And she saw years of disappointment fall away from him in that instant. He'd waited a long time for her to step up.

Everything that was laid out before her now was unknown—except the secrets. "I know it's probably all going to come out—everyone else's part in it." She didn't doubt for a minute that April Vaughan would use it. Maybe that was the difference between April and the ten thousand people who wanted to *be* April.

Dan looked straight at Annie, then reached down to pick up another rod and pull out a length of line. He changed the fly to a chironomid, something that would sink in the faster current running by here, finding the fish that had found the quieter, cooler depths. His hands, she saw, were shaking.

They stood together in this ordinary place—as though each had already assumed some ancient preordained role. Knowing that it was in repetition that ritual gained its power and resonance. And that what she'd already said a thousand, thousand times, into a hard and empty silence, could be said at least once more, here, to him. The one who'd waited longest to hear it.

"I *did* speak to her that night, you know—Mrs. Sternberg—through the door," Annie began. "Usually, she would just leave the chain on and talk to me through the crack. But I'd done it too often in those last few months. And I knew she was getting pretty fed up with me by then. I knocked a couple of times, I remember. But she didn't even answer the door. So I just shouted to her, said I was going out for a few minutes—to get milk or something. I don't know why I bothered—she didn't believe me any more anyway. She'd seen me stumbling in a few too many nights as it was. I don't think she even heard me. I know I didn't wait to find out."

When they'd first moved in, Mrs. Sternberg had been friendly, bringing over baking, inviting Charlie to go there after school when Annie was a bit late getting home from work. Over a few months, though, as Annie's absences became more frequent, as she began to impose more often, Mrs. Sternberg became less available. Maybe she should leave the boy with her family if she was going to be out so often at night, the old woman would say.

Mrs. Sternberg was hard of hearing, Annie knew. Charlie would have had to knock—hard—if something bad happened, or if he really needed help.

"That night, you know, the sirens went right past the bar," she said. "I remember thinking I didn't give a shit—it had nothing to do with *me* any more. At that point, I was fighting with everyone—mostly Bill. And I was going to show him. My shift was long over. The only thing on my mind was to finish that last double and walk back home. But then the sound didn't disappear—I could still hear it, sticking, somewhere nearby.

"I left a twenty on the counter. Never risked running a tab anywhere in those days—that was the kind of thing that could get you suspended. Then I was going towards my place for a while. And before I noticed it, I was getting too close to the sound."

That part was a lie—she *did* know, long before she saw the fire trucks outside her building, that she was heading right for them. Even before she saw the greasy black smoke rolling out of every window up one whole side of the five-storey building, the firefighters already inside. It was in its early stages, when it was still possible for a single street cop to keep her back and away, along with the rest of the curious crowd gathering on the sidewalk. She didn't think to start screaming until several seconds later, and then whatever sound she made blended and disappeared into the voices of the sirens.

"I'm not even sure what I did say or who I spoke to, in the end. But I don't remember ever thinking that I wouldn't be telling the truth that night. Maybe I just kept waiting for someone to ask me."

Was it her father who'd said something to her in a broad whisper?—like, "I'm not having you hurt our people. Just to make yourself feel better. You can't change this now." Or something close to that. And she'd let it happen.

Only afterwards, when she found herself alone in the corridor of the hospital and nothing could possibly matter any more, did she realize that whatever opportunity had existed to speak about it was already gone.

Her family was there—her father, her brothers, Harry and Jack. The division commander. Her lieutenant. Bill, devastated and grieving. Confused. And Dan Hewitt.

There was an argument and she remembered, above all, that it was Dan's voice rising sharply in protest at one point, an echo of it reaching her down the entire length of the hallway.

Then she was being told by someone else that she was in shock, that the burn on her hand wasn't as bad as it looked—maybe requiring a small skin graft—that she should probably try to get some sleep. After they said all that, she finally noticed that the sun was already shining high in the sky outside the windows. Which was odd, because it was still night—or had been, only a moment ago.

A young police constable she didn't recognize was stationed at the entrance to the ward and no one approached her. Not with questions or blood tests or accusations. The newspaper had to end up using her old police academy graduating class photo. Her son's school picture, taken only three weeks earlier, was published beside hers on the front page of the newspaper.

Below them, the third, smaller photo was of a woman they reported that Annie had left to look after her son—a Mrs. Sternberg, a seventy-year-old neighbour. The old woman, who'd perished in the fire as well. Found by firemen on the floor of Charlie's bedroom, overcome by smoke, not strong enough to carry him out in the end . . .

Over the next many nights she dwelled in a safe room of silent, soft, grey nothingness which finally gave way to a vortex of lurid and complex visions. The sedatives gradually cleared from her system, replaced by the dreams—the same ones that recently had started once more.

"Dan, I don't know how to do this without hurting everyone again," she said finally.

Hewitt stood facing her directly, as he'd probably wanted to that night more than ten years ago. "Maybe it's simple," he said, "but it's not always easy. I think we *all* want to be better than we can be, sometimes. You made a mistake—but telling anyone about it wasn't going to bring your boy back." He wiped his eyes, unashamed. "We chose to be there too." There were seven who'd lied for her that night. Seven who'd protected her. For reasons, she knew now, that spoke of honour or loyalty, all-too-human need and regret. In judgment and in fearing judgment. All bound together in the same place, held in the same way a ship might be trapped in Arctic ice.

All of them held in the same lie for so many years. And it had diminished each of them in some way.

She stood quietly beside Dan for a long time, both of them looking down at the Stoney River.

"Ever since that night, I ask myself the same question—is there a sin beyond all forgiveness? I haven't been able to answer that yet. But I *am* going to try to do everything I possibly can to protect Kyle Mallick. And I know they're about to come at me with everything they've got."

"Who is?"

"The people who want him to go before he should. A symbol. A way to rationalize their right to kill him."

"You really think that's what's goin' on out there?"

"I think someone's going to try and make money out of a *lot* of people dying just a little sooner than they're supposed to."

"Mercy-killing?"

"Not the way we've ever wanted to think of it up till now, Dan," she responded. "It's not to relieve pain. It's more like therapeutic suicide. They won't fund counselling for the incapacitated, the terminal, the poor, the depressed. But they'll pay for the drugs to end it, if we ask. A formal program of state-sanctioned euthanasia. State-directed euthanasia. State-mandated euthanasia. Because they *want* people to ask—to *choose* it. They'll encourage us with financial incentives, with social pressure. Whatever it takes, all customized on a mass scale. And they'll *sell* it to us. That's Leah Mallick's great contribution. She's shown them how to create the climate for legalized murder. And make us all want to buy it."

Dan stared at her for a moment, then looked away, saying nothing.

She smiled at him. "You've been a cop too long, Dan—you don't even seem particularly surprised."

"Well, I'm getting to an age when I'm a little more aware how mortal my coil really *is.*" He shook his head again. "But it looks like I shoulda taken retirement five years ago. Shit . . . it's getting too rough for *me* out there," Dan said gruffly. He reached down to grab the lighter of the two rods resting against the bridge railing.

"So, why now?"

"I can't seem to make the tough decisions any more. Guess I just don't want to have to," he said. He passed her the rod. "Go ahead."

She leaned over the railing and looked at the drop to the river's surface below. "We're a long way up."

"Ah. It's just practice, anyway. Give it a try. See how much you remember."

Standing slightly behind her, he placed his large, roughened hand over hers. Together they pulled the rod back to the two o'clock position, then, feeling the looping line gather strength above them, changed its direction and sent it out, straight and far. Fine and fair . . .

Let me remember all of it, she thought. Grant me the grace to remember everything.

It was a large storage room, built into one end of the cavernous basement, framed in by wire mesh and a flimsy lock, with a dozen rows of shelves up to the ceiling, holding whatever had to be held in inventory: the warehouse of all crime evidence compiled by the department going back maybe twenty-five years. Probably the site, too, of more than a few private late night poker games. Here they kept whatever was left of the cases after everyone took their piece. Certain things went to the state crime lab and were filed there: hairs, fingerprints, blood and tissue samples. A few had to go to the FBI. The Lockport PD couldn't afford the proper facilities to store that kind of thing, anyway. They were left with everything else: clothing, shoes, wallets, glasses, papers, sporting goods. Items were held, sometimes, to be returned to the next of kin, then never claimed. But the room stood as a perpetual embarrassment. DeVries, for one, had been pushing all along for a real forensics department.

But until *that* happened, every few months someone would get ambitious and dig in to clean it up. They always began the job with the best of intentions, usually undone after only a few hours. Left dirty, dusty, frustrated by the confusion of an arcane system reflecting no planning, only too many hands. Items that might have been so significant that they had changed whole lives forever were now, literally, spilling out of boxes.

There wasn't sufficient staff time available to cover the room for more than a regular eight-hour business day, so there was a sign-in sheet attached to a clipboard hanging on the wall. Annie knew that its entire security system hinged on hiding a key in one of a few little niches nearby. That hadn't changed, she was certain. She found it in the second place she looked. Taped to the back of the fire extinguisher mounted on a bracket nearby

Annie let herself in the gate, then stopped and looked up at the mountain of information in front of her. Even if it *was* a mess, she knew that the most recent stuff was always closest to the front. She allowed herself a short sigh and began to tunnel in. Within only a few minutes, she'd found what she was looking for. Three large boxes. In among the Ms, filed right where she expected—between the Rs and the Zs.

The slam of a metal door at the far end of the basement sounded like a gunshot. She heard someone approaching. She looked around quickly for a spot to tuck into. Just have to stay out of the way for a few minutes, she told herself. Whoever it was would probably leave. There was nothing doing down here, anyway. Maybe, if it was someone she knew, she could come up with a reasonable excuse for being here—at midnight . . .

Before she could move, a young man came around the corner, busy shuffling through a bundle of file folders he was carrying. She recognized him right away this time. The new cop she'd met at the Mallick house, the same one she'd sent to look out for the children at the bus stop on Scott Boulevard.

As he swung the gate open, he happened to look up and saw her standing directly in front of him. He jumped, startled. He hadn't expected anyone to be down here either.

He was in old jeans and a T-shirt covered in grime and sweat. That was the other thing that happened down here—sometimes cops drew grunt work like this as first-year hazing. Annie was confident now that she could brazen it out. He was already intimidated by her.

"Hi. Sorry to scare you. I'm wrapping up something on one of my outstanding files. I forgot to ask Lieutenant Williamson to follow up for me. I thought I'd just come down and finish it myself. Looks like we're the only ones working tonight." She indicated the piles rising up behind her. "I see it's still as much of a mess as ever." She smiled a bit.

His eyes went to the box set on the desk in front of her. It was marked clearly, "Mallick, Tim." In big bold letters.

"Yeah, I guess. They told me to take a run at it. I've been stuck down here for a few days. I don't think I've made a dent." He moved something on the floor to another pile in the corner, then looked at her again. A little resentfully, she thought. "Aren't you supposed to sign in?"

"Yeah," and she gave a short laugh. "You're right, I should've. But I was in a bit of a hurry. I can do it on the way out. We're in and out of here all the time anyway . . ."

She watched his glance slide away from her and over to the box again. Why *that* one, she could see him asking himself. He'd been on the force probably less than a year. The murder-suicide in Belford—the Mallick case—had to be the biggest thing he'd ever seen. And he'd somehow managed to tick someone off. She was just another senior officer, now watching him intently. Maybe judging him too. "So, am I supposed to help you or what?"

She shook her head. "It's OK. I can do this by myself. Maybe you should go." She said it slowly and carefully, not taking her eyes off him, willing him to leave.

He looked confused for a moment. Nodded then, as though it might help him better understand what was happening. She could see him thinking so hard that frown lines formed. He didn't know what was going on, just that it wasn't the right procedure. Not sure what he was supposed to do here. And there was no one else to ask. His decision, she knew, wasn't an easy one to make. Things like this could affect entire careers.

"It's OK, then?" he said finally.

Annie nodded. "Sure. Go on," she said again, more gently this time. "I'll only be a minute. It's late. I'll lock up. Promise . . ."

She waited until he was gone then opened the box and unfolded the soiled bedsheet to lay it across the desk. It felt thick and coarse in her fingers, no longer a luxurious silk-like fabric that had been so carefully selected to complement the beautifully designed decor. It had been handled, roughly, by many. Examined, tagged, then thrown aside. Slightly crushed now, by being in storage.

She knew all it took was a couple of inches square, a piece no one would ever notice missing. From the very centre, where she knew the semen stain had been spread. She stared at the sheet in her hand.

Shit. I forgot the goddamn scissors. The thought came to her suddenly, and her nerves jumped for a moment. She tested the fabric in her hands. Could she somehow tear a neat little square out of the middle? Maybe, but only if she was willing to destroy the rest of it completely. She couldn't afford to be caught here again. She stood for a minute, trying to decide what to do. Then she remembered something, a vague detail from long ago, in the distant past, her own first year in the department.

It was almost twenty years ago. They'd been summoned to a trailer park on the south edge of town. It was perhaps the tenth time the police had been called there over a single three-month period, responding to persistent complaints about noise. Always the same thing—hour upon hour of nighttime shouting, always coming from the same house. Maybe they *were* a bit slow getting there that once.

But by the time they arrived, all was quiet. The wife was calmly smoking a cigarette, a fresh, cold beer opened on the kitchen table in front of her. She offered no objection when they placed her in the police car outside. Then they found her husband, sitting in his La-Z-Boy in front of the TV, dead.

Annie searched her memory. What was the name? That woman . . . It was something very simple. Dean, Davis? Dear . . . it was Dear, of all things. Annie hoped that D was still part of the regular alphabet. She glanced around quickly, spotting a Dealey and a Dennis. Pushing another aside, she pulled out the single box containing all evidence relating to the long ago Dear murder. Obviously, no one had ever bothered to claim these old bits and pieces. Annie gingerly felt through the contents until she touched something long and hard, still wrapped in plastic. She lifted it out and looked at it.

By now, in all likelihood, Mrs. Dear had been released—having served perhaps eight years of a twelve-year sentence. Annie was almost nostalgic. It had been her first murder scene, in her very first month. All the experienced cops had expected her to have a problem with it, but she hadn't. That was the night they'd accepted her as one of them, she knew. And here she was again, holding that same murder weapon: a razor-sharp fish-gutting knife.

Well, she said to herself, it'll just have to do.

14

Annie adjusted the shutters slightly, keeping herself far back in the shadows. She saw a news crew still parked in a van across the street. The cameraman was pacing in slow, bored circles, grinding another cigarette into someone else's lawn.

She could picture her neighbours, up and down the block, hidden behind their windows, wondering what the fuss was all about.

She could tell them—it was about her. Rumours of her resignation had begun to leak out. Roy Warren had given a terse "No comment" to the morning paper. But it didn't stem the interest in the range of possibilities. An editorial had been able to offer several reasons why she *would* resign. Reports, rife with innuendo. They all knew about a special session being convened by the police board. But the only television, so far, was a clip of Paul DeVries stepping from his car and disappearing up the steps into City Hall.

As scandals went, she didn't expect this one to go far, even locally. A ten-year-old story? Most likely, up and down in a three-day news cycle. Because this time it wasn't about sex or money or power. It was only her own involvement that stirred up attention. Well, live by the sound bite, she told herself, die by the negative spin.

Annie left the window, already dressed to go. A baggy sweatshirt, her oldest shorts, a baseball cap pulled down low over sunglasses. She could blend in at any mall, and it was the only way she could think to get out of here without trailing them all behind her like a raggedy circus parade.

She'd forbidden Bill even to drive down the street—not with *them* out there, waiting for anything to come into view. And whenever they talked on the phone, she heard the new tension in his voice, a tempered frustration. No one ever knew how they'd get through something like this until they had to. He wanted to help, needed to believe that he really could.

But for the moment at least, her need trumped his. And what she needed, most of all, was to keep him—all of them—safe and away from as much unwanted curiosity as possible. It was her problem alone. If the world was looking for a signal, she was giving them one. This was how she wanted the news media to read it when it all came out—that the story ended with her resignation. No one else had any part in it.

She went into the kitchen and looked out the screen door onto an ordinary summer day, the backyard in all its familiar, dismaying fecundity. At least there was no one lurking in the laneway beyond that she could see. She patted Ben as she passed. He barely stirred. Then she folded the envelope into her backpack and pulled the door closed quietly behind her. As usual, the reporters were busy watching only the front of the house. Typical. To them, news in Lockport was strictly a two-dimensional experience.

Annie crossed the yard to confront the unpainted board fence that enclosed her property. It was her own fault, she realized. It had never once occurred to her that she might need a back gate to escape through. The fence towered almost two feet above her, an insurmountable wall. *Ich bin ein Berliner,* she thought.

She looked around quickly for a ladder, even a rope, then noticed the folding lawn chair, rocking on its rickety legs in the summer breeze. Better than nothing. She wedged it tight against the fence. Still unsteady. At best it gave her only an extra foot or so. She hesitated, then threw her backpack high and heard it thud on the gravel road outside. Nothing like having an incentive, she thought. And with that, she grabbed the top of the fence and performed her first successful chin-up in more than five years.

That was as far as she got. She hung on, limbs flailing wildly. Finally, nearing exhaustion, she was able to hurl one leg over the top and pull herself up, sitting astride the swaying fence like a nervous bareback rider. She sucked in her breath, a staccato hiss—ow, ow. *Ow!* Caught on splinters, she threw herself over to the other side in a semi-controlled fall, landed by rolling sideways on weak ankles. She found herself sitting in the dirt, the backpack a couple of feet away. She grabbed it and hobbled down the alley at a slow jog towards St. Edward's Park, feeling the sting where the inside of her thighs had been scraped raw.

Callie Christie was already there, waiting for her, as arranged, on the park bench near the children's wading pool. Wordlessly, she held out a Starbuck's café au lait as Annie walked up.

"Thanks. I hope I didn't keep you waiting long."

Callie smiled. "Better than some parking garage."

"Yeah, well, I don't think they do it that way any more. Too many surveillance cameras." Annie dug the envelope out of her backpack and traded it for the coffee.

Callie flipped the package over, back and forth, a couple of times. It felt thin. "Is this it? Why we're here?"

Annie rested on the bench for a moment. "That's just context. It'll save you a couple of hours' research."

She was still winded from the short run. It was the excuse to say nothing for a moment. But she really wanted one last chance to look around and consider how any decision she made would play to these people, the ones in the park. Midspring, midweek, midday. An old couple shuffling along the uneven path. A young mother guiding a toddler ahead of her on a bicycle with training wheels. A guy laid out flat on the grass, his shirt opened to a blue-white chest, trying to catch some rays. It wasn't enough to know that they all had stories too. Hers was going to be the one on the suppertime news.

"You know that I've submitted my resignation to the department."

Callie nodded slowly, her eyes narrowed in concentration. Of course she already knew.

"I'm going to tell you why. But there's something else I want to discuss first." Annie looked at her now, taking a long time. Maybe this *was* a mistake.

The scrutiny made Callie uncomfortable. "Annie, what . . ?"

"I intend to sue for custody of Kyle Mallick," she said.

Callie stared back, waiting to understand. "You're what. . . ?"

"Riverview Hospital intends to kill him. They've already tried it once and it didn't work. So they're setting themselves up to do it again. And they won't fail this time." She watched Callie's face assume the expression of someone who suspected she was in the presence of a madwoman.

"You talking about when they removed his life support? And you think you should stop them?" Callie was speaking too carefully.

"I have to try."

"You really think the hospital wants to murder an eight-year-old child?" She seemed embarrassed. "Annie, he's already gone. *Everyone* knows that."

Annie was breathing in a kind of rush now, scooping air like she was about to be sick.

Callie leaned closer. "I'm sorry—but is there any reason to expect he's going to come out of it?"

Annie shook her head, angry tears welling up. "No. And that's the point. We have to understand what it means."

"But you know, don't you, that there's all kinds of different boards and permissions and legal procedures? Social Services is involved. They're not just going to . . . just *do* something to him. Why would you think that?"

Annie covered her face with her hands for a moment. She felt a hundred years old. "Don't talk to me like I've gone insane. They won't make it *look* like murder, for God's sake. They won't call it that . . . But they're intending to use him as a way to make it look completely acceptable to do exactly that, to finish someone off. Maybe only a day or two sooner, a week, a month. But, in the end, it won't be just him—it'll be for everyone. The gold standard throughout the state."

Callie seemed more puzzled than alarmed. "What do you mean, 'gold standard'?"

Annie took a few more deep breaths, until she felt herself beginning to calm down. "It's going to become normal operating procedure in the hospital. They'll start by changing the regulations to allow for an updated version of 'Physician-assisted suicide.' And when that happens, they finally get to define 'quality of life' for all of us. A list of all of the qualifications you're going to need in order to be allowed to stay alive. Doctors will become de facto judicial agents. And everything we're ready to accept now—from living wills to advanced medical directives to riders for health insurance to pre-natal screenings to genetic testing—will become part of that same program. They will have transformed the purpose of medicine in some fundamental way we can't even begin to understand yet. They'll offer us choices that aren't choices at all. Maybe they'll still call it 'terminal care.'" Her sarcastic laugh sounded loud, even to her.

Callie frowned. "Where are you getting all this?" She glanced down at the envelope in her hand, then up again at Annie, the question written on her face.

"No, that isn't it." Annie reached over and tore open the flap. Old, yellowed news clippings spilled out all around her. They fluttered to the ground now, forgotten. "Before she was killed, Susan Shaw and I had already begun to put it together. She kept saying there was a pattern. She was right. She'd already submitted some of the cost-benefit analyses they were going to use—"

Callie interrupted more impatiently now. "But you mentioned this . . . 'list' thing?"

"I don't *have* a list. They don't leave it lying around."

"But if you're my source—"

She couldn't help herself. "Callie," she said impatiently. "I'm not your source. I'm *a* source. At best. And probably not much of one any more. It's time for you to graduate. Jesus."

Callie immediately looked hurt. "You do think I'm stupid, don't you?" she said, after a moment. "You always have. This is just more 'spin.'"

"No, I . . ." Annie stopped, exasperated. But it was true. She did think that. And this was spin. "Yeah, it is. Because I need you to help me protect some people I care about. It's been such a long time and they shouldn't have to suffer through everything again. They did nothing but try to help me. And I let them, knowing full well it was an utter lie." Dan, Bill, her old captain, even her father and brothers . . . "They don't deserve to be dragged back into this."

She turned to Callie again. "But if I've ever seemed concerned about your . . . abilities, I guess it's because I know now that very little in life ever presents itself as black and white, good or bad, the way you can still believe it does. It was only an unkind comment about youth and experience—not a real or fair judgment."

"Then why *are* you talking to me?" Callie had crossed her arms and sat frowning extravagantly like a five-year-old.

Instead of someone like April Vaughan, she was asking. That *was* the right question, Annie said to herself.

Because you'll run at the wall as though it's not even there, Annie thought. And not understanding the dangers, you won't be afraid to take them on. And because, like a hundred generations before me, I'm completely willing to sacrifice your innocence and hope that leads to something better. "Maybe because it *is* still black and white to you," she said

Callie continued to pout.

Looking at her, Annie laughed a bit. "OK. You want honesty . . . ? It's because *they* do—I chose you because *they* think you're stupid. That you won't begin to understand what they're proposing. Or that you won't care even if you do. And they're so damned arrogant, they won't see you coming for them. April Vaughan didn't start *out* being invited to weekends at Hyannis Port for touch football with the Kennedys. She was a terrific reporter first. This is how you *get* to be April Vaughan, Callie."

Callie relaxed only slightly. "They're always telling me that kind of research stuff doesn't matter any more."

No, it's all about personalities these days. Annie shook her head and smiled faintly. "I'll just bet they are." She stretched wearily and closed her eyes for a moment, just listening to the sound of kids and their moms splashing in the decrepit wading pool, a guy urging his dog to chase a Frisbee. Was she was the only one who could remember the halcyon days before *Headline News*?

Then she pulled herself up straight and turned to Callie again. "Look, I know Kyle's never going to come out of it.

Maybe what made him what he was in this world is gone. But what's left there—whatever *that* is—it's still his."

"Then what are you going to do?"

"I'm going to force them to acknowledge that. I don't care if he has only one more minute—that minute is his, not theirs. I want to protect it. We should *all* want to. I don't want to lose that minute to any political agenda, or to some corporate price-to-earnings ratio. When a decision has to be made, I want it to be made by someone who confronts all the guilt and the fear and the doubt, with all the imperfect and irrational ideals of some constant moral value. I want it to be someone who'll stand there and see *him,* above anything else, and understand what the loss of one child means to this world."

Callie looked overwhelmed, her voice very small. "So, it's a human interest story—"

Annie let out a long, deep sigh. "It's a *war,* Callie, and it's already cost the lives of Tim Mallick and Leah and Susan Shaw and a man named Brian Clarke. Over a principle. And whoever wins gets to determine how we see ourselves. We have to make them explain, to all of us, what they really mean when they say 'a worthwhile life.' Because if we let them do this on the basis of some return on investment, our economic function in this new world, we're going to be lost. And eventually, every one of us—everyone but the gifted and the educated, and the rich and the genetically favoured—is going to be forced to prove that they have an equal right to be cared for too." The ultimate negative option. "At first we'll simply be inconvenient, then we'll be unworthy of the expense of keeping us alive. And I can tell you, when your life isn't worth the same as theirs, your suffering won't mean much to them, either." *We can look Africa in the face without blinking . . .*

Annie almost smiled, reminding herself that this was still Callie, after all. And when you were young, healthy, educated, pretty, maybe it was hard to fathom that any other quality of life could be considered equally worthwhile. "I don't want to hold him past the time of going," Annie said. "But I don't want it left to the Cross Corps of the world to say when it's time to leave.

Annie heard Callie take a deep breath. She was trying to decide it all for herself. Probably an unfamiliar sensation, Annie thought dryly. But still—

"This place is a mess, isn't it?" Callie said. She was staring at the park in front of them.

Annie glanced around too. "Yeah, I guess it really is." Even the bench they were sitting on was missing one of its splintered, weather-worn slats. And what wasn't simply fading away was being beaten into submission. Someone had obviously taken a bat to the painted hobby horses in the preschoolers' area. And there'd been only half-hearted attempts to cover over a year's worth of graffiti everywhere else, obscenities mixed with multicoloured tags and the usual "so-and-so was here" messages. It's all so fragile—this whole precious idea of community, she thought. "You should do a piece about that."

"Not what my audience is going for, these days."

"Maybe they go where you lead."

Callie looked thoughtful, then laughed shortly. "I suppose. If I knew where . . ."

"Well, right now, all your audience wants to know is why I'm resigning. That's our deal."

Surprisingly, Callie pressed her lips together and shook her head firmly. "No—"

"Ask me the hard question. That's the reason you came."

"I'm not going to do it—"

"Don't disappoint me. Be a real reporter, Callie. Ask it. I'm a news story, not your friend. That's what it's going to take."

"No," she said again.

"Ten years ago, I lost my son—" Annie began.

Callie held up a hand to stop her. "Annie . . . I already know."

Without looking at her, Annie continued. Her heart was in her throat. "I was responsible for it. I was a drunk and I used to leave him and go out almost every night to some bar. I should have been prosecuted for criminal negligence. Reckless endangerment. Child abandonment. And if something hadn't happened that night . . . But I lied, to everyone, in order to protect myself—" Then she felt Callie's hand on her arm and fell silent again.

Neither spoke for a moment. They watched the kids run at the swings across the park. "It's been a rumour for years," Callie said finally. "Someone up at the hospital once told me. They'd guessed you'd been drinking." She paused. "Annie, you know you can't change what happened. And you can't save Kyle Mallick now. Don't do this—"

Annie gathered herself again. "You're really going to have to do your legwork, this time.

"Follow the money. . . ?" Callie advanced tentatively.

Annie gave a small, pained smile. "Yeah. Right. Follow the money. Begin there . . . Then you confront the politicians with their own campaign platforms." Even with a few false starts she might be ready just in time for the election, stumbling into their midst, her small-market media crew in tow. Callie Christie was the wild card they wouldn't be expecting. After all, Woodward and Bernstein weren't fucking *geniuses* . . . More importantly, it might force the major media organizations to step up to the plate.

Callie took a few notes dutifully. But her face was forming another expression now.

Annie waited. It was the *other* hard question. "Go ahead . . ."

"You had *him* removed from life-support, didn't you? Your own son?"

Annie nodded wordlessly.

Callie let her notebook fall closed and gazed across the park. She suddenly seemed overly interested in the man with the Frisbee-catching dog. "And you believe you know the difference."

Annie lowered her head.

It was Callie who spoke again. "You *are* my friend. It's hard to be the one asking too."

Annie could feel something of her own brittle self-control beginning to give way. "Callie, I know. It's always going to be. But decide to do this now. Start the right way. And do it before you realize you have far too much to lose. Why *you* . . . ? Because you can sell this. Because you're not April Vaughan yet."

And, please God, you never will be, Annie said to herself.

~~~

After Callie left, Annie sat alone in the park, finishing the last of her stone-cold coffee as she watched the sun move slowly across the sky.

She realized even now that some idea of perfection still existed for her, though the Church had done everything to convince her otherwise. Annie envied the true believers. They were like something out of the Renaissance. Perfection, for them, existed in God, in the same pure mathematics her aunt had once taught. In Bach and Mozart. All the rest was charity and God's grace, Aunt Ell had always said.

Though, these days, Annie imagined a God who'd already moved on to better things. Who, bored and not a little disappointed in them all, had abandoned this world for another that might offer Him greater potential. Even now He was taking slime and bacteria, double helixes and multiplying cells, and fashioning an alternative—like any parent, wishing for the chance to do it again, and do it better this time.

Grass was pushing open cracks in the sidewalks everywhere she looked. The chain-link fence around the empty lot next door had partially collapsed on to the patchy, neglected lawn. From where she was sitting, the windows set deep into the brick walls of the surrounding housing project looked dull black. This was not a place of mercy. The liturgy she'd once loved was void: "I ask forgiveness for what I have done, for what I have failed to do—and to pray, for me, to the Lord our God . . ."
~~~

~~~

She was skirting the edge of a primeval forest, the trees grown so close together that it was impossible to penetrate more than twenty feet into its depths. Beyond what she could see, there was a deep carnivorous sound, not an animal, as much as a *thing.*

She had a choice. She knew that she could travel in there simply by willing it, not through the trees but as a part of them for a split second. They were like great spears piercing the sky above—black, pinpricked with stars.

And there was water within. She was being drawn towards a rush of water. A spillway, something constructed, disguised as a falls.

Another cry went up, long and sustained. It blended into the distant whistle of Palladian Steel.

Annie awoke with it, her face damp. The rain was beating in the open window. She crawled out of bed, felt the floor wet and cold under her bare feet. As though winter had returned in the night.

~~~

Bill came through the side gate.

Annie glanced up quickly. "Anyone see you?" She'd made him park a couple of blocks over.

He shrugged. "Yeah, some old guy with a Shar-Pei. Between the two of them, they had enough skin hanging off 'em to make another dog."

Annie smiled distractedly. She was busy changing the

arrangement of plants in the flower bed. It didn't look anything like she'd hoped. She'd planned for something big and curving, commanding one whole side of the yard. But the ground was harder here than she'd expected. It had taken her more than two hours just to dig a small section of the overly optimistic grand outline she'd made.

The rest of her purchases—the two large balled-and-burlapped trees, the dozen five-gallon pots of robust shrubs, flats of exotic perennials, twenty or thirty other things that had looked nice in the garden centre—were now clamouring for her attention. They were like demanding children left at a day-care centre. They'd been delivered that morning. It had all seemed easy enough then, with a convoy of strong, healthy young men in tight jeans bringing them in one at a time. But after that the responsibility for them had fallen to her, as though their parents had simply decided not to come back for them.

Annie hated every one of them now.

"Thinking of getting someone in to do it?"

"I don't know. I was sort of hoping . . ." She looked around. She was going to say "to do it myself," but at this rate . . . She kicked a clod of dirt halfway across the lawn.

Bill stood with his arms folded across his chest. He seemed to be enjoying her aggravation. After a few minutes he issued a loud groan. "Oh, man, I can't stand this. Where's your shovel?"

She pointed, swallowing with difficulty. She was parched already and the sun wasn't even at its hottest yet.

Bill walked over to her pile of old tools, swung a shovel and a mattock onto his shoulder and went to the spot where one of the new trees sat. "Here?" He indicated it with the tip of his shovel. Then he sank it in up to its hilt, dislodging a two-foot section of sod and soil. Within seconds, it seemed, the hole was deep enough to edge the tree into position. He cut the binding cord and folded the cloth back, away from the trunk. He glanced up, catching her staring at him.

"Good to have a man around the house, eh?" he said.

Three hours later, everything was safely in the ground.

She was still fussing with the last of the perennials, but more content with the overall result. This, at least, was something close to what she'd seen in her mind's eye. Not perfect, but in some idiosyncratic way reflecting a kind of personal style. She'd finally released her inner gardener.

Bill splashed water from the hose over his face, then took a long drink. "I meant to tell you that we brought in a few of the staff from the Creighton Hotel. Had them go through some mug shots in case we'd missed anything."

"Yeah. . . ?"

"Yeah. One of them thought he recognized you."

That wasn't unusual. They always included a few "ringers" in the mix to get rid of undependable eyewitnesses, the ones who'd pick anyone who looked vaguely familiar just to be able to come up with an answer. Their testimony wasn't solid enough to build a case upon. "*Only* me?"

He started smirking. "And Condoleezza Rice."

She laughed. "Why don't you take the first shower. I'll finish up here."

∿∿∿

She was making supper in the kitchen, when she heard the shower shut off. A few minutes later, Bill came back down.

He was wearing another shirt, a Denver Broncos souvenir-edition jersey. "I can't believe you *kept* this," he said with a note of surprise. They'd picked it up during the one weekend they'd ever travelled together, an impulsive, dangerous gesture, counter to departmental policy. In those days, it could have earned both of them a suspension, or reassignment back to patrol. "It still fits." He tugged at it in a few places, but he was right.

Damn men and their metabolisms. "I was going to tear it up for cleaning rags."

"Oh, honey, did you sle-e-e-e-p in it?" He leaned close to her. He smelled clean and warm and healthy.

Without intending to, she reached up and put her arms around his neck. "I did. I still do."

A grin spread across his face. He gathered her tighter in his arms. "You have to say it, then. I'm the one who asked ten years ago. It's your turn, this time."

"Say what?"

In answer, he began to sway as he sang to her. It was the old 5th Dimension song, "Wedding Bell Blues." He sang all the parts, a rising falsetto in the chorus. "Please marry me, Bill."

Annie giggled, as tears gathered in her eyes.

He grabbed her more tightly. She was helpless, held there. He hummed, forgetting most of the words, and still refused to release her. She gave up and laid her head on his chest where she could feel the music rising.

After another chorus, Bill had stopped moving. He rested his chin now on the top of her head. They'd always fit together this way.

After a moment, though, she finally leaned away from him, her face serious, looking up into his. "Is this the part where one of us notes that we're not getting any younger? Bill, there's too much water under the bridge. I don't know what's going to happen. I'm out of a job. I'm looking at an Internal Affairs investigation, probably a criminal indictment. I've got half the town convinced I'm completely insane. *This* is not what you want to take on."

I can protect you . . . But in response, he only started to sing again, more softly. Not dancing, simply holding her.

"Say it," he whispered. "Say 'I want you to marry me.'"

∿∿∿

Her first meeting with Children's Services, the initial interview, began with a solitary intake worker who, as soon as Kyle Mallick's name was mentioned, abruptly excused herself and ran for her supervisor.

The second meeting was with the high-priced adoption lawyer she'd called to force them back to the table.

Then the third. Everything about it had seemed unusual—including their insistence that their own legal counsel be permitted to join them.

This was the fourth. But they were determined to maintain the illusion of objectivity, providing her, however grudgingly, the information any applicant would have been entitled to. And while they watched, Annie took an hour and a half in a hot, windowless room to deliberately read and complete the pile of material they'd unceremoniously dropped in front of her.

The next required step was for a medical examination. A new regulation, she observed mildly. Annie agreed to it and made the arrangements at Riverview Hospital.

The clinic had left her waiting more than three hours past the scheduled appointment. It was just one more thing she figured they could do to make everything as difficult and humiliating as possible.

When she finally arrived, the doctor at least seemed genuinely apologetic for the delay. She was younger than Annie had expected. Friendlier too. She left Annie alone in the examination room to undress, then returned after a few minutes with a soft knock on the door. "OK? All ready in there?"

"Sure." Annie was already seated, up on the table, the sheet tucked under her arms, unsure what to expect. They'd said a complete physical exam, and it had to be someone other than your regular family physician. A little late for them to get queasy about apparent conflict-of-interest, she thought.

Blood pressure, heart rate, lungs—*no, I've never smoked*—eyes, ears, nose, throat.

Then, "Could you just lie back down, with your feet up here." The doctor pulled the stirrups into position and adjusted them. Annie sighed. No matter how many times she'd gone through this . . .

Dr. A. Grace. Annie focused on the name tag. It saved her from having to look directly at the woman's face, and gave her something else to think about. "A." Alice. Alicia,

Alyssa. She didn't look like any of those. The speculum slid in, a bit cold. Alberta. Alabama. Arizona. Though obviously, she wasn't part of the recent trend in naming children after states. Amelia, perhaps. Old-fashioned, no-nonsense. Shortened to Molly. Annie looked at the eyes now, gazing absently into her own. Molly. The hands were off doing something else, hidden under the paper sheet. A small shooting pain. Then only a slight irritation, remembered. Yet apparently she'd made some sound or movement.

Dr. A. Grace stopped, a note of impatience. "Sorry. Did that hurt?"

"No. I didn't mean to . . . react. I'm probably just a little tense."

"Umm. That's natural. But just a little further now. I want to make sure. In women of your age, particularly, we have to sometimes . . ."

She didn't complete the sentence. Annie felt the mechanics of it probing, felt the two fingers of the instrument suddenly expand against her, harder than usual. Dr. Grace straightened, her hand held aloft. "Try not to tense up now." She glanced at Annie casually.

Annie had torn a bit of skin loose on the inside of her lip and worked it with her tongue. "I *am* trying."

Dr. Grace was still looking at her. "It tends to pinch more if you do, you know."

Annie carefully counted the ceiling tiles and then the holes in the ceiling tiles. And tried to put as much distance between herself and what was being done to her body . . . Just finish. *Finish.*

"What, are you rearranging the furniture in there?" she said finally, forcing a half-laugh. She was feeling a kind of claustrophobia. Get this thing out of me, she wanted to say.

"Almost done." But the pressure, rather than lessening, actually increased.

Annie let out a solid gasp this time.

"You've had a child." The doctor's voice was unchanged. They might be chatting over coffee. Annie could feel a slick of sweat covering her face. Not the precursor of a hot flash this time, but an old-fashioned fainting spell. She was actually about to swoon.

She gripped the sides of the narrow platform, her feet still splayed in the stirrups, thighs held apart now with trembling muscles. *Jesus God, don't let me pass out like this.* "Doctor, you're going to have to—"

"Have to what, Lieutenant?" A small adjustment and, surprisingly, the pressure took on another character. Not imagination this time, but real pain, and what felt like something tearing inside. She'd bitten her tongue hard, instantly numb and throbbing now in her mouth. When she realized she had to open her eyes, seconds later, the doctor's face was hovering only a few inches above her own. "Now you're going to feel a bit of a pinch . . ."

That was all Annie heard before a white flash ignited in front of her eyes. She blinked helplessly, trying only to hold her attention on the ceiling tiles straight ahead of her. If she didn't think about what had just happened, the pain would subside immediately. "Doctor—"

"Grace," the woman completed automatically.

It wasn't a damn name she was trying to say. Annie bit her lip. She could feel small tears forming at the corners of her eyes. "Dr. Grace. Stop. Now."

Annie wanted to sit up but knew she couldn't, not without hurting herself. The doctor's face loomed above her again, cutting off a view of the fluorescent tubes flickering on the ceiling.

"Anne." The doctor now planted her hands firmly on either side of her, the latex gloves making a quick rubbery squeak on the steel frame of the examining table. Everything had its fragrance, Annie noticed—the gloves, the fresh laundry smell of Grace's white coat, morning toothpaste overlaid with coffee on the doctor's warm breath spilling on to her face. "If you co-operate, we'll be done in a moment. You know how this goes. I'm just taking a small sample—"

"No, you're not." Annie couldn't stop one of the tears running down into her left ear. Her eyes were wide open now and she stared hard into the other's, just above her face. "You're trying to make a point." Her voice sounded shaky and unsure. In the next moment it seemed a ludicrous remark to have made.

Grace said nothing, but straightened up and walked to the foot of the table, disappearing once more behind the frail paper curtain. Annie closed her eyes again, against a sharp wave of nausea, gone as quickly as it began. The pain abated immediately and Dr. Grace held up the smeared speculum. A small spiral brush was disposed into a glass tube and sealed. "I'm going to ask for a yeast culture too. Might be a little something there. No big deal." She smiled reassuringly. "Everything looks good. I'm sorry that seemed uncomfortable . . ."

Annie heard the sliding snap of the gloves being removed. She knew what that felt like, the sudden cool air on warmly damp fingers. A relief. Dr. Grace tossed the gloves into a garbage can, allowing the lid to drop noisily. Annie began to wonder if she'd imagined it, some implied threat. Had it been any worse than usual? Of the probably twenty times she'd had the procedure, had this one really been that different?

Grace was making a couple of notes. "How old is your child?" She scribbled something more before looking up again.

Why was she still harping on that? "How do you know I had—" Annie began, then stopped. Anyone who read a paper could know that much.

Grace looked at her, smiling thinly. "I'm a gynaecologist, Anne. We *can* tell, you know." As though addressing a five-year-old.

Annie felt silly now. And so completely on edge. Maybe she was reading too much into this.

But this woman could say or report anything untoward, the smallest thing, to be used against her. Even incipient paranoia. Like preparing a case for prosecution. And there was something else happening to her now. Under the too bright lights, tears formed again for no reason. "I did have a son. But he . . . he died. He would have been eighteen. This summer." She didn't care if the doctor already knew; she just wanted to say it.

She was surprised when, in the next instant, she felt the

doctor's cool hand on her forehead. She'd closed her eyes tight without intending to.

"Listen to me. I know this means a lot to you, this guardianship you're proposing. But do you really think this is the best way? You've always wanted another child, I can imagine. Any normal mother suffering such a loss would *think* about that, anyway. But have you tried? Recently? I mean, to conceive?"

Annie shifted on the table uncomfortably, her feet still splayed awkwardly in the stirrups, made ridiculous with their little blue paper booties. "In case you haven't already noticed, Doctor, I'm a little past—"

Grace shook her head. "You can cover up now." She'd stepped away again. "No, you're not. In fact, there are several very viable procedures we could consider for you. Some rather stunning new therapies. It's not voodoo. You must have heard about it—how every second movie star is getting pregnant in her late forties and early fifties? It's becoming quite fashionable. And we can almost guarantee positive results now. I just wondered if you'd seriously looked into all the possibilities?"

Annie remembered the many times it had come up. With friends, even a few lovers. But it always ended when she said she never wanted to bring another child into this world. Not with anybody. Maybe it was a lie, but—just her luck—it was the one prayer God *had* answered.

Was it really possible again? Annie wondered. Another son. Or a daughter, another matriarch-in-waiting in the long line. The mere thought of that almost made her smile. For all the times she'd tried or even hadn't tried, there was nothing, no going back and making it right. But here, maybe some slim hope was being offered to her again—long after she had believed it impossible.

Could someone really do that now for her? Make even *that* happen, after all these years, after all hope had been extinguished? It was a moment of such unanticipated magic that the thought rose on a soaring, euphoric note she hardly recognized in herself.

What was the real beginning of the questions she should ask? Where did anyone start? What rational judgment could be brought to bear, was even useful in the face of this cosmic art they held so closely in their hands—the ability to stop time, to turn it backwards on itself. To fix, amend, what had always been immutable. The inevitable passage away. Abracadabra.

Only give me back what I've already lost, Annie thought. Even lying down, she felt faint. Dr. Grace spoke again. This time briskly, a dwindling effort at warmth. "If you like, we can schedule you for some more advanced tests, present you with some real options. You could be looking at substantive results within six or eight months."

As soon as that? "Are you actually telling me I could still become pregnant?"

"Admittedly, it's a somewhat drawn-out process—but I can't see why not. You're healthy now." Dr. Grace tapped the file nervously, her chin thrust out a bit.

Annie turned her head to look at her, and doubt began to intrude again.

She'd almost had her.

But this was no Leah Mallick. The hand was tipped too

easily, too clumsily. There was no evidence of Leah's skill in letting an unwelcome suggestion slip smoothly into the unwary unconscious. This was a programmed approach, by rote, line and verse, with none of the passion—and subtle patience—that Leah Mallick herself would have brought to it. This one had pulled on the line a little too quickly, before the hook could be truly set.

"I'm just here for a medical, Doctor," Annie said.

Dr. Grace's expression remained unchanged. "Of course. I understand. But I just thought you should know. That there are other possibilities. One of them might be having another child of your own. If you want to." A breath's pause between each point counted off.

Annie felt her uncertainty rising again. Maybe she had misunderstood. She resented being made to come here; she'd made that much clear. And the doctor's bedside manner was more than a little perfunctory. But the option laid out for her seemed to be very real. And Dr. Grace still smiled, unconcerned. Perhaps nothing had happened, then; she had simply tensed up at the wrong moment. If this had gone badly, maybe it was her own fault.

When she could, Annie sat up. Then she saw that the paper sheet now stuck to various parts of her, almost comically, caught in patches of sweat that had gathered along her sides in some more natural response. Whatever had happened, the pain she remembered had been real. Her body had immediately recognized what her mind couldn't afford to.

"You might have a little spotting. I'll leave a pad for you here," Dr. Grace said. And just as she spoke, Annie felt a warm stream run between her legs, a watery red stain spreading in a fan, brighter red after a moment. Not sharp pain, really, but something tight and uncomfortable inside her, as though some hidden part of her body still held itself rigid in contraction, a muscle spasm that wasn't letting go.

"So *have* I made it, Lieutenant?" The smile, Annie noticed, was completely erased, nothing but a memory. Dr. A. Grace watched as Annie slid clumsily off the table to set her bare feet on the sour green floor, her only protection the flimsy paper sheet that she clutched uselessly in front of her. "Have I *made* the point?" she said.

The question, like a slap, struck sharply. "I'd like to get dressed." Annie heard her own voice tremble slightly. She knew that A. Grace could hear it too.

"By all means. Take whatever time you need." Dr. Grace pulled the door open. "We should have the results back in a week or so. Feel free to get in touch if you have any follow-up questions. I think you'll find we're very well positioned to give you what it is you really want."

The door closed silently on the flash of a disappearing white coat.

∿∿∿

Annie took a long, scalding shower. It didn't help—she still felt dirty. The fingers on her skin, the voice inside her head. After forty minutes she turned the water off and stood there. Almost immediately, the phone began ringing. Dripping wet, she wrapped herself in the closest towel and went into the bedroom. "Hello?"

"Hi. I was about to hang up and try later. Interested in some company when I get out of here?"

She was tired. Beyond tired—depressed. "Bill, I don't . . ." she said faintly.

"I thought you should know . . . we just got back from delivering the rest of Susan's stuff."

He hadn't mentioned they were going to do it in person. "Oh?" The process was usually nothing more than handing over a simple paper bag, tagged with the date, the name, an ID number.

"Yeah. I was kinda surprised—a few of Acton's staff showed up. I gave them some excuse about taking so long. They signed the receipt. I think they just want to get it behind them. We talked a bit about what they've heard on the case so far. The state police have nothing more than we already gave them. They don't want to say it out loud, but you can tell most of them still believe she got caught, maybe, by some guy she'd picked up in the area. No one knows where she spent those last couple of hours."

Annie used a corner of the towel to wipe her face. "You know how I feel about that. There was no sign of any struggle. She was struck from the front. And she carried a gun, Bill. It had to have been someone she knew, someone she had every reason to trust."

Bill paused. "I did notice that one of them seemed kind of shook up. A guy named Peter Donovan—Acton's chief of staff. I get the feeling he might have had a little something going with her. Kept pretty much to himself while I was there. Maybe we should ask him a few questions."

"Maybe," she responded doubtfully. It was only reasonable to assume there were other romantic entanglements. Maybe they should be looking in that direction. "But it went OK? You gave them back the laptop?"

Bill laughed. "Yeah, no problem. I told them that the two of you had been working over at your place that afternoon and she'd just forgotten it. Then one fella came out with some story about an FBI agent he knew who had his laptop stolen out of the trunk of his car while he was at an NBA playoff game. The only one who didn't find it funny was this older woman—Acton's personal secretary. She actually got pretty irritated when we started cracking jokes about it, like we were trying to lay something off on Susan. I gather *they* were pretty tight too, Susan and her. Seemed kind of a motherly type. Blowing her nose with this little lace handerchief, wiping her eyes. She just kept saying it couldn't have happened that way, Susan leaving the computer with you. Got fairly defensive about it, in fact—like she still wanted to protect her."

Annie's mouth was suddenly dry. "What—exactly—did she say?"

Bill stopped for a moment before speaking. "I think it was . . . Well, as I recall, what she *said* was, just that it was completely impossible. Though why she believed that . . ."

Annie closed her eyes. If the governor's personal secretary believed it was "impossible," it was because she already knew that Annie was lying.

15

Annie drove into the capital complex on a sunny Friday morning. There were more empty spaces than cars in the parking lot. It was the start of a long weekend.

Regular security for the main building had been stepped up somewhat in the wake of a shooting incident two years earlier—a fired state employee who'd "gone postal." That was the explanation they used, anyway. Disturbing, how easily that summary phrase was thrown off these days; no one even thought it ironic any more. But if maniacs were going crazy in Gap stores all across the country on a regular basis, she thought, they would have had a congressional committee investigating khaki cargo pants by now.

They'd installed a basic metal detector at each public entrance. Annie passed through one of them and presented her ID at the small sign-in desk. Then she was inside it, the People's Palace. The hallways were completely empty of everyone but data entry clerks, trying to kill the last few hours of the workweek. The governing classes were already on the road, commuting to their country houses and home constituencies for the weekend.

The building had that same look and smell she remembered from her own parochial school days. Antiseptic, rather than clean. Benches set where no one would ever sit upon them. Expensive, but you could never figure out where all the money went.

She knew the Office of the Governor was a large operation, taking up an entire wing on the second floor. It had grown significantly over the last three years; recent editorials had already used the adjective "imperial" once or twice. Annie took the wide staircase rather than wait for the ancient elevator.

Several staff with indistinguishable titles filled the first and larger of the two outer offices. Past this, obviously, were the conference areas, the cabinet room, the communications offices—probably an election war room set up by now—and rows of desks for the assistants of the assistants of the assistants. Outside of campaign periods it was as somnolent as the backroom at the DMV, but now it looked like it was quickly filling up in preparation.

Every person in the reception area seemed completely oblivious to her. Almost overnight she'd become invisible. No one looked up, and she had to wait another minute before the one nearest even noticed her standing there, waiting. His shirt sleeves were rolled up, the bookish glasses giving him the slightly outdated look of a hotshot stockbroker and an air of self-importance. Probably making twenty, maybe twenty-one thousand a year. Most of them, she knew, served only enough time to rack up an impressive Rolodex.

He looked up at her, surprised. "Sorry. Can I help you?"

"My name's Anne Shannon, from Lockport. I wondered if I could talk to someone here—someone who works for the governor?" She was drawling out the words, deliberately painting the word "hick" across her forehead. Non-threatening.

He looked at her without interest, blankly. "Do you have an appointment?" He was vamping for time, trying to figure out what to do with her. She saw his hand creeping towards the phone on his desk. Probably security. "Maybe a card . . . or something?" He was probably wondering how she'd even made it past the lobby.

"No. But I'm in the middle of this custody case and . . . well, a friend told me that the governor's secretary might be willing to meet with me for a few minutes. Mrs. Gagnon?

He narrowed his eyes in an expression of disbelief. "Why don't I check that out for you," he said. She was left to wait again.

She watched him lean down to speak with someone a few desks over, a woman who peered over at her without bothering to get up. After they whispered for a few seconds, he returned, slightly emboldened. "Listen, I can maybe try to get someone to help you. If you could tell me a little something of what this is about. . . ?" He smiled and rested more casually against the front edge of his desk, close enough to her that she could smell the Paco Rabanne he was wearing. "Who was it suggested you come?"

She was prepared to overrun him now like a division of Sherman tanks. "Susan Shaw. Tell Mrs. Gagnon that Susan Shaw sent me." *Call her, you vile little bastard, or I will strangle you with that bloody ugly tie.*

She stared at him until he squirmed in discomfort. His hand slipped again towards the phone on his desk. Without taking his eyes off her, he spoke. "Mrs. Gagnon, I'm sorry to bother you, but . . . there's a lady here, named Anne Shannon—from Lockport. She wants to discuss some custody case." He wound and unwound the cord around his finger. "She says she's a friend of Susan Shaw's—"

He didn't get any further. In the next moment, "Of course. Sure." Then he set the phone down. "Mrs. Gagnon asked me to see you in. Would you follow me, please?"

Then she was being led into the small sitting room right beside the governor's private office, and Georgia Gagnon, Acton's long-time personal secretary, was rising to greet her. Surprising—she was such an ordinary-looking, older woman. No nonsense about her. Motherly.

"So it *is* you," Gagnon exclaimed. "About time we meet. Susan told me a little bit about what the two of you were doing up there, everything you went through together. She seemed so impressed—" There were already tears welling up in Georgia's eyes. "I still can't really believe it happened. She was like my own daughter. Did you bring some more news?" She was gently guiding Annie to a chair in the small seating area.

Annie, a little overwhelmed, looked around the office. It was more like an elegant suite—a well-equipped workstation, a conference area, a comfortable couch draped with a handmade quilt, between two large chairs in front of a fireplace. Dark panelled, with tall, sweeping windows looking out over the steps and plaza in front of the capital building. There were fresh flowers everywhere, interspersed with the subtle glow of several computer screens. Annie could hear others working somewhere nearby—a fax, a photocopier.

And there was a full silver tea service already set up on the tiny table in front of one of the upholstered chairs.

Georgia smiled another welcome. "I've just stopped for my 'elevenses.' Let me get you a cup and you can join me. Susan always used to. She'd laugh and called it my 'japanese tea ceremony.'"

Annie smiled weakly as she tried to balance the delicate china cup and saucer on her knee. She was far more comfortable with the cardboard carry-out version these days.

Then Georgia passed her a plate of what looked like homemade cookies. It was almost too much. Lacy edges, with sprinkles of sugar.

"She loved those, too. I always made her a special box of my baked goods at Christmas. She complained I was trying to make her fat. No danger of that—she was a beautiful girl. Inside and out." Georgia shook her head again slowly. "So, dear, tell me about yourself. Is your family from Lockport?"

Annie smiled politely. "Yes, mostly. A couple of generations, in fact."

"That's the stuff. People don't really understand the value of roots sometimes. I'm going to be heading out of here and home soon too. To a little place called Butler. It's not even on the map any more." She laughed. "But once you're out of *this* business, the capital quickly becomes a rather cold place. All those people not returning your calls. I'd prefer to be somewhere where it's a bigger problem if they don't return your casserole dish." She picked up her cup. "But you can't take it personally." A shadow came across her face again. "Susan didn't have a family to go home to. That's what I always told her. When it's over, it's over. You have to know—"

"—when it's time to go?" Annie completed.

Georgia glanced at her sharply but saw nothing in Annie's flat expression. She pushed the cup and saucer away for a moment as a young assistant entered the office quietly and leaned down to show her a couple of heavily annotated pages. Georgia reached for the glasses hanging on a thin gold chain around her neck. She read it out aloud. "'If we are unwilling to name the problem as Ignorance, to confront this enemy of all progress, our great gifts will forever remain unclaimed. What we need is not power, but strength of purpose . . .'" Her voice faded into a mumble as she finished another few sentences. "So this is the section that comes just before the line item?"

The assistant nodded.

"OK. Good. I'll see it again when it's all together. Thanks."

After the door closed, she turned back to Annie. "Sorry. We're drafting a rough version of the State of the State. It's early, but I've learned it's usually better to get out in front of the curve."

Annie looked at her. This wasn't just early—it was arrogantly premature. The governor's annual address was always made to the combined House in January. *After* the election. *If* Acton won. Clearly, they were confident.

Georgia poured herself another cup of tea. "I must say, your people have been co-operative, looking after everything." Her eyes narrowed, though she still smiled. "For the most part." Just a subtle hint that their performance might have been something less than stellar.

Annie opened her briefcase. "That's part of the reason I'm here. To talk about our continued co-operation. I still had a couple of files sitting at home. Susan and I were working on them right up till . . . well . . . as you know, everything happened so fast—" Annie looked around the office, not wanting to meet the other woman's eyes quite yet.

After a moment Georgia released a deep sigh that shuddered right through her. She ignored the silk handkerchief decorating the pocket of her blazer and reached instead for a Kleenex, holding it to her suddenly reddened eyes. Her sorrow was obvious in her every move. After a moment she wiped her eyes and indicated the small stack of files Annie had laid on the table. "You did quite a lot of work together, then? What sort of things were you—"

Annie continued as though she hadn't heard. "I kept copies of all of it, of course. These files, the e-mail records, reports, flow charts, cost-benefit analyses, inter-office memos . . ." She saw Georgia's glance slide over the pile, a nervous twitch appearing as she dabbed the Kleenex to her damp eyes again, hiding behind it. "In fact, it's everything that was on her computer."

For the first time Georgia looked uncertain. "That's *hers?* Where—" Then she stopped abruptly.

Annie paused before continuing. "I heard you were asking about it. I figured you'd be concerned that the information might have fallen into the wrong hands." She looked at the files. "But, as you can see, it's fine. It's all here. Even though someone tried to delete it."

Georgia picked up one of the files, making a show of reading. Annie knew it was a sham.

"Delete?" Georgia furrowed her brow for a moment. Then her face cleared. "Well, that's easy enough to explain, of course. Susan was always very careful. She had access to all types of confidential information with her high-security clearance, financial data, draft policies. Even, to be honest, some early party campaign strategy. Not strictly kosher, according to our current election laws. You can't be surprised that she would have gotten rid of it at some point. In fact, we advise all our senior employees to back up their files to a secure mainframe. Clean it out on a regular basis. It's not a very smart idea to carry everything around on something that can be so easily lost or stolen like that, is it? I'm sure you've heard *those* stories."

"I see. Then I feel obliged to confess something *else* to you. Susan didn't forget it at my house. I took it, from her hotel room. All those deletions were made *after* Susan was killed."

At first, Georgia offered no reaction. Then she gave Annie a grim smile as she stood up and moved towards a computer open on a nearby desk, beckoning Annie to follow. "Let me show you something here. How much do you know about computers, Ms. Shannon?

"Enough—"

"Well, then, you'd know that you can set it up to run routine maintenance programs." Georgia moved with assurance into a task menu. Within seconds she'd isolated a dated record. "You see? Automatic. Two a.m. Every Sunday morning. This is my portable. We all do the same thing. She could have overridden it, of course. But otherwise, by modem, right back to the office. Thereafter, erased. Deleted."

Annie looked at it, nodding.

Georgia sat back down, more heavily, in her chair. She forced a laugh. "The fact that you could so easily recover it tells me we're going to have to substantially upgrade our security measures. And I don't know everything that might be here, but if there's more, I'd certainly suggest you return it before the real possibility of serious charges presents itself." She poured another cup of tea—"One sugar. Right, dear?"—and held it out to her. "Now, maybe we can discuss that custody issue you mentioned."

Annie made no move to take the cup this time. Instead, she looked directly into Georgia Gagnon's eyes and asked, "Why was it 'impossible'?"

Georgia was startled. "I'm sorry—?" The cup vibrated on its saucer very slightly. She set it down again.

"You said 'impossible.' Why was it *impossible* that I had that laptop?" She indicated the files again with a tilt of her chin. "Why did you say it was impossible that Susan might have left it with me? Accidentally. Unless you don't believe in accidents either."

Georgia smiled now. "As I told you—she might have been many things, but I'm sure you learned that she wasn't irresponsible. Or careless. About her job, at least. Maybe you didn't know her as well as you thought. Other women never go anywhere without their purses. Susan rarely went anywhere without her laptop. She would never have left it with anyone, even someone she'd recently begun to think of as a friend." She shrugged.

"But you certainly knew it wasn't with her *that* night. Down at the river, where they found her. You didn't say anything about it then."

"No. I was in shock. And the same as everyone else, I suppose I assumed it had been stolen. Pawned or sold. Something. That's why it was on the list. A formality, for insurance purposes. It's still government property, dear." She stirred her tea. "Why is this such a concern to you?"

"Because it *wasn't* missing the night Susan was murdered. It was still in her hotel room the morning after, when *I* took it. And I think you knew that. You knew it was still there, because you'd already spent considerable time working right from here to wipe out all the files you didn't want anyone to see."

Georgia's reaction wasn't very satisfying. She just blinked behind her glasses, frowning and shaping her mouth into a gesture of disapproval, as though Annie had deliberately chosen to be rude.

"The funny thing is," Annie continued, "there's nothing there that would implicate you. Read it yourself. Maybe a few social policies that are going to cause quite a ripple. A brand-new economic development strategy the opposition would give its eye teeth to get its hands on before the election. But nothing about you, Mrs. Gagnon. Unless you count a couple of instant messages she saved. Particularly the last ones . . . You're right. She wasn't careless."

Georgia spoke in a low tone. "You're leaning rather heavily on that one word—'impossible.' And I'll tell you right now that it is. I'm a little disappointed, Anne—Susan said you were clever, even though it was obvious to her you were still very troubled by everything that happened a few years ago. But are you seriously trying to imply that I might have had some part in harming her? It's impossible that I was in any position to do that. And it's impossible anyone would *ever* believe that I had. Ask them. Ask anyone. My heart literally broke when she died." She dabbed at her eyes again.

Annie felt a stab of betrayal that Susan might have really told this woman anything about her . . . She steeled herself again and chose to believe it was another lie.

Annie forced a smile. "I *am* clever. And I know you're the only one who could have gotten that close. She trusted you. Maybe the one person she really did, any more. So, while I'm sure it was probably *hard* for you, in the end it wasn't impossible. You had something, and someone, else to protect. Susan's job was done—she'd helped you secure Leah Mallick. Then, when that went wrong, you told her it was time to go, but she couldn't accept that. She'd finally put together the whole picture. And she still thought you would want to stop it." Annie stood up. Georgia, she saw, was fighting for self-control.

"But *your* job's not quite finished, yet." Annie said. "You're setting up Thomas Acton for a run at the Presidency during his second term, aren't you? He's the one who's going to make Cross Corp's program national."

Georgia Gagnon raised an eyebrow.

"And he's going win. With tax cuts, a re-energized high-tech sector and a brand new initiative for universal medical care."

Georgia stood abruptly and went behind her desk.

"That sounds like an impressive record for anyone, don't you think, Ms. Shannon?"

"But that's going to be the test, isn't it—when people really begin to understand what it is you're proposing. What will they ask? Unless you seriously believe you've found a way to control even their questions."

Georgia smiled suddenly. "*Whose* questions? The medical ethics panels we've assembled? The palliative care conferences we're sponsoring? The grass-roots coalitions clamouring for patients' right to choose? The economic white papers we're releasing? The bipartisan legislative commission we're going to convene?" She paused. "'What does mercy look like to you?' That's the only question they're going to have to ask—and answer. And in the end it will give us affordable public health care, second to none in this country. When you think of it, *we* won't have to do very much. Just read the polls a year from now."

Annie shook her head. "As long as you can dictate when it's the right time to leave. As long as you can leave virtually nothing to chance. Nothing between us and the big sleep . . . but a checklist. I've tried to imagine everything that you're going to have to put on it. Birth defects? Chronic disease? Permanent physical incapacity? A genetic propensity to neurological disorders? What's fair game?"

Georgia smiled. "An informed and equitable assessment, based upon reasonable and measurable criteria. Across the board. Without bias or prejudice."

"Except for those who can afford more. . . ?"

"A little early in the day to foment a class war, don't you think? No one's going to campaign against continuing life-enhancement strategies, the right of anyone to pay for elective surgery, experimental drug programs, MRI full-body scans, alternative therapies, vitamins, high-protein diets, health club memberships. It's a free market. People demand choice. But it means that we're going to be able to provide every citizen in this state with advanced palliative care and compassionate terminal treatment. And, yes, maybe offer that to the country. Because *that's* what people want."

"Or *think* they want—until the death sentences start being handed out. Until the state-mandated early-term testing says you must abort anything less than a perfect baby or take on the costs of lifetime care on your own. Until a genetic analysis denies you access to benefits. Or until your impaired 'quality of life' is stacked up against some bottom line." What will be enough to qualify? Paraplegic but not quadraplegic? A minimum IQ of 60? Depressed no more than three days a month—"

"Don't pretend to be naive, Anne. You must know that doctors are already making those same decisions on their own. I think you'll find that most people *want* us to regulate it for legitimate medical cases. Create clear, unequivocal guidelines. Finally provide some adequate protection under the law—for both sides."

"But who put doctors on one side and patients on the other in the first place? You're going to force us to choose, aren't you?"

Georgia threw up her hands now, tired of discussing it. "Susan couldn't have harmed Governor Acton. Neither can you. Check further, Lieutenant. You'll find that she was trying to blackmail him. Their affair had been over for almost a year, but she wouldn't let go. And everywhere you look, you or anyone else will find incontrovertible evidence of that. There are people who will say that she called him day and night—until he had to threaten her with an injunction. She was distraught. She disappeared, more than once, without telling anyone where she was going. To Lockport, for example. She misrepresented herself. We believe that she may have absconded with funds. We're already commissioning an audit of her department to confirm that. Do you want me to go on?"

"None of that's true."

"It will become the truth." Georgia smiled again, politely. "Or I could tell you that Susan was the one who actually put Leah Mallick forward. They'd met at a dinner party, just before last Christmas. Susan ended up introducing her to someone on the board of Cross Corp. At least, I think it was that same evening. Of course, it could have been another night—I understand they became very close friends after that. Whatever. For some reason, she certainly believed Dr. Mallick might be good for business. She became desperate when Dr. Mallick suggested withdrawing because of family concerns. In the end, it was Susan who pressured Leah Mallick to accept the appointment . . . even though she was already under considerable strain." Georgia had wandered to the window.

Now she turned to look at Annie and, surprisingly, there were tears in her eyes. "But what I'll always remember is how excited she was, the last time we spoke. She talked about some place you'd taken her to—a particular section of abandoned buildings along the river in Lockport—she said it gave her an idea about trying to create a new hub of biotech development. Or something like that. She was excited by all the possibilities. She wanted to show it to me sometime."

Annie felt something sour rise into her throat. She swallowed hard. "You won't stop me."

Georgia sighed and wiped her eyes one last time. "Well, for now at least, I'm going to have security escort you out without too much fuss."

Annie smiled grimly. "You could just ask me to leave."

"I think it's more *useful* my way."

Annie turned to see two state troopers arrive in the doorway. One had already edged a few inches into the room.

Georgia was right—that's what would be reported. She spoke loudly to Annie now. "I understand how difficult this must be for you. Obviously, you're very frustrated, coming here like this. But I really will *try* to do whatever I can to help you with that custody case. We're not hardhearted. Promise. The governor has a few friends on the Children's Services board who owe him a favour or two. We'll call someone for you. I think we can make that adoption problem go away. You'd be a wonderful mother to that boy." She scribbled something on the back of a business card and pressed it into Annie's hand.

Annie stared at her. That's how these things were played. She, all of them, everyone, still so willing to use the child.

Then, before she knew it, Georgia had swept her into an embrace. A low laugh into her ear: "Accept my offer. You really have no idea what you'd be taking on, Ms. Shannon."

Georgia's eyes met hers. There was no mistaking the threat. It was probably the last thing Susan had ever seen.

"They say that people are more motivated by fear of loss than the possibility of gain. I guess we'll see," Georgia said, patting her arm.

Annie laughed shortly. "The difference is, Mrs. Gagnon, I have very little left to lose."

Georgia responded with a sad, private smile of her own. "I only wish that were true. Life might be so much easier for all of us."

"Maybe it isn't *meant* to be easy," Annie said.

A few staff were crowding the open doorway now, whispering. Annie found herself being led out through the middle of them. The capital police joined her escort at the bottom of the stairs, under the vault of the soaring lobby. One of them accompanied her all the way to her vehicle.

He waited until she was seated behind the wheel of her car, then he passed her something through the open window. "I'm sorry, but security is a pretty high priority these days. So I'm obliged—here ya go—to provide you with this record of notification. It informs you that you'll be refused entry and may be subject to prosecution if you try to get back in without a prior appointment." He handed her the paper. It was as innocuous-looking as a parking ticket.

"And I bet I'd really have to jump through hoops to get one, wouldn't I?" She let the notice flutter to the floor.

He smiled uncomfortably and shrugged, then stepped back as she started the car. "Don't forget your seat belt, there. And you have yourself a safe trip," he said.

She looked down at the business card in her hand. Georgia had scribbled a phone number on the back of it.

One call. At one word from her, they'd be willing to look for another "hard case" to make their point. With one call Kyle could be set free. An eight-year-old boy, free at last to encounter the sacred on his own terms. Leave the rest to worry about what happened after that.

But it wasn't up to her. She wasn't Leah Mallick, in control of the universe. And Kyle's fate wasn't in her hands alone. It couldn't be, or shouldn't be. Children belonged to the larger world, and the world had to answer for what it was about to do to him—and in his name.

Annie stopped the car and called the guard back. She passed him the card. "Could you return this to Mrs. Gagnon for me. Tell her the answer is no."

Annie sat at her desk and breathed in the tropically warm evening air that was pushing the curtains aside. The only sounds were crickets and the infrequent swish of a car going by on the street below. It had become too dark to read anymore. But it didn't matter. She was done.

She'd worked straight through for the last two weeks, rarely leaving the house, never turning on the TV or radio. No drinking.

But finished finally and in front of her now, were the two orderly piles, completed. One established a clear direction in which to take the prosecution of Georgia Gagnon, all the specifics the department would need to establish an official investigation: reports, timelines, jurisdictions, completed requisitions for a series of search warrants, the request for a subpoena to seize computer records. It would take them all the way into the governor's office.

The second, larger stack was for Callie Christie. This was how she'd need to begin, starting with context: Leah Mallick and her relationship to Cross Corp, Cross Corp to the election and the election to the choices being offered. Why Kyle still mattered. The story had found her. But Callie was going to have to come up with a way to sell the truth without buzz, beautiful pictures, or sound bites this time.

In a memo Annie set out the whole road map for her: "Callie—don't rely on your regular channels. Get new quotes on the record from city and state officials, especially about recently proposed economic development. Ask them about Cross Corp. Ask about something called the Fortinbras Foundation. Compare everything they say with previous statements and published reports. Analyze the new tech centre building permits. As soon as possible, they're going to start arranging seminars at medical conferences throughout the state, sending speakers to community presentations, likely emphasizing the ethics and right-to-choose stuff. Check out who's sponsoring them, then who's behind *them.* Look at any new academic studies on health care scheduled for release in the next couple of months—especially if they have private or foundation funding. Who's on the boards. Get a hold of social service agency projections for the next three to five years—palliative, home care, that kind of thing. Work low- to mid-level contacts within the department of Health and Human Services. They may not know how everything fits together yet—but they'll be flattered and give you a piece of something, if you play them right. Pay special attention to any polls related to single-payer health insurance, especially if they're privately commissioned . . ." *Yeah, follow the money.*

This isn't a television show any more, she thought. The spin cycle is over—let the real debate begin.

Annie went back downstairs.

There was a large, untidy pile scattered beneath the slot in the front door. Today's mail. She hadn't heard it arrive—it would have been hours ago now. Ben had already made an effort to sort through it. She gathered everything up, idly leafing through it. All junk. Except for one envelope. Toothmarked and damp, but intact.

As she looked at it, her heart jumped a beat. Ordinary-looking, plain white, with a Wichita, Kansas, postmark. From Medix Express. It was addressed to her pseudonym: Pepper Anderson. She smiled to herself. Maybe it had given someone in Wichita a laugh too. The only thing that really mattered, she knew, was the $680 fee she'd sent in with the sample. No one cared who was doing the asking any more.

Annie took the time to make herself a cup of tea before she finally sat down at the kitchen table, the thick white envelope resting in her hand. She needed to take a moment. For one last time she wanted to put herself in Leah Mallick's place. To find, if not understanding, then at least something more than just hate to bury her with.

It was an easy enough assumption—that there would have been months of private despair and slowly rising horror before Leah had suspected the truth. In the end, she would have ordered a report like this one for confirmation, having taken every necessary step to ensure its confidentiality.

And for a fleeting instant she might have even found a strange comfort in it when it finally arrived—the measurable outcome, the clean, numbered conclusion of a highly technical, predictable scientific process she could trust, the one sure thing left in her collapsing universe. It gave her an objective reason for what was happening. Proof that it wasn't her fault.

Maybe, too, Leah would have paused in just this way, knowing that once the envelope was opened, it could never be closed again. Because she also knew that the report would identify the specific genetic indicator—the mutated chromosome—tagging the inexorable development of neurological devastation in her husband. And the statistical certainty of a precipitant death sentence pronounced upon her own son. Leah had witnessed the evidence herself: her husband's increasingly erratic behaviour, her son already evoking his father's same strange, debilitating neediness. Science was telling her that neither had a right to live.

The test results would be couched in probabilities, determined within several decimal points of absolute. The report would be objective—relentlessly, resolutely, heartlessly, undeniably, implacably neutral—and as accurate as the world's leading-edge technology could make it. And the scientist in her would have had to admit that there was nothing inherently good or even bad about it, no matter what it said. It was just information. It had only the value assigned to it. That, and the cost of a stamp.

Annie hesitated another few seconds, then slipped the papers out of the envelope to read them for herself. It was exactly as she'd expected. The complex charts, terms like "limited sampling field," "alleles," "kilobases," "locus," "autosomal dominance." One page was actually a brilliantly coloured graph showing where some important line met, then fell away from accepted, nominal standards. A separate sheet set out rows of gradated bars in shades of black and grey, columns of figures. Another showed a pretty design of neon threads.

Damning enough—here a predisposition to asthma, a warning about adult-onset diabetes, there the indication of an inherited tendency to colour-blindness. But she finally stopped when she saw the larger truth it revealed—that nowhere here, throughout the entire seven pages, was there a single reference to any known degenerative neurological disorder. None of the rampant dozens that had been classified. None of the tags, the probabilities, even given the margin of error. Not ALS or Alzheimer's. Not Parkinson's or Friedreich ataxia. And there was nothing, anywhere, of the deadly diagnosis trumpeted by April Vaughan, in her televised revelation of Tim Mallick's medical record. *Nothing.* Nothing "pathological" anyway. His own childhood, his own father's failure—who knew what that had left him? A too-aware child, living in chaos . . .

Annie let it all finally sink in. She was holding the proof that Leah had been deceived by an elaborately staged lie.

Someone had found the one way to present Leah Mallick with "irreducible fact"—the tenet of her secular faith, knowing that her entire career had been built on the search for it, the need to collapse all doubt to crystalline certainties. Cross Corp had divined her one blind spot: that she, who knew better than anyone else how malleable human hope could be made to be, would be swayed by the simple appearance of objective truth. The science of the brain, not the ephemeral nature of a mind.

And it was all so ironic, Annie thought. Whatever weakness *had* destroyed Tim Mallick's own equilibrium, his fragile grasp upon the universe, it wasn't *that.* It wasn't what Leah had diagnosed—only what she'd always exploited in others. Everything for which she'd always expressed such complete contempt. His all too human need and response—to myriad fears, doubts, inadequacies. In the end he'd passed on nothing to his own son, except perhaps his love for astronomy. And a sensitive nature. And what life created out of those two things.

Cross Corp had shown her the very future she was helping to create, in stark black and white.

But how could she have bought the lie so easily? Annie wondered now. Wasn't it Leah Mallick herself who'd long ago set out to gather every string of fate into her own hands, ready to spin choices that offered no real choice at all. Leah who'd never been one to underestimate the power of advertising and blind self-interest. According to her, Adam and Eve didn't have to be thrown out of Eden; they could be seduced. Step by step.

She was able to do it only because almost everyone who'd ever met her had come to believe that she could walk on water if she wanted to. And people like that never have to take control, Annie knew. The world is always too willing to *give* it to them.

If there was a reason to hate the dead, to wish her ill for all eternity, Annie *did* hate her now. For exploiting her uncommon power. For exercising her extraordinary gifts with such rich contempt for the consequences. For abdicating every fundamental obligation, violating every oath and promise she'd ever made on earth. *For choosing to destroy her own child.*

Annie didn't want to know about Leah's pain anymore. Of hearing his voice calling for her when an unfamiliar noise in the night awoke him. Urging him down into his blanket to stay warm, tucking it tight around him with hands already trembling from too many pills. Closing the door, while she promised everything would be all right. Picking up the keys to an expensive car sitting waiting in the garage . . .

Leah Mallick *had* held the strings. Until they took them back—and drew them tight enough to choke her. Cross Corp didn't want a Leah Mallick. They wanted only her work, what she could do for them. Not her needs.

In the end, all they'd really had to do was allow her to define herself—what she would do, how far she would go. And when the time came, they used it against her. They slowly, deliberately, unwrapped her greatest fear, her only vulnerability, and presented it to her as the final, objective truth: that all her skill and talent and wanting could not change the inevitability of her own son's fate. In the brave new world she'd designed, there was no place for the child she loved. Her science said that he had no intrinsic right to live. It was only her heart that told her otherwise.

And they knew, far better than Leah herself did, what she would have to do. It was her last mercy killing. And her most human act—that she wouldn't let him go alone.

This was the only thing a good reporter would really need. The ultimate smoking gun.

Annie walked back upstairs and put the package on top of Callie's pile.

In the front hallway she saw Ben waiting patiently for her, excited at the very sound of her steps, and completely willing to forgo any possibility of a treat in the kitchen for a walk. Tired, she stared at him. He stared back. It was impossible, she realized, to argue with an implacable English springer spaniel. And it was relief, not exhaustion, she felt now. A walk was, in fact, a brilliant idea.

She took a moment to leave a phone message for Bill. "I think I've got some good news for you. Call me as soon as you can. Love you, hon." They'd both waited such a long time to leave the past behind. Now maybe they could.

She bent down and attached the leash to Ben's collar, giving him the other end as usual, and opened the door. He trotted outside, down the stairs, and turned, without hesitation, to the left. He kept an intermittent pace in front of her, stopping only to sniff at every piece of windblown flotsam in their path. Without planning it, they were headed for the community garden again.

It had become the most pleasurable part of her routine, seeing what was new there, seeing what had changed. She always looked forward to bringing a new idea home, as though the woman who'd created it was trying to teach her something.

As they neared the corner, Ben suddenly lunged forward. Annie watched in dismay as the dog threw himself at a shadow she could barely pick out in the distance, someone bent over under the dim light from the old street lamp. She ran up, already apologizing.

The voice came out of the darkness with light, musical quality. "Hel-lo. My first visitor." The woman had risen up on her knees from where she'd been digging in the soil, and was allowing Ben to lick her face while she ruffled his fur, the dog all wagging hind end and short yips of excitement.

She looked up expectantly, greeting Annie with a broad smile. "Hello, Anne Shannon," she said. She pronounced the name distinctly, punctuating it with a mock stern look. Then she shook her finger at her. "You pass by, but you never stop. Someone has to tell me you're a famous police-woman. I should be so lucky that you're my neighbour, eh?" She wiped her hand on her slacks, then held it out, broad and rough, and clasped Annie's warmly. "I'm Margrid Brezchinski."

Annie obligingly laughed a little. "Mrs. Brezchinski. Hello. How are you?"

The woman was beaming. "I'm doing very well, thank you."

"I can *see* that." Annie looked around. "It's beautiful. You've done so much work." There was no one else around. "But do you really think you should be here, all by yourself, at night? It's really not the best area . . ."

"It got dark before I knew. But I'm fine here. There's neighbours all around. I see them, peeking out at me," and she mimicked a gleeful child hiding behind a curtain. "They think I'm crazy, I guess." Mrs. Brezchinski indicated the empty flats piled beside her on the ground. There were already several new rows of flowers, planted in freshly turned soil. A hose was coiled nearby. "But they are watching out for me, I think." She pointed in the direction of a window across a yard. Annie saw a thin figure framed in the light from inside. "You see? That's Mrs. Helmer in there. She give me this hose so I can use her water. She's too sick to do it herself, but she enjoys the flowers." Mrs. Brezchinski waved at the little figure. "She ask me to come for coffee when I'm finished. She just lost her husband too."

Maybe that was why she was here, building a garden that few knew existed. A memorial.

Wherever Annie looked, she could see the outlines of other things planned. The empty lot was now a kind of landmark, an oasis, where there'd so recently been nothing. "It's a lot of work," she said again. Up close she could see that its details were even more impressive. Succulents were tucked into the tiny crevices between rocks. Trailing stems spilled out of shards of weathered old pots, as comfortable as if they'd been growing there for years.

Mrs. Brezchinski nodded agreeably. "But what else can you do," she shrugged, "if you want a garden." She set out a couple more annuals, quickly and expertly. "If it's not weather, it is bugs, eh?" she said, brushing off her hands as she struggled to her feet. "Maybe even a dog who comes by to visit sometimes," and she looked at Ben again, smiling. "Some years good, others not. But Mother Nature—she always wants to keep going."

Mrs. Brezchinski stood up stiffly, parking her hands on her hips, a bit out of breath. She looked at the one flat left to go. "Too hot to leave these out." She motioned to Annie.

"You come here, Miss Big TV Star. You can do our last row for us. My back is not as strong as it used to be—rheumatism, maybe. I'll hold the flashlight."

She pulled close and leaned heavily on Annie's shoulder as they knelt down together on the soft ground in the dark. Annie could still feel the sun held in the soil from the long summer day just behind them. The grass was damp and fragrant.

It occurred to Annie then that she could always walk past here. Each night, taking the long way around. Maybe she could donate something to it, a garden bench to encourage others to stop and sit for a few minutes.

Mrs. Brezchinski set the last tray of impatiens on the ground between them and settled back more comfortably to gaze at the expanding starry sky. She pointed upwards. "I think now that's where my Olaf is. Right there. Watching me." She hummed something different this time, a bit of what Annie recognized as vintage Lennon and McCartney. "In My Life."

Annie took the first small container Mrs. Brezchinski passed to her and gently removed the young plant from it, careful not to disturb the fragile roots. Then she sank her hands deep into the earth.

An hour later, as she neared her home again, there was something else unexpected.

She glanced up ahead towards it, as casually as any stranger might have, and saw, for the first time, that in the most important way the house was actually finished. It was finally done. Simply seeing it there now gave her a rush of surprisingly sweet pleasure she'd never expected to feel again. The lights she'd left on glowed warmly through the windows. The wide porch sat solid and generous, clematis vines already twining around its columns. It had, despite her own inconstancy, been restored complete in itself, to this street, in this neighbourhood. Not a folly after all.

Annie Shannon had never been a sentimental woman. In a few months, she knew, she'd probably find herself bored by the gentle monotony of it all, the neighbours repeating all the usual rote things that people said, every time they met on these same old sidewalks shaded by chestnut trees—banal complaints about rising taxes and prowling cats who dug up flowerpots and attacked the songbirds. But there were worse things in the world to worry about.

As she opened the front door, Ben pushed roughly past her, running towards the kitchen, hoping beyond hope that more food had magically appeared in his bowl while they were gone.

The phone rang. Annie automatically reached for it, then her hand fell away. Let the machine pick up. But the ringing had already stopped before the tape cut in. It wasn't Bill.

She went into the kitchen, put down fresh water for the dog and plugged in the kettle for herself.

She looked, again, at the report she'd left on the table, at everything still spread out, It was only charts and graphs, but the details seemed almost too intimate to absorb. Like an autopsy, it was the evidence of living. But cold and empty of life. She pulled out a chair and sat down to go through it once more.

Leah would have been so frantic to protect her privacy . . .

Annie picked up the top page and began to reread it. Maybe this helped to discredit Tim Mallick's medical report—prove it had been counterfeit. But what if *that* hadn't been a lie? How could *anyone* ever expect to stand up to such inhuman scrutiny. If companies like Cross Corp were really prepared to use this sort of thing from now on . . . What would ever stop them?

The phone started ringing again. The machine was set to pick up at six. There were five rings, then it stopped. No message. She shrugged. As Aunt Ell used to say, if it's important, they'll call back.

As if someone had heard her thoughts, the phone rang again. Three, four five . . . stopped. Then three more times. Five rings, then nothing. No message.

Annie glanced up more nervously, waiting. It sounded like someone was actually trying to reach her. In the thick silence that followed, she heard a package hit the floor underneath the mail slot in the front hallway. Ben barked half-heartedly and went to investigate. She could hear him take something and tear it open, then yelp frantically. Fucking dog. She stalked down the hall. He was growling at whatever it was that had slid under the chest of drawers. She reached out to grab him as she opened the front door. There was no one on the street in either direction.

She turned and looked at the dog. The hurt expression on his face didn't move her. He stared at her, retreating, still trying to wag his tail—his entire hind end going hard side to side. Then he peed on the floor. The combination of fear and apology finally stopped her. She saw there was a drip of blood on his lip. He'd bitten down too hard on something. She sank down heavily beside him. "Ah, Bennie. Sorry. Sorry. Sorry," her arms wrapped around his neck, her face buried in his fur.

Annie picked up the nondescript cardboard sleeve he'd been gnawing. Though slick-wet, it was still in one piece. Simply addressed to "Anne Shannon." Just more junk mail.

She tried to quiet the dog as she crawled over to reach under the bureau, her fingers stretching to find whatever it was, while he bayed beside her ear. "They're *dust* bunnies, Ben, not real ones, for Crissake . . ."

Her fist closed around it and she drew out her arm, sneezing at the cloud she'd stirred up.

It was nothing but a key chain. He'd bitten down too hard on some cheap trinket someone had sent her. She held it up to the light spilling out of the kitchen.

Probably a dime-a-dozen promotional thing. She was always getting pens and pins sent through the mail. Now, another key chain. This one was brushed gold, solid-looking. Nice weight in the hand. But how many of them could you really use? She knew they'd stop sending her things soon enough, when people realized she wasn't going to be famous any more.

Annie took the key chain and the envelope back into the kitchen where the light was better. There was a fancy medallion attached to it. Probably something promoting a local car dealership or a travel agency.

But the design on it, she saw now, was actually some kind of hologram. Tipping it in the light, she watched a few thin, random filaments, brightly coloured threads, arrange themselves into a pattern. And only because she had just studied one almost exactly like it, did she recognize it. It was a design representing the configuration of a DNA molecule. Like the one decorating the report about Tim Mallick.

The phone rang again and she jumped. This time, she counted it aloud. "One. Two. Three. Four. Five." She held her breath, waiting for the sixth. Instead, silence again. Someone knew she was there. She didn't want to answer.

Instead, Annie twisted the key chain in her hand, snapping off the medallion. In the light, she caught a glimpse of what appeared to be two lines of small print beneath the design. She tilted the hologram again, back and forth, trying desperately to read it even as she began to tremble. She was suddenly nauseated, too. Maybe it only meant that another migraine was coming on. Probably time to go upstairs to get her glasses . . .

The words faded and reappeared almost magically as she worked to steady her hand. It took her at least five times, probably ten, to read them over again, until what they said finally registered in the rational, thinking part of her brain.

She stared at the medallion now through a new kind of pressure gathering in the air all around her. She saw *his* name, *Shannon, Charles.* In the space marked *File ID,* she recognized his social security number.

On the second line—*Access #*—was the confidential code she'd set up herself, to enter the secured police computer network: *080684.* Tina had warned her that it had to be something she couldn't forget. It was hers alone—even the system operator couldn't get at it. And the sequence she'd created was simple, easy for her to remember: Charlie's birthday. August 6, 1984.

Annie turned the medallion over. On the back, she saw a long list of numbers and letters, stamped into the gold-coloured metal—*D8S1358, D13S317, vWA, StR*—a series of them, so tiny they were difficult to read, even in this light.

In a kind of summary line at the bottom, embossed on the surface and raised so that she could actually feel it running under her finger, she read: *Data Storage Provided by Cross Corp, Inc.*

She remembered every minute of those last days spent in the hospital with him. Tests. Vials taken and stored somewhere. She hadn't had to *give* them anything; they'd always had it. Or knew exactly where—and how—to find it, if they decided to.

Annie picked up the envelope again. She could feel something else inside it. Her heart was pounding unnaturally now. She pried the flap open. It was a simple photograph, a digital picture, so lacking in apparent detail that it was almost abstract. But it was clear, even to her untrained eye, that she was looking at a microscopic field of embryonic development—so much clearer than the old ultrasounds had ever been.

And she recognized it all. The pink, translucent curves. The origins of appendages from a pearly mass. Denser, darker tissues, antecedent to the spine or cornea. She'd seen it before, as a child, in the sequence of a photographic pictorial in *Life* Magazine. Dirty pictures, her parents had called them, discarding that particular issue. Like looking into God's own dream, her aunt had said, letting her hide another copy.

Charlie's name was printed on it. An inventory number. Bold and formal.

Annie didn't have to ask what it was, what it meant. Or even what they were offering to her this time. Somewhere in the world, somewhere beyond blunt law and dry debate, they were prepared to give her the only thing she'd ever wanted all these years.

To have her son returned to her. And be allowed to start over.

One cell joining to the next, transmogrifying into bone and skin, brain and heart. Human only in its potential, but the moment another journey began. Now held in some distant laboratory, just waiting now for her to say "yes" to a minor medical procedure. An implantation? She was fifty, in reasonable health. What could stop her? Who was she ever to have bet against them and their miracles?

She knew that at the end of that telephone line was her answered prayer. What *would* God's voice sound like, she wondered.

The phone rang again.

She tried to imagine what she would hear when she eventually picked it up. Probably little or no preamble. In all likelihood, a woman's voice, persuasive and corrupt, like Leah Mallick's. Maybe they'd even found a way to paste *her* together again—bits and pieces of old tape, in anticipation of just such a moment as this. They could pick and choose from amongst so much. After all, what was a "Leah Mallick" anyway?

Five rings. Annie counted each of them again without intending to. Like the half-heard tolling of a distant clock . . .

I thought you might want to discuss some of the options available to you.

Some . . ?

The woman on the other end laughs pleasantly. *Well, one, at least. But I'm sure you understand how important it is that we have a meeting, as soon as possible.*

Of course. Calmly. *It's really him, though, isn't it? It's Charlie.*

But before the voice could answer, Annie saw that she wasn't really holding the phone. And that the phone itself was ringing again.

She walked away from it for a moment to look out the back door. The cover of night was slow to come now, an extended twilight, and sounds floated over the trees and through the hedges and across the lawns. Late barbecues. Music. Laughing adults, overtired children, fighting off the shadows. Not light any more, but an even glow reflected from the smooth bowl of sky above.

Not surprisingly, it was Leah Mallick herself who stood in front of her now. An assembly of pieces, finally coalesced around the bare structure, like a computer-generated model laid upon an armature. In the end, what was a human life anyway? The photographs, the gossip, the interviews. The inventories, records, receipts and transcripts. The proverbial stone in the water, the ripples spreading all the way to the end of the universe, the origin of time.

We all begin, Annie thought, with the energy of impulse and passionate intent. All symphonies and skyscrapers. Then, one morning, all that remains is the smell of blood and ripening flesh, the cognac fragrance of Chanel No. 5 still clinging to the sheets.

Of the rest, the thick meat in the middle, it was only ever a matter of degree. And fate.

The phone had been ringing, on and off, for almost ten minutes now—maybe a hundred times in total. Annie knew that she would answer it. This hesitation, this deliberate simulation of uncertainty, was only the necessary illusion of careful thought and sober consideration. The end of debate. The beginning of the bargain. She would answer the phone and say, "Yes. I want my child back." No mother would say anything different.

And they already knew that. They knew, by now, that she was about to climb the stairs to tear each detailed report about them into a thousand pieces. And erase a dozen, damning computer files. And agree to forget every crime to which she was about to be witness. *I was distraught. I was confused.* She couldn't be responsible for the world . . . She had her own son to think about.

When the phone began again, it took her a few seconds to register—*six* rings, this time—that the machine was already picking up. She heard Bill's voice through the tinny speaker. "Hey, babe. You there?"

She lifted the phone. Her own "Hi" sounded sleepy and far away to her.

"Annie. . . ? Hey. Just picked up my messages. I was on my way over there anyway, but you said you had some good news. . . ?"

She stopped, momentarily confused. Then vaguely remembered that she'd already left an earlier message for him: something about bringing Cross Corp to its knees—

"Hey. You OK there?" he said. "Everything all right?"

Annie closed her hand tightly around the medallion she still held.

"Annie. . . ?"

It's true, she thought—there will never be one moment when all your decisions are behind you. "Yeah. Sure. Sorry. No, everything's fine, honey," she said finally, forcing a short, bright laugh. "It's just that I think I might be pregnant."

ABOUT THE AUTHOR

BARBARA J. STEWART is a former filmmaker. Her productions have been shown at festivals in Montreal, Yorkton and New York, and distributed internationally. Originally from Waterloo, Ontario, Stewart now divides her time between Winnipeg and Vancouver. *The Sleeping Boy* is her first novel.